Homeward

COLORADO

HOMEWARD COLORADO (Hart County Series Book 5)

Ebook Cover Photography: Regina Wamba

Cover Design (Ebook and Print): Angela Haddon

Produced by Diana Road Books

HART COUNTY BOOK 5

HANNAH SHIELD

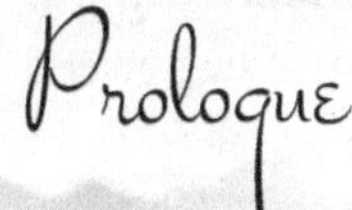

Prologue

Then

I LEANED into Grace's side and whispered, "What about him? He's cute, right?"

She glanced at a sophomore guy drifting past on a skateboard. "I give him a five out of ten."

"*Harsh*. What about that guy?"

"That's Mr. Miller, dork. He teaches geometry! Ew!" Grace elbowed me, and I cackled so loudly a few other freshman girls turned and stared as they crossed the parking lot.

"Okay, okay. But you're making this really difficult. How am I supposed to find you a date for our first homecoming?"

"*You* don't even have a date, Piper."

"I am not the issue here." I twisted on the bench, crossing my legs. "How about Trey Finley? I saw him checking you out in the hall."

"He's a second-year senior and wolf-whistles any time a girl bends over to pick up a pencil." Grace stuck out her tongue, and I did the same back.

"Older guys are hot, though," I said. "Come on. You have to have a crush on someone. Zach Kirby? He's cute."

But good-girl Grace was having none of it. "Nope. I have too much homework for boys."

I groaned, almost falling off the bench, which made her laugh. "Fine then," she said, giggling. "Who's *your* crush?"

Guilt zinged in my stomach.

I tapped my chin, pretending to think. "Mr. Miller. He's totally an eight out of ten. That tweed blazer? Yum. Think he'll be chaperoning at the dance?"

Grace sighed. "Piper Landry. I know you're kidding, but seriously. What am I going to do with you?"

Being best friends with Grace O'Neal had never been a conscious choice on my part. It had been as natural as breathing.

Her family had lived across the street from my family for our whole lives. Grace was there in all my earliest memories. In all the good things about growing up in Silver Ridge, Colorado, our small mountain town.

In the bad things, too. Like her mom dying and her dad taking off. Or when my mom was on a bender and I had to drag her home from some dive bar.

Good times.

There was only one thing I couldn't tell Grace, and that was the identity of my real crush.

My stupid, impossible, embarrassing crush.

What would Grace think if I confessed my obsession with her oldest brother, Grayden? A man who was eleven years older than me and my own brother's best friend?

I was beyond pathetic.

"How about we forget about the stupid homecoming dance," she said, "and go get cherry limeades."

I nodded sagely at her. "You really are a genius."

"Thank you for acknowledging that."

We both grabbed our backpacks. Grace tugged me away from Silver Ridge High and down the sidewalk, heading toward Main. My arm looped with hers.

It was a Monday afternoon, with the rest of the week looming ahead of us, but at least we were together.

A few minutes later, we had a corner table at the coffee shop with glasses of icy cherry limeade in front of us, extra cherries.

I wrapped my lips around the straw and took a sip. "I have so much math homework to get through tonight it's not even funny. Quadratics are evil."

"I can help you later. If you can explain what the heck is going on in this book." Grace dug out a worn copy of *The Giver*, our current assignment for Honors English class.

"Deal. But just to be clear, you're still the super-smart friend, and I'm the wild one. When we get to college, you'll be dragging me to class and I'll be dragging you to bars."

She stirred her drink around and around in the glass, barely smiling, just staring at the crushed cubes floating on top.

"Sorry," I said. "Didn't mean to bring up college. I know you're worried about the financial aid part."

We'd been dreaming of going off to school together in some city, but at the same time, neither of us knew how we'd pay for it.

"No, it's not that. It's about my brother."

Heat raced over my skin. "Yeah? Which one?"

Grace had a framed picture of her three older brothers in her room. There was Grayden, the intense one. Ashford, the grumpiest one. And Callum, the golden retriever goofball. All of them tall, athletic men, all known to females throughout Silver Ridge as extremely hot and extremely eligible.

But Grayden was the only one who made my gaze linger and made longing stir in my chest.

"It's Callum. He's talking about enlisting."

My lips flinched into a frown. This wasn't a surprise, since Grayden and Ashford were already in the Army. But still.

I took another sip and swallowed. "When?"

"I don't know. Maybe soon." Then she added in a whisper, "Piper, I'm scared."

"Hey. It's okay. It *is* scary."

I wasn't sure if she was scared about the two of us being entirely on our own, because my mom certainly didn't count as an authority figure. Or if she was afraid of having three brothers in the service and the risk that one of them wouldn't make it home.

I understood both fears. My brother Teller was a soldier too, and the O'Neals were like family to me.

"Everything will be alright." I put my hand over hers on the table.

She tilted her head, lips curving sadly. "If anyone could make me believe it, it's you. You're the best. I love you."

"Love you too."

Yep. It was settled. I could never in a million years confess my dirty thoughts about Grayden to her. Grace would be horrified. So would Teller, though for different reasons of course.

We finished our lime-aids, then walked the couple of blocks back to school to get our bikes. I had homework and chores to take care of. With Teller stationed on the other side of the country, if I didn't clean up my house, nobody would.

Maybe Grace would, though. She was kind of elf-like. All cute and short and helpful.

Wind streamed through our hair as we biked home. "Dinner at 6:30?" Grace asked when both our houses were in sight. "Callum has work, but there's leftovers from that pot of spaghetti he made last night."

"Yum. Definitely. See you then."

Grace and I had still been in elementary school when Grayden left for the Army. Teller—who was ten years older than me—hadn't been far behind, eager to join his best friend. Then Ashford enlisted a few years later.

Callum had graduated from Silver Ridge High last year, and now he was waiting tables at a diner on Main Street. But it didn't surprise me much that he wanted out of Silver Ridge, like the rest of them.

Sucked to know another of our brothers wanted to leave us behind, though.

Of course, they had good reasons. They wanted to make something of themselves, more than they could in our small town. And they sent money to us every month. We were proud of them. Teller had just joined Special Forces, making him an elite Green Beret.

Yet Grayden was the one we all looked up to the most. There was just something about him. Grayden had acted all grown-up even as a teenager. Taking care of his siblings, always gentle and watchful with his intense, sad eyes.

His broody stare, which seemed to go right through me, as if I wasn't even there.

Then, the last time he came home on leave, I finally noticed how incredibly, absurdly sexy he was.

He was twenty-six. I was a freshman in high school. What was wrong with me, having a crush on him?

What are we going to do with you, Piper?

An excellent question.

The lights were off when I stepped inside my house. I dumped my backpack by the couch and marched straight to my mother's bedroom. The door was cracked open, and the smell of vodka hit me from across the room.

"Mom?" I called out. "Are you up yet?"

A groan came from the pile of blankets on her bed. "The hell does it look like, Piper? I was out late."

Yeah, no kidding. She'd stumbled home when I was making myself breakfast before school, even though her shift had ended at midnight.

Sunlight filled the room as I yanked the curtains open. "Time to get up. It's almost five. You can't be late again. You already got your final warning."

She grumbled and cursed at me, but I finally got her moving and into the shower. Then she was out the door with barely enough time to make it. I prayed she wouldn't do something stupid like stop for cigarettes on the way.

With a sigh, I turned to the dirty dishes in the sink. After that, I would tackle my homework before heading to see Grace for dinner. Best part of my day.

I was halfway through my first algebra problem when there were heavy footsteps on the front porch and the door burst open. Hell. What was Mom doing back?

I got up and rushed down the hall toward the door. "Mom, you're definitely going to be—"

But it wasn't my mother standing just across the threshold. It was Grace.

Tears tumbled down her cheeks, and they kept falling. There was something about the way she was looking at me. I knew. I *knew.*

"Who?" I asked, voice thick.

Which of her brothers wasn't coming home? They weren't deployed right now, but things happened. We both knew the stories.

She could hardly get the words out. "It's Grayden."

No.

Oh please, no.

Guilt and fear and nausea rushed through me all at once. I hurried over and crushed Grace in a hug. Her head fit against my collarbone. She'd always been small, but I'd shot up during our middle school years. Made me feel like I was the big sister, though I was only six months older than her.

"I'm sorry," I kept saying. "Oh God, I'm so sorry, Grace." All the while feeling sick over the secret grief I felt. The tragic, foolish hope I'd carried in my heart.

"But it's not..." Grace hiccuped. "It's not what you think."

"*What*? What do you mean?"

She pulled back enough to wipe her face, even though the tears hadn't stopped. "Ashford called. Callum answered it on speaker, and I heard them talking. That's how I found out. Something happened with Grayden."

"But he's alive?"

She nodded, lip trembling. "He's alive. He's not hurt."

Relief crashed over me, so strong I could hardly breathe.

"But Ashford said… Piper, he said Grayden was arrested."

"*Arrested*? Are you sure?"

Her eyes were glazed. "Ashford was notified by military police from where Grayden's stationed. They say Grayden killed another soldier in a bar fight on the base. That's all we know so far." She choked out the words, "But he confessed."

I was shocked speechless.

This couldn't be real.

"There might've been some mistake," I said, my pulse racing. "Or there's a reason. Like self defense. Teller probably knows important people as a Green Beret. Maybe he can help."

But if Grayden had confessed, did that mean he was guilty?

Something vicious clamped around my chest and squeezed.

Grace put her head on my shoulder. "What if he doesn't ever come back to us? Why does this keep happening? Everyone leaves, and they don't come back. My mom, my dad…"

"I don't know why, G," I murmured, hugging her again. "But we have to stay positive. It could all turn out okay."

Yet even as I said them, my words rang hollow.

I thought of Grayden's sad, serious dark eyes. The brave tilt of his chin in that photo of him in uniform.

Grayden was a good man. I knew it down to my bones. But what if that wasn't enough?

Maybe a good man could still fall so far he wouldn't make it home.

ONE
Piper

Now

I STEPPED out of the warmth of my house and into the chill, not bothering with a coat. Outside, the air held the kind of quiet that comes only before a heavy snowfall or on a winter holiday.

Today, it was both. But Ollie was out here, and usually the word *quiet* wasn't found anywhere near my nine-year-old.

Two legs dangled from the hole in the treehouse platform. "Ollie-bear?"

No answer.

The wooden ladder creaked as I climbed. The sky hung white and heavy above our heads, and the air smelled of wood smoke. It was going to snow again later. I could feel it in my chest, the way the cold seemed to press down on everything.

Yet it was a comfortable feeling. Familiar and nostalgic, making me think of hot cocoa and a roaring fire.

My head popped up through the opening in the platform, and I rested my arms on the weathered wood. "Hey, bud."

Ollie looked at me with those big hazel eyes. "Mom, I don't think he's coming."

Ugh, my heart.

Reaching over, I playfully tugged at his jacket. He'd been sitting out here for two hours, and the thing wasn't even zipped up. Usually, Ollie would be moving too fast for me to worry about him getting cold. The kid had energy that could power half the town.

It was disconcerting to see him sitting so still.

"That means you get to come to Thanksgiving at Aunt Grace's house with me. We're going to eat so much. You know how delicious her gravy is. I'm going to have thirds. You'll have to roll me out the door."

He shrugged, no sign of a smile yet.

"Uncle Callum said he and Zandra are making a special pumpkin pie. If you're really nice, I *might* be able to convince him to sneak you a slice before dinner."

Ollie's gaze remained downcast. "Are you sure Dad didn't call?"

I sighed. "I'm sure, bud." Just in case, I pulled out my phone and checked it again. "He must've gotten caught up with something."

Ollie picked up a stray twig and chucked it at the platform railing. "No. He's just an asshole."

A stricter mother would probably scold him about language. Also, I tried to stay neutral where Danny was concerned. But the kid was right.

"Yeah. He can be at times. A grade-A asshole."

My swearing brought out a snicker and a twinkle in Ollie's eye.

It used to be that when Ollie was little, he assumed something life-or-death had come up to explain his dad's absence from baseball games or school events. Either that, or he'd get sad and then bounce back with a Lego set or some cartoons on his iPad.

But Ollie was nine years old now. Old enough to understand how much things just sucked sometimes. People we love can let us down.

From the moment I'd gotten pregnant in college, I'd sworn to myself I'd be a better parent than my mom or dad ever were. And I was, even if I'd made the mistake of giving so many years to my now-ex-husband.

But in most other ways, my life had been a lucky one. Teller, Ashford, and Callum had come home safe and sound after their military service. Grace had stayed a part of my life at every stage.

She'd been the first person I told when those two blue lines appeared. The maid of honor at my wedding to Danny. The first number I called after I asked Danny for a divorce.

Since my childhood, I'd had my brother Teller and the O'Neals standing by me. And they were Ollie's family too. I didn't want my son to ever think he was alone in this world.

"Hey, Maisie's going to be excited to see you," I pointed out. "Just imagine the hijinks you two will get up to. I'll have a head full of gray hair by the end of the night." I lifted a lock of my blond hair. "Oh no, it's already happening!"

Not entirely a joke. I was only thirty, but I was pretty sure I'd spied a gray hair or two in the mirror. I blamed Ollie's father.

He rolled his eyes. "Mom..."

"Come on. You can help me finish cooking. I'm running a little behind schedule."

"You're always behind schedule," he said with a laugh.

"But that's how I fit in exercise. Running to get to things at the last second. Life lessons, Ollie. I'm giving away these nuggets of wisdom for free. You should be writing this down."

"Love you, Mom." Leaning over, Ollie wrapped his arms around my head and hugged me. I almost lost my balance on the ladder as I returned his hug, my throat getting tight. My sweet boy.

"I love you too, Ollie-bear."

I climbed down and only cringed slightly when Ollie jumped five feet to the ground and ran ahead.

Inside, a playlist of mellow rock hummed from my phone. The kitchen looked like a minor explosion had hit, with most of my ingredients mid-prep to make green-bean casserole. A pot of coffee burbled, filling the room with one of my favorite scents in the universe.

Made sense, considering I owned Silver Linings Coffee on Main Street. I was a total sucker for a worn wooden table, a used paperback book, and a steaming cup of joe in a mismatched mug. My idea of heaven.

For tonight's festivities, an insulated carafe waited on a counter nearby, which I'd borrowed from my shop. I was very particular about sourcing my beans from regional roasters, and I couldn't possibly have my pumpkin pie tonight without a quality cup alongside it.

Coziness was my love language, and in my opinion, coffee tipped the scales toward cozy any time of day.

"Grab the wooden spoon and get ready to mix," I said, dumping blanched green beans into the casserole dish.

Ollie poked at the skillet of sauteed mushrooms, sneaking his fingers in to snag one. But when he put it in his mouth, he made a face. "Tastes weird."

"That's because I added wine. We're going fancy." I was a canned-soup girl for this recipe, all the way, but I'd decided to dress things up this year.

"Wine?" His eyes lifted, and I recognized that mischievous glint.

"Calm down, my dude. The alcohol's cooked out. Now hurry up. Get that stirring spoon ready."

Once the casserole was in the oven, Ollie dashed off to grab some games to bring along for this evening. A pile of dishes waited to be loaded into the dishwasher, but before I even touched the mess, I folded my arms on the parmesan-dusted counter and put my head on the butcher block, letting out a huge sigh.

Phew. I loved the holidays, but this time of year could be tough.

I didn't waste time on regrets. That wasn't my style. Life had blessed me with a wonderful son, a beloved local business, and dear friends.

But sometimes, my ex-husband... Oh, that man made me wonder.

How did my Ollie share an ounce of Danny's DNA?

A few days ago, Danny had called and asked to spend Thanksgiving with Ollie. Finally making an effort with our kid, or so it seemed. Danny was supposed to pick up Ollie at noon and take him to a family-friendly hotel and hot spring for the long weekend. I'd agreed, of course, and Ollie had been over the moon.

Should have known better than to let Ollie get his hopes up.

Yanking my phone from my back jeans pocket, I opened my messaging app and scrolled to Danny's thread. I'd toyed with the idea of changing his contact name to "That Dick," but then Ollie might see it. The kid made enough jokes about bodily functions as it was.

In front of my eyes, a message appeared in the thread, and I sucked in a breath.

DANNY

Tell Ollie sorry. Something came up

ME

Something always comes up, right? You're unbelievable

Don't lecture me, P. You don't know what's going on

And I don't want to know. Just want you to do better

Ollie was smart and funny and caring. Also a handful at times, and I loved that about him. I loved my son with every fiber of my being. I'd move every mountain in Hart County for him. How dare Danny not feel the same?

Whenever my brother Teller was in town, he spent quality

time with Ollie. He'd built that treehouse in the front yard. Ollie had so many aunts and uncles looking out for him.

Yet the loneliness of single-momhood struck me sometimes, right at my center.

"Mom?" Ollie's voice drifted from somewhere in the house. "I'm ready! Is it time to go?"

I pressed my palms against my eyes for just a second and then plastered on a smile. "Almost!"

By the time Ollie came back to the kitchen, I was myself again. Cheerful, capable Piper who had almost everything under control. For my kid, I could do anything.

"Can I bring my skateboard?" he begged.

"Absolutely not."

TWO
Piper

Ollie rang the doorbell about five times in quick succession before I could stop him.

"I think two rings was enough," I said with a laugh, balancing the casserole dish and my bag with the rest of my contributions to the potluck.

"I had to make sure! I bet they're already having fun in there without us."

The door swung open, and Grace appeared.

"Happy Thanksgiving!" Ollie shouted.

"Happy Thanksgiving. I'm so glad you're here!" Grace's eyes found mine over Ollie's head, her eyebrows lifting in a silent question. I gave a tiny shake of my head.

Yes, Ollie was here, instead of with his dad like we'd planned.

And no, *let's not mention it*.

Because Grace was my best friend, she understood all of that without a single word. "Get in here, you two." She grabbed the bag I was carrying. "I was just about to serve up the spiced apple cider. Maisie's in the backyard throwing the tennis ball for Stella. Or maybe building a snowman? Not sure. And Ashford and Dane are arguing about the football game on TV in the living room."

"See, told you they were already having fun," Ollie muttered before dumping his backpack of comic books and board games right there in the entryway. I nudged it aside with my foot, smiling fondly at Ollie's back as he ran deeper into the house.

"Thank God we're here," I said with a sigh.

"Come on. Let's get you some spiced cider. Or wine?"

"Definitely wine."

Grace's kitchen was slightly more organized than mine. Probably because it was a lot bigger. Grace and her boyfriend Dane had renovated the house after moving in almost a year ago, putting in top-of-the-line gadgets and appliances while keeping a rustic, upscale-mountain feel.

Maybe a little too much like the ski resort that Dane owned, but nobody had asked me.

Turkey roasted in the lower oven, and yeasty rolls overflowed the baking pan in the upper one. The place smelled incredible.

I set my casserole on the counter, saying hello to Emma—Ashford's wife—who was ladling hot apple cider into cups. As soon as my hands were free, it was hug time. A big hug for Emma, and another for Grace.

Grabbing the wine bottle, Grace pushed her glasses up her nose and pursed her lips into a frown. "So. Ollie's hot springs Thanksgiving trip with his father..."

"I should've known Danny would find something better to do."

Emma set a mug of cider on the counter with a thump. "Better than spending time with his kid? What is wrong with that man?"

"I've asked myself that question more times than I can count. Some mysteries have no answer. But we're with all of you lovely people, and that's what matters."

"Hear, hear," Grace said. "Now let me find my biggest wine glass for you."

"Have I told you how much I love you?"

While we cooked and laughed and gossiped, I let myself sink

into the moment. The stress from earlier began to melt away, replaced by the easy comfort of being surrounded by the people I loved.

Over the years, we'd all had our ups and downs. Once, I'd jokingly named our group of friends the Lonely Harts club so we could all commiserate over our bad luck when it came to relationships. We all lived in Hart County, so the pun practically wrote itself.

I could never resist a silly pun, as Ollie would probably attest.

But one by one, the Lonely Harts had been falling in love. First it was Ashford falling for Emma, who loved his daughter Maisie like her own.

Then Grace caught the bug. She and I used to have a no-dating pact, back when we were both cynical about love and convinced we were better off without it. But then she met Dane, the billionaire playboy from New York who only had eyes for her.

My brother Teller succumbed next, quitting his job as Silver Ridge Chief of Police so he could be with Ayla Maxwell, international pop star. They were spending their first Thanksgiving as a couple in Los Angeles.

It was obnoxious, really. What right did they all have to go proving romance could be healthy, fulfilling, and downright magical?

Kidding aside, I was the first to cheer all of them on. I'd even played a key role in some of their love stories, if I said so myself. But seeing most of my closest friends and family pair off hadn't changed my resolve one bit.

I would *never* make the mistake of falling in love again.

About an hour later, Callum and Zandra showed up. Our latest adorable couple. I'd thought Callum would hold out and stay single like me, but that was until Zandra came back to Silver Ridge.

"We're here!" Callum announced. "Party can officially begin."

Maisie and Ollie tried to tackle him, while Callum held his precious pumpkin pie out of harm's way. I wrangled the kids into the living room for Ashford and Dane to manage, and Zandra and Emma went to finish decorating the dining table.

In the kitchen, Callum immediately stuck his pinky into Grace's gravy and tasted it. "Needs more fresh pepper."

Grace swatted his arm. "Go find somebody else to bother!"

Callum moved to the counter, surveying the spread of dishes. "You did remember to make things Zandra can eat, right?"

"I promise I've been very careful. Even used gluten-free flour in the gravy."

"Thanks, Grace!" Zandra called out from the dining room. "You're amazing!"

I laughed as Callum opened his mouth to say something else, and Grace pointed a wooden spoon at him in warning. Callum wisely retreated to the living room.

Grace nudged me with her elbow, her voice dropping low. "Do you think, by next year, it could be *all* of us together? Teller and Ayla, and..."

She swallowed, as if just saying the rest of that sentence was a big step.

"Grayden too," Grace finished, almost in a whisper.

I rolled my tongue against my teeth, considering. It was not a straightforward question, and there were a lot of big feelings attached to it.

Not *my* big feelings, of course. But for Grace and her brothers.

Grayden hadn't been back to Silver Ridge for well over a decade now. More like a decade and a half. After his guilty plea and all that had happened during that awful time, it was almost like he'd died.

For year after year, there'd been no contact. Grayden had been completely gone from our lives.

Then last year, Dane hired a private investigator to track down the oldest O'Neal brother. Apparently, Grayden lived in Seattle now. He'd served his time in military prison, and from what Grace told me, Grayden had thought none of his siblings wanted anything to do with him.

Where Ashford was concerned, that was still true.

But Grace and Callum had both forgiven him. They spoke to him at least once a month, even though Grayden continued to stay away from Silver Ridge so long as Ashford didn't want him here.

When I'd mentioned the situation to Teller, he just said we should stay out of it. Let the O'Neals figure this mess out for themselves. My older brother wasn't chief of police anymore, but he was still a cop part-time.

It was hard to imagine straight-laced Teller, a decorated war veteran, reconnecting with a dishonorably discharged ex-con. Even if they'd once been best friends.

But as for me... I wasn't sure.

I knew how much heartache Grace had suffered over losing her oldest brother. And how much relief she'd felt after finding him again.

My long-ago schoolgirl crush was irrelevant.

I squeezed Grace's shoulder. "I really hope so. It would be great to have everyone together again."

"If Ashford lets that happen. He's still so angry with Grayden over everything."

"Ashford just needs time." I tapped my finger against my chin, pretending to think. "And we'll need a bigger table. Especially if you and Dane start popping out adorable tots. Or maybe Teller and Ayla will. We'll have to rent out the entire rec center."

She smiled and laughed, though the sound was tinged with sadness.

We all gathered around the dining table. A bounty lay before us. Platters of turkey, bowls of mashed potatoes and gravy and roasted veggies, my green bean casserole next to Grace's rice stuffing and rolls.

Callum and Zandra's pumpkin pie waited on the sideboard, along with my coffee and Ashford and Emma's cherry pie and chocolate-chip cookies. The whole house smelled like roasted meat and herbs and home.

Ollie sat with Maisie at one end of the table, the two of them giggling as they sneaked a bit of turkey to Stella. Ashford and Emma sat across from each other, that easy partnership they'd built on full display. Dane kept his hand on Grace's back, while Callum and Zandra shared a private smile.

My phone buzzed in my pocket. I pulled it out under the table and glanced at the screen.

DANNY

I know you're angry, but I swear I'm working on something important. Just give me time. You'll see

Disgust rolled through me. I shoved the phone back into my pocket.

"You good, Piper?" Callum asked from across the table. "Everything okay?"

I glanced at Ollie, making sure he was distracted. "Just some stuff with Danny," I said under my breath.

A wrinkle appeared between Callum's brows, and Zandra gave me a sympathetic look. But they both knew better than to get into it at the dinner table, not with the kids nearby. Besides, I just wanted to focus on the positive.

I noticed Callum checking his phone too. Maybe thinking of the one O'Neal sibling who wasn't here, like Grace had been doing.

Romantic love didn't fix everything. Sure, if you fell in love with a billionaire or a massively successful pop star, love could solve a few monetary problems. I had some money worries myself, not that I wanted to think about that on a holiday like this.

But even with a partner, adulting was still hard. You still had bills and leaky roofs and crappy exes. Family rifts that wouldn't heal.

You had to find joy wherever you could, every single day.

And I didn't need a man in my bed for any of that.

The doorbell rang, cutting through the conversation. Callum raised his eyebrows at Grace. "Expecting anyone else?" he asked.

Grace shrugged, hands full as she ladled gravy onto Maisie's plate. "Can you get it, Cal? You're the closest."

Callum stood and walked to the door. He opened it, and I heard him say one word.

"Grayden?"

Everyone at the dining table went quiet. Grace's mouth dropped open. Ashford's fork clattered against his plate.

Maisie looked up at her father. "Daddy, who's Grayden?"

THREE
Grayden

People who've experienced something traumatic, something life-changing, often talk about how their existence breaks down into *before* and *after*.

The years, minutes, even seconds before everything changed. And then, picking up the pieces and trying to understand. To move on, as much as that was possible.

That dichotomy made perfect sense to me. The entire timeline of my life broke down into the time before my sentence to the United States Disciplinary Barracks at Fort Leavenworth, Kansas, and the five years since my release.

Of course, there were also the years in between. The ten years I'd been incarcerated, serving my sentence. Wondering how everything had gone so wrong.

The black hole at the center of my life story, big enough to swallow every bit of light, everything good, if I let it.

But I wasn't there anymore. I was in the *after*. Standing outside my sister's new house in my hometown of Silver Ridge, Colorado, wondering what in the hell I was doing.

Grace's porch light was off. Voices, laughter, and light came from inside, but out here, it was still dark and deathly quiet.

Before. After.

Here goes nothing, I thought, and reached out to press the doorbell.

The chime rang out inside. I retreated to the porch steps.

Then I turned my face up to the night sky, feeling the bite of the cold against my skin. Snowflakes drifted lazily in the air and brushed my face, while my heart beat out a contrasting chaotic rhythm.

I hadn't been this nervous about anything in a long, long time. This was probably stupid, but here I was, doing it anyway.

Story of my damn life.

For a moment, nothing happened. I wondered if they'd even heard the bell. Then there were footsteps, the porch light switched on, and the door opened.

A breath got stuck halfway in my throat.

Callum stood there. My little brother. I'd spoken to him over video several times over the last few months, but seeing him in person was completely different. He certainly wasn't expecting me to show up tonight.

My inhale went stale in my chest as I watched his face change, going from calm to recognition and then surprise. Was that bad surprise? Good surprise?

Hell, the suspense was killing me.

"Grayden?" he finally said.

"Hey." My voice came out rough. I cleared my throat and tried again. "Hey, Callum. It's me."

All these years I'd had to imagine this meeting, and those words were the best I could come up with? Fuck, I was shaking. I would've had my hat in my hands too, except I'd left my beanie in the truck.

"Happy Thanksgiving," I added.

A huge grin broke over Callum's face. "Holy shit. You're here? I thought you were still in Seattle. I can't believe it." He opened his arms. "Get over here and give me a hug, man. This is crazy."

Oh, thank fuck. He was happy to see me.

I stepped forward, my own arms opening. And then we were embracing tightly, my arms wrapped around my brother. Deep relief flooded through me.

I'd known it was a big risk showing up here this way, but a hug from Callum made it all worth it.

Then a happy scream came from the doorway, and a petite figure streaked across the porch toward me in a blur, jumping into my arms. I caught my sister, laughing as I held on tight.

"Gracie. God, I'm glad to see you." I buried my face against her hair for just a second, fighting to keep my composure.

Fifteen years.

All those years I'd missed, all the moments I'd thrown away—even if I'd never meant things to turn out the way they had—and somehow she was still willing to hug me like this.

"How did you get here?" Grace asked. "When? Why didn't you say you were coming?"

"When did you get to town?" Callum asked at the same time.

"Um, it was kind of spur of the moment. Relatively speaking." I set Grace on her feet. She was taller than I remembered, but still didn't reach my shoulder. "I wasn't even sure I'd make it to Silver Ridge in time for the holiday."

I'd also needed to get out of Seattle on short notice, and calling my siblings had seemed like something I could worry about later. Or maybe I'd just been worried they would tell me not to come.

The last time I'd shown up suddenly in Silver Ridge, not too long after my release from Leavenworth, Callum had told me to get lost and never contact any of them again. But last year, Grace got in touch with me out of the blue. Biggest shock of my life, and one of the best things that ever happened to me. Knowing she still cared.

Then Callum had agreed to talk to me too. Apologized for telling me to stay away.

We'd talked some things through since then, though certainly not *everything*. There was so much Grace and Callum didn't know, and I wasn't sure if it would make me look better or worse in their eyes if I confessed the whole story.

But our brother Ashford was the biggest *if* of all. I had no idea how Ashford would react to seeing me again. He'd refused to even have a phone call with me so far. But I was hoping for the best.

Hope, like stupidity, was infinite.

"This is a surprise." Grace's boyfriend Dane stepped outside, holding a coat for her. He draped it around her shoulders, then extended his hand to me.

"I'm just glad to be here. Good to meet you in person." I shook Dane's hand, and he put an arm around Grace's waist.

"Same."

I kept marveling at my baby sister. "How did you get so grown-up and beautiful, kid?"

"You saw me on video a few weeks ago," she said, laughing and crying at the same time.

"But this is real life. Trust me, it's nowhere near the same." I knew firsthand that pictures and videos were pale copies when it came to the people we loved.

For maybe a solid minute, I just smiled at them. Taking my time and soaking it in.

Callum's girlfriend, Zandra, came out to the porch next, and I waved hello. I recognized her from calls with Callum. She shocked me by rushing over and giving me a hug too.

"Welcome back," she said.

"Thanks, Zandra. That means a lot."

I noticed a tall blond hesitating just inside the house, arms crossed over her sweater with a curious frown on her face. One of my siblings' friends, maybe?

Then she stepped outside. My gaze lingered on her stunning features. And I was the jerk staring at her when I should be focused on my siblings.

As I turned back to Grace and Callum, a tidal wave of guilt tried to pull me under. God, so much had gotten messed up. If I got to thinking too much about all the years we'd lost because of the choices I'd made, it would crush me. It *had* crushed me in the past.

My chest tightened and my eyes burned with everything going through my head. "I'm sorry," I said. "I know this is a lot."

Grace hugged me again, head resting on my arm. "Why are you sorry? This is amazing. You're welcome here, okay? Always." She gripped my hand. "Whatever else has happened, you're our brother. It's Thanksgiving. We're supposed to be together at Thanksgiving."

"If he comes in here, I'm leaving," a low voice said. "And I'm taking Emma and Maisie with me."

Ashford stood in the doorway with the light of the house behind him. Seeing my younger brother was like looking at a mirror of my past self. I'd probably worn a scowl that intense, back in the days when I wanted to rage at the world.

Who was I kidding? I still wore that same scowl more often than not.

"Hello, Ashford," I said softly.

He stepped onto the porch, shutting the front door behind him. "Grayden, what the fuck are you doing here?"

I flinched like he'd thrown a punch, not just some strong words. I'd known this would be the hardest part. Had I expected a different reception from him tonight? Not realistically.

"I just wanted to see you all. Figured this was an efficient way to do it. If a bit dramatic, I'll admit."

"Well, I don't want you here." Ashford's voice was hard. "Not around my family. Not around Maisie. She doesn't even know you exist."

I breathed through each new blow, just absorbing them all. Anything Ashford could say wasn't half of the hate I'd thrown at myself in the past. I didn't blame him.

"Don't do this, Ashford," Grace murmured, trying to stand in front of me, and I was glad when Dane wrapped his arm around her waist to pull her back.

"No, I understand," I said, keeping my voice calm even though my heart was pounding. "I know I don't have any right to just show up like this. But Ashford, I'm trying to make things right. I want to be part of this family again."

"Not gonna happen."

"If we could just talk—" I stepped toward him, reaching out.

Ashford shoved my hand away. "Don't touch me."

Grace gasped, and Callum put his palms out. "Hey, come on," Callum said. "Let's just take a breath."

Ashford's eyes never left mine. A surge of anger rose instinctively in me, making my pulse thrum. An involuntary reaction. I breathed through the feeling.

I couldn't get angry at my brother. I was a better man than that. Now, anyway.

"You don't belong here," Ashford said. "You made your choices, and now you have to live with them."

"That's not fair," Grace said, her voice shaking. "He's still our brother."

"He stopped being my brother a long time ago."

The words cut deep. I'd expected this, known it was coming, but hearing it out loud still felt like something vital was being torn out of my chest.

"Ashford, please." Grace's eyes were bright with tears. "It's Thanksgiving."

"Then he should have called ahead instead of ambushing us. That way, I would've known not to come." Ashford stormed back into the house.

"I'll talk to him," Grace said, and followed. Callum murmured something to Zandra, who went in along with the tall blond.

I blinked at the wooden slats of the porch. *Fuck*. What a fucking mess, and I was at the center of it. But since when was that a new position for me? Infinite hope, infinite stupidity.

"I apologize for bringing this to your house," I said to Dane, who'd remained outside with Callum. "Hoped he would react better. I figured I was pushing my luck, but...yeah. I know Ashford's a close friend of yours. You must care about his opinion."

"And Grace is the woman I love. If she wants you here, then that counts even more." Dane was the same in person as he was on video. His confident demeanor hadn't faltered for a second. "Ashford and I always work things out. I'm more concerned about Grace right now."

"I'm sorry," I said again, though the words felt weak and inadequate.

Callum shifted with his hands in his pockets. The night air had gotten chillier, and his breath puffed in front of him when he spoke.

"Maybe we should let things calm down for tonight," Callum said. "You can try again with Ashford later. Another time."

Dane nodded his agreement.

"Yeah." I swallowed hard. "The last thing I want is to cause a fight between the rest of you. Or upset Ashford's wife or daughter. I'm just grateful I got to see you in real life."

Dane shook my hand again. Callum pulled me into another hug.

"Tell Grace I love her," I said when we pulled apart.

"Where are you staying?" Callum asked.

"Not sure yet."

He cursed, indecision written across his face. "Want to stay with me and Z? We're happy to have you."

"Nah, that's not necessary. I can find a motel."

"Dammit, I don't feel right about this. We've barely gotten to see you. I should go with you. Grace will probably try to chase you down when she realizes you've left."

"Callum, I am *fine.* I promise. I'm tired after the drive. I'll see you all again soon." Whoever was willing, anyway.

"You won't leave town, right? You're sticking around?"

I smiled and clapped his shoulder. "Drove a hell of a long way to get here, so I'm definitely sticking around. Don't worry about me. Tell Ashford I'll be here when he's ready to talk."

If he was *ever* ready to talk.

"I love you, Cal," I added. Something I was sure to say every time I spoke to my brother or sister. Just trying to make up for the years that I couldn't.

"Love you too, brother."

I kept my chin up as I walked back to my truck. I'd gotten to hug Grace and Callum. I'd seen my family, even if only for a few minutes. That should have been enough.

But as I climbed into the driver's seat and the dome light faded, leaving me in darkness, all I could think about was Ashford's face. His absolute certainty that he was better off without me.

That had been one of the most humbling experiences of my life, and hell, I'd had more than enough of those.

Maybe Ashford was right. Maybe I'd broken us too badly to ever put the pieces back together.

I sat there in the cold truck, watching snowflakes gather on the windshield. Then I started the engine and drove away.

FOUR

Piper

GRAYDEN WAS *HERE*. In Silver Ridge. Right outside.

I couldn't figure out how to feel.

The moment we heard Callum say his brother's name out on the porch, Grace was the next to jump up and run for the door. She squealed with joy and leaped into his arms.

I followed but didn't go outside, glancing through the front window at them instead. I caught a glimpse of the tall man hugging Grace.

A tall, rugged, rough-around-the-edges man who was even more handsome than when we were younger.

I remembered him with a buzz cut and a clean-shaven face. But now, Grayden's brown hair had grown to almost his chin, all tousled and messy with a slight wave to it. His beard was in need of a trim, and he had far more lines around his eyes and mouth than before.

A tattoo of black roses peeked up the side of his neck.

But all that toughness was softened by his wide grin as he talked to his sister.

I startled when Ollie tugged the edge of my sweater. "Mom, who is he?" Ollie must have noticed the tension, because he was whispering. "Maisie asked who Grayden is, but her dad didn't answer."

"You don't need to worry about that right now."

"But—"

I walked Ollie back to the dining room. Behind me, I heard Grace and Callum talking loudly outside. Dane brushed past me, and it sounded like he'd shut the door, dampening the sounds of their voices.

But in here, it was like time had stopped. Ashford was just staring into space with a look of sheer horror on his face. Like he was watching a train wreck that was on fire and about to get eaten by Godzilla.

Emma stood up, grabbing Maisie's hand. "Hey, Maisie-doodle. I just realized we haven't called my dad and stepmom to say Happy Thanksgiving. Come help me."

"But Emma, I'm still eating. And Daddy's—"

"Your daddy needs a minute." She didn't let Maisie argue, just ushering her down a hall toward one of the guest rooms.

Ashford hadn't broken free of his catatonic state yet, but storm clouds were gathering behind his eyes.

I turned to Ollie, who looked like he was ready to rush outside and find out for himself what all this fuss was about.

"Ollie, go play with Maisie for a while."

"No way! I want to see what's going on. What is all this?" He tried to push past me, but I held on to his shoulders.

"This is a grown-up moment. Just listen to me for now, and I'll explain later."

"Grown-up moments suck balls."

"*Excuse* me? Oliver Carmichael, get your butt out of this room and go with Emma and Maisie. Right now." I jabbed a finger toward the hallway.

Ollie stomped off. When he was gone, I turned and saw amusement dancing in Zandra's dark eyes. "Grown-up stuff does suck balls sometimes," she murmured. "That's objectively true."

I snorted a laugh, covering my mouth.

But once Zandra and I got outside, I wasn't laughing. Especially after Ashford finally made his entrance. Said what he said.

The look on Grayden's face... There'd been a glimmer of hurt before he shut down, turning to stone.

Then Ashford stormed into the house, and Grace tried to follow and argue with him. By the time Grayden had left and everyone else was back inside, it felt like a bomb had dropped in the middle of our Thanksgiving.

What the heck had Grayden been thinking, showing up like that?

But also...wow. That had taken some nerve.

Emma, Zandra, and I dished up pie for the kids and put on a movie for them in the guest room. Then we joined the adults gathered around the dining table. Half-eaten plates of food sat haphazardly at our places. The gravy had congealed.

The wine glasses, though? Those were empty. Any minute and Dane would break out the expensive whiskey.

Grace glared across the table at Ashford. "It didn't have to be like that," she said.

"Agreed. It would've been better if he didn't show up and ruin our night."

"Not what I meant. If anyone ruined our night, it's you."

"*Me*?" Ashford leaned back in his chair. Emma put her hand on his leg, and I wasn't sure if she was comforting him or trying to stop him from saying whatever he was about to say.

"Grayden's trying to fix things," Grace said. "So we can all be a family again."

"Not my family." Ashford's volume rose. "He's a killer, Grace."

"It was involuntary manslaughter," Callum said calmly. "A bar fight that got out of hand. You already know that. He served his time."

"But has he explained everything else that happened back then?" Ashford glanced from Callum to Grace and back again. "After he got arrested, he refused to defend himself, shut us out, wouldn't even talk to us. Probably because he was guilty as sin. Grayden cut *himself* out of our lives. Has he said one single thing to excuse any of it?"

For several long seconds, there was no sound except breathing and the faint sounds of the kids' movie in the other room.

"No," Grace muttered. "We forgave him anyway, and we're letting him tell us the rest when he's ready."

"Then nothing has changed. I don't want him around my kid. You invited him inside with zero regard for how I'd feel about it. What the fuck was that?"

Dane put his hand on Grace's shoulder. "Hey, could you not talk to her that way?"

"This is between me and my sister, not you," Ashford snapped at him.

"If it involves Grace, it involves me."

"Guys, can't we just let it go for now and try to enjoy the rest of the evening?" Callum asked. Zandra opened her mouth like she wanted to speak, though she held herself back.

But Grace and Ashford were getting into it again. I'd never seen them so angry at each other. And Dane and Ashford looked ready to come to blows, even though they were supposed to be best friends.

Geez, this was going downhill fast.

Maybe it was a good thing Teller wasn't here too. When it came to Grayden, I didn't know which side Teller would be on. But I could guess.

I jumped up, grabbed my wine glass, and whacked my spoon against it. Everyone's head turned at the high-pitched clinking.

"Okay, okay! Quiet, please! We're all going to shut up and stuff our faces with pie for the next hour, or so help me, you're all banned from Silver Linings for the next week."

Grace frowned at me, and Ashford's jaw stayed tight.

Zandra stood. "I'm with the coffee lady. I can't live without my pistachio lattes."

"Agreed," Callum said, taking a deep breath before his usual grin slid into place. "I made a killer pumpkin pie. Everyone needs to try it."

Zandra poked his shoulder. "You seem to forget I made the pies while you sat on your ass and played with our new kitten."

"I supervised!"

A glimmer of a smile crossed Grace's expression. Dane kissed her temple. Emma leaned into Ashford, whispering in his ear, and he nodded.

There. The problem wasn't fixed, but at least we could take a break before the inevitable next round.

While everyone was busy clearing the table, I grabbed Grace's hand and tugged her down the hallway toward the laundry room. "Hey, I'm sorry it all went down like that," I said quietly.

"Me too." Grace hugged me, and I rested my cheek on her head. "I tried texting Grayden after he left to see if he's alright, but he hasn't written back. I don't even know if he has a place to stay."

"I'm sure he'll figure it out. He did show up tonight out of the blue. He had to expect it might not go well."

Grace looked like she wanted to disagree, but then nodded. "Yeah. I was shocked to see him. But it felt good to hold him." Her voice faltered. "He's my brother, Piper. I hadn't hugged my brother for half my life until tonight. It isn't right. I just want this to work out. It has to."

"It will," I said firmly.

"You always say that."

"I'm always right. Sometimes it just takes a while for the rest of the world to catch up."

Dessert helped everyone settle down. We shoveled pastry crust and sweet fillings into our mouths, taking comfort from all those calories. I poured cups of coffee from the carafe I'd brought and declined Callum's offer to spike it. Didn't want to be tipsy when I drove Ollie home.

After more hugs and lingering goodbyes, I grabbed my container of leftovers and managed to get a yawning Ollie into the back seat of the car. He was tall enough to be out of his booster, but still too small for the front.

Of course, the first thing he said when I started the engine was, "Mom, I want to know who Grayden is."

Shit.

Whatever I said to Ollie, it would probably get back to Ashford's daughter Maisie. Those two were so close. As good as cousins. And I didn't want to ask him to lie to his friend. What kind of example would that set?

Though I did stretch the truth sometimes myself for perfectly legitimate reasons...

I bought myself a minute or two by studying the road and tapping my fingers on the steering wheel. "It's one of those complicated family things, Ollie-bear. Grown-up things."

"Mom," he whined.

"Hold on, I'm getting to it, okay? Just let me explain."

Ha, like all this made sense to me. But I was the parent. I was supposed to have all the answers, even though I was still trying to figure out life myself.

"The thing is, Grayden is part of the O'Neal family."

"How?"

Well, I couldn't avoid it, could I? "He's the oldest brother. It was Grayden, then Ashford, Callum, and Grace."

"I didn't know they had another brother! Maisie doesn't know either!"

"Yeah, that's the complicated part. Ashford doesn't talk to Grayden anymore. And he doesn't want Maisie to talk to Grayden."

"Why? Is he bad?"

"He's...no. He's made some mistakes, but I don't think he's bad. Grace and Callum don't think so."

"What did Grayden do? Why doesn't Ashford like him?"

Phew, couldn't we just have the where-babies-come-from talk again?

"Grayden hurt someone. He had to go to prison. I don't know exactly what happened. It was a long time ago."

Ollie's face scrunched up. "So Ashford thinks Grayden would hurt Maisie?"

"I don't think so. Not exactly. I think Ashford's afraid of getting hurt himself. His heart, I mean. Because of...a lot of things."

Nice and awkward there, Piper.

How did I explain to my nine-year-old that us adults were carrying deep wounds that rarely showed on the surface? That Ashford, a man Ollie idolized, had once been a scared kid who lost his mom and dad.

Sure, I could say those things, but how did I make Ollie understand?

"Families are complicated," I finished. "We're all just doing our best, even if we mess things up. Ashford, Grace, me. And Grayden too."

"And Dad? Even though he didn't take me on our trip today like he said he would?"

Ugh. I wished Danny would live by his better instincts instead of his worst. I had zero faith where my ex was concerned.

"I hope so," I said. "I do know your dad loves you. Very much."

Ollie looked out his window and nodded, but a crease remained between his little eyebrows.

Snow fell in big, soft flakes, gathering on the windows and the edges of the windshield beyond the wipers. The world was a blur of white and shadow until we got closer to Main Street, where there were more street lights.

I drove slowly past a gas station on the edge of the commercial district, mindful of the ice on the road. A figure emerged from the tiny convenience store. Tall and broad shouldered, with a knit cap pulled over his messy hair.

My heart did a strange stuttering dance.

Grayden held a small shopping bag in his hand. The gas station shop was probably the only business open tonight, given the holiday. I watched as he walked at a casual pace toward an old, beat-up Dodge parked on the curb, seeming not to mind the snow gathering on his jacket and hat.

He reached the truck. But instead of getting in the driver's seat, he opened the rear door of the extended cab and climbed into the back.

Wait a minute. He wasn't…

"Mom?" Ollie craned his neck to see what I was staring at. "Why are we stopped? Is the storm getting bad?"

"Uh, no, it's not too bad to drive. But I need to pull over for a moment."

"What's wrong?"

"I need to check on something really quick. Okay? Just stay in the car."

Turning the wheel and pressing the gas, I steered my Subaru to the same curb where Grayden was parked, but with my hood facing his. My car was probably too low for my headlights to blind him, but I switched them off just in case.

"Stay in the car," I said again to Ollie, hoping he'd listen.

Then I got out and walked toward Grayden's truck.

FIVE

Grayden

A GAS STATION Thanksgiving dinner wasn't the worst I'd ever had. Not by a long shot.

After spending over an hour trying to find a cheap enough motel to justify spending my hard-earned money, I finally gave up and headed toward Main Street. Nearly every business was closed, but old-fashioned street lights lit the route, and strings of cheerful lights crisscrossed overhead. Pretty.

In a couple more weeks, there'd be holiday greenery and red ribbons decorating every spare surface. And a Christmas tree in front of the town hall.

Brought back memories. Like when Teller and I used to cruise down this stretch of road in high school, thinking we owned this town.

Teller became chief of police, a local hero. While I turned out to be the bad guy. The villain in the O'Neal family story.

Also, Teller had scored himself a pop star girlfriend. I'd heard all about it in articles and videos online. While I was here perusing the gourmet offerings of a tiny convenience store for my holiday meal.

The man behind the register grunted, "Happy Thanksgiving," without looking away from the football highlights on his phone.

"You too," I said as I considered what to eat. There was a tiny machine rotating two hot dogs that looked drier than the Colorado desert in summer. But I grabbed one dog anyway, stuck it in a bun, and slathered it with ketchup.

Again, not the worst I'd ever had.

Next I selected a bag of chips, an overripe banana, and a few granola bars, along with a big bottle of water, and brought it all to the counter. The man rang it up without much comment, but when I held out a few wrinkled bills to pay, he scrutinized me.

"You look familiar. Got family around here?"

I figured the man recognized the features I shared with Ashford and Callum. Maybe I'd even known this guy back in the day, but my memory drew a blank. I decided not to identify myself.

I assumed every old timer in Silver Ridge knew the name Grayden O'Neal, and I didn't want to deal with that tonight.

"If I did, I'd be eating better food tonight than this. No offense."

"None taken," he grunted.

I accepted my change and dropped half of it into the tip jar before taking my bag.

Then it was back out into the snow. Which was a blessing. Yes, it was cold out, but the snow would cover the windows in my truck before long, almost like curtains. Nice and cozy.

Made me think of the warmth I'd glimpsed through the windows of Gracie's house. I loved that she had a nice place like that. A man who adored her.

Callum had Zandra, a strong spitfire who could keep him in check. I smiled as I thought of the trouble my youngest brother used to get into as a kid.

And even though Ashford had looked at me like something he'd scraped off his shoe, I was so damn proud of the way he'd talked about his wife and daughter. Like he would sacrifice anything for them.

Ashford might be surprised, but I would do the same for the people I loved. Sacrifice everything. I *had* done it. With devastating consequences.

I hadn't earned back Ashford's trust yet, but I would. I just had to be patient. A skill I'd gotten very good at over the years.

Couldn't wait to meet my niece Maisie, though. Grace had sent me a photo via text a few months ago, taken on Ashford and Emma's wedding day. Maisie's smiling face had been front and center. She looked so much like Ashford. And, I guess, like me. I got choked up whenever I looked at it.

The old hinge of the door to my truck fought me, but this Dodge had made it all the way here from Seattle, so that was yet another thing to be grateful for. I settled into the backseat, taking off my snow-dusted hat and ruffling my hair. Time to dig in to Thanksgiving dinner.

Then headlights swung in my direction, making me squint. The vehicle parked right in front of me, nose to nose. Like it wanted to keep me from leaving.

You gotta be kidding me, I thought.

The car was low slung. Could be a state trooper or something. The cops had found me already? Shitty fucking luck. Unless... could Ashford have called and reported me? Given them the description of my truck?

I immediately started to sweat, heart kicking. It was an involuntary reaction when dealing with police after my history. The moment any cop ran my driver's license, he could find out that I had a record. Computers and nationwide databases worked at light speed these days.

But you're the idiot who decided to take the risk of sleeping in your truck this close to town.

I had nothing to hide though. I hadn't done anything wrong, and I could say I just wanted to relax and eat before I kept driving. Couldn't be a law against that, right?

Unfortunately, I doubted it would matter. If the cops wanted to make trouble for me, they could.

There was a knock at my window. My pulse increased.

But when I saw the face through the glass, my heart tripped over itself in a different kind of way.

It was the pretty blond from outside Grace's house.

What in the world was she doing out here in the snow? It was getting late.

I carefully opened the door and stepped out, shutting it most of the way to keep the weather out. She moved back a couple paces, but she was still close.

"Grayden. Sorry. Hope I didn't startle you."

I dug my hands into my jeans pockets to keep them warm. "Not much."

"I'm not sure if you remember me."

I searched her face but came up blank. "Sorry, I—"

"Piper. Teller's sister."

Damn.

Little Piper Landry?

Piper had changed a lot. Not so little anymore. She'd grown. Blossomed, really. She was just a few inches shorter than me, which would put her close to six feet. Her features were delicately beautiful, and the lights of Main Street spun her blond hair into gold.

"Piper Landry," I said. "How are you?"

I hadn't recognized her, but now, it all came rushing back.

I'd lost myself in memories of growing up in Silver Ridge plenty of times over the years. Piper had been there, kind of a vague presence orbiting my sister, her features not quite distinct. Even though I'd been around Piper pretty much since she was born until I left Colorado.

But I could almost picture the gangly kid she used to be. The teenager I'd sometimes caught staring a little too long at me. Who blushed whenever I stopped by the Landry house to see her brother, especially when I was in uniform.

Piper wasn't gangly anymore. That was for sure.

And her brother wasn't my friend anymore.

"My last name isn't Landry now," she said. "But anyway. I just noticed you out here, and I decided to stop."

"Alright." I wasn't sure what she wanted me to say to that. Was she going to lecture me about what happened at Grace's? Curse me out?

"You're not sleeping out here in your truck, are you? It's freezing." She wrapped her arms around her coat, emphasizing the point.

An edge of annoyance worked its way under my skin. "I haven't firmed up my plans yet." Like I had a packed social calendar.

"You should go back to Grace's if you need a place to stay. Or at least find a hotel. That's what Grace would want."

"Thanks for the concern, but I'm fine."

Piper glanced behind her toward her car. I couldn't make out if anyone else was inside. "Grayden, if you need money or something—"

Oh, for fuck's sake.

"I don't need charity. I can afford a hotel if I want one." I was trying to save every penny of my savings toward getting myself established here in Colorado, not blow it on overpriced hotel rooms. That wasn't her business though. I could sort out my own shit.

Besides, this wouldn't be the first time I'd slept in my truck. In fact, I'd slept in my truck just last night. The drive to Silver Ridge from Seattle was a long-ass way.

"Well, I can't just leave you out here. I need to know you'll be alright."

I barked a sudden laugh as a memory came to me. Little Piper bossing her brother around about doing the dishes, though Teller was ten years older and had weighed at least twice as much as she did. There'd been something fearless about her.

He'd listened though. Always. Teller had been just as doting over Piper as I'd been over Grace.

Piper frowned and put her hands on her hips. "Something funny?"

"Not really. Just thinking."

Thinking about what a bossy mouth you still have on you. And how you grew up into a hell of a sexy woman.

If I said all that out loud, it would absolutely make her back off. Not that I would. I had a strict rule about not being an obnoxious dick.

The back door to her car opened, and a boy of around ten stomped toward us through the snow. "Mom, that's him, right? The one we were talking about?"

"Ollie, I told you to stay put."

"But I wanted to make sure you were okay." He eyed me like I might pull a knife any second, and he had every intention of defending his momma from me.

The corner of my mouth ticked up. What did we have here? Piper had a kid. A feisty one at that.

I held up my hands. "It's all good. Your mom was just checking up on me, little man. Which I appreciate. But I'm fine."

"I'm not little." His scowl deepened. "See, he's fine, Mom. Can we go?"

"No, we are not going. Not until I'm satisfied."

Ollie sighed like he was well familiar with that tone of voice. His mom meant business. She looked at my old truck, then at her own vehicle, then at the gas station. And finally, back to me.

"Here's what's going to happen. You'll sleep on our couch tonight."

Ollie's mouth dropped open. "Mom, seriously?"

I ran a hand over my beard, tilting my head.

She didn't take her eyes off me. "It's either that, or I call Grace and Callum right now and let them know where you are. You decide. But I'm not letting their brother freeze to death in a rickety truck on Thanksgiving."

"Rickety? My truck takes exception to that."

"Your truck will get over it."

I glanced at Ollie, lifting my brows. "Your mom drives a hard bargain."

"You have no idea," he muttered.

SIX

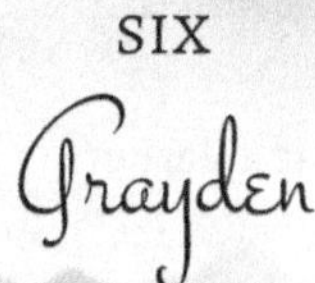

I FOLLOWED Piper's car in my truck. It wasn't a long drive. Meanwhile, the snow continued to fall.

After maybe three minutes, we pulled up to a little cottage about a block off Main. I grabbed my duffel from the backseat.

The rest of my stuff was in the truck bed, covered by a tarp, and it'd be fine. But these were the items I couldn't afford to lose. My tablet computer, chargers, art portfolio, and my tattoo equipment. A couple changes of clothes and a toothbrush.

I followed Piper and Ollie to the front door. He kept glancing back at me suspiciously. Piper pulled out her keys, balancing a container of leftovers with her other arm.

"I can get that for you," I offered, but Ollie grabbed it first, sending a glare my way. I held up my hands, backing off, and my duffel swung against my side on its long strap.

The moment we stepped inside Piper's house, welcoming scents enveloped me. Savory home cooking, fresh flowers, and something sweet like cinnamon or nutmeg blended with the rich aroma of coffee.

The walls were painted in bright colors with white trim. Shoes and boots were lined up beside the door, with coat hooks above.

I took a few steps inside, lowering my duffel to the ground, and reached to untie my boots. Piper and Ollie took an immediate left through an archway into a small kitchen. I could see them from the entry. It wasn't a big place.

After Ollie set the leftovers on the counter, he went to open a cookie jar. "Oh no, don't even think about it," Piper said. "It's late. You need to go to bed."

Ollie tipped his head back, lamenting. "I'm not tired."

"Brush your teeth, mister. Go." She nudged him out of the kitchen.

Ollie passed me on his way. He pointed to his own eyes with two fingers, then jabbed his pointer finger in my direction. The universal symbol for *I'm watching you, so don't get any ideas*.

Fuck, I kinda loved this kid already.

I almost laughed, but I didn't want to belittle his protectiveness. Far from it. I respected that Ollie wanted to take care of his mom. So instead, I put a hand over my heart and nodded solemnly.

He and Piper had nothing to fear from me.

"Have you had dinner?" Piper asked from behind me. I turned and saw her leaning against the kitchen counter.

I scratched my beard. "I had a hot dog, but I left it in the truck."

"A hot dog for Thanksgiving dinner?" She turned around and grabbed the container of leftovers. "Come on. You must be hungry."

"How do you know what I am?"

I was starving actually, but my orneriness was rising to the surface. I'd never been that great at dealing with authority. Funny when you considered the years I spent in the Army, but not so funny when you thought about how all that ended up.

"Because you were willing to eat a gas station hot dog at eleven at night. I'm sure they're good some of the time, but this late on Thanksgiving, it was probably slim pickings."

"Yeah, you've got me there. But I've got my bag of chips. Those won't go bad until after the zombie apocalypse."

Smirking, she opened the lid on the container, revealing a whole spread of seasonal favorites. "Quit arguing and eat. Grace won't be happy if I keep her brother from having a decent holiday meal."

"Well, if it's what Grace wants, I guess I can get onboard."

Piper offered to warm up the food, but that was more fuss than I wanted to put up with. So she handed me a fork. "At least sit at the table."

"Eating at the counter isn't civilized enough for you?"

"I'm a counter-eating girl. Believe me. But..." She tucked a few golden strands behind her ear. "You should sit at a proper table for a holiday meal. It's important."

I waited while she set out a green placemat and then added a paper napkin with fall leaves printed on it. "Thank you," I murmured, and Piper nodded, taking the seat across from me.

This was nice. Also kind of embarrassing. I didn't want anyone's pity, and the thought of Piper seeing me that way made me bristle.

Some people might not think it, but I had plenty of pride left.

Then she asked, "Can I have a mushroom? I added them to the green beans this year. Put wine in the skillet and everything."

"Go for it." I held out the container. She plucked a mushroom with her fingers and popped it in her mouth.

There was something so familiar and casual about the move that it diffused any tension I'd been feeling. Made me feel less like some drifter she'd taken pity on.

Also, the way she moaned as she chewed had me sitting up straighter, all my attention on those pretty pink lips.

"Mmm," she hummed. "Try it. Try everything. It's all good."

"Don't have to tell me twice."

"I definitely had to tell you more than twice."

Smirking, I practically inhaled the first bites. There was turkey, mashed potatoes and gravy, stuffing and the green bean-mushroom casserole.

"Like it?" Piper asked, watching me with her light-green eyes.

"Might be the best meal of my life. Except the hamburger and greasy fries I had that first day after leaving Leavenworth. That tasted pretty damn amazing. I put on quite a show at the fast food place with the way I licked the salt off my fingers. It was getting R-rated." I forked up another bite of stuffing.

She sputtered a laugh that died too soon. "So we're talking about that? The prison thing."

I shoveled half the slice of pumpkin pie in my mouth. Possibly a delay tactic.

When I swallowed, I said, "Makes no difference if we talk about it or not. It is what it is. But I'm not gonna dance around it, and you don't have to either. I'm a convicted felon."

I watched her expression for any misgivings about inviting me into her home. I'd been some part of Piper's life before. But that had been a lifetime ago. She didn't owe me a damn thing.

Maybe she was doing this for Grace's sake, but Piper had no reason to trust me. Ashford certainly didn't. Hell, I didn't always trust myself. I had a habit of leaping before I bothered to look.

"And now you're an ex-con with a full stomach," Piper said.

A surprised laugh burst out of me. "That I am. Thank you again. The food was delicious."

"Better than a stale hot dog?"

"Much. But you don't have any leftovers."

"That's okay. I ate so much at Grace's I won't be hungry for two days anyway."

"What about your growing kid?"

"Ollie? He'd much rather eat Oreos and tortilla chips than turkey and green beans."

After washing my plate over Piper's protests that she'd do it in the morning, I stopped by the hall bathroom.

When I emerged, the living room was empty. But Piper had set up the couch with a sheet and a blanket. Looked a whole lot more comfortable than the backseat of my Dodge.

Fuck, I was tired enough to sleep for a week. Especially with a belly full of comfort food, the cozy warmth of Piper's home, and soft snowflakes drifting down outside the window.

I stripped my long-sleeved tee over my head, folding it carefully before setting it on the coffee table. I could just wear my jeans to sleep, since changing into pajama pants felt a little too casual.

There was a small sound behind me, an intake of breath, and I glanced back over my shoulder.

Piper stood a few feet away holding a pillow. Her lips were parted, and her eyes were on my back, her gaze moving like a slow caress I could almost feel.

No, I *could* feel it. Pleasant tingles of awareness spread across my skin, down through my belly and then lower.

She seemed to be admiring my tattoos. I knew they looked good. And I didn't mind being admired.

Her gaze continued down my spine to the low waistband of my jeans. I wasn't wearing underwear. That hadn't seemed like a relevant issue to anyone except myself when I got dressed yesterday. But it was probably obvious.

My cock stirred, thickening a bit.

Suddenly Piper jolted, like she'd just realized I was watching her from over my shoulder. Clearing her throat, she stepped forward and held out the pillow.

"The piece on your back is impressive."

"You like it?" Those words had come out low and husky, not entirely on purpose.

She nodded, swallowing.

"My design. A buddy did the ink." Now that I'd turned around, the angle of her eyes had shifted to my chest. My nipples tightened, and two blooms of pink appeared in Piper's cheeks.

If she kept looking at me like that, it would soon be extremely obvious I was going commando.

I found myself wondering about the life Piper had led here in Silver Ridge. Was Ollie's father still in the picture? She'd mentioned her last name wasn't Landry anymore. Was she married? Was she seeing anyone?

All things I had no right to be thinking about. She was pretty much my little sister's age. I was forty-one and more banged up than the old Dodge I'd left parked at the curb.

My ink was eye-catching, that was all.

I lifted the pillow she'd given me. "Thanks for everything."

Her eyes found their way back to mine. "Don't mention it." Her voice was rougher than it had been before. "Happy Thanksgiving." She turned to go.

"Hey, Piper," I called out.

When she turned back around, she looked uncertain for the first time tonight. "Um, yes?"

Did she think I was going to proposition her? Not that I wasn't tempted.

"Look, I'd prefer if you don't mention tonight to Grace or Callum," I said. "Unless they ask, and I don't think they would. The last thing I came here for is anyone's charity, especially theirs."

If Grace or Callum heard I'd been ready to sleep in my truck, they'd try to fix it. I didn't want that. Certainly didn't want Grace thinking I'd shown up here to mooch off her rich boyfriend.

I was back in Silver Ridge for good, but I intended to do this my own way.

Piper considered me for a moment, carefully keeping her eyes on my face. Then she nodded.

"I just don't need anyone to feel sorry for me. I had a solid gig in Seattle, and I ran into some issues, but—"

She crossed her arms. "Issues? Like what?"

I hadn't wanted to get into that, but I'd also made a deal with myself. If anyone asked me a question head-on, I'd answer it. Full honesty.

Piper had just asked.

I tossed the pillow onto the couch. "I was renting space to see clients in a shop along with a buddy. Another artist. Thought I could trust him, and it turned out he was selling shit to customers on the side."

"Drugs?"

I nodded once. "The owner of the shop found out and my supposed friend blamed *me*. Owner kicked us both to the curb, regardless of the rent and deposits I'd paid. Thank God he didn't call the police. I can't afford to be near anything illegal. I'm the one with a record, so who would the cops believe?"

Her lips twisted with empathy rather than judgment.

"But that gave me the push I needed to come back to Silver Ridge," I went on. "I'm going to make things right with my family."

"Good."

"So I don't need anyone worrying about my welfare."

"Anyone, such as me?"

Heat flared low in my stomach again. Something about the teasing sarcasm in her tone. Because I liked it.

I shrugged, figuring her question had been rhetorical.

"Just...take care of yourself," she said.

"You do the same."

"I plan to."

SEVEN

Piper

First thing in the morning was my favorite time of day at Silver Linings. Especially a winter morning like this one, when it was still dark out, and the day was fresh and new.

Chatting with my customers and seeing their smiling faces was also my favorite part of the day. But a girl could have more than one favorite, right?

I brushed the snow from my coat just before walking into the inviting warmth of the coffee shop interior. The scents of butter and sugar hit me as I strode into the kitchen.

Dillon's broad shoulders hunched over the counter as he scooped balls of dough onto a baking sheet. "Morning, Dillon," I called out. "It smells absolutely incredible in here. Is that cardamom?"

He looked up and gestured to a cooling rack. "Wait till you try these. New recipe. Here."

He set down his scoop, picked up a scone from the rack, and held it out to me. I broke off a piece and took a bite. The texture was tender, with bursts of sweetness from dried apricot and the spicy bite of crystallized ginger. Cardamom accented the finish.

"This is dangerous. People are going to start camping out

front before we open." I took another bite. "Make a double batch tomorrow."

Dillon smiled and nodded. "You got it, boss."

I grabbed my apron and started on my tasks for opening up the shop.

Silver Linings had been mine for about five years now, and I still got that little flutter in my chest every time I walked through the door. My pride and joy, second only to Ollie.

Not that the path here had been what I'd planned. Once upon a time, I'd been working on a literature degree, my head full of Joyce and Hemingway and ideas of maybe being a teacher.

Grace had been my college roommate, naturally, the star student of her accounting classes.

While I'd taken out loans to fund my education, Grace had received a full-ride scholarship from an anonymous alumnus of Silver Ridge High, based on her impressive test scores.

I was still paying those loans off, even without the degree to show for it. At least Danny had agreed to move to my hometown, probably because he wasn't at all close to his own family.

I'd wound up a barista right here. Worked my way up until I took over the place myself while also caring for Ollie, no thanks to my ex.

It had been my idea to add shelves laden with well-loved paperbacks for sale, and to refurbish the old fireplace so we could have a blaze going in the winter months. I'd even come up with the Silver Linings name and hand-painted the wooden sign outside.

Now, I had a half-dozen employees who worked various shifts, plus seasonal help in the summers. About once a week, I helped open up the shop in the morning, but I spent the others with Ollie.

Speaking of my employees, wasn't there supposed to be another here right now?

On cue, Rina charged in five minutes late and out of breath. Her dark, wavy hair stuck out with static as she whipped the beanie off her head. "So sorry, Piper! Couldn't find my ice scraper, and then I slipped on the driveway. My feet were over my head."

I looked her over, but she seemed uninjured. "You alright?"

"Landed right on the snow-people my little brother made yesterday. Squashed them flat. But I swear, my entire life played out like a movie in my head. Scene by scene."

Dillon placed a tray of muffins on the cooling rack. "Only you could have this much drama before seven a.m."

I chuckled and handed Rina an apron. "Glad you're safe and sound."

Rina Collins had moved to Silver Ridge last year and always seemed to be skating through the door at the last second. She was far worse than me about keeping to a schedule. But her milk foam artistry was legendary. Seriously, she had her own Instagram account devoted to it. And she kept us laughing.

Dillon Kirby was a former baseball player. Not the most likely type to wind up my best baker. But he was one of those quiet men with hidden depths. He'd been through far too much tragedy and loss already in his life, having lost his father and sister in a fire when he was a kid.

Then he worked his way to becoming a college baseball star before he tore his rotator cuff so badly that surgery couldn't fix it.

Lucky for me, he'd discovered a passion for high-altitude baking techniques.

Within a couple of hours, we were busy making lattes, boxing up pastries, and chatting with customers.

There seemed to be one topic of conversation on everyone's mind today: a certain handsome, mysterious, tattooed bad boy who'd just reappeared in town.

It seemed most of Silver Ridge had heard about the drama at Grace's house. Including the way Ashford had yelled at Grayden and told him to leave.

It was still hard to believe he'd sat at my kitchen table that night, eating my leftovers and throwing out casual mentions of his prison time. And afterward, when I'd walked into the living room and found him shirtless, all those muscles and tattoos on display...

Yikes.

Grace's brother, I reminded myself. I'd had a pathetic crush on the man when I was a teenager, but I had far more sense now.

Besides, I doubted Grayden would stick around that long, regardless of what he'd said the other night about staying in Hart County.

Around mid-morning, I took a ten-minute break and retreated to the kitchen, where I downed a mocha and ate half a bran muffin while I scrolled my phone. No urgent messages waited from Ollie's school, thank goodness. Like the time he'd played chicken on the monkey bars and the other child wound up with two broken arms.

Rina's head popped in. "Piper, you need to get out front."

"What's wrong?" We didn't usually get slammed at 11:30 on a Monday. "Did you spill another twenty-pound bag of coffee beans?"

"No. It's way more exciting than that. Two words. *Double. Espresso.*"

"What?" I shook my head, as if that would help me understand what in the world she was talking about. "Aren't you supposed to be on the register?"

"Yeah, I was. That's my point. You need to get out there. This is *big*."

I let her push me along through the kitchen toward the front. She stopped me before we reached the counter and peeked comically from behind a partial wall at the tables.

"See? It's *him*. The guy everyone's talking about. He's *here*."

My gaze first went to the register, confirming there weren't any annoyed customers waiting with no one to help them.

Only then did I let my eyes wander in the direction Rina was pointing. The far table in the corner by the bookshelves.

Grayden was here.

I ignored the tiny increase in my heart rate. "So?" I asked. "He's allowed to drink coffee."

"Double espresso, Piper," she stage-whispered. "Who orders just espresso in Silver Ridge? This isn't Italy. But he was so cool and confident about it, I was all, *Bellissimo, Signore*, like I'd been transported to Roma."

I was doing my best not to roll my eyes. "Plenty of people order plain espresso." Okay, not a lot, but it happened. Sometimes.

Rina kept up her stream of consciousness. "And he smells like...I don't even know, something a really hot anti-hero smells like. Broken promises and virgin tears."

I snorted. "He's not an anti-hero. He's just a guy. And he smells more like..." I cut myself off, realizing I should *not* finish that sentence.

For the record, he smelled like black pepper, cedar, and pure man. And his eyes were dark brown with subtle hints of amber and gold.

"Piper." Rina leveled a glare at me. "For heaven's sake, look at the guy."

Nope. Didn't need to do that. "I just did."

"No, you glanced." She nudged my chin. "Take a nice, long look."

Ugh, did I have to? I'd seen more than enough of Grayden the other night.

Trust me, I'd looked my fill.

But reluctantly, I went ahead and focused on the secluded corner table again. Grayden sat with his head bowed as he read a battered paperback. He wore a black button-down with the sleeves rolled up his forearms to show off his tats. His unruly hair hung into his face, and as I watched, he pushed back the strands with a large hand.

A shiver passed through me, and a sigh whispered through my lips. No denying the man was fine as hell.

His head tilted, giving us a better view of the black roses inked on the side of his neck. His beard was a bit more trimmed than the other night. But today, he wore a pair of thick black-framed glasses.

That was just unfair.

"Didn't know about the glasses," I muttered weakly.

"Yeah, sexy-guy glasses. And the tattoos?" Rina made a choked sound. "I wonder how far they go over his body."

That, I had a pretty good idea about.

A huge design of tropical leaves and flowers covered most of Grayden's back. His right arm was mostly unmarked except for a starburst on his bicep. But an intricate sleeve of ink covered his left arm and stretched up to his shoulder, where the design extended across his upper chest to the stylized roses just visible right now above his collar.

I hadn't been able to take my eyes off him when he stood there shirtless in my living room. I'd remembered him being in good shape back when I was a teenager. But not like *that*. There was no way his upper back had been that broad years ago, or that his pecs had been so...round.

I'd gone to bed with my blood pumping, my nipples peaked, and very naughty ideas swirling in my brain.

At his table, Grayden turned a page of his paperback. Lifted his tiny cup to sip the espresso.

Then his eyes shifted upward and met mine, which made me jump and duck back into the kitchen.

Yeah, he probably hadn't noticed.

Getting flustered around handsome men was not something I did. But Grayden O'Neal wasn't just a random hot older man. He was a guy who'd spent the night on my couch a few days ago, then vanished by the time I stumbled out of my bedroom the next morning.

Which was fine by me. Not like I'd cared either way about seeing him again. I cared about Grace being happy and working out her siblings' differences, but this wasn't about *me*.

I had no idea what he'd done since. If he'd gotten a hotel or ended up sleeping in his truck for the rest of the weekend. Maybe I should've asked for his number to check, but he'd made it clear he didn't want my help or my interference. Grace and I hadn't texted much the rest of the weekend either.

"I guess he's okay looking," I finally said to Rina.

That was definitely a lie.

"What are you two staring at?" Dillon asked behind me.

Rina turned around. "Only the sexiest man to set foot in Silver Ridge, Colorado, since history began. Even if Piper won't admit it. You were there, weren't you?" she asked me under her breath. "Is it true he and Ashford got into a knock-down, drag-out fight, MMA style? Please tell me you got some video footage."

"That is *not* true. And no, there's no video. It's a family matter, and the O'Neals deserve privacy about it. As far as we're concerned, Grayden is just another customer." I was determined to view him that way. "Now we all need to get back to work."

Dillon huffed. "Pretty sure I'm the only one who was working."

"Don't argue with the boss," I said, winking as I headed back toward my office.

Not because I planned to hide from Grayden. Not at all. I simply had a lot to do.

"Piper, wait." Dillon followed me into the kitchen. "Is that guy a problem?"

I spun to face him. "You mean Grayden O'Neal?"

He dipped his chin in a nod. "I've heard about him. If he's bothering you, I can get rid of him."

I almost laughed. Dillon was always being thoughtful, but he had the wrong idea about Grayden.

If anything, I was the one who'd been sexually harassing the man with my eyes.

"*No*. It's nothing like that. But thanks. I doubt he'll stay too much longer anyway."

"At Silver Linings? Or in town?"

"Both."

Dillon was still frowning as I turned away and escaped toward my office.

Unfortunately, the moment I closed the door to my tiny office space and glimpsed the stack of waiting bills on my desk, I remembered what else I'd been avoiding. Dang it.

Bills, invoices, and more bills.

Couldn't I go back out there and keep ogling Grayden instead? Keep making a fool of myself, because he had one hundred percent noticed me staring, both the other night and just now?

No. I was an adult. A mom and a business owner who had a lot of people relying on her. The last thing I needed was to get any further into Grayden's drama.

Shit. I had a lot of people relying on me.

The reality was that running a small business was more expensive and stressful than I'd ever imagined before I took this place over. The cost of ingredients kept climbing, the old building needed repairs. Add to that the challenge of fairly compensating my employees and making my student loan payments every month.

Meanwhile, Ollie kept growing like a weed, shooting out of his clothes and shoes at an alarming rate. And Danny hadn't bothered to make a child support payment for the last six months.

All of my friends and family had been stepping up since the divorce to help care for Ollie. Nobody knew how tough things were getting for me financially.

I didn't want them to know. This was *my* mess to handle.

But there was something I'd been putting off for a while now, and it was time to tackle it. I pulled up a new document on my computer and started typing.

HOUSE FOR RENT, mixed-use zoning, perfect for commercial and/or residential. Lots of potential!

Potential, meaning *Needs a shit-ton of work*. But I preferred to look on the bright side.

I added a few more details and printed it out. The people of Silver Ridge were still an analog bunch, and they'd be far more likely to see a notice on my bulletin board than a rental listing on some website.

Then I made myself busy doing other things for an hour until I glanced out and confirmed Grayden was gone.

Phew.

I carried the rental notice to the bulletin board and pinned it front and center. I snipped the little tabs so they stuck out, practically begging people to grab one. Maybe not a solution to all my problems, but a step in the right direction.

Things would work out. They always did, one way or another. You just had to keep moving forward and believe that somewhere up ahead, there was a silver lining waiting.

EIGHT

Grayden

I'D BEEN BACK in Silver Ridge less than a week, but from the glares I'd been getting, it seemed like every last person in town knew who I was on sight. And had very strong opinions about my presence here.

Actually, the hostility was comfortable in some ways. I knew what to do with people who hated me. I'd had plenty of practice.

My baby sister, though? Hell, Grace was determined to smother me with love and acceptance. Something I craved but wasn't all that comfortable with yet.

My phone buzzed. Probably my sister, because who the hell else texted me this early in the morning? Callum was more an afternoon/evening guy.

GRACE

Morning! How's today going for you? Another beautiful blue-sky day in Hart County, riiiight?

I blinked at her message. That was a lot of cheerfulness to spring on a guy before he'd had caffeine.

With my lips creeping into a smile, I wrote my response.

ME

Don't sprain anything with that optimism. Since when are you all sunshine and daisies and frigging rainbows? That was always Cal

Hey, I can do sunshine! I've learned a thing or two from Piper over the years. And Callum is NOT the sunshine of the O'Neal family, he's way too annoying

I shifted, glancing up from my phone screen because of Grace's mention of Piper. I was on Main, right across the street from Silver Linings. Which Piper apparently owned.

I'd been catching up on a *lot* of developments in the last few days.

Piper hadn't told Grace or Callum about me spending the night on her couch. She'd kept her word. I was grateful for that, but at the same time, I didn't know how to read it.

Did it mean she was protecting my privacy, like I'd asked? Or that she wanted nothing more to do with me?

I'd dropped a few strategically subtle questions with Callum and Grace in the last few days. From them, I'd learned Piper was divorced, her ex was a waste of space, and she wasn't seeing anyone. In fact, they couldn't remember her dating anyone since splitting from her husband.

Interesting facts, that was all. No harm in collecting them.

GRACE

Doing anything fun or exciting today?

No

Any leads on apartments?

No

Did you know you're terrible at texting?

Yes

Fine be that way! But if I can help with anything, let me know. Please?

Don't need you to be my cheerleader. Or my mom. Or my parole officer.

OK, grumpy. What about a good dinner? Dane and I would love to have you over again

I'll think about it. Got lots to do

Good luck conquering the world today, but if you need me...

I know, I know. Thanks. I love you

love you 🩶

I'd already done Sunday dinner at her and Dane's place, and it had been great. Really great, actually. Good food, easy conversation. Yesterday, it had been lunch with Callum and Zandra.

But I didn't want them to feel like they had to take care of me or fuss over me. Didn't want to disrupt the usual flow of their lives. I was used to navigating my days as a loner, and my reappearance in Silver Ridge hadn't changed that.

In Seattle, I'd had a decent life. Acquaintances and occasional hookups instead of real friends. But I'd never fully settled in there. As if I'd always known I would end up back here in Colorado.

When I'd arrived in town, my plan had been to find a new gig as a tattoo artist. But I hadn't found any tattoo shops operating in Silver Ridge, and my forays to operations in nearby towns had not been successful.

No help wanted currently, thanks.

I'd handed out my portfolio, but hadn't heard a peep back.

Which left the idea of opening up my own place. I would need to rent a suitable location, jump through any regulatory hoops, pay for insurance and buy supplies and studio furniture.

Fuck, it was a lot, and I didn't have a ton of wiggle room in my savings.

I had to figure something out soon, or I'd be applying for other jobs. Ranch or farm hand? I could lift heavy shit and work hard, if they could look past my record. Or I could wait tables. Callum would probably hook me up, since he ran Hearthstone Brewing. I didn't want favors, but I'd pay him back by working my ass off.

Didn't love the idea of my little brother being my boss, though.

As for a place to live, I'd been staying at a lovely spot called the Pine Cone Motor Lodge. From the yelling I sometimes heard outside my window, the place attracted trouble. I did *not* want trouble. So I needed out of there sooner rather than later.

I was giving myself another day or two to consider my options and wait for something to pop up. But with so little happening on the job front, I'd had far too much time to think. Time to sit around and read and enjoy the scenery.

Which explained why I was jogging toward Silver Linings right now. For the second day in a row.

I pulled open the door. The little bell chimed overhead. The guy behind the counter was the same clean-cut, athletic-looking kid from yesterday. His name tag read Dillon.

I walked up and nodded at him. "Morning. Could I get an espresso? Double shot."

He eyed me for a moment. I started to wonder if I had something on my face. But then he said, "Coming right up," and turned to the machine.

While he made the coffee, I glanced around the shop. A few customers were scattered at tables, mostly older folks with newspapers and laptops. A fire flickered behind an iron grate. A couple of women perused the bookshelves.

No Piper.

I'd left her place early the morning after Thanksgiving, not wanting to bother her after she'd already done so much for me. I'd figured things between us were okay.

But when she'd seen me at the coffee shop yesterday, I'd caught her staring. And then she'd hidden like I was someone she needed to avoid.

The smart thing to do would be to steer clear of her. Give her space. Let her pretend Thanksgiving night had never happened.

But if I steered clear of everybody who had some kind of issue with me in Silver Ridge, I wouldn't be able to walk down Main Street.

"Is Piper here today?" I asked.

Dillon's shoulders stiffened. He finished pulling the second shot and poured it, then slid the cup across the counter with a scathing look. "She isn't available right now. Did you need something?"

"Just wanted to say hello. Is that not allowed?"

"Depends on your intentions." He put his hands on the counter, lowering his voice. "I know who you are. I know you're trouble. Piper doesn't need that."

"Is that what she told you?"

A blush crept up his neck. "She didn't have to."

Seemed like he had a crush, and that was cute. I picked up the espresso and took a sip. "Thanks. Nice and strong."

Dillon didn't respond, just kept watching me like he was waiting for me to do something that would confirm whatever suspicions he had.

Whatever. Hardly the only person in town who didn't like me. My own brother couldn't stand me, so take a number, kid.

I left an overlarge tip, just to prove I could.

On my way toward the exit, something on the bulletin board caught my eye.

HOUSE FOR RENT, mixed-use zoning, perfect for commercial and/or residential. Lots of potential!

I stopped and read it again. *Lots of potential.* That meant it was probably a disaster, which, honestly, sounded about right for me. The price was definitely right. As in, cheap.

I pulled out my phone and typed the phone number into my messaging app.

Maybe it wouldn't work out. Maybe the landlord would take one look at my background check and tell me to get lost. But I had to take the shot.

It was that, or let my little sister take over as my life coach. I wasn't quite there yet.

After downing my espresso, I sent a quick text to the number for the rental.

ME

Hi, interested in the commercial/residential lease. Still available?

UNKNOWN

Yep! Feel free to swing by in a couple hours. I'll be there. I'll text the address.

Wow, this person was trusting, not even asking for my name or a copy of my ID first. But that was living in a small mountain town, where they didn't worry about a potential renter being a serial killer.

Big city, this was not.

Shaking my head, I waited for the address to come through. When it did, I blinked at it, shocked by the coincidence. Not the house where I'd grown up, but the one right across the street.

The Landrys' old place.

There were so many reasons I should forget about that rental notice and look for something else, not least of which the possibility that Piper's family still owned it. After all, I'd seen the notice in her coffee shop.

But this was the only decent, affordable option I'd found that could fit my needs.

I'll be there

If Piper was the landlord and decided to slam the door in my face, so be it. I'd already told her the story of my last commercial rental in Seattle, which had gone all kinds of wrong.

I'd just have to wait and see.

NINE

Grayden

I SPENT the next two hours in a quiet park, reading a paperback with my knit hat pulled low and coat zipped high. My glasses kept fogging up. It was cold today, and the snow from Thanksgiving Day was still thick on the ground.

The words of my paperback pulled me in. Transported me to another time and place, another identity, which was the thing I loved most about reading. This one was set in the far future with heavy symbolism and social commentary, but also a fast sci-fi plot and some hot sex thrown in too. I was tearing through it.

Maybe I'd stop by Silver Linings to look for another read after I finished. Assuming I was still allowed in there, between Dillon's evil eye and Piper's wish to avoid me.

When it was time for my appointment at the house for rent, I took off my glasses, jumped in my truck, and drove out to my old neighborhood.

This was a different side of Silver Ridge. Only a ten-minute trip, yet we were far from the cutesy, touristy charm of Main Street. A humble mix of homes and businesses spread out before me, with tall pine trees and dead grasses dotting the spaces between.

I drove past an unassuming barber shop on a corner. A

motorcycle repair shop, with a row of bikes for sale out front, all gleaming chrome and leather.

Reminded me of the Yamaha Supersport my buddy had in the Army. He used to let me borrow it. *Before.*

A pang of bitterness hit me in the center of my chest.

Then two clapboard houses appeared up ahead. I parked my truck at the curb and got out, glancing around.

My childhood home sat on the right side of the street. But I barely recognized the place. The former O'Neal residence was now tidy and freshly painted a cheerful yellow, and the sidewalks were cleared of snow.

My memories of this house were complicated. There were the Christmases before our mom died. Dinners laughing around the kitchen table with tiny Grace and our brothers.

And nights when my dad and I would scream at each other, back before he took off for good and before I left for the military.

My hands flexed at my sides. Shoving them in my pockets, I made myself breathe slowly through my nose.

I turned left, toward the Landry house. Where Teller and Piper had lived.

There was a For Rent sign out front that looked brand new, but the rest of the house had seen better days. The paint was faded and peeling in places. The roof was missing some shingles. Not falling apart, exactly. Just tired. I could relate.

Fuck, this was strange. The present and the past colliding, and I didn't know how to make sense of it all.

Instead of going straight up to the front door, I walked around the side. Telling myself I was just checking out the property, getting a feel for the place. Not avoiding anything.

Sure.

That's when I heard Piper's voice. "I'm sick of your excuses, Danny."

So she was the owner after all.

Sounded like Piper was in the back yard. My boots crunched

in the snow as I edged closer. I wasn't meaning to eavesdrop, but she sounded upset. Was someone back there with her?

"And what about our son?" Her voice cracked slightly. "I know not to believe anything you say. But Ollie still does."

My jaw tightened. The conversation was clearly one-sided, so she was talking on the phone. I assumed this Danny was her ex.

"Whatever bullshit scheme you came up with this time, it's nothing to do with me."

I thought about walking away. It was rude to eavesdrop. Yet I found myself standing there, frozen in place, as she spoke again.

"*What*?" She sounded confused now. "No, I'm not lifting a finger for you. What I want is for you to pay the child support you owe and be a part of Ollie's life. That's it. Those are the only subjects I'll discuss with you, not some... I don't even know what you're going on about." She sighed heavily. "I'm hanging up now."

I heard fabric rustling, like she'd put her phone away. I was about to retreat and go to the front door.

But then Piper let out a roar of pure fury that would've been impressive if it hadn't sounded so anguished. What the hell was going on?

I hurried around the side of the house just in time to see her bend down, grab a lump of snow from the ground, and hurl it at the enclosed back porch. It landed with a smack against the screen door.

"Piper?"

She was already stooping down to grab another handful of snow when I said her name. She whirled to face me, gasping, and the snowball flew. Caught me square in the chest with a solid thud.

I looked down at the wreckage of the snowball on my jacket. Her eyes went wide, her mouth forming a perfect O of shock.

"Grayden? I'm so sorry."

I brushed the snow away. "No big deal. I think I'll live."

Her face was turning pink. "I was just...um. Didn't know anyone else was around. You startled me."

"No, I get it," I said gruffly. "You're the type to shoot first, ask questions later."

She made a scoffing sound, staring like she didn't know if I was serious. "Can you blame me? You're a big guy. You kind of snuck up on me."

"And now you're saying I was asking for it."

Her lips slid into a smirk. I returned it, hopefully letting her know I wasn't actually offended. Because this was kinda funny.

Seemed like we both needed a laugh.

I bent down, scooped up my own handful of snow, and packed it into a ball. "I don't think I can let this stand."

She laughed. "Okay. No need to—"

My snowball hit her right in the middle of her purple wool coat. For a second, she just stood there, glaring at me.

Then she reached for the nearest patch of snow.

I moved fast, but Piper's next throw caught me on the side of the head, almost knocking off my cap. "Ouch. You're vicious."

"Then forfeit, O'Neal."

"Hell no. Never." I dodged her next one and charged, pelting her with the biggest clump of snow I could grab on the fly.

"Half that went down my coat!" She screamed and danced around, breathless with laughter. Her hair was in a long braid and it flopped against her shoulder. "Not fair. Your arms are longer than mine."

"Should've thought of that before you started a fight you couldn't finish." I launched another one, and she tried to avoid it, but her boot slipped. She stumbled, arms windmilling, and went down hard on her backside.

The laughter died in my throat. "Shit. Piper, you okay?" I started toward her.

She looked up at me with wide, innocent eyes as I approached. "I think so. Just help me up?"

I bent down, reaching for her hand. That's when she grabbed

my wrist and yanked, throwing her weight backward. I went down like a felled tree, landing in the snow beside her with a loud *oof*. Before I could recover, she started scrambling away while she giggled like a kid.

I grabbed for her. Piper lost her balance again, her weight falling back toward me.

Somehow, we ended up with her sprawled on top of me, both of us breathing hard as we lay on the ground.

Piper's hands were braced to either side of my shoulders, while I had my hands on her waist. Her hair had come partway loose from its braid. Blond strands trailed down and brushed my face.

Her cheeks were flushed, plush lips parted as she caught her breath. Her pale-green eyes were brighter than usual.

Fuck.

Then she reached down, scooped up a handful of snow from beside us, and smushed it against the side of my face.

The shock of cold against my overheated skin made me gasp, and she rolled away, laughing. "Truce," she said, sitting up and holding her hands in the air. "I surrender."

"You surrender after a cheap shot?" I sat up too, brushing snow from my face and hair. My heart was still pounding, but the cold had done its job. Cooled me down.

Which was for the best, even if every part of my body was raring to heat things up even more.

I got to my feet, then reached down to help her up for real this time.

Piper let go of me as soon as she was standing, patting at her hair to tuck away the loose strands. "So. Um. What are you doing here?"

I rubbed the back of my neck. "I'm the one who texted about the rental."

She blinked. "That was you?"

"I saw the notice at Silver Linings this morning. If it's still available." I glanced at the building behind her.

"Yes," she said, though she didn't sound certain. "I just didn't expect it to be you. Or to have an impromptu snowball fight." She laughed nervously. "That was fun, though."

I picked up the knit cap I'd dropped, brushing off the snow. "It was."

"I guess you want to see inside."

"If you don't mind."

"Right. That's why you came." She started toward the back door, then paused and looked over her shoulder at me. Snow still clung to her hair, melting on her eyelashes. I wondered if she was going to say something else.

But instead, she led the way into the house.

TEN

Piper

"The place needs some work," I warned him.

Grayden followed me through the back door and onto the sunporch. "That's okay. I don't mind work."

I shrugged out of my coat. I'd turned on the heat earlier, but the air inside still held a chill. It had never gotten warm enough to be toasty in the winter. Just tolerable.

But my pulse was still racing from our snowball fight, heating me through. I couldn't remember the last time I'd felt so exhilarated.

I'd had plenty of snowball fights with Ollie, sure, but those were silly and fun. Mother-and-son bonding time. What just happened with Grayden had my blood pumping and my stomach fluttering like I was sixteen again and had just been noticed by a sexy bad boy.

When he'd grabbed me, and I landed on top of him in the snow, he'd looked at me like he wanted to bundle together to conserve body heat. Preferably naked.

My younger self would've been rejoicing. *He noticed me!*

My older, more responsible self was trying to rein in my wilder side. I did *not* need to be getting those kinds of ideas about Grayden O'Neal.

"I'll give you the grand tour. Such as it is."

Grayden unzipped his jacket, revealing a snug waffle-knit shirt beneath that hugged his chest. "Ready when you are."

His deep voice hummed inside me. I had no idea if he was doing that on purpose or if it was just the effect he had on me. But Grayden sounded like pure sex whenever he spoke. It was distracting.

No, Piper. You may not flirt with Grace's brother.

"As you can see, the house is pretty out of date. There are two bedrooms, one bath. The sunporch can function as a third bedroom."

"I remember," he said in that rumbly yet soft tone of his. "That's where Teller slept. Been a while, but I've been here before. Thousands of times, probably."

I breathed out a laugh. "Right. Of course."

It was surreal having him here. This man I'd grown up around. Who'd been Teller's closest confidante. My first intense crush.

Gah, how many nights had I fantasized about Grayden while living in this house?

Grayden was that same man, and yet different too. Like a distorted double image. Fifteen years was a very long time.

We went into the kitchen. I gestured around us, trying to be professional. As if real estate agents commonly had snowball fights with prospective tenants and wound up lying on top of them.

"My mom kept living here until she died. She left the house to me in her will. Surprised the heck out of me."

There. The perfect subject to erase any pleasurable feelings. My mother.

Grayden took in the dusty stove, linoleum floors, the cabinet doors that didn't close all the way. The boxy white fridge straight out of the 1990s.

"That was good of her," he said.

I smirked, the bitterness impossible to hide. "Maybe it was

consolation for all the years I took care of her and she told me daily how much she hated me. Teller was gone for a lot of it, but Mom never failed to remind me he would've done a better job. After Teller was wounded and took his medical discharge, he tried to do his part. But Mom would freak out every time she saw his scars."

Grayden winced. "And I assume your husband wasn't much help with her?"

"Danny? Not at all. Mom couldn't stand him. Said he was all facade with nothing beneath, and it turns out she was onto something. You know what they say about broken clocks being right twice a day."

I forced a brilliant smile, pushing away the ugly memories this house always brought to the surface for me.

"Anyway, after Mom passed, I rented the place as-is to a neighbor from down the street. She used it as a quilting and sewing space until pretty recently. But then she passed away too, and her kids didn't want any of her stuff. Told me to get rid of it, but I haven't had much time to focus on it."

We'd moved on to the living room, where piles of scrap fabric still lay in heaps. A huge work table with an ancient sewing machine occupied the space where a couch might've gone.

Lint and loose threads were *everywhere*. Not to mention boxes of my mom's old stuff in all the storage spaces.

From here, the open doorways to the bathroom and one of the bedrooms were visible. Those views weren't much better. Grayden walked the short distance down the hall, peering into each room.

I gritted my teeth, staring at the mess in the living area. I'd seen it all a few minutes ago, but now it seemed to have grown, like something alive and multiplying.

Grayden had not only witnessed my near breakdown after that awful conversation with Danny. He was seeing my utter failure to manage this place as a landlord.

What had I been thinking, putting up that rental notice? I

should've at least brought a vacuum in here and sprayed some air freshener first.

Like that would've made much difference.

"I know it's not much," I said when he returned to the living room.

"Good thing I don't need much. Just want to open up my own studio. If I can live in the back and set up the front rooms for clients, that would be ideal."

"The zoning is mixed use, so I don't see why not. Depending on local regulations about tattooing and that kind of thing."

"I've been checking on it. Shouldn't be an issue." He made a slow circle, hands on his hips as he studied the space. "Yeah. I think this'll work well."

"But it's such a mess right now. It needs repairs and there's all this old stuff, both the last renter's and my mom's. There's probably something better out there for you."

A frown creased his mouth. "You changing your mind about renting the place? Or you just don't want to rent it to *me*?"

"No. I don't have any issue with you, Grayden."

"Seems like you do. You hid from me yesterday when I was at Silver Linings."

"I didn't hide. I was very busy."

"Sure, busy staring at me and gossiping with your employees."

My mouth dropped open. "I was shutting down their gossip. But can you blame people for being curious? Everything about you is mysterious."

"That's your excuse for not renting to me?"

"That's not what I said!"

He crossed his arms, his body language making a clear accusation. Defensiveness made me keep talking.

"You were gone for years, then showed up in town with no warning. You spent the night at my house and took off in the morning without any word or even a note."

"You expected a note?"

Geez, I sounded like a disgruntled one-night stand. "Not necessarily. I'm just giving examples."

"About how I'm mysterious," he deadpanned.

"And add to that your broody aura, the neck tattoo and scruffy hair, the hot-guy glasses—"

"Hot-guy glasses?" The frown hadn't left his face, but I could've sworn he was smirking.

"Look, that isn't the point. I'm just trying to say, I don't have a problem with you."

"You sure? You did just call me scruffy."

Was he kidding or not? I sighed and rubbed my eyes. "Let's sit down and talk. We can probably work something out with the rental."

After a moment, he nodded. "Okay."

"Do you want some tea? I'm pretty sure the kettle in the kitchen can handle that much. And there are some tea bags somewhere. Quilting lady loved her chamomile."

"Sure. I'm an herbal tea guy."

"When you're not drinking double espressos?"

"Exactly."

I snickered, which turned to a genuine smile when I saw Grayden giving me a soft yet sardonic smile back.

At least we weren't lobbing snowballs at one another. Or perceived insults.

ELEVEN

Piper

In the kitchen, I started opening cabinets. "I swear the kettle was here somewhere. Ah ha." A survey of a lower cabinet revealed an aluminum antique, bright blue with the classic splotches of white.

As I stood, I bumped up against him. The kitchen was tiny, and he was *right* behind me. His hand reached out to steady me.

Then his arm brushed my shoulder as he reached around me, pulling a box of tea bags from a shelf. "We'll need these too," he murmured.

I cleared my throat. "Thanks."

I busied myself filling the kettle and setting it on the stove, hyperaware of every movement he made. He was glancing through the cabinets, and when he opened the corner one, he made a sound of amusement.

"Instant coffee crystals," he said, holding up the jar like it was a dead mouse. "I'm guessing this isn't yours?"

I wrinkled my nose. "Ew. I'd rather drink a cup of muddy water from the backyard."

"I figured." He set the jar back in the cabinet and closed the door. "The espresso at Silver Linings is fantastic, by the way."

"Should be. I buy my beans from the best regional roasters."

When I glanced over, I found him listening intently. "Costs have been going up though. My margins have been getting a lot tighter lately. That's why I decided to finally rent this place out again."

I hadn't told anyone else about my financial stresses. Not even Grace. But after a few minutes alone with Grayden, the words had just tumbled out.

"I overheard some of your phone conversation earlier," he said quietly. "With your ex."

I stiffened. "How much did you hear?"

"Enough to know he owes you child support."

I huffed, grabbing two mugs and rinsing any lingering dust under the faucet. "Yeah. Danny is the king of bad investments. He cares more about whatever new scheme he's dreamed up to make a quick buck than about his son."

"What does he do for a living?"

"He's a dentist."

Grayden's eyebrows shot up. "A dentist? Aren't they supposed to be stable and boring and make a great income?"

"You'd think. But Danny managed to get himself into debt, which of course he blames on our divorce, and then he pissed off so many people in Silver Ridge that he had to leave town. Moved his practice hours away, which is a common excuse for why he can't get here to see Ollie. He also loves bringing up the fact that Teller is dating a superstar now, so I should just ask my brother for money if I need it."

Grayden was nodding along. So he'd clearly heard about Teller dating Ayla. "But you won't."

"Last resort. I know you feel a similar way about Grace and Callum. You said you don't want anyone feeling sorry for you. Or to feel like you're a charity case."

"True."

The kettle started to whistle, and I poured water over the tea bags, watching the liquid slowly take on color. I set the kettle down and handed him one of the mugs, and we sank into chairs at the kitchen table.

"Danny failed to show up to spend Thanksgiving with Ollie last week. Now he wants me to look for some box that belonged to my mother." I shrugged, thinking of his odd request. "Supposedly it has something valuable in it, though of course he won't explain himself. Not that I want to know."

After Mom died, Danny pawed through her belongings like he might find some priceless antique buried here. He was disappointed then, so why this sudden interest in my mom's things?

"But Danny rarely cares about what I want," I went on. "He expects me to do what he says or else."

Grayden rubbed his jaw. "That sounds ominous."

Clearly I hesitated too long.

"Piper?" Grayden's voice was still a low rumble, but far more dangerous than soft this time. "Has Danny ever hurt you?"

"Not physically," I rushed to say. "That's not what I meant. Danny's said plenty of cruel things. That's his favorite way to manipulate me. But he's not physically violent. He definitely wouldn't ever hurt Ollie. Mostly I'm just frustrated with his failings as a father. Ollie deserves better."

Grayden studied me another moment. Then he said, "From what little I've seen of your son, he's an amazing kid. Protective of you. It's sweet."

That made me smile, the tightness in my chest unwinding again. "He *is* pretty amazing. Sometimes he still acts like a little kid, wanting cuddles and bedtime stories. And then he turns around and seems to think he's going to fight the whole world to take care of me." My voice went soft. "I love him like crazy. I'd do anything for him."

Tears pricked at my eyes, and I blinked them back. But before I could pull myself together, Grayden reached across the table and put his hand on my arm.

The touch was gentle, warm through the sleeve of my sweater. It lingered for a moment, his thumb brushing against the inside of my wrist, and then he pulled away.

"Ollie's not the only one who's protective," he said. "The kid behind the counter at Silver Linings this morning nearly bit my head off when I asked for you."

I set aside the brief rush of pleasure I felt, knowing Grayden had been asking about me, and focused on his words. "That must've been Dillon. If he's protective, it's because he lost his older sister years ago. His father too. They died in a house fire."

Grayden's expression went serious. "Fuck. That's awful."

"It was ruled arson, and the culprit was never found." I wrapped my hands around my mug again. I hadn't even taken a sip, but it felt nice to hold. "Anyway, Dillon tries to look out for me and the other employees at Silver Linings."

"Especially the female ones?"

"I know how it sounds. But it's not like that."

"Maybe," Grayden said slowly. "Or maybe the kid just has a crush on you."

I nearly choked on my tea. "What? No."

"Why not?"

"I'm his boss. He's eight years younger than I am. He's not truly a kid, like you keep calling him, but he's way too young for me."

Grayden leaned back in his chair, his eyes never leaving mine. "I'm more than eight years older than you."

The implication hung in the air between us, thick and weighted. Heat crept up my neck and into my cheeks.

"Dillon's not interested in me," I said firmly. "If he was, I'd shut him down."

"Good to know. Are you seeing anyone else?"

"No."

"That's surprising." Again, there was so much more meaning in Grayden's tone than the simple words suggested.

Did he mean… Was Grayden flirting with me?

My heart was beating up into my throat, and desire spread all over my body as I imagined Grayden touching me. Tilting my chin with those thick fingers and kissing me. Nitro fuel for my former teenage fantasies.

There was definitely chemistry between us. I'd wanted him for a long time, and it seemed the attraction was mutual now.

If I'd met Grayden somewhere different, in some other life where he wasn't Grace's brother or Teller's former best friend, I wouldn't have a problem letting him know I was interested.

But when it came to sex, I usually liked to keep things simple. If I had a rare night to myself, I would find a handsome guy at a bar and go home with him. Get sweaty and satisfied, then say my goodbyes.

Falling into bed with Grayden would be anything but simple.

"So. The lease application." I got up and grabbed the copy I'd printed from the kitchen counter. "I'm open to negotiation on the rent given the work involved in cleaning it up. It needs some drywall, plumbing and electrical repairs. This isn't a small project. Are you sure you want it?"

"I'm handy, and I'm fine taking on a project. I think the original rent you asked is fair." He was quiet for a moment, his jaw tensing like he was chewing on something he didn't want to say. "Unless any of your neighbors has a problem with you renting to me."

"The neighbors can mind their own business."

"I'm well aware most of the town doesn't like me. Not that I mind them taking Ashford's side. The thing is, I don't want there to be sides. I don't want to cause problems."

"People are live-and-let-live on this street. Just like when we were kids. That much hasn't changed."

"Alright. I have some savings to get through the first few months of rent. And you probably want a security deposit as well."

"That's not necessary. Just first and last months of rent, and we're good. You can let me know about materials for repairs. I'll subtract them from next month."

"No deposit in case I trash the place?"

"Look around." I gestured around us. "Besides, I trust you."

Those words had come out all breathy, like I was a flirty, innocent ingenue in a movie. Good lord.

His sexy little smirk said he'd heard the same thing.

"I'll fill out the application right now," he said.

"It's just a formality. We can sign the paperwork next time I see you."

"Yeah? That's fantastic. I'll get you the check. Actually, would you mind if I start on clean-up today? Sooner I can get out of the Pine Cone Motor Lodge, the better."

I made a face. "That motel is notorious. I'll leave you the keys, and we can get everything else settled later."

"Thank you, Piper. I appreciate this. I look forward to seeing you again."

More flutters. What Grayden was selling, my body was clearly buying.

We shook hands, which somehow morphed into him just holding mine. We stood there for another moment, neither of us moving.

Then I pulled my hand away and shocked myself by saying, "I'll be at Hearthstone Brewing tomorrow night with Ollie. You could join us if you want. We can exchange paperwork over dinner."

Grayden's expression was hard to read. But finally he said, "I'd like that."

"Great." I stepped into the sunporch and grabbed my coat from where I'd left it. "Around six?" I called out.

"I'll be there."

"See you then," I said over my shoulder. "Leaving the spare key on the hook here! Good luck with the mess!"

The moment I was outside, I rolled my eyes at myself. I'd nearly lost my mind over just holding his *hand*.

But inviting Grayden to Hearthstone didn't have to be a big thing, right? I was just being friendly. Proving that I didn't have any issue with him, and I wasn't picking sides.

Just landlord/tenant stuff.

Shit, this could be bad.

Yesterday, Dillon had asked me if Grayden was dangerous. I'd said no. But now I might change my mind.

Of course, Grayden wasn't a threat in the way Dillon had meant. The danger wasn't physical. It was in the deep timbre of his voice and his intense stares. Those sexy-as-hell tattoos.

Grayden called to my former bad-girl side, and she was far too eager to answer.

And if he put those glasses on again? *Gah.*

I was going to have to be very, very careful with this man.

TWELVE

Grayden

HEARTHSTONE BREWING COMPANY was already crowded and lively when I walked through the door. Laughing faces, the aroma of fried food and hoppy beer, the sound of glasses clinking and conversations overlapping. I didn't see Piper or Ollie yet, though I definitely felt plenty of eyes on me.

That was life in a small town for you. Especially when you were the newly returned ne'er-do-well.

At least there were plenty of people here who seemed more like tourists than locals, probably here for the skiing. They didn't know who I was or what I'd done. To them, I was just another guy here to grab dinner and a beer.

I spotted Callum near the bar and headed that way, weaving through the crowd. When he saw me, his face lit up, and he pulled me into a tight hug.

I still wasn't used to this yet, the easy affection with him, but I liked it.

"Grayden! Good to see you. Didn't know you were swinging by tonight."

"Grabbing dinner. Still hard at work?"

"I'm finishing up manager duties for the day, making sure these knuckleheads stay in line." Callum gestured behind himself, where a couple of bartenders were busy pouring brews from the taps.

"Where's Zandra?"

"She's in the office in the back right now. But later, we're going to try out this new restaurant in Hartley that does everything gluten-free. We're meeting up with Ashford, Emma, and Maisie."

There was a beat of awkwardness as Callum seemed to realize what he'd just said. His smile deflated at the edges.

I waved it off. "I don't mind hearing what Ashford's up to. It's the opposite, really. I like hearing that he's doing well and his family's happy."

"I've been talking to him about giving you a chance. Grace has too. He's been stubborn so far, but we won't give up."

"It's only been a week. I'm here whenever he wants to talk, but I'm not going to push it. That's got to be his call. And I don't want you or Grace stressing about it either."

Callum leaned against the bar, studying me. "So how are things going? You settling in okay?"

"Actually, yeah. I found a rental where I'll be able to open up a tattoo studio after some work to the building." I would need to comply with health protocols as well, but there were no state-level licensing requirements. Passing the inspection and finding clients would be the main obstacle.

At least I still had friends in the community in Seattle who'd vouch for my skills. If that helped.

Callum's eyebrows shot up. "Seriously? That's big!"

"It'll be good once I'm done. Drove out to a hardware superstore today to pick up supplies." I rubbed a hand over my beard. "I'm thinking of doing a mural on one wall inside. To showcase the kinds of artwork I do."

Callum grinned. "That sounds awesome. I can't wait to see that. Is the location close to Main Street?"

"Uh, about ten minutes away. Not too far."

It felt good to have something to work toward. Something

productive instead of being so much in my head, a place I didn't always love being.

Also, I'd finished reading the sci-fi novel, and I hadn't had the chance to grab a new one.

Last night had been a little strange, spending the night in the Landry house. Sleeping in a cold, dusty sunporch under a pile of threadbare blankets, surrounded by boxes of sewing supplies and the ghosts of old memories.

It was just a house. A house that needed some TLC, and I was happy to provide it. Especially knowing it would benefit Piper too.

For some reason, though, I hesitated to mention to Callum that Piper was my landlord.

And that was probably the *exact* reason I should be open about it.

"Actually, I'm renting the place from Piper. It's her mom's old house."

Before Callum could say anything to that, I heard a familiar voice behind me.

"Grayden! You made it."

I turned to find Piper smiling up at me. She touched my arm briefly, her fingers light against my jacket, and I had to resist the urge to cover her hand with mine.

"Hey," I murmured.

I'd been thinking about her nonstop since seeing her yesterday. Maybe I'd succeeded in getting those old memories from years ago stuffed into the back of my mind, but Piper as a grown woman seemed to take up the rest of my mental space.

Like the sight of her skin all flushed and snow in her hair. Or the adorable wobble in her voice when she'd asked me to have dinner tonight.

There was some fiery chemistry between us. I had no doubt about that. Where Piper wanted to take it, I wasn't sure yet. Or even if I *should* go there.

As if I could resist.

Ollie ran over to Callum, throwing his arms around my brother. "Uncle Cal!"

Callum grinned and returned the hug, then held out his fist for a bump. "What's up? You and your mom stopped by for dinner?"

"We're here to meet *him.*" Ollie turned to me next, giving me the stink eye, before he focused on Callum again. "Uncle Cal, will you eat with us too?"

Callum aimed a curious look at me as he responded to Ollie. "Can't tonight, buddy. Another time, though. Promise."

Piper put her arm around Ollie's shoulders. "We'll grab a seat before they all fill up. Grayden, could you order us a couple of barbecue bacon burgers and a side of tots?"

"Sure thing."

They headed off toward the tables. I felt my brother's loaded gaze.

"Barbecue burgers and tots?" he said. "I can put that food order in for you."

"Three burgers. But no tots for me. Make it a side salad."

"Watching your figure in your advanced age?"

I flipped him off, but yeah, he was on the right track. Keeping in shape over forty was not the same ball game. "And I'll take a golden ale. What do you think Piper and Ollie would want to drink? Or I could go ask them."

"Nah, I've got it." Callum tapped at the screen, punching in the order. "Piper likes the golden too. And Ollie always gets root beer."

"Thanks."

Callum poured the beers from the tap, taking his time. Then he said, "So. You're renting Piper's old house. And meeting her and Ollie for dinner. Didn't know you'd been spending so much time with them."

I kept my tone neutral. "That's not a problem, is it?"

"No, just...interesting." He made a face. "Are you and Piper on some kinda date? Was that the vibe I was picking up just now?"

"We're supposed to exchange paperwork for the lease." Though we didn't need to have dinner for that, technically. "It's a friends thing."

Callum shrugged, though from the way his shoulders stayed bunched, he was far from comfortable. "Friends is good. I wouldn't want to be the one to tell Grace if you and Piper are having some kind of fling. That would be weird for all of us."

An unpleasant thought occurred to me, and I couldn't stop myself from asking. "Did you and Piper ever...?"

"What? No. God, no. Piper's practically my sister."

Not my sister, though, I thought. Not even close.

But clearly my siblings wouldn't be comfortable with me and Piper as more than friends. Not sure what else I'd expected. Grace and Callum were happy to have me back in their lives, but that didn't mean I was good enough for Piper.

Fuck, they were probably right. What was I even thinking?

That you want her, my brain responded. It was true. Didn't mean I should go after her. I was supposed to be setting up my new life here.

I picked up the two beers and the root beer, balancing them carefully in my hands as I started toward the table. Then someone bumped into me, hard. The icy drinks sloshed over their rims, splashing down the front of my shirt and unzipped coat.

Shit, that was cold.

Beer soaked through to my skin, and I cursed under my breath, looking up to see who'd just run into me.

It was that guy Dillon. Piper's employee from Silver Linings.

"Sorry," Dillon said, not sounding sorry at all. If anything, he looked satisfied. "Didn't see you there."

I felt my anger rising, a familiar heat in my chest and a growl building in my throat.

It would've felt so good to just let it out. Wipe the smirk off

Dillon's face with my fist. But I shoved it back down, clenching my jaw.

"Might want to open your eyes then. I'm taller than you, kid."

"Silver Ridge doesn't want you here," Dillon hissed. "You should get back in your shitty truck and move on."

Callum appeared with a bar towel. "Everything okay?"

Dillon disappeared into the crowd as I stared after him, glaring.

"Accident," I said. "It's nothing."

I forced a smile, aware of people watching. Like they were waiting for me to get angry. Fly off the handle. Prove that I was exactly the violent good-for-nothing they thought I was.

Whatever. A few spilled drinks didn't matter, and random people's opinions of me didn't matter either. Not like I was going to start brawling over some twenty-year-old having a jealous tantrum. Or whatever Dillon's problem was.

The people of Silver Ridge could come after me with pitchforks if they wanted. I wasn't going anywhere.

I dried off as best I could while Callum got us new drinks. Then I made my way to the table, weaving through the crowd with more care this time.

I reached the table and set the drinks down. Piper's eyes widened when she saw my wet shirt. "What happened?"

"Small mishap. It's fine." I passed a beer to Piper and placed Ollie's drink in front of him. "I hear root beer is your favorite, buddy."

"Don't call me that." He pushed the glass away without looking at it.

"Ollie," Piper scolded under her breath. "You love Hearthstone's root beer."

"No worries," I said. "Sometimes we're in the mood for something different. I could grab another drink for you if you want."

Trying too hard, I told myself. But what did I even know about kids?

"Root beer is fine," Piper said firmly.

Ollie stared at the table for a long moment, then pulled the root beer toward himself. "Mom, can I go play the arcade games?"

Piper sighed. "Yeah. Okay. But don't go anywhere else."

"I won't." He got up and was gone before I could blink.

She turned to me with an apologetic expression. "I'm sorry. I don't know why he's being so difficult tonight. Usually he loves coming to Hearthstone for dinner."

"He hates me," I said with a laugh. "It's fine."

"He doesn't hate you. He doesn't even know you."

"Believe me, plenty of other residents of Silver Ridge have an issue with me, and they don't know me either." I leaned in slightly. "Is it just me," I said, keeping my voice low, "or does it feel like half the people in here are watching us and pretending not to?"

Piper laughed, the sound warming me from the inside out. "Like I said yesterday, the local population is curious about you. It'll wear off soon."

"I hope so. By the time I have the house fixed up and open my studio for business, I don't want people to be afraid to trust me with a tattoo gun. That could be a problem."

"Are you kidding? Your sexy bad-boy reputation will be an asset as a tattoo artist. You've got that rebel factor going."

I raised an eyebrow, smirking. "Sexy bad boy? That's my reputation?"

She looked down at her beer, tucking her hair behind her ear. "I mean, that's what I've heard."

"Really. You've heard that. Just generally, around town?"

"Yep."

"And what's your opinion on that subject?"

"I think..." She sipped her drink. "I think you know exactly how attractive you are."

I remembered her eyes on me last week at her place, when I

took my shirt off. Women did like my tattoos. That was nothing new or particularly exciting.

But Piper's attention had felt different. Like something I knew I shouldn't have, but couldn't resist.

The baskets of food arrived. Ollie came back from the arcade games and slid into his seat, picking up his burger without enthusiasm. We ate in relative silence for a few minutes.

The burger was good, the beer was cold, and Piper was sitting close enough that I could smell her shampoo. Some kind of vanilla and honey scent that was making it hard to focus on eating.

Then, halfway through his meal, Ollie set his food down and looked at me. "You're Maisie's uncle, right? Her dad's brother?"

"Yes, I am."

"Then why didn't you try to come back here sooner?" Ollie's voice was accusatory. "Why doesn't Maisie know who you are?"

"Ollie, maybe we should talk about this another time," Piper said, but I shook my head. I'd figured this interrogation might be coming. And honestly, I respected the kid for bringing it up.

I set down my food and wiped my hands and mouth. "I made some mistakes in the past. I had to go away for a long time because of them. But I never, ever wanted to hurt my family. All I wanted was to protect them."

I could feel Piper watching me as I spoke, her gaze steady and unwavering. Ollie seemed to be listening too.

"I plan to fix things, and I want to meet Maisie. But only when her dad is ready for me to do that."

"But why did you come back to Colorado *now*? Was it because you just got tired of wherever you were before? You couldn't get along with those people, so you thought you'd try with us instead?"

This kid was relentless. "Not exactly."

"My mom said you hurt someone." His voice went quieter, but no less intense. "You're a criminal, like the people my Uncle Teller puts in jail. I want to know what you did."

"Ollie, that's enough," Piper said. "This isn't a conversation to have in the middle of Hearthstone."

"I don't see why we have to be here with him at all." Ollie pushed his food away. "I'm not hungry. I want to go home."

I didn't blame Ollie for his questions or his attitude toward me. His mom was right, though. This wasn't the best place to confess all my mistakes, and maybe the subject matter wasn't entirely kid-appropriate anyway.

Piper closed her eyes briefly, then opened them. "Okay. We'll go." She started gathering their things. "I'm sorry," she whispered to me.

I stood. "It's okay."

She grabbed her jacket and Ollie's, guiding him toward the door with a firm hand on his shoulder.

I followed them out, the cold night air hitting my still-damp shirt and making me shiver, even after I'd zipped up my coat.

THIRTEEN
Piper

THE MOMENT we reached the sidewalk, Ollie ran ahead down the block. I called out for him to wait, then turned to Grayden. "I'm really sorry. I thought this would be nice, grabbing dinner together, but..." I trailed off, shaking my head.

"It's alright. Ollie's entitled to not like me. He's hardly the only one."

"But he's not entitled to be rude. I taught him better than that."

Grayden shrugged, brushing his hands over the damp spots on his coat. "Still had a good time with you tonight. For what it's worth."

I bit my lip. "Same." For a while there, I'd been enjoying dinner with Grayden. Until Ollie had decided to blow up our evening.

My stomach twisted with embarrassment over what my kid had said and the way he'd acted. Even though he'd asked some legitimate questions.

Ugh, why was this so hard?

"I've got the rent check for you in my inside pocket," he said. "Might be slightly damp from the spilled beer though."

"Don't worry about it. I'll get it later." The paperwork could wait. I didn't care about the damn paperwork.

"Can I walk you both home, at least?" he asked.

"You haven't had enough of us?"

"Nope. Not yet." Grayden didn't smile, but I'd detected a hint of his deadpan humor.

I didn't want him to go yet either.

Ollie stayed ahead of us for the minutes it took to walk back to my place. When we reached the house, Ollie jogged up the steps and stood right beside the door, frowning at me with his feet tapping the porch.

"Mom, come on!"

I glanced sheepishly at Grayden. "I need to get Ollie settled, but if you don't mind waiting, I can come back out and talk more. Unless you want to take off."

He stuck his hands in his pockets. "I'll stay."

"You're not too cold? I'd invite you in, but—"

"Go on, Piper. Take care of Ollie, and I'll hang out here. I don't mind."

Pulling my keys from my purse, I walked up the porch steps and went past Ollie.

"Mom, can I—"

"Don't even think about it, mister. You were rude to Grayden after he was perfectly kind to you all evening. You're going to bed."

"I'm not tired."

"Same thing you say every night."

"Cause it's true. Maybe you just need more sleep than me."

A smile threatened to appear on my lips, but I kept it at bay.

I unlocked the door, pushing Ollie inside as I switched on lights. "Brush your teeth, then pajamas and bed. Right now. If you're not tired, you can read. But I am one inch away from grounding you for the next week. Don't give me a push. Got it?"

"Why am I in trouble for just asking what he did?"

"Because there's a time and a place for difficult questions, but dinner out wasn't it. Also, that's grown-up stuff."

"Yes, Momma," he mumbled.

I kept an eye on him until he was tucked under his covers with his copy of *Charlie and the Chocolate Factory* and a pile of comics. Then I sat on the mattress beside him and pulled him into a hug. "Ollie, I want you to give Grayden a chance."

"*Why*? We have enough friends. We have Uncle Teller and Callum and Ashford. We don't need *him*."

"Because there's always room for more love," I said automatically. Even if the thought of Grayden O'Neal and the word *love* in the same sentence was enough to have my nerves rattling.

"And you might not need more friends," I added, "but Grayden does. Did you ever think of that? He wasn't perfect in his past, but he's really trying to make up for it. The world would be a far better place if people could admit their mistakes and try to do better."

"Yes, Momma," Ollie grumbled again, before holding his book in front of his face.

Once Ollie was settled, I brewed some coffee, my ultimate peace offering. Grayden was still sitting there on the porch steps. Good. He hadn't left.

"Coffee?" I asked. "I assume you take it black. Considering the espresso."

"Black is perfect."

He went to stand, but I crossed over to him, holding out a mug. "Here. Don't get up. This is a good spot to sit."

"Thanks."

I'd left the porch light off, and the street was mostly dark, which left the stars arrayed above us. My mug was toasty in my hands.

I felt Grayden's warmth beside me too, crossing the narrow space between us.

"Ollie shouldn't have said those things to you," I began.

"He made some fair points."

"It must be exhausting, though. Having people throw your past in your face. I don't just mean my kid. Small town doesn't have to mean small minds, but sometimes..."

"It's okay. I can handle it. I chose to come back here, knowing what the residents of Silver Ridge would probably say."

"Doesn't mean it's right."

Grayden sipped his coffee. "You know, Ollie is actually the first person in Silver Ridge to ask, point blank, what I did to wind up in prison." He blinked, gaze bright in the dark. "Even you haven't asked."

My breath stopped in my chest. Did Grayden want me to ask?

"I know it was a bar fight." There were some official records about it, though I hadn't seen them.

"But you don't know the details. Even Grace and Callum haven't asked. Because they're afraid of the answer."

"Should they be afraid?"

He glanced up at the sky. "Fear is a subjective thing."

I huffed a laugh, wrapping my arms around my coat. "You're different from what I expected. You're pretty philosophical sometimes."

"A guy who spent years in prison can get very philosophical. Trust me." His eyes crinkled as he smiled, and I smiled back. Couldn't help myself.

Maybe Grayden's smiles were like shooting stars. Even more arresting because they were rare.

"Grace and Callum might be afraid to ask the nitty-gritty details about your arrest and conviction, but you could just tell them. Tell Ashford too. That's one of the things he's still angry about. Not knowing, and feeling like it's some secret you're keeping."

"I've thought about it. From the moment Grace called me, and I heard her voice for the first time in so long, I wanted to tell her everything. But the truth will hurt her. I'm afraid she'll feel guilty."

"Why would Grace feel guilty?"

Grayden breathed out slowly, staring into his coffee mug like it was a code to decipher. "It's a long, fucked-up story. Plus, aside from upsetting Grace, I would've sounded like I was making excuses for myself, and it's not like I'm innocent in the whole thing. A lot of it wasn't my choice. But some of it was."

We sat in the quiet for a while longer until the coffee was gone. The words were on the tip of my tongue. *What happened? What did you do?*

But I didn't ask any more questions, and Grayden didn't volunteer anything either. I couldn't decide if I was disappointed.

"I should get going." He handed me his mug and stood.

I nodded. "I might not see you for a while. The holidays are pretty crazy at the coffee shop, and then we're going to see Teller and Ayla in California."

I was rambling about my schedule when there were so many other things I wanted to say. But he didn't call me on it. Probably because he was holding back plenty too.

"Night, Piper. Happy holidays." Grayden walked down the steps.

He turned back, as if he wanted one last look at me in the starlight. And then he was gone.

FOURTEEN

Piper

I PULLED up in front of my mom's old house and cut the engine.

It wasn't my mom's place anymore though, was it? It was Grayden's now.

Grabbing the bag of pastries I'd brought, along with the to-go double espresso, I got out. The fizzy feeling in my belly increased at the thought of seeing him again.

The last time had been the night we had dinner at Hearthstone. Weeks ago. I had *not* been avoiding him.

I had just been...busy.

As I'd mentioned to Grayden, the holidays were always an action-packed time of year in Silver Ridge with all the festivities. Like brand-new holiday latte flavors, the annual toy drive Silver Linings hosted, and our obligatory Santa visit at the coffee shop.

Zandra's grandfather, Manny Alvarez, had volunteered to play the big man this year. Which turned out to be a big mistake, after Manny made three kids in a row cry when he interrogated them about whether they were on the naughty list. *Yikes.*

Then Ollie and I jetted off to Los Angeles to spend Christmas with Teller and Ayla. We'd enjoyed the warm temperatures and the stunning views from Ayla's house in Malibu. Ollie had loved playing in the Pacific Ocean, even though it was downright *freezing*, and Teller taught him to boogie board.

But now the holiday gauntlet was officially over, and it was way past time to pay my tenant a friendly visit.

I didn't like the way we'd left things last time. That tension between us. Questions I wouldn't ask and things he wouldn't say.

But pastries and coffee would solve everything, right?

Approaching the house was a surreal experience. Grayden had lived here for three weeks, and it looked so different already. All the weeds were gone. The dry grass was trimmed back. The siding had been scraped in preparation for repainting, and the broken slats on the porch were fixed.

I noticed Grayden's truck wasn't out front, but didn't think too much of it.

Until I knocked at the door and there was no answer. Dang it. But if he wasn't here anyway, it wouldn't hurt if I did a little more harmless spying, right?

The view through the front window revealed the inside of the house was transformed too. The mess in the living room had vanished, along with the dirty old carpet. Instead, planks of laminate covered half the floor, with boxes of more waiting nearby. The new overhead light fixture was sleek and modern, and tasteful roman shades had replaced the ancient curtains.

Thankfully, Grayden had left the shade up for me to snoop.

I imagined him busy at work, kneeling as he laid the new flooring. Probably in a tight T-shirt, tattooed muscles flexing. Ass prominent in his snug jeans.

I might've fantasized about him over the holidays. Once or twice.

Strolling around the side of the house, I peeked at the carport at the end of the driveway, confirming Grayden's truck wasn't there either. I had time before my next appointment, so I could stick around to wait for Grayden to come home. No big deal. It was the friendly thing to do, since I'd brought him coffee.

Of course, I had a key, but I didn't want to go inside without giving Grayden a heads up.

I was contemplating whether to text him when I heard a noise near the back of the house. It had sounded like a loud thump. As if someone had just dropped something heavy.

Was Grayden in there after all?

But as I reached the next window, which overlooked one of the bedrooms, it wasn't Grayden I saw inside.

It was *Danny*. My creep of an ex-husband.

What on earth was Danny doing here?

Instinctively, I ducked back so he wouldn't see me. Then inched forward to spy on him. Danny was pawing through the contents of a cardboard box. He tossed it aside and opened another.

I'd had no idea he was even in Hart County. And he had no right whatsoever to be inside a house that I owned.

Fury ignited in my chest as I marched to the back of the house. The door yawned open. Danny had broken the lock.

I stepped inside the enclosed sunporch, setting the coffee and pastries down on a side table along with my purse. It looked like Grayden had been sleeping back here, judging from the twisted blankets and pillow lying on top of a new futon.

His duffel slumped against a wall, clothing spilling out. It made me feel a brief pang of tenderness toward him.

But unless Grayden was a complete slob who typically left all his belongings strewn over the floor, Danny had been in here too.

My body went hot and then cold with mortification. Danny had been rifling through Grayden's personal things.

There were books thrown around haphazardly, papers with pencil and ink designs. Art supplies. Plastic bottles of tattoo ink. One was broken, with vivid red smeared on the tile.

I would not let my ex get away with this.

My fists clenched as I stormed into the bedroom where I'd seen Danny before. And there he was, dumping out yet another cardboard container, this one full of fabric. Probably stuff Grayden had carefully boxed up from the previous tenant.

"Danny," I choked out. "Have you lost your mind? What in the hell do you think you're doing?"

He had the decency to look ashamed for one split second. Then his mouth slid into a sneer. "You got rid of it, didn't you? Just to spite me."

"Got rid of what? What are you talking about?"

He brushed his sweaty hair back from his forehead. Danny's cut was usually styled with enough gel to withstand a hurricane. I'd seen how long it took him to get that wave just right in the mirror. But today, his hair was as disheveled as his wrinkled polo and khakis.

"The last time I talked to you." He jabbed an accusatory finger at the air as he spoke. "I asked you specifically on the phone about that box with your mom's old jewelry in it."

"My mother's jewelry," I repeated.

I did remember him saying something about a box in my mom's basement. That was the day Grayden overheard my conversation. I also remembered telling Danny I wanted nothing to do with it.

"Yes, Piper. That's what I said. How stupid are you?"

My insides shrank. Danny had always known which insults hurt me the most.

"What, you want her gold-plated cross necklace and her wedding ring with the fake emerald?" I asked. "You think that stuff is worth anything?"

"It's not the jewelry I wanted. There was something else, and it's fucking *important*. Like I told you."

"*This* is your latest scheme? A box with my mom's unwanted stuff?"

Danny was pacing, gripping his hair again and he glanced around frantically at the mess he'd made. "It used to be in the basement. The old crap you couldn't bring yourself to get rid of.

But it's not down there, and it's not anywhere else either. So where *is it*?"

"How am I supposed to know?"

Danny had done some twisted things for money over the years. Like selling gossip about Ayla Maxwell to paparazzi.

But this was just...bizarre.

A laugh started in my chest, sneaking up into my throat.

He went still. Slowly turned. "Are you fucking laughing at me right now, Piper?"

"Yes, because this is absurd! If this box of Mom's junk is so important to you, maybe you should try the dump. I'm guessing that's where Grayden has been hauling things."

Danny's expression went even harder. "So that's who's renting this place now? Grayden O'Neal? I heard he was back in town, but I had no idea you were so close to him." He looked me up and down with disgust. "You're so desperate for money you'd rent this place to a felon?"

"I've had enough of this, Danny. Time for you to leave." I would ask him to clean up his mess, but since when had he ever done that?

"What else are you doing for money, huh? Are you screwing him too?"

My face flushed with heat. "You have no right—"

"Answer the question." Danny advanced on me, and I backed up instinctively until I hit the wall of the bedroom.

"Stop. I'm not doing this with you."

"The only reason I'm here, doing this *at all*, is for Ollie and for *you*. To make things better for you two, like you're always nagging me to do. And now I find out you're slutting around with a criminal?"

My heart hammered against my ribs. "You're trespassing. I'm calling the police."

I started to take a step away, reaching for my phone in my pocket, and he shoved me back hard. My head thudded against the wall.

Shock had me in a daze. I couldn't believe this was happening.

His hand came up just below my throat, pinning me. "I've put up with a lot from you over the years." Danny's voice was cruel and spiteful. "The disrespect. The lies you've spread about me in Hart County. I'm sick of it, Piper. So fucking sick of *you*."

Fear spiked through me. I'd never been afraid of Danny hurting me before. We'd had our fights, our ugly moments during the divorce, but he'd never gotten physical. Never.

Right now, standing here with his hand at my throat and fury blazing in his eyes, I was genuinely scared.

"Danny," I said, trying to keep my voice steady. "Let me go."

"Not until you tell me where that box is. See, I think you know. You're playing a little game, thinking you can outsmart me."

"I don't even know what box you're talking about!"

"Liar."

"Danny, stop—"

His hand pressed against my throat, cutting off my words.

FIFTEEN
Grayden

My palms drummed a beat against my steering wheel as I drove my truck toward home. I leaned back in my seat, singing along with the radio.

I was in a fantastic mood today, and nothing was going to get me down.

I'd driven out to Pine Creek, a nearby town, where another tattoo shop had been looking to sell some gently used studio furniture. I'd even stayed to chat with the artists there for a while.

Fine by me that they assumed I was a new transplant. Since they were in Pine Creek, they didn't know my name or my face on sight.

After loading the couple items of furniture into the bed of my truck, I'd grabbed some food at a drive-through on the way back. A damn good morning, all in all.

I'd considered stopping at Silver Linings too for an espresso fix, but I still hadn't been back there in weeks. Not after that disastrous night at Hearthstone with Piper and her son. I hadn't seen Piper a single time since.

Aside from a few holiday get-togethers with Grace and Callum and their partners, I'd spent plenty of nights alone the last several weeks. Which wasn't so bad.

Just meant more time to work. The sooner I could get myself established, the sooner I could prove to everyone I had a right to be here.

As I drove up the street toward my place, I spotted a Lexus halfway down the block. A much nicer car than I'd seen around here lately. Most of the other people in this neighborhood were far more humble, like me.

As Piper had said before, they had a live-and-let-live attitude, and nobody had made any trouble about me moving in here. Thank goodness for small favors.

Pulling into my driveway, I spotted Piper's car parked right in front of the house, and anticipation started pumping through my veins like something heady and addictive.

She was here. She'd come to see me.

Maybe it was just landlord business. But I'd dropped off the first and last months' check back in December, and I wasn't due to pay next month's rent just yet. Or maybe some neighbor had complained about me after all. Maybe I'd been too noisy on the nights I'd been working late on the house.

Or maybe, just maybe, Piper had been thinking of me as much as I'd been thinking of her.

Taking a steadying breath, I got out of the truck and started toward the house.

Glancing around, I didn't see Piper anywhere. She'd probably already gone inside, and I didn't mind. In fact, the idea of her seeing all the progress I'd made gave me a warm glow of pride.

As I neared the house, I caught my reflection in the front window and paused to check my hair. Ran my fingers through it like that would make any difference.

Ridiculous. I was acting like a teenager trying to impress a girl.

The moment I stepped through the front door, I heard a loud thump. Followed by raised voices. My mood shifted instantly, my muscles tensing as I listened.

That was Piper, and she sounded angry. And someone else who I didn't recognize. A man.

Their words became clearer as my long strides took me near the bedrooms.

"You're playing a little game, thinking you can outsmart me."

"I don't even know what box you're talking about!"

"Liar."

"Danny, stop—" Piper's voice cut off abruptly.

I rounded the corner, stepping through the open doorway, and I saw them. A preppy looking guy had his hand on Piper's throat as he pinned her against the wall. She stared at him with wide, frightened eyes.

Rage exploded in my chest, turning my vision to static, blood roaring in my ears.

Hell. *No.*

I crossed the room in two strides and ripped him away from her, throwing him back hard. He stumbled on the debris-strewn floor, his arms pinwheeling.

"Hey!" Danny caught himself before he toppled all the way to the ground.

"What. The fuck. Do you think you're doing?" I growled.

So this was Ollie's deadbeat father. Piper's piece-of-shit ex.

I kept advancing, and he managed to stand up, squaring his shoulders in his green polo. "This is between me and my ex-wife. Stay out of it."

Glancing back at Piper, I saw her coughing and rubbing her neck. He'd hurt her.

Don't be stupid, O'Neal, I told myself. *You need to calm down.*

But all the work I'd done over the years to quell my temper were no match for this feeling. He'd hurt Piper, so I would make him pay.

I grabbed Danny by the front of his polo shirt and slammed him against the nearest wall, holding him there. "You think you can put your hands on her?" My voice was rough and dangerously quiet. "You think you can come into this house and threaten her?"

"Let go of me."

"Like you did, when she asked you to stop?"

My fingers clamped onto his throat and squeezed. His face was turning red, his breath coming in short gasps. I could feel his pulse hammering against my palm, could see the fear starting to creep into his eyes.

Good. He should be afraid.

"You don't know what's going on," he choked out.

"I know plenty. I know you're a coward who doesn't take care of his own kid. And you just assaulted the mother of your child."

Each word came out harder than the last. I was struggling to keep my righteous anger in check, to not do something I'd regret.

To not be the person most of Silver Ridge already thought I was.

"Grayden." Piper's hoarse voice cut through the fury clouding my mind. "That's enough. You need to stop."

I looked back at her. She stood by my shoulder, chin up and gaze steady. And that was what I needed for reason and logic to take over.

I released Danny and stepped back. He doubled over, sputtering, one hand clutching his throat.

"Are you okay?" I murmured to Piper. "Say the word and I'll call the police. We'll report his ass."

Bringing the authorities into this situation was far from my preference. I'd have serious questions to answer about roughing up her ex.

But I didn't care about that right now. Only about what Piper needed.

She shook her head. "I just want him gone."

My fingers brushed her wrist, the barest touch. "Then I'll take care of it. Stay here, okay? I'll be right back."

Piper nodded, eyes glassy. I grabbed hold of Danny shirt again and shoved him toward the door. He tripped over his feet the first few steps, but then let me march him out of the hallway and toward the front door.

When we were almost there, Danny yanked himself out of my

grasp, spinning to face me. "You're a dumbass if you believe everything she says. I'm not the problem here."

This joker was treading on my last frayed nerve. "Stay away from Piper and Ollie."

"You've got no right to tell me that. I can see my kid whenever I want." He sneered. "You're sleeping with her, I'm guessing? Piper's been a lying slut since I met her, and she's—"

I took a menacing step toward him, pulling back my fist. He backed up, reaching for the front door handle.

"I've known plenty of men like you," I said. "Only brave when you're terrorizing someone you think is weaker. But your days of hurting Piper are over. Because *I'm* here now. And I won't fucking stand for it."

Danny's glare was pure hatred. "I know who you are, asshole. You grew up in this trash neighborhood just like Piper did. Even your own family doesn't want you here. She's scraping the gutter by getting involved with you."

"That supposed to hurt my feelings?"

"I can destroy you if I want, O'Neal."

"Go ahead and try."

So he'd recognized me. That meant he knew about my manslaughter conviction, and at the moment, I was happy to play the bloodthirsty killer. I hardly cared what this guy had to say about me.

"Piper and Ollie are *mine*," he hissed. "They always will be."

"Hurt either of them again, and I'll break every bone in your body. Now get the fuck out."

SIXTEEN

Grayden

DANNY SLAMMED the door on his way out.

I turned around and stopped short. Piper stood just inside the living room, staring at me in shock.

"So you heard all that?" I asked.

"Hard not to."

"Are you alright? How badly did he hurt you?" I crossed the room to her, but when I got close, Piper flinched.

"I'm fine." Her voice was shaking.

Sticking my hands in my back pockets, I left a couple feet of space between us, realizing how badly I might've just fucked up.

She'd seen me almost take her ex-husband's head off. Heard me yelling. She'd seen my temper, the pure, unrelenting rage living inside me that I tried not to let anyone see, but *especially* not someone like Piper.

My eyes closed for a brief moment as shame spread through my insides.

"If you'd prefer that I go—"

"What? No." Piper reached for my arm. "Grayden, I'm sorry."

Wait. *She* was sorry?

"Hey." Carefully, I rested my hands on her shoulders over her coat. When she didn't flinch away again, I put a little more weight behind my touch, hoping it would ground her. "None of what just happened was your fault. Why would you be sorry?"

"This house is your home now. And my ex shows up and causes trouble for you."

"I've had much worse trouble, believe me."

Piper's shaking got worse, tears filling her eyes. "Can I sit down for a minute? I'm...I'm dizzy."

Fuck, I really was doing this all wrong. "Of course. C'mon."

Keeping her upright, I led Piper to the sunporch. I was distantly aware of my belongings strewn all over the floor. Damn, Danny had been in here too. Doing who knew what. But I'd deal with cleanup later.

Right now, Piper was the only thing in the world I cared about.

"Have a seat." I gestured at the futon, unzipping my own jacket and tossing it on the edge of the thin mattress.

Piper reached for the buttons of her coat, but her hands were shaking.

"I've got it." I unbuttoned her coat and eased the wool fabric from her shoulders. Once it was off, revealing a sweater and jeans, I grabbed my blanket and draped it around her. Her fingers clutched the fabric.

"That okay?" I asked.

"Yeah."

I sat beside her, the thin mattress dipping. Piper's weight fell against me, and she let me hold her up. We sat like that for a long moment. Neither of us spoke.

I could feel the tension slowly leaving her body as she breathed.

"Your espresso's going to be ice cold," she said finally, her voice muffled against my shirt.

"My what?"

"I brought you a double espresso and some pastries. On the side table."

My expression was probably half smile, half confusion. "Okay. Thank you."

"And—" Piper gasped, sitting up. "I need my phone. Where's my coat?"

"Right here, sw—" I cleared my throat. I'd almost just called her *sweetheart*. The hell was I doing?

I fished Piper's phone from one of the pockets. As soon as she had it, her fingers started flying over the screen.

"What is it?" I asked.

"I'm texting the principal at Ollie's school. Making sure if Danny shows up there, they notify me immediately." Her jaw was tight as she typed.

"You think he'll go after Ollie?" I was ready to put Piper in my truck and drive to the school right now.

"No, I..." She shook her head. "I don't know. I have custody, so they won't let Ollie leave with him without my prior authorization, but I'll feel better if I say something." She finished the text and set her phone down, pulling the blanket tighter.

"Can you tell me what happened before I got here?" My voice was gruffer than I'd intended, but thinking of Danny had me fighting back anger again.

What I wouldn't give to break a few of the teeth in his pretty-boy mouth. But that thought really wasn't helping right now.

Piper took another shaky breath. "I came by thinking you and I could talk, catch up. But you weren't here, and then I heard a noise at the back of the house. When I looked through a side window, I saw him inside. Danny." Her voice cracked on his name.

I put a hand on her knee over the blanket and massaged it gently. "Take your time."

"He was looking for something," she continued. "A box of my mom's old stuff. Jewelry, mementos. Things like that."

I cursed. "Are you kidding? Your mom's jewelry?"

"I know, it's absurd. All that stuff couldn't have been worth more than two hundred dollars, and he owes me a whole lot more than that in back child support."

This was the reason he'd lashed out at her? Two hundred dollars worth of jewelry? If that was true, Danny Carmichael was far more unhinged than Piper had told me. Unless something had drastically changed with the man.

Hard to believe that guy had been married to her. But I knew what it was like to put faith in someone and have that trust get stomped on.

"Danny claims there was something else that's valuable in that box," she went on. "He asked me about it on the phone last month, and I told him I wanted nothing to do with it. I didn't think he'd break in here trying to find it."

"He didn't tell you anything more about this mystery item?"

She shook her head, frustration creasing her brow. "I didn't even know he was back in Hart County. If there was something valuable, and Danny knew about it, why wouldn't he have taken it before? Then he blamed *me* for hiding whatever it is, as if I was plotting against him. As if you and I..."

She didn't finish that sentence. Didn't have to.

You're sleeping with her, I'm guessing?

Joke was on Danny, because I wasn't sleeping with Piper. But I sure as hell wanted to. If I could be so lucky.

"I haven't seen any boxes of jewelry," I said, wracking my brain. "Or your mom's mementos. I would've given it to you if I had."

"No, I know. None of this makes any sense."

There'd been plenty of boxes in the basement, but I'd sorted through them. I was planning to donate most of the contents. None of it was very personal, certainly not valuable. Same with all the sewing supplies from the previous renter.

"Do you think he'll go to your house next? Will he look for the jewelry box there?"

"No, Danny knows I wouldn't want anything of my mom's at my house. I left it all here to deal with later. For my ex to throw all over the place, apparently. Along with your things. Ugh, what a mess." Piper's shoulders slumped, blond hair hanging in her face. "I'll help you clean everything up. And I'll replace anything that's broken."

I reached up to tuck her hair behind her ear. "Fuck the mess," I grumbled. "I'd much rather try those pastries you brought me. I'll brew a fresh pot of coffee for us."

"You don't have to do that."

"Hell yeah, I do. It's kind of our thing now. Sitting. Drinking coffee. That's what we did a few weeks ago on your porch."

"But we had chamomile tea last time I was here."

My shoulder bumped against hers. "Here's my deep, dark secret. I actually hate herbal tea." That stuff was disgusting.

She snorted. "Oh my gosh, so do I."

"I would throw it all in a bonfire and burn it. Every last little dried flower."

It was good to see her smiling again.

"Come on," I said. "Carbs and caffeine will make us both feel better."

"Those are words I live by."

I stood and held out a hand to help her up. "That's exactly why I like you."

SEVENTEEN

Piper

ON OUR WAY into the kitchen, Grayden grabbed the bag of pastries from the side table. He stuck the to-go cup of coffee in his fridge for later. No point wasting good espresso.

After placing a couple of croissants in the toaster oven to warm, he pointed to the new coffeemaker and bean grinder on the counter. "I've upgraded the equipment around here."

"Thank goodness. I hadn't seen you at Silver Linings for so long, I thought maybe you'd given up caffeine altogether."

He hummed contemplatively as he poured beans into the grinder.

I sat at the table, his blanket still around my shoulders. My nerves were jittery, but at least my heart had finally started to slow down.

I touched my fingers to my neck, remembering Danny's fingers there. He hadn't pushed very hard, but in that moment, I hadn't known what he might do. I'd been terrified.

Then Grayden had shown up exactly when I needed him, and he'd been *fierce.* Now he'd completely switched gears, taking care of me and making sure I was okay.

I was still struggling to catch up.

"Is there a reason you haven't been to Silver Linings lately?" I asked.

He moved around the small kitchen to get the coffeemaker started. "You said you'd be busy over the holidays. And I wasn't sure if you wanted to see me after that night at Hearthstone."

"I thought you had a nice time."

"I did."

"I made you coffee that night," I teased. "It's our thing, remember?"

He smirked, leaning his hip against the counter. "But then we were talking about my prison time, and it got a little awkward. Unless that was just me."

I looked down at the table, tracing the grain of the wood with my finger. He wasn't wrong.

"What would Teller do about Danny if your brother were here in Silver Ridge?" Grayden asked, changing the subject.

"He would probably start a manhunt to track Danny down and throw him in a jail cell."

"Still an option. Even without Teller as chief of police."

"I don't know if they can do anything except cite Danny for trespassing."

"He attacked you." Anger flashed across Grayden's face. "He had his hand on your throat."

"But getting charges to stick isn't so simple. Even if I get a restraining order, it wouldn't keep him away in reality. And if there's any chance of Danny making things right with Ollie, I don't want to prevent that."

Grayden studied me for a long moment. "You're a good mom."

"Even though I have no idea what to do? Things have always been tense with Danny, but this is awful." I ran a hand through my hair, frustration coursing through me. "I feel so helpless."

"You're not helpless."

I thought of what he'd said to Danny. *Your days of hurting*

Piper are over. Because I'm here now. And I won't fucking stand for it.

What man had ever stood up for me that way? Except for Teller, but my brother had his own life to live now. He deserved his happy ending with Ayla.

Grayden hadn't defended me out of obligation. He'd done it simply because he wanted to.

Before long, we had cups of coffee and plates with toasted croissants. The first bite of buttery pastry melted on my tongue, and for a moment I just let myself enjoy the simple comfort.

Like sitting next to Grayden earlier on his futon. He'd made me feel better just by being there, being himself.

I cleared my throat. "This is the second time we've sat at this table in, what, a month? Most of my memories of this kitchen aren't nearly so pleasant. I'm glad you're the one renting the house."

"Might be easier if it were a stranger, though. Somebody who didn't have his own baggage overlapping with yours. Someone without my messy past."

I shook my head. "I don't agree. You're making the house into something new, and the fact that it's *you*, it's somehow...better."

"If I can find a way to wipe my slate clean, there's hope for anyone, right?"

"Maybe I'm just trying to say I missed you the last few weeks. I've been thinking about you." I looked up suddenly, shocked I'd said that. But it was true.

Grayden's brown eyes were locked on me. "I've been thinking about you too. A lot."

My heart rate kicked up again, but not from anxiety this time.

He brought his hand alongside mine, his pinky stroking my pinky, and my heart bunched right up under my throat.

My gaze fell to Grayden's lips before I blinked and looked away.

"I'm embarrassed you heard those things Danny was saying about me." My face heated.

Lying slut.

"Don't be, Piper. He's nothing but a bully. He doesn't get to define you."

"I know that logically. But after years of hearing those kinds of insults... If Grace or Teller or your brothers had ever heard Danny talk that way, they would've been furious. But nobody else knows."

I was so glad they didn't know.

Grayden's pinky stroked mine again. "You're one of the best people I've ever met. You make my day brighter every time I see you. You've always been that way."

"I thought you never noticed me when I was a kid."

"Sure I did. Just not the way I notice you now." He laughed softly. "Now you're... Fuck." He whistled. "You're a knockout. Not just the way you look, either. First night I got back to Silver Ridge, on Thanksgiving, I had no idea what was about to hit me."

"You make me sound like a natural disaster or something."

"Am I that far off? It's useless to argue with the weather, and it's useless to argue with you. You always win."

I wiped my eyes, finding my smile again.

Grayden was right. I was a pretty awesome lady with a vibrant personality, and nothing Danny said could change that. I knew who I was.

"Thank you," I said.

"Just being honest."

I was staring at his lips again, so I saw the exact moment they creased into a frown.

"Piper, I went too far earlier with Danny. I apologize for that. My temper blew up when I saw him hurting you."

"You were defending me."

"But then there's my prison record. My shitty reputation, far as Ashford and most of the town thinks. Also the fact that I curse too much and I'm not always in the best mood."

"Cursing is hardly a major character flaw. Or being grouchy."

"What I'm trying to say is, I never want you to be afraid of me. *Ever*."

I met his eyes and saw so much sincerity there.

"I think of you as complicated. But if you're asking if I feel safe with you, I do. I always have."

"You *are* safe with me."

"If I didn't feel that way, I wouldn't be sitting with you. I'd be using every dirty self-defense trick in the book to bust my way out of here."

"Glad to hear it."

But I still had questions. The longer I waited to ask them, the more those unknowns stood between us. The more the questions grew into something I couldn't ignore.

And then, like he could read my mind, Grayden murmured, "Ask me. You can just ask me."

I knew exactly what he meant.

Instead of speaking, I got up and went to the coffeemaker to refill my mug, needing something to do with my hands. Grayden stood too, setting our plates in the sink, and leaned against the counter beside me. Waiting.

My throat was thick, and fear gathered like storm clouds inside me. Grace and Callum were afraid of asking this question, and I was too.

Afraid. But not of him.

I had to do this for both of us. Because for some reason, Grayden couldn't just come out and tell me. Maybe fear was holding him back too.

He'd served his time for involuntary manslaughter. If he felt remorse, as he seemed to, then did it matter what mistakes he'd made? Didn't he deserve a second chance either way? Forgiveness? Grace and Callum had already given that to him.

I hadn't known this version of Grayden very long, but my heart told me he was still the good man I'd grown up knowing.

But the truth *did* matter. I had to square the man in front of me, this man I enjoyed being around, with the man who was supposedly a killer.

When I next spoke, the words came out small. Almost like I was a kid again, on the terrible day when Grace had told me the news. We'd been standing in this very house.

"They said you killed someone in that bar fight. Beat another soldier until he died. Did you?"

The question hung between us.

"No," he finally said. "I didn't kill anyone."

I exhaled sharply, shocked by the relief I felt. "But you pled guilty."

"I did. I took the fall for someone else."

That revelation went through me like a shockwave. "You have to tell them. Your family."

"I would tell my brothers and my sister anything if they asked me. But they still haven't. I'll tell you the whole ugly saga if that's what you want. But Piper, don't expect me to come out of it sounding like the hero. I'm not."

"Then who are you?" I asked desperately.

"You want the honest truth?"

"I do. I want to understand you."

The sudden heat in his dark eyes seared me to my core.

"I'm just a man who wants to kiss you more than any fucking thing in the world right now."

I leaned into him without a conscious thought. Our lips brushed, then pressed harder and lingered.

God, it felt good.

His tongue licked the seam of my lips, then slid gently into my mouth. He groaned, setting off an ache of pure want between my legs.

I felt like I'd slipped into a hot bath. It was like every moment of each of our lives, every mistake and wrong turn, had led us here to this shared moment. The two of us finding common ground when nothing else made sense.

Grayden's calloused hand moved to cup the side of my neck,

thumb tracing my jaw. I got swept up in the deep strokes of his tongue, the hungry pulls of his lips.

After a perfect, breathtaking minute, he broke the kiss.

"I care about you, Piper. I probably shouldn't say that, since we have all kinds of history and I'm your renter now, and I'm still working on sorting my own shit out. But I haven't stopped thinking about you since you demanded I sleep on your couch weeks ago. Bring home a stray, and that's what you get."

"You're not a stray. An adorable rescue, at the very least."

"That's one of the nicer things someone has said about me."

"I can be much nicer."

His hands rested on my hips, tugging me closer. Our mouths found each other again. His lips were soft, and I liked the rougher brush of his beard against my skin. His tongue glided against mine.

We stopped for air. His smile was hypnotizing. "I'd like to take you out sometime. Just you and me."

"I'd like that too." I almost pointed out that it was just the two of us *right now*. We could do anything we wanted. But the mess Danny had left wasn't such a turn on.

Then again, I was feeling pretty into this right now...

My hip brushed the thick erection in his jeans. Oh, I wanted that. Wanted to feel his cock in my mouth, my tongue driving him wild. My hands and mouth tracing all that ink on his skin. That beard against my inner thighs.

I could imagine our bodies naked and moving together. My legs wrapped around him while he thrust inside me. My panties went damp from thinking about it. Those well-worn fantasies. *Years* of imagining what Grayden would be like in bed.

He pressed a kiss to my cheek, then nuzzled his beard against me in a way that made me shiver.

"You should know, Callum made it pretty clear he wouldn't be okay with this. Grace might not either. And you can guess what Ashford and half the rest of Silver Ridge would say. Not to mention your big brother."

I cringed, imagining Teller's reaction. "But why on earth would we tell them? I don't make a habit of telling my older brother about my sex life. And I certainly don't need to tell Grace if I sleep with hers. Nobody needs to know what kind of fun we have."

Grayden pulled back and looked at me, a crease appearing between his brows. "Piper, I'm trying to ask you on a real date. Not some secret hookup."

"A *date*?"

"Would that be so bad?"

"But I don't date. That's not something I'm looking for."

"You just want to use me for my body?" When I didn't answer, the humor in his eyes disappeared. "Oh. Shit. Not sure if I'm flattered or offended."

"I, um, I guess we had different things in mind."

"Oh, believe me, I love the sound of what you have in mind. I was just hoping for more."

I forced myself to untangle from him. Take a step back.

"It's not about you," I said. "It's me. After my divorce, I promised myself I wouldn't ever get in that kind of situation again. No dating, no marriage. No falling in love. I'm done with all of that."

Please don't judge me for it, I added silently.

"But you and Ollie both deserve to have someone who's devoted to you. You deserve a guy you can always count on."

"And you think *you're* someone we could always count on?" I squeezed my eyes shut. "Oh God, I'm sorry. That sounded terrible. I didn't mean it."

The muscle in his jaw ticked. "Nah, I understand."

"I don't know what I would've done if you hadn't shown up today. I'm grateful."

"You don't have to be. You owe me nothing. But I also know a few hot hookups with you wouldn't be enough for me."

Wow. I'd pretty much offered him casual sex, and he'd turned me down. But I'd turned him down too. So we were both disappointed.

It wasn't fun.

"Friends?" I asked lamely.

"Friendship happens to be an untapped talent of mine," he said gruffly. "Along with interrupting holiday dinners, feeding the small-town gossip machine, and impromptu snowball fights."

"You also make a pretty good cup of coffee."

"That's a serious compliment coming from the likes of you."

"It is."

"Since we're being so honest..." He touched my chin. "Just know, I'll be thinking of your kiss for a very long time."

Because I was a mess of contradictory feelings, I leaned in and brushed my lips against his again.

Grayden held my face, his kiss softer this time. Like it would be the *last* time, and he wanted to savor it. Then he kissed my nose, pulling back after an achingly slow moment.

I tried to insist on cleaning up the mess Danny had made, but Grayden refused. "You have far better things to do with your time," he said.

He grabbed my coat and purse from where I'd left them. Returning to the kitchen, he held up the coat, and I slid my arms into it.

"Let me know if you have any more issues with Danny. So I can be there. As a friend."

Ugh, why did that word sound so inadequate all of a sudden?

"I will. Thanks."

Grayden tucked a lock of my hair behind my ear. My breath caught, my gaze lingering on his. Suddenly, I didn't want to leave. My hands wanted to grab hold of him and never let go.

But that thought alone was scary enough to have me running for the door.

EIGHTEEN

Piper

"HEY PIPER? Isn't that your phone ringing?"

I blinked, pulled from wherever my mind had wandered. "What?"

Dillon gestured toward my apron pocket, where my phone was indeed vibrating. "The buzzing sound. Pretty sure that's a phone call."

"Oh. Yes." I fumbled for it, pulling it out just in time to see Teller's name on the screen before I missed the call entirely. Whoops.

I sighed and set the phone down on the counter.

"You okay? You've been super distracted today."

"Yeah, sorry. A lot on my mind."

Ever since that awful confrontation with Danny a couple of days ago, I'd been on edge. Unsure if Danny was still in town or if he might show up again. I'd gone from begging my ex to come to Silver Ridge to being afraid to see him.

But Danny's asshole tendencies, or his bizarre interest in my mom's old stuff, was hardly the only thing taking up space in my brain.

Such as the incredible, epic kiss that I couldn't stop replaying.

"A lot on your mind. Hmm." Dillon's expression was carefully neutral. "Anything to do with Grayden O'Neal? Heard he's renting your mom's old place."

How rude of Dillon to be one hundred percent correct.

I'll be thinking of that kiss for a very long time.

I shook my head to chase away the memory. If only that would work. "Grayden is a friend. If you've heard any rumors about him, you shouldn't be so quick to believe them."

"But you also shouldn't be too quick to trust," Dillon mumbled.

"And that's my call to make, not yours."

He looked chastened. "Didn't mean any offense, boss."

"I know you meant well." I regretted how irritable I'd sounded. "If you want, you can head home a little early." As my head baker, Dillon was always here before the crack of dawn. He only had another half hour on his shift anyway.

"You sure?"

I gestured around the nearly empty coffee shop. The only non-employee here was Ollie, because his after-school activity had been canceled.

Ollie was over in the corner by the bookshelves, building a complicated, precarious tower out of used paperbacks. Also, pouting about not being allowed to skateboard on the busy Main Street sidewalk.

"This place is dead right now anyway," I said. "Rina and I have got this."

Dillon studied me for another moment, then nodded and grabbed his jacket from the back.

After he left, Rina came over from where she'd been sweeping up crumbs near the window seats. "So what's the real story?"

"The real story?"

"About you being so distracted you keep staring off into space? Is your mind still stuck on the handsome bad boy with the naughty glasses?"

I snorted. Should've known she'd been listening. "How can glasses even be naughty?"

"Grayden manages it."

I glanced at Ollie to make sure he was fully absorbed in building his paperback tower. Then I stage-whispered, "I kissed him."

"You *what*?"

"Shh!" I glanced toward Ollie again, but he was ignoring us.

"Piper Carmichael. You must tell me *everything*."

Rina poked my arm with the broom handle from across the counter until I glared at her. She scurried around to the other side of the register, putting the broom away as she went.

I grabbed a pair of tongs to top-up the pastry display case. "There's nothing to tell," I said quietly. "It was just a kiss."

"Just a kiss," she scoffed.

More like three kisses, I corrected silently. Rina didn't need to know that. "It won't happen again," I said.

"But you want it to happen again."

"I didn't say that."

"You didn't have to. It's all over your aura, babe." Rina was practically bouncing on her heels now. "This is the most exciting thing that's happened since Manny Alvarez cursed out those snooty tourists while dressed in his Santa costume."

I snorted a laugh. Yeah, that had been funny.

It was also a relief to tell *someone* about kissing Grayden. I certainly hadn't told my best friend that I'd made out with her oldest brother and then offered up my body for sex.

And he'd turned me down.

"It wasn't even just the kiss," I whispered. "Grayden is renting my old house. A couple days ago, Danny broke in. I confronted him, and he was being awful. Grayden came home and kind of went...*feral* on him."

Rina's jaw dropped open in slow motion. "Piper, that is *so. Hot*. When are you seeing him again?"

"I'm not sure. We're friends, but it can't be more than that. I'm not *interested* in more than that."

"Not what your aura says," she muttered.

"I'm going to go call my brother back."

I wasn't avoiding Rina's hints about my feelings for Grayden. Nope, not me.

"I'll keep an eye on Ollie and hold down the register." Rina glanced around the utterly silent, completely empty coffee shop. "You know, in case we get swamped in the next five minutes."

"Thanks," I said, already heading toward my office.

I had to get myself together. Had to stop thinking constantly about Grayden, because this wasn't healthy.

After Grayden had told me he was innocent and took the fall for someone else, it had been hard not to go straight to Grace and repeat everything he'd said. His siblings needed to know. Especially Ashford.

Wouldn't the truth make a difference? Maybe Ashford would finally give Grayden a chance.

But before, Grayden had said the truth would hurt Grace. That she would feel *guilty*. I couldn't understand why or how, but Grace had already been through so much. She didn't need more pain heaped on top of everything else.

This time, it was probably better to stay out of it. Just let things unfold between the O'Neal siblings naturally. They'd talk everything out when they were ready.

Besides, Grace had been in New York City with Dane since New Year's. She wasn't around right now to notice how overwhelmed I was, unlike Dillon or Rina.

For my entire life, I'd been able to confide in Grace about almost everything. The only exception? Grayden. Both when we were teenagers, and right now.

I didn't like having secrets from my best friend.

In my office, I closed the door behind me and sank into my desk chair.

Teller answered on the second ring. "Hey, sis."

"Hey, yourself. Sorry I missed your call."

"No problem. Just in between meetings and I thought I'd say hello."

I swiveled in my chair, propping my feet on the edge of the desk. "Listen to you, taking meetings with music execs. What did you do with my grumpy cop brother?"

"No execs were present," he said with a chuckle. "Which is lucky for them. I hate all that bullshit. I just coordinate with law enforcement and our bodyguard team."

Teller was still a part-time Silver Ridge PD officer when he visited Hart County, but he also served as Ayla's head of security. She was about to start a months-long national tour, so Teller had plenty to do.

The two of them were adorable and sweet together, and I never imagined I'd say that about my brother.

"How about you?" he asked. "Anything new?"

Uh oh. I knew that tone of voice.

I sat forward, dropping my feet to the floor. "What do you mean?"

"Callum mentioned that Grayden O'Neal is renting mom's old house from you."

Yep, there it was. "That's true."

"Why didn't you tell me?"

Because I knew you'd be weird about it, I thought.

Out loud, I said, "It didn't seem like a big deal. I needed a tenant, he needed a place to live. It made sense."

"Are you sure that's a good idea?"

"Why wouldn't it be?" I challenged. "Are you taking Ashford's side? Because I happen to think he's wrong about Grayden."

"I'm not taking a side. It's Callum I've been talking to, remember? I respect that Callum and Grace have worked things out with Grayden. I'm just not sure it's a good thing for Ollie to be around the man. Considering...you know, *everything*."

I made an exasperated sound.

Teller would be surprised to learn the real *everything* involving me and Grayden.

"Also, it sounds like Grayden's more than just your tenant. You're seeing him socially too. With Ollie."

"Callum told you about the dinner at Hearthstone?"

"Yes. A dinner that took place *before* you came to see me and Ayla for Christmas. But you didn't mention any of this then."

"Do I have a right to an attorney for this interrogation, Officer?"

"Not an interrogation. You're the one who's hiding things. I'm just trying to find out why."

I stood up from my chair and started pacing the small office. "This is my business, Teller. I'm a big girl. I don't need you and Callum ganging up on me about who I rent my property to. Or who I spend time with."

"Piper—"

"He was your best friend once," I interrupted. "Remember that? Now you're talking about him like he's some random creep. Grayden is a good man."

The line went quiet for a moment.

When Teller spoke again, his voice was softer. "Grayden and I were friends a long time ago. It's clear I never really knew him that well."

Yet I remembered the two of them laughing quietly about some inside joke. Or talking late into the night. They'd both been so serious, but they'd opened up around each other. Best friends. *Brothers.*

"There's a lot more to the story than you know," I said.

"Usually that's the case."

"If you ask Grayden, he'll tell you."

"Piper, I haven't spoken to Grayden since we were in our twenties. I have nothing to say to him, and I figure he feels the same about me."

"Which you couldn't know. Unless you *ask*."

Teller sighed. "Look, I'm sorry. I didn't mean to upset you. I'm just concerned, that's all. You're my little sister. I want to make sure you're okay."

The fight drained out of me. "I know. I'm sorry for getting testy with you."

"I'm also missing Ollie. Maybe I'm just feeling guilty about not seeing him since I've been gone from Silver Ridge so much."

Look at my brother, so in touch with his feelings these days.

I sat back down in my chair. Even when I was annoyed with Teller, even when he was being overprotective, I knew it came from a place of love.

Exactly why I couldn't tell him about my latest issues with Danny.

Teller knew all about Danny's failings as a father. If I told my brother about Danny's latest affront, the way my ex had put his hands on me, Teller would drop everything and fly out here to Hart County.

But Teller had already given up things he wanted in the past because he thought he had to protect his little sister. He'd put his own life on hold. I wasn't going to let him do it again.

"Ollie's doing well," I said.

"Still can't believe Danny flaked on him for Thanksgiving."

I could. "Actually, Cal is taking Ollie to Denver this weekend to see a Broncos game. Just the two of them. Ollie's really excited. I'm surprised Callum didn't tell you, since you two have been gossiping so much."

Callum had wanted to do something special for Ollie to help make up for the failed Thanksgiving trip with Danny. Because Callum was a sweetheart.

Teller made a happy sound. "That's fantastic. I'm jealous."

We talked for a few more minutes about nothing important. When we finally hung up, I sat in my office for a long moment, staring at my phone.

I hoped that whatever scheme Danny had been up to, he was finished with it now. He rarely stuck with anything too long, so he was probably already back home and out of Hart County.

Out of my life again, at least for a while.

But I'd been over and over it in my head, trying to figure out what possible item of value my mom might've had that Danny would want. And every time, my mind drew a blank.

Just one of those mysteries about Danny Carmichael that I'd never figure out. Like what I'd ever seen in him in the first place.

Rina looked up from her phone as I walked toward the counter. The shop was still quiet, no sign of any new customers. Maybe because the weather was beautiful outside, much warmer than the typical January day, and the snow had melted.

Kinda made me want to get out in nature too. Maybe I would take Ollie to the park after this. Let him skateboard to his heart's content.

"How's big bro?" Rina asked. "Everything good with him and the pop princess?"

I laughed. "Yeah. He was calling about me, actually. Making sure I'm okay."

"Overprotective big brother mode?"

"There's no other mode for him."

My thoughts drifted to Grayden again, the way they kept doing. I appreciated what he'd done for me a couple of days ago. I liked having him around. As a friend, since we couldn't be more.

But I didn't *need* him. Right? I couldn't allow myself to rely on him. I'd learned that lesson the hard way already.

For now, Ollie and I were okay. We were safe. Whatever happened next, even if Danny showed up again, I'd deal with it. I always did.

I glanced over at the tower of paperbacks. Only then did I realize who *wasn't* there.

"Rina, where's Ollie?"

NINETEEN

Grayden

I'D BARELY SLEPT a moment the last couple nights.

First, I'd scoured the old Landry house top to bottom, searching for the mystery box Danny had been looking for. Not because I wanted to help that waste of breath, obviously. But for Piper.

If there was something valuable in that house belonging to her mom, then I wanted Piper to have it.

No luck. Aside from some photos and mementos from Piper's younger days that made me smile, I didn't find anything worth ransacking the place.

Then I'd been on cleanup duty. Putting away all the stuff Danny had thrown around, the boxes he'd upended, my ink bottles he'd broken.

Thank goodness he hadn't done any damage to items I couldn't afford to replace. Like my tablet computer, which held all my digital designs, and my sketchbook.

Danny had broken the old lock on the back door to the house, which probably hadn't taken much effort. So I'd replaced it with a nicer one. The house was pretty much back to normal now, and I was back to making progress on my various studio-prep projects.

But the other reason I hadn't been sleeping? My mind had refused to stay quiet about the beautiful blond who'd become my obsession.

I'd been trying not to dwell on Piper, but it was hard. Part of me wondered what the hell I'd been thinking, turning down her offer of a no-strings hookup. It had been an impulsive move on my part, not just kissing her but wanting more. Wanting to try something real with her.

I could've spent some quality time getting horizontal with her that day. But no, I'd had to get a bug up my ass about dating her. On the very same day her ex had hurt her. Of course she'd shot me down.

We were beyond complicated, and I was hardly the picture of stability just yet.

There was exactly one person in Silver Ridge who believed I could deserve her. And that was *me*. Overconfident, perhaps?

But I didn't regret anything I'd said to her that afternoon. It had been freeing to tell her the truth about my guilty plea, even if I hadn't explained exactly why I would take the fall when I was innocent.

She'd listened. She'd believed me. That meant everything.

I'd kept my phone nearby the last two nights, just in case Piper called needing anything. Because I was a complete sucker for that woman. If Piper snapped her fingers, I'd probably start running.

And I didn't even feel bad about it.

But Piper hadn't texted or called. No news was probably good news, since it likely meant Danny hadn't bothered her again. Yet it also meant I needed another excuse for seeing her.

Which explained why I was driving down Main Street right now, scanning for a parking space on this beautiful blue-sky winter day.

There were plenty of spaces near Silver Linings, so I pulled my truck into one. The door to the coffee shop flew open as I approached, and the tall blond of my dreams dashed out, running straight into me.

I caught her before she could stumble, my hands on her arms. "Whoa, Piper, what's going on?"

"I can't find Ollie." She glanced back and forth with wide, frightened eyes. "He was inside a few minutes ago, and now he's gone. His skateboard is too. Ollie has a basic phone so he can always reach me, but he left it inside. What if Danny—"

"Hey, don't panic," I said, keeping my voice calm. "Ollie wouldn't just take off, even if his dad showed up, right? If he's on his skateboard, he can't have gone far. You think he'd go somewhere specific? The park?"

She pressed her fingers to her temple. "Maybe Main Street Market? Rosie always gives him candy."

"You check there. I'll walk around the block and see if I spot him."

"I'll text Rosie and some of the other shopkeepers. We have a group thread."

"Sounds good."

"If we don't find him in five minutes..."

She trailed off, the rest of that sentence implied. She would call the police. Kids probably ran around half-wild in Silver Ridge all the time. Teller and I certainly had as kids, and so had my siblings.

But Piper and her ex had argued just days ago. I understood what she was afraid of.

"Five minutes," I agreed.

Piper nodded and took off toward the market while I circled around to the side of Piper's building. The alley was quiet except for the hum of an exhaust fan and the scrape of my boots on pavement.

Then I heard it. Soft whimpers.

I found Ollie beside the back door to Silver Linings, slumped against the wall with his skateboard lying a few feet away.

"Ollie?"

He rubbed his face with his arm, trying to hide his tears. His hands were scraped up, palms raw and bleeding.

He squinted at me. "What are *you* doing here?"

"Just stopped by for a coffee fix, and your mom couldn't find you." I pulled out my phone and sent Piper a quick text.

Found Ollie behind the building. He's okay.
Just a few scrapes. I'll bring him inside

I approached and kneeled beside him. "Rough landing, huh?"

Ollie kept swiping at his face with the back of his wrist. He sniffled and nodded, not meeting my eyes. "I only wanted to skateboard around the building a couple times. I tried a trick and I fell."

"Was it a cool trick?"

"Huh?" Ollie's eyes scrunched up like he suspected I was making fun of him.

"I assume it was a cool trick. The ones that make you wipe out usually are."

"I guess. Yeah, it would've been. If I'd made it."

"Maybe next time. Need help getting up?"

"*No.*" He squirmed around. "But the back door is locked, and I didn't wanna go around to the front because my mom would see what happened. Forgot my stupid dumbass phone inside because it's boring. Doesn't even have games or the internet."

I forced myself not to smile at his cursing. "Come on. Time to face the music."

"What's that mean?"

"It means you need to face your mom even if she might be mad."

Grumbling, Ollie got to his feet. My fist rapped on the glass just below the *Silver Linings Coffee* logo. A familiar face appeared, one of Piper's employees. Rina, according to her name tag.

Rina pushed the door open, looking past me at Ollie. "Dude, you ran off on me! I was supposed to be watching you!"

"Sorry." Ollie shuffled through the back door as I held it open.

"Does Piper know where he is?" Rina asked me.

"Yeah, I texted her. She's probably on her way back."

Rina opened another door, revealing a tiny office space with a desk piled with papers. "Take him in here. I'll grab the first-aid kit."

Ollie went through the open door of Piper's office and sat in a chair, cradling his hands. Piper appeared a moment later, out of breath and wearing a thunderous expression.

"I told you no skateboarding until later. I cannot believe you just left, Ollie."

"I was bored. Rina was doing stuff, and you were busy, and I didn't think anyone would notice."

"Of course I noticed." Piper crouched in front of him, her face a mixture of relief and frustration. "Ollie-bear, you're all scraped up."

"I'm *fine*, Mom," Ollie said adamantly, glancing at me with his chin jutting out. Even as more tears were welling in his eyes.

Poor kid.

Rina popped her head in again. "Um, boss? I can't find the first-aid kit."

Piper sighed and got up. "It was right on that middle shelf." She squeezed past me, going with Rina, and I realized how much of the space I was taking up in the small room.

I shifted my weight. "I'm going to head back out to the front and let your mom take care of you. Okay?"

"Wait." Ollie's voice was quiet. "Can you..."

I paused, studying him.

He dropped his gaze to his scraped palms. "My mom always puts hurty stuff on cuts. It stings, and I don't..." His voice went even smaller, and the next few words came out in a rush. "*Donwanna cry in fronofher.*"

As soon as I figured out what he'd said, my chest twinged with empathy for him. He was trying so hard to be brave. "You can probably do the bandages yourself. You're pretty grown up, right? I can show you what to do."

He nodded, blinking the tears away.

When Piper came back with the first-aid kit, Ollie said, "Mom, I can do it myself."

"Bud, I don't think—"

"Grayden's going to help me. I asked him to."

Piper gave me a questioning look, and I smiled sheepishly. "I've got plenty of experience with bandages in my line of work. I'm happy to give him some tips."

"Please, Mom? Could I have a hot cocoa? I know you're mad, but I'll pay for it from my allowance."

"I'd love a double espresso," I said softly. "I've been saving my allowance too." I added a subtle wink, and a tiny smile appeared on Piper's lips.

"Okay. Both of you can turn off the charm, because the drinks are on the house. I'll put your orders in with Rina, and I'll be back soon. Just call out if either of you needs anything."

"Yes, Mom," I said.

She smiled bigger and shook her head, retreating from the open doorway.

When I was a kid, my dad never would've patiently shown me how to clean my hands after a scrape, making sure I got all the dirt and bits of gravel out. Nah, my father had been the *Shut up and quit being a crybaby* type. Piper and Teller's father had been the same way.

Made me wonder how Danny would've handled this, if he'd been the one to find Ollie instead of me.

Not that I was trying to be a father figure. But it took surprisingly little effort just to be kind and decent.

I pulled another chair up in front of Ollie and opened the first-aid kit. "Alright, let's see what we're working with."

We started with the antiseptic wipes. Ollie flinched a few times, one tear rolling free. "You're doing great," I said. "That's the hardest part."

"I know." He sniffled, dabbing at the cuts.

Ollie spread too much ointment over the scrapes, making a mess, and I held back a smile. I asked, "Why don't you want your mom to see you crying? If you can cry in front of anyone, it should be your mom, right?"

He was quiet, and the hum of conversation between Piper and Rina filled the space along with the hiss of the espresso machine. "My mom has enough to deal with already. I don't want to make her more sad or worried than she already is."

I didn't like hearing that. "Your mom's been sad?"

"She thinks I don't notice, but I do." He stared at the smears of ointment on his fingers, and I held out a tissue for him to wipe off the excess. "My dad doesn't come around that much anymore. He makes promises and then breaks them. It sucks. But the worst part is how my mom gets this look in her eyes."

I nodded slowly, unwrapping a bandage and helping Ollie position it. "I know a few things about dads who don't keep promises."

"You do?"

"Sadly. It hurts, doesn't it? It always hurt me, even though I tried not to show it. And then I got mad, and that didn't feel so good either. In the end."

Ollie stared at his bandaged palms. "Did it get better?"

"Eventually," I said with a sigh. "When I accepted that my dad's problems weren't about me at all. Or about my brothers or my sister. It was all on him."

After a breath, Ollie mumbled, "Sorry for bein' rude and stuff when we were having dinner at Hearthstone. I wasn't trying to." He flinched. "Maybe I was. But I just didn't know if you were a bad guy or not. My mom says you're not. I guess I believe her."

I replaced the supplies in the first-aid kit, glad to have at least a slight vote of confidence from the kid.

"You asked what I did to wind up in prison, and that's a valid question. I would've told you that night, but I wasn't sure if your mom wanted me talking about it in front of you."

Ollie perked up. "I can handle it. I read all kinds of bloody stuff in my comic books. I'm really mature."

I smiled. "Seems like it."

"Except for crying when I fall." He slumped a little. "That's kind of babyish."

"Nah," I said smoothly. "Everybody cries. Including me. Cried plenty of times when I was in prison. I missed my family a lot. Wished things hadn't turned out the way they did."

Ollie tilted his head, studying me with those serious eyes. "My mom told me you didn't really hurt anyone, but that I shouldn't talk about that with anybody else. Like Maisie. Because it's not my story to tell."

I sat on the edge of the desk. "I confessed to a crime because I thought I was protecting someone."

"Was it the right thing to do?"

I wished I knew the true answer. Had it been right? Noble? Or just stupid? Until it went completely sideways, of course, and I couldn't take it back.

I'd turned those questions over in my head a thousand times during my years inside, and I still wasn't sure.

"I thought so. At first. By the time I realized what was really going to happen to me, it was too late to tell the truth."

"My mom says it's never too late to tell the truth."

"No, she's right. Telling the truth is important, and it's never truly too late. But sometimes, things get complicated."

His brow furrowed, and he picked at the edge of the bandage. "I don't like when stuff is complicated."

"Yeah, Ollie. Me neither."

We headed out to the front of the coffee shop, where a hot cocoa and a double espresso were waiting on the counter. The place was busier now, with both Rina and Piper serving customers. Piper silently pointed at the stack of paperbacks on the floor by the bookshelves, eyeing her son sternly.

Ollie dragged his feet in that direction. "I'm supposed to clean my mess." Then he looked at me hopefully. "Want to team up? It'll be faster."

I chuckled. "Sure. I'll help."

Ollie sat at a nearby table and instructed me on where to put the various books, acting like a foreman on a construction site. So the kid was smart and resourceful, too. He'd put me right to work.

I couldn't help sending sly grins to Piper, who was clearly watching us.

"My mom likes you," Ollie said under his breath.

I turned back to him, grabbing the chair beside him and taking a sip of my coffee. "As a friend."

"But she talks about you a lot. Like all the time."

Hope spread through my chest. I told myself not to read too much into it. "Was she saying good things?"

He rolled his eyes. "Yeah. I said she likes you, didn't I? Are you going to be her boyfriend?"

The word hit me with longing. I wouldn't mind that. Wouldn't mind it at all.

But reality was a different story.

"I don't think your mom's looking for a boyfriend."

"She seems not as sad when you're around, though. I mean, she always smiles all the time, but around you, her smiles seem more, I don't know. Real. Like she doesn't have to think about them."

"How do you feel about that?"

He shrugged. "I guess it's not the worst thing. I think my mom's right. You're a good guy. Even if you don't look like one."

"What's a good guy supposed to look like?"

"I don't know. Not all tattooed and stuff. My dad would say you need a haircut."

I raised an eyebrow, amused.

"But maybe I don't care what my dad thinks. As long as you keep making my mom smile."

He pulled a book from the shelf and started reading, apparently done with our conversation. But man, I was still reeling. And trying not to overthink it, but that wasn't easy.

When the rush of customers died down, I carried my cup over to the counter where Piper was wiping down the espresso machine. Rina was doing something in the kitchen.

"Thanks for all your help today with Ollie," Piper said quietly. "Being so patient with him."

"He's a great kid. Honest, brave, and adores his mom. And he talked me into unpaid labor. Seems like he's headed for management."

She laughed, a beautiful tinkling sound that played every one of my heart strings. "I just want him to be okay."

"With a mom like you, he's got everything he needs."

Something complicated passed across her face. Then she kissed my cheek, her lips soft against my skin.

I stood there like an idiot after she pulled away, the spot on my cheek still tingling.

TWENTY

Grayden

I PUSHED my glasses up the bridge of my nose, tilting my head this way and that as I studied the sketch in front of me. My charcoal pencil moved across the paper, tracing the outlines of familiar peaks and valleys.

I'd started this sketch without a clear picture in mind. But here I was, drawing Silver Ridge. My hometown for some of the best and worst moments of my entire life. Inescapable.

Wasn't enough that I was back living here now. This place had taken root in my psyche once again, as if I'd never left.

Because this had always been home.

I let inspiration guide me. Added buildings along the base of the mountains. More details made the structures recognizable as the quaint architecture of Main Street. Silver Linings Coffee materialized prominently in the foreground, more detailed than the rest. Because of course it did.

At least I hadn't just drawn a dozen portraits of *her*. Piper smiling and holding out a cup of coffee. Piper with a sarcastic smirk, hair in a bun with wisps framing her face. Piper with her arms crossed and a bossy, *I-mean-business* frown on her full lips.

This is sad, O'Neal. How much more evidence do you need that you've got it bad?

Sitting back, I stretched my arms up until my spine cracked. I'd gotten lost in my work for a while, and that had felt good, even if being hunched over wasn't so great for my back these days.

I was in the front room of the house, sitting at my thrift-store table that would eventually serve as my studio's front desk. The laminate flooring was in place now, and it looked damn great if I said so myself. The walls were freshly painted.

I'd even hired a guy to paint the exterior siding on the cheap, and he was scheduled for next week, weather permitting.

As for these sketches, I'd been trying to brainstorm ideas for the big blank wall behind me. It would be the first thing clients saw as they came in. A crucial first impression. Not just a chance to show off my art style, but to make clients feel welcome and let them know they were in good creative hands.

And the best I could come up with was the landscape outside my door? The same view everybody around here saw every single day?

If I was going to be a cliche, I might as well just come up with a clever variation on the Colorado flag for the mural. People around here ate that kinda thing up. I could work the name of my studio into the design too.

Unfortunately, I didn't have a name for my studio yet either. Another annoying detail.

Incarcerated Ink? *Convicted Custom Tattoos?*

Sorry, my dark humor was out this morning, it seemed.

A knock at the front door pulled me out of my thoughts. I lifted my head, heart thrumming hopefully.

Despite daily trips to Silver Linings since Ollie's skateboarding fall, I still hadn't seen much of Piper. But if that was her at my door, my day was about to get a lot brighter.

To my epic disappointment, I did not find Piper on my doorstep.

My expression tightened as I glanced over the three men standing outside. None of them were smiling.

"You Grayden O'Neal?" the one in front asked. He was dark-haired, a bit shorter than me, wearing a black leather jacket. The other two flanked him, like he was their leader.

I lifted my chin, keeping one hand on the door. "That's me. What can I do for you?"

"You're Ashford's older brother, right?" the leader said.

The guy on his left was stocky, a spark plug in his Harley Davidson sweatshirt. And the one on the right was straight-up massive, with a mountain-man beard and a brown leather vest over a short-sleeved tee despite the cold.

Fuck. I hadn't experienced any kind of issues with the neighbors so far, but I still got dirty looks everywhere I went in Silver Ridge. Were these guys about to give me the *You're not welcome here* talk?

"Look." I leaned against the doorframe, going for casual. "If you're here to run me out of town, you should know other people have already tried and failed. I'm not going anywhere."

The middle guy in the leather jacket blinked.

Then he laughed, a genuine bark of amusement that completely changed his face. The tension in my shoulders eased a fraction.

"That's definitely not why we're here," he said, shaking his head. "I'm Milo. You and I went to high school together, but I guess that's true of most people around here."

He offered his hand, and I took it.

"Nice to see you, Milo." Though I couldn't remember him at all. Not that I'd been Mr. Popular or everyone's friend back then. But high school had been *before*. Some things just weren't as clear all these years later.

Milo jerked his thumb at his companions. "And this is Zach and Earl. They have resting angry faces, but don't believe it. They're both softies."

The big one with the beard, Earl, cracked a slight smile. The guy in the Harley-Davidson sweatshirt, who was apparently Zach, just rolled his eyes.

"We work at the motorcycle shop the next street over," Milo

said. "Thought we'd stop by and say hello. You're opening up a tattoo joint?"

"Yeah." I hadn't told that many people aside from Piper, Grace, and Callum, but word had a way of traveling. "A studio. Appointment-only kind of place."

"High class," Milo said.

"Not sure I can pull off high class, but we'll see. Probably another month or so until I can open, but I've made a lot of progress. Any of you in the market for some ink?"

"Seems likely." Milo grinned. "We've been trying to convince Earl to get his first."

"I have a low pain tolerance," the big, gruff man muttered.

Zach elbowed him. "He's our delicate flower, this one."

"See?" Milo said. "Softies."

I hooked a thumb at the room behind me. "You're welcome to come in and check out the space."

"We're not bugging you?" Milo asked.

"Nah, I could use a break from the monotony."

Their appearance had been unexpected, but this was promising. My first potential clients.

The front room looked a thousand times better than the first time I'd walked in here, but there was still plenty to do before this place looked like an actual business.

Over the last few days, I'd been taking boxes of Mrs. Landry's old stuff to donate or thrift. But I'd triple-checked all of it carefully. No sign of any jewelry.

No word from Piper about Danny either.

In truth, I was in a holding pattern. Slowly moving forward on the studio, but with my head unable to focus on much except Piper.

"This is the old Landry place, right?" Milo asked.

"Yep. I'm renting from Piper Carmichael."

My belly swooped just from saying her name. I was ridiculous.

"According to Piper, the previous renter was a quilter who

never met a piece of fabric she didn't want to keep," I said. "I've got boxes of the stuff in the back bedroom, but not totally sure who might want it. I tried a thrift store, and they said they don't take scrap fabric. Donation didn't want it either."

Earl perked up. "Fabric? Quilting cotton?"

I brushed a hand over my beard. "Uh, I guess? Lots of colors and patterns. Why?"

"Fat quarters?"

I stared at him. "No clue what that means. But if you know anyone who might be interested, feel free to take a look. I'd love to get rid of it all."

"Uh oh," Zach said. "Earl, don't you already have a ton of fabric you haven't used yet?"

"Motto of quilters everywhere," Earl replied. "There's no such thing as too much fabric."

I pointed toward the hall. "Help yourself. Back bedroom, stack of boxes against the wall."

Earl headed that way immediately. Zach trailed after him while making some comment about Earl's Pinterest account.

I turned to Milo, and he laughed at my expression.

"Didn't expect him to be a quilter, right?" Milo asked. "Earl looks like he's more likely to bash heads than sit behind a sewing machine. But it's the opposite."

"Well, more power to him. I'm familiar with people making assumptions about me. It's annoying as fuck. You three work on bikes for a living?"

"Yep, plus buy, trade and sell. You ride?"

I shrugged. "Not for a long time. Since my Army days." My teeth dug into the inside of my lip as I considered how to say this next part. "I'm guessing you've heard about my record?"

"Sure, man. What else are small towns for, but making sure everyone knows everyone else's business? But we don't care about that shit."

I nodded gratefully, and was even more grateful when Milo

didn't ask for my story. Instead, he stopped by my desk, angling his head to look over the sketch I'd been working on.

"Damn, this is good. You drew it?"

"Yeah. Trying to come up with ideas for a mural." I gestured at the large blank space that was just begging for artwork. "I'd like it to double as decor and showing off what I can do."

"You do all your own designs?"

"Sure." I pulled up my sleeve, showing him the ink on my left arm. Geometric patterns interwoven with flowers and vines and trees.

Milo leaned in, examining the work. "Fantastic." He pushed up his own sleeve, revealing the tribal designs on his forearm. "Got these a while back, and I'd love to add to it, but I want something more unique next time."

"Well, once I get this place up and running, you know where to find me."

"I'll take you up on that." He glanced around the room again. "You need help with any of this? I can do a little plumbing work. Maybe you could give me a discount when I want to get some ink done."

My grin was genuine. "Absolutely."

Milo pulled out his phone. "Give me your number. We'll set something up."

Damn, had I actually made a friend? Aside from Piper, Milo would be my first in Silver Ridge since my return.

We exchanged contact information, and I was just starting to think this whole neighbor thing might actually work out when Earl walked back into the room carrying a cardboard box.

He dropped it on the floor with a heavy thud. Zach followed behind him, and both of them had stormy looks on their faces.

"The hell is this?" Earl grunted out.

"What?" Milo said, strolling over. "You don't like the fabric selection? Geez, how picky can you be?"

I was equally incredulous. What were these two scowling about?

Then Milo went over to the box and looked inside. His expression turned hard. He looked up at me. "You want to explain this?"

Okay, they were making me nervous.

I moved closer and looked down into the box.

A rectangle wrapped in clear plastic lay on top of the fabric. A brick of white powder, compressed and sealed.

The *hell*?

My stomach dropped. "That's not mine."

"Right," Zach said. "It just appeared in your house by magic. I'm not judging anybody's recreational use, but this is enough for felony intent to distribute."

Waves of nausea-inducing heat rolled over my skin.

"I'm serious. That wasn't there the last time I went through these boxes." I looked at Milo, willing him to believe me. "That was a few days ago. I was sorting through all of this after someone broke in, and there was nothing but fabric and sewing supplies and stuff that belonged to Piper's mother."

"Someone broke in?" Milo's tone was skeptical.

"Yeah. Danny Carmichael. Piper's ex. He ransacked the place looking for something."

"You suggesting he planted this?" Earl's voice was flat.

"I don't know. I went through all this stuff as I was cleaning it up. But..." I ran my hand through my hair, my mind racing. I'd been here almost every day. But not every hour. There'd been gaps.

Could Danny have done this?

Racing into the back bedroom, I went to the window.

"Wouldn't have been hard to jimmy that lock open," Milo said behind me. He must've followed me in.

The lock on the frame wasn't latched. I was sure I hadn't left it like that. And Milo was right. The thing was an old piece of junk.

Of course, plenty of things around this house were falling

apart. Replacing all the window locks was on the endless list of things I hadn't done yet.

I turned around. "Look, you know I have a criminal record." I heard how defensive I sounded and hated it. "I'm here to get my life back on track, not wind up in prison again."

Milo's expression was uncertain. But finally, he nodded. "I have a cousin who was dealing, and he was throwing off shifty vibes I could sense a mile away. I don't get anything like that from you."

At least one of them believed me. But that still didn't solve my problem.

"Hey, we've got company," Zach called out from the living room.

Fuck, what now?

When Milo and I returned to the front of the house, Zach was peering out the window toward the street. "This ain't good."

A Silver Ridge PD vehicle had just pulled up in front of the house.

Icy cold shot through my veins.

My mind worked frantically. This was a setup. It had to be. Danny had broken in before. He could've come back, planted the drugs, and then made an anonymous call to the police. It was exactly the kind of move a guy like him would pull.

I can destroy you if I want, O'Neal.

And I was the idiot who hadn't taken him at his word.

"Wherever that brick of powder came from," Milo said quietly, "you'd better get rid of it. Right now."

TWENTY-ONE
Piper

I ALWAYS FELT a jolt of nostalgia when I stepped into Silver Ridge Elementary.

Maybe it was the aroma of cafeteria food mixed with that particular smell of construction paper. Or the motivational posters I could've sworn had been up since I was in school here.

Hang in there, kid.

"Hi Piper, you brought snacks?" another mom asked, holding the door for me. She was decked out in pristine yoga gear with her hair blown out. Meanwhile, I was pretty sure I had latte stains on my jeans and my hair was half out of its messy knot.

I shifted my tray of mini cupcakes, all gluten and dairy free, to my other hand. "It's for career day in my son's fourth-grade class. Our new baker does them."

"Dillon Kirby, the cute one?"

"Uh, yep. That's him."

"I see his mother at yoga." She nudged me. "Dillon's grown up a lot, hasn't he?" Her tone dripped with innuendo.

"Um, I guess. But I like my guys older, personally."

"I sense gossip. Who's the lucky older man?"

"Oh, *no one*. There's nobody. Not at all."

"Uh huh." She did not look convinced.

Hopefully, I wasn't blushing.

I said goodbye and took the hallway for Ollie's class. Time to pick up my pace. I wasn't late, but it was close.

I was here today to wax poetic to Ollie's class about the joys of running my own coffee shop. Most of the kids had been to Silver Linings before, so my career day presentation would at least have some relevance to them.

Never mind the fact that the cozy atmosphere of my coffee shop sometimes felt out of step with the stresses of my real life. Especially lately.

But Ollie's teacher hadn't invited me to hear my complaints about bills or ex-husbands. Or my confusing feelings for handsome, older men with the last name O'Neal.

Nope, I was here to make owning a small business sound like never-ending fun. And if all else failed, bribing fourth graders with cupcakes certainly couldn't hurt.

A hum of happy kid voices came from Ollie's classroom up ahead. A handful of other parents waited outside in the hall, checking phones or chatting quietly.

I stopped so abruptly the tray of cupcakes almost went sideways.

Danny stood near the classroom door, leaning against the cinderblock wall and smiling his perfectly white smile. He was wearing pressed khakis and his typical polo with an expensive coat over his arm. Clean-cut and professional. Every inch the respectable dentist and the devoted father.

My stomach roiled, bile inching into my throat.

"Danny." I kept my voice low as I approached, aware of the other parents watching. "What are you doing here?"

He straightened, offering that smooth smile that had fooled me completely, once up on a time.

"Career day, Piper," he said patronizingly. "I was on the email list the teacher sent out, just like you. Thought it would be nice to surprise Ollie."

"A surprise. Wow. Could I have a word, please?"

"Maybe you don't mind being late, Piper, but—"

"*Now,*" I hissed.

My pulse was racing as I led Danny away from the cluster of parents and down the hall. When we were far enough, I turned on him, still keeping my voice to a harsh whisper.

"You can't just show up with no warning. Not after what you did last week."

"And what exactly did I do?"

Beads of sweat broke out along my sides. "You broke into my rental property," I said through gritted teeth. "You *choked me.*" The last two words shook on their way out, and I hated how broken I sounded.

Danny grimaced. "God, Piper. I'm sorry about all that. Seriously. It was a misunderstanding."

"A *misunderstanding*?" I repeated, still feeling his fingers at my neck. My own hands shook so hard I was afraid I'd drop the cupcakes. "You attacked me."

He glanced back at the other parents. "Don't blow it out of proportion. If anyone got attacked, it was *me*. By your criminal boyfriend."

"Grayden is not my boyfriend."

"I'm willing to forget about it, okay? I've already moved on. You should too."

Bullshit, I wanted to shout. Danny was gaslighting me, and I wished it were the first time.

Yet that wasn't even the worst part of his so-called surprise.

"This isn't fair to Ollie," I sputtered. "You can't stand him up at Thanksgiving, make pathetic excuses, and then waltz in here like everything's fine. It's beyond manipulative."

"I'm here now, aren't I? I'm trying, Piper. I thought this would be a good opportunity to reconnect with him. And as his parent, I have every right to be here at a school event."

Legally, he was correct. That didn't make me any less furious.

"Fine. But after this, we're going to have a real conversation about scheduling and consistency. Ollie deserves better than occasional surprise appearances."

Danny nodded, his expression contrite. "You're right. Absolutely. We'll talk."

I didn't believe him. But there was nothing I could do about it now, not with a handful of other parents watching us from down the hall.

We headed back toward the classroom. The door opened, and Ollie's teacher smiled at all of us. "Thank you so much for coming, everyone. We're ready for you now."

I walked in first, still carrying my tray of cupcakes. Ollie's face lit up when he saw me. Then his gaze shifted past me, and his eyes went wide.

"Dad?" The pure joy in his voice made my chest tighten like a vise.

Danny grinned and gave a little wave. "Hey, champ."

I pasted on a smile as the presentations began. Somehow, I got through mine, barely aware of what I was saying.

Seeing Ollie's happiness crushed me, because I knew how much it would hurt later when Danny let him down again.

My phone felt like a lifeline in my purse. I could text Grayden. He'd asked me to let him know if Danny showed up again, and he'd been so amazing with Ollie the other day.

But I'd spent years dealing with Daniel Carmichael, and I would continue dealing with him for years to come.

Grayden was... I didn't know. Just a friend. He'd been there for me and Ollie more than once over the past week, but I couldn't allow him to fight my battles for me.

By the time the career day presentations wrapped up, it was the end of the school day. After cleanup, the kids grabbed their backpacks and filed outside together, as they always did.

Danny walked beside me, not saying a word. I didn't speak either. I was too busy stewing in my anger.

As we headed toward the parking lot, Ollie was practically vibrating with excitement. "Dad, I can't believe you came!"

"Wouldn't miss it, champ."

A flicker of hesitation passed over Ollie's features. "Are you staying in Silver Ridge for a few days?"

"For as long as I can. Yeah. Cleared my schedule."

No mention of the fact that he'd been in Silver Ridge days ago. Had he been in Hart County the whole time? Or had he been driving back and forth? I had no idea what was going on with Danny's new dental practice. If he'd driven it into the ground the way he'd destroyed his practice here.

Danny's gaze moved to me, turning calculating. "How about the three of us grab an early dinner?"

Ollie stared at me with a worried frown as he waited for an answer.

"I can't," I said stiffly.

Danny shrugged like he hadn't cared either way. "Hey Ollie, you've got a three-day weekend, right? No school tomorrow. That's what the schedule said."

Ollie nodded. "I guess."

"I was thinking. How about we do a guys' trip this weekend? Just you and me. We could head up to the ski resort, do some snowboarding. Have steaks in the fancy restaurant they have up there. Piper, Grace's boyfriend is the owner, right? He could hook us up."

"Really?" Ollie's eyes went huge. "That would be amazing!"

"Absolutely not," I snapped, then I softened my tone. "Ollie, you're already going to Denver this weekend with Uncle Callum. Remember? The Broncos game?"

That was setting aside the fact that Danny expected Grace and Dane to arrange a free vacation for him.

Ollie's face fell. He glanced between me and Danny, clearly torn.

"Oh, come on," Danny said. "He can reschedule with Callum. This is father-son time."

I opened my mouth again, but Ollie shook his head, beating me to it. "Sorry, Dad. I can't do that to Uncle Callum."

My chest lifted with pride. My kid already showed more responsibility and thoughtfulness at nine years old than his thirty-five-year-old father.

Danny's smile tightened, but he recovered quickly. "Okay, I get it." He crouched down to Ollie's level. "How about you and I still grab dinner tonight. The two of us. We can hang out, catch up, get some burgers."

Ollie barely seemed excited. Like all his happiness from earlier had deflated, and he couldn't manage the effort again.

But he still said, "Can I, Mom? Please?"

And here I was, trapped.

If I kept saying no, then I would be the bad guy. I didn't want to keep Ollie from his dad. I'd been begging for Danny to do exactly this for months. Be more involved. Spend time with Ollie. Make an effort.

Love him, dammit.

"Sure. But Ollie needs to be back by seven. I'm taking him to Callum's in the morning, and he needs to have some quiet time before bed. I'd also like to know where you're going, please."

"What exactly are you afraid of, Piper? You think I'm going to kidnap my son?"

Cold fear sliced through my insides. *You bastard*, I thought. How dare he even joke like that after what he'd done to me the other day.

Danny gave me a pitying look. As if he was going out of his way to be reasonable for his hysterical ex-wife. "Fine, I'll pick a restaurant on Main Street, if that makes you feel better. You can meet us in the park at seven. Usual spot."

My jaw clenched, but I nodded. "Good."

Danny clapped Ollie on the shoulder. "This is going to be great, champ. Just like old times."

When we neared Danny's Lexus, I caught Ollie's arm before he climbed in. "Have fun, Ollie-bear. Text me if you need anything. Okay?"

"I will. Thanks, Mom!" He hugged me quickly, then scrambled into the car.

Not that I really thought Danny was going to take him away. My ex was capable of plenty, but if I'd believed he might cause Ollie harm, I never would've left our son alone with him. Visitation rights or not.

Yet as I watched them drive away, Danny's Lexus disappearing down the street, the unsettled feeling in my stomach wouldn't go away.

I prayed that he truly just wanted time with his kid, but Danny had lost my confidence a long time ago.

As I drove away from the elementary school, I was still fuming. The audacity of my ex, showing up like that without warning, acting like father of the year in front of Ollie's classmates and the other parents.

And now Ollie was with him, probably getting fed a bunch of empty promises over burgers and fries. *Urrgh.*

I'd meant to check in at Silver Linings after the school event, make sure everything was running smoothly. But I was too upset to be the boss right now.

All I could think of was talking to Grayden. I could tell him what had happened with Danny. Soak in the comfort of his presence. He always seemed to make me feel better, even when he wasn't trying. Just being around him steadied me.

Maybe hearing Grayden's voice would help me calm down, help me sort through this mess of anger and worry churning in my gut.

But when I grabbed my phone, I was still so mad I wasn't sure I could articulate the words to describe it. Everything would come out in a furious jumble.

I just needed to see him.

And that's how I found myself driving toward the opposite side of town.

Every day it got harder to ignore the way my heart lifted when I saw him, harder to keep myself from reaching for him.

I should stay away. Give myself some distance. Figure out how to untangle these feelings before they got any scarier. But I couldn't seem to do it.

I turned onto his street.

And immediately saw a Silver Ridge PD SUV parked in front of Grayden's place, along with two uniformed officers heading up the walk toward the house.

TWENTY-TWO

Grayden

MILO STEPPED toward the cardboard box, like he was going to pick up that plastic-wrapped brick of powder and get rid of it.

"Don't," I said.

He stopped, glancing back at me with his eyebrows rising. "Thought it wasn't yours."

"It's not. But I know my rights. I doubt the police have a warrant to come in here." I kept my voice level. "If they don't, I'm not letting them inside. If they do, then I'll deal with it. But I'm not going to go scrambling around acting guilty or ashamed."

That was exactly what the Danny Carmichaels of the world wanted. For me to never be able to stop hiding from my past, to always be looking over my shoulder, waiting for the next accusation. Exactly what I'd done in Seattle when trouble got too close.

But now that I was finally home in Silver Ridge, I was finished running.

Was I being stupid? Probably. Hardly the first time.

I used my foot to kick the flaps on the cardboard box closed, then shoved it into the corner behind my table where it was out of sight.

The knock came a moment later at the front door. Three sharp raps.

"You're welcome to leave through the back if you want," I told the others.

Zach and Earl exchanged a glance, but Milo shrugged. "I'm good. I can serve as a witness to whatever goes down."

"Same," Zach grunted. "Neither of us touched that package. If we need to, we can explain how we found it."

I felt a rush of gratitude as I went to the door. But the nerves quickly followed.

I did not have a good track record with the authorities, and these local cops had to know it.

If they'd looked up the exact details of my incarceration at the US Disciplinary Barracks? And the reason I'd served my full sentence instead of getting early release? That certainly wouldn't help.

So I kept my expression neutral and non-confrontational as I opened the door.

"Afternoon," I said.

Two officers stood on my porch. The first was a woman in her fifties, gray hair pulled back, her expression professional. The second was younger, maybe mid-twenties, and he kept his hand near his gun holster, his eyes trained on me like I might attack at any second.

Not the best start. Sweat beaded at the small of my back despite the winter air.

"Grayden O'Neal?" the woman asked.

"That's me."

"I'm Chief Susan Nichols, Silver Ridge PD. And this is Officer Chad Bronski." The other guy squinted at me as Nichols continued to speak in a monotone. "Just following up on a tip. Mind if we step inside?"

"A tip." I leaned against the doorframe, trying to keep my posture relaxed though every hair on my body was standing on end. "What kind of tip? From who?"

"It was anonymous."

Of course it was.

Footsteps pounded up the walkway. Piper appeared, out of breath, her skin flushed and hair falling out of its knot. "What's going on?" she demanded, glancing between the cops and me. "Chief, what're you doing here?"

Protectiveness surged through my veins, mixed with elation at just seeing Piper's beautiful face. The whiplash was enough to make my head spin. Wanting to pull her close as much as I wished I could send her away.

I didn't want her here for this.

But Chief Nichols had already turned to her. "Piper. I tried to call you, as a courtesy. Since you're the property owner. Left a voicemail."

"Well, I didn't get it. I've been busy all day. What the heck is this?"

"Let me handle it," I said softly.

Piper sent a quick glare my way. Bossy Piper was out in full force. But I was ready to stand firm, too. She didn't need to be defending me.

Officer Bronski, the younger guy, puffed up his chest. "We got a tip. Drug activity going on at this property. Are you aware of your tenant's criminal record, Ms. Carmichael?"

Piper aimed that withering glare at him next. "How is that your business?"

"Your tip is wrong." I kept myself still, avoiding any sudden movements. Because Bronski hadn't taken his hand from the butt of his gun.

"How about we sort all this out right now?" the police chief said. "Mr. O'Neal, if you have nothing to hide, then there's no problem. Let us take a look around."

"No." My voice was exactly the same volume, the same tone as hers. But the chief braced like I'd shouted the word.

Nichols tried Piper next. "Do we have your consent to search the property as the owner?"

"No, I do not consent. You clearly don't have a warrant or any kind of evidence to create actual probable cause. My brother was the chief of police before you, in case you forgot."

"I didn't forget," the chief deadpanned.

"You should be investigating whoever made that anonymous tip. Because they're just trying to make trouble for Grayden based on his past. It's bullshit, and I bet you know it."

The chief glanced down, seeming to absorb these words. But Officer Bronski was turning red in the face. "If Teller Landry was still chief of police, he would've been over here a lot sooner. Letting Mr. O'Neal know what is and isn't acceptable in this town." Bronski turned his sneer on me.

Wonderful. So this guy was yet another member of my fan club.

Chief Nichols's eyes flashed in a brief show of emotion, and it was aimed at her employee. "Alright. Enough. Piper, Grayden, if either of you has any more information, then give me a call."

She pulled a business card from a pocket. I accepted it without comment.

Chief Nichols and Officer Bronski walked back to their vehicle. We watched them pull away, neither of us moving until the SUV disappeared around the corner.

Then I finally let out the breath I'd been holding.

Piper pressed her hands to her face, taking a shaky inhale. "I think it was Danny. He must've called in the tip."

"I think so too. But you should've let me handle it. It's not your job to defend me."

"Are you *kidding*? This is all because you defended *me*, and now Danny's here in Silver Ridge again today and he's—"

"Whoa, slow down." I finally gave in to the urge to touch her, holding her by the shoulders. "You saw Danny again?"

"He showed up at Ollie's school this afternoon. Ollie's going to have dinner with him, and it's probably fine, but I do *not* believe this is a coincidence."

Yeah, neither did I. "We can go get Ollie right now if you want."

"No, that's probably what Danny is hoping will happen. For me to freak out and make a scene in front of Ollie like *I'm* the problem. I just hate it. I'm sorry you got dragged into it. *Again*. And I'm sorry for defending you because apparently that was wrong too."

"Piper—"

Milo cleared his throat, reminding us we had an audience.

She looked past my shoulder to see into the house. "Someone else is here?"

"Some friends. Come on. Come inside."

"You sure you want me to?" she snarked. "I'm not interfering? Your annoying landlady, showing up when she's not welcome?"

"You're always welcome." I put my arm around her shoulder and ushered her through the door.

I still had dangerous contraband to deal with. But if I told Piper to leave now and insisted on handling all of this myself, it was entirely likely she'd never forgive me.

I was just trying to figure this out one moment at a time.

"Piper, this is Milo, Zach, and Earl. They work at the motorcycle shop."

She nodded at them distractedly. "Sure, I know Milo and Zach. Nice to meet you, Earl. You were all here when the police showed up?"

Earl stroked his bushy beard and lifted his equally bushy eyebrows at me, probably unsure of how much I wanted to say in front of Piper.

The answer: everything. Now that she was here, I couldn't do this halfway.

"It was more than just an anonymous tip." I grabbed the box from the corner and dragged it over. Pulled back the flap, showing her the plastic-wrapped brick inside.

Piper stared at it, her face going pale. "Oh my God," she whispered.

"Zach and I found it in the bedroom when I was looking at

the quilting fabric," Earl said. "Just sitting there inside the box, right on top. Wasn't even hidden."

Milo crossed his arms over his leather jacket. "Piper, you really think your ex planted this?"

"Danny?" she said hoarsely, her eyes fixed on the package. "Yeah. I think so."

Yet she sounded far less confident than she had moments ago with Chief Nichols.

"Danny doesn't like Grayden," she added.

"Yeah, no shit," Milo muttered. "Good luck, man." He clapped me on the shoulder. "You better get rid of that stuff before anything else happens."

I nodded. "Planning on it."

Once they were gone, I shut and locked the door. That had been far more excitement than I was anticipating for today.

What a damn mess.

When I turned around, Piper was pacing back and forth across the front room. She still had her coat on, her arms crossed over it like she was cold, though I had the heat on.

Every time she came here, something bad seemed to happen.

"There's just something I don't understand," she said.

"And that is?"

"Where would Danny even get the money for a bunch of drugs? He can get access to prescription painkillers and anesthesia as a dentist, sure, but not whatever *that* is." She jabbed a finger at the box, which lay where we'd left it, flaps hanging open to reveal its nasty contents. "He's capable of plenty, but this just doesn't feel like Danny."

The message made its way through my thick skull. Fuck.

"You don't believe me."

Piper stopped pacing, head swiveling toward me in shock. "I didn't say that."

"No. But it's okay." I felt my shoulders drop, resignation settling over me with a familiar weight. I'd been through this so many times before. The questions, the suspicion. Even with people I'd thought I was close to.

Didn't make it hurt any less.

This was like what happened at my previous gig in Seattle. My colleague had been dealing, and the shop owner believed I was in on it too. I'd been honest with Piper about that, but maybe that story planted a thread of doubt in her mind about me.

And now that thread was twisting into a whole pattern, probably as elaborate as one of Earl's quilts.

Grayden O'Neal, the lying criminal.

"I understand if you doubt me," I said calmly. "But I have never seen that package before in my life. I would never bring something illegal into this house or anywhere near you. Never."

Piper exhaled and shook her head, her expression crumpling. "No, I know you wouldn't do that. And even if you did..."

"I didn't."

"I *know*. But if it was yours, why would you invite your new friends inside to have a look? Unless they were here for that, or..."

I gripped the bridge of my nose. "Maybe a guy like Officer Bronski believes leather jackets, bushy beards, and tattoos equal drug dealers, but it's not actually true."

"Don't put words in my mouth."

Holding up my hands in surrender, I took a few steps away. Not because I was mad at her. I wasn't. I would never, ever, take out my anger on Piper. I'd promised her she was safe with me, and she was.

I was just tired. So fucking tired.

Piper pressed her fingers to her temples. "If Danny really did this, then I don't want him anywhere near Ollie. But it's another thing to prove it. If that's even possible."

It could be possible. If the police investigated who'd made the call. But they'd have to *want* to investigate it. Besides, the tipster had probably made an effort to stay anonymous. Using a burner phone or a VPN or something.

For similar reasons, I knew it would be pointless to turn over the drugs to the police as evidence and report the latest break-in here.

What do you mean they didn't find the real culprit? Didn't they call their forensics experts to take DNA swabs and examine the broken lock with a giant magnifying glass?

Yeah, right.

I stuck my hands in my pockets. "Honestly, I'd much rather have Danny bothering me than him taking it out on you or your kid."

"But you don't deserve this. You never would've met Danny if not for me."

True. But either way, it wasn't her fault. "I can flush the stuff to get rid of it."

Piper looked horrified. "And poison a bunch of innocent fish with fentanyl or whatever that is? *No.*" She went over to squint at the offending package again. "There's an anonymous drop box for contraband at Silver Ridge PD headquarters. I can get rid of the drugs there."

"I don't want you getting mixed up in this any more than—"

"I'm already mixed up in it."

Well, she was right about that.

I'd thought my presence in Piper's life wouldn't cause her any harm. Maybe I'd been wrong, and that was bad enough.

But that truth would've been far easier to bear if I wasn't in so deep already where Piper was concerned. If I didn't crave having her in my arms so damn badly.

TWENTY-THREE

Piper

THE SILVER RIDGE PD contraband drop box was behind the station. I'd driven by it a thousand times at least.

And never had I imagined I'd be dropping off something here myself.

If Teller could see me now... Ugh, that wouldn't be pleasant.

The sun was sinking as I pulled a baseball cap low over my eyes and got out of my car. Then grabbed a paper bag from my trunk. There were always cars in the station parking lot, but it wasn't a shift change. Nobody was out and about.

There were still cameras, and at least one would be trained on the drop box. But according to official department policy, contraband could be left here anonymously, no questions asked.

And if Chief Nichols recognized me in the security footage and decided to ask questions, well, my memory would conveniently come up blank.

It was also possible Nichols would report all of today's events to my brother. The two of them were still pretty close. But I would have to worry about that later.

Somehow, Danny was responsible. This was indirectly my fault. So I was going to fix it.

Moving at a steady walk, I headed straight for the drop box.

Once I reached it, I lifted the lid and tossed the bag inside. The lid slipped from my fingers and clattered as it fell, making me jump.

Gah, I was wound up tight. My pulse wouldn't slow down, and my breaths were shallow enough to leave me light-headed. Pivoting on my sneaker, I tried not to run as I made my way back to my car.

A relieved groan left my throat as I collapsed into the driver's seat, shutting the door behind me. Thank goodness that was over.

I drove off. After taking a couple of turns, I pulled behind Grayden's Dodge, which he'd parked several blocks away from the police station.

When I slid into the passenger seat of his truck, the cabin was toasty warm. His fingers were drumming a nervous rhythm on the dashboard.

"All set?" he asked.

"Yeah. It's done."

"Did anyone see you?"

"No? I don't think so. Except the cameras."

He groaned. "Cameras?"

"I knew about the cameras. It's not a big deal."

I explained about the department policy and my backup plan to deny, deny.

Grayden rubbed his eyes. "This is so fucked, Piper. All of it. Drugs showing up in my place, and then *you* having to get rid of them for me. If Ashford and Teller knew..."

"They're not going to know."

"Unless Teller's friends in the department decide to inform him. For all I know, Officer Bronski is Teller's new bestie and already texted him the gory details."

I scoffed, though just minutes ago I'd been worried about Teller getting an earful from Chief Nichols.

Guess what your little sister has been up to?

"Hardly," I said. "Bronski is a newer hire. The department's had a lot of turnover. Teller barely knows him. But that's beside the point. If any of our family hears about this, we'll tell them the truth. That you didn't do anything."

"Why would they believe that? From the outside, it looks like I'm backsliding into illegal shit and taking you with me."

Just tell them the whole truth, all the way from the beginning, I wanted to shout. Because there was still so much Grayden hadn't shared with his siblings. There was plenty he hadn't even shared with me.

But I understood what he was feeling. From Grayden's perspective, the truth wasn't always enough to fix everything. And that really sucked.

"Then we'll just be Bonnie and Clyde," I said. "Partners in crime."

He snorted. "I shouldn't be laughing. This is a mess."

"But it's *our* mess. Let's get some dinner. Turns out a life of crime makes a girl hungry."

He side-eyed me. "It might be better if you're not seen with me."

"So dramatic. Come on, let's go to Main Street. I'll get my car later. I've had a completely shitty day, and I want comfort food before it's time to pick up Ollie. I think you owe me. I risked arrest for you."

Shaking his head, Grayden put his truck in gear. "Alright, Bonnie. Comfort food, it is."

As Grayden drove us toward Main Street, I checked my phone, just in case Ollie had texted again. All I'd heard so far was, *Getting burgers and shakes!*

Didn't take much to make a nine-year-old happy. I was glad Ollie was having fun with his dad, though I was more on edge than ever.

"Has Ollie written?" Grayden asked.

"Yeah. He's fine." After confirming the GPS location of Ollie's phone—a diner on Main—I tucked my phone away. "I'm meeting Danny at the park for the hand-off at seven."

"Then we have a couple hours. Where would you like to eat?"

I considered the usual options, but only one place had the high level of comfort I craved right now.

"Let's go to Silver Linings."

"Thought it was already closed for the day."

"Exactly."

There was plenty of street parking available when we reached my coffee shop. My employees had closed up an hour ago, so I unlocked the back door, switching on more lights as I went inside and made a beeline for the kitchen.

The heat was turned down low, but the chill would be gone in no time once we had the fireplace going. I hung my coat on a wall hook.

Grayden followed more slowly, hesitating on the big winter mat designed to catch the worst of my employees' muddy snow boots.

"Flip the lock?" I said over my shoulder.

"Got it."

I was already heading for the fridge. "I don't think you've tried my panini yet. What do you like? Ham? Turkey? Goat cheese?"

When I glanced back, he'd taken off his black canvas jacket. He pushed up his long sleeves, revealing his tattoos.

"I'm not picky. I trust you."

A brief thrill lit up my chest. I remembered saying the same thing to him weeks ago when he first rented my mom's house.

But a twinge of guilt followed. Because today, for one split second, I *hadn't* trusted him. I'd seen that block of white powder wrapped in plastic, and I'd wondered if he could be lying to me.

"I'll make you my specialty then." I piled sandwich fixings on the stainless steel work table.

"Can I help?"

"Actually, if you get a fire going in the fireplace, that would be amazing. Instructions are right in that drawer." I pointed. "Everything else is on the hearth. It's easy, I promise. If Rina can handle it, anyone can."

"I'll be careful."

He'd said that all husky and soft, sending tingles racing over my skin.

I believed Grayden. He wouldn't be involved with anything illegal. I refused to be one of the people who made assumptions about him simply because of his prison record.

We'd been through all this before. And yet, he kept on proving himself.

The split-second of distrust I'd felt was less to do with Grayden and everything to do with Danny. My ex had taught me how risky it was to give my trust away to the wrong man. To give my *heart* away.

But I wasn't giving my heart to Grayden. No matter how much I felt drawn to him. So...I had nothing to worry about anyway.

After stuffing our house-made sourdough with all the goodies, I placed each sandwich on the panini press. "Drink?" I asked. "Espresso?"

Grayden was kneeling by the fireplace in the dining room, all his intense focus on his task. "Give me something different tonight. Whatever you're having."

After thinking a moment, I decided on flat whites. Something different, but not too different, and not too sweet.

Grayden approached the counter just as I was setting out the drinks. He brushed off his hands. "Smells great already. Fire's going."

"Thanks. Sandwiches are almost up. I'll pour some glasses of water too."

Once the cheese was good and melty, I piled everything onto a tray and carried it to the loveseat near the fire. Flames licked at the split logs beyond the grate, sending out light and warmth.

Ugh, I'd needed this.

The loveseat was the coziest spot in the entire coffee shop. Out of sight of the front windows and the door.

The tray fit perfectly on a little side table made from a tree ring. I took off my shoes and curled up on one side of the small couch, pulling my plate onto my lap.

"So this is what you meant by comfort food?" Grayden asked. "No shoes required?"

"Hush and sit down. Just wait until you taste this sandwich. I'll have you know it won a blue ribbon at the last Hart County Fair."

"Well, with a recommendation like that..."

Grayden sat heavily on the cushion beside me, shifting as he settled in. His thigh brushed the tips of my socked feet. I tucked my toes under his leg, and a tiny smile graced his lips as he grabbed his plate.

Then he took a big bite of the melty, cheesy panini, the crusty bread crunching in his teeth. And he groaned. "Damn, blue ribbon all the way. Fucking hell, Piper. How did I not know about this heavenly sandwich?"

"You could've ordered one before. It's right there on the menu. Ask and you shall receive."

The sideways look he gave me made those tingles start up again.

I took another bite of my panini, slowly chewing. The coffee shop had all its familiar scents, like ground coffee and hints of butter and cinnamon mingling with wood smoke.

Most of the main lights were off, which made the place feel smaller and more intimate than during the day. And outside, the sun was setting, which added to the pink and orange tint of the light coming from the fire.

Somehow, all of that just made Grayden stand out more. His strong silhouette, the cut of his profile. The dusky lines of the black rose tattoos on his neck. He looked like the coziest thing of all, and also by far the most exciting.

My heart sped up, forgetting a beat or two along the way.

When he'd almost finished his meal, Grayden asked, "Are you going to say something to Danny about the police showing up to my place? Might be better if you don't."

I set my plate on the tree-ring table. "I won't in front of Ollie. But I have to. I have to do *something*. If Danny has anything to do with drugs, I can't let him take Ollie for days at a time. Earlier today, he wanted to take Ollie for the entire weekend. No advance notice."

"But you're not letting him?"

"No way. Ollie already has a trip to Denver planned with Callum for the three-day weekend. But in the future..." I picked up my coffee, though I didn't feel like drinking it anymore. My stomach was too jumpy. "Maybe I should call my lawyer. See what we can do."

But those billable hours were expensive, and Grayden's rent payments had just barely put my finances above water.

"I'm making things harder for you," Grayden said gruffly.

"*What*?" My toes wiggled under his thigh. "What would have happened if you hadn't shown up the day Danny broke in and put his hand on my throat?"

"Piper, I would step in and defend you or Ollie, anytime, anyplace. But Danny can use my history against you. What'll happen when you speak to your lawyer and you tell her about how Danny has a grudge against your tenant? And how your tenant has a record. If you have to go in front of a judge, how will it look for you to have *me* as a friend?"

I hated what Grayden was saying. Yet it did make a twisted sort of sense.

How was it possible that Danny seemed so smooth on the surface, given his clean-cut looks and his Lexus and his professional career, when he had a rotten core underneath?

While Grayden, the truly good man, had a stain that would follow him for the rest of his life.

TWENTY-FOUR

Grayden

PIPER LOOKED SO DOWNCAST. She'd come here for some comfort, and I'd just given her a cold splash of reality.

I took a gulp of the coffee drink Piper had made me.

"Not trying to make you feel bad," I said. "It's just something to think about."

"I hate the world sometimes. So many things aren't fair."

"Truer words."

But Piper was essentially agreeing with me. Her situation would be harder with me around.

I never should've kissed her the other day. She was the wiser one to turn me down.

Of course I would never regret defending her, but I could've backed down a little with Danny when I confronted him that day. Instead, I'd escalated the tension. Now he hated me, and I worried how far he'd go as a result.

If Piper or Ollie got hurt because of me, directly or indirectly, how could I ever forgive myself?

These were some dark fucking thoughts. Piper deserved some time to relax and smile, and I realized I might have just the thing.

I placed my empty plate on the tray. "Hey, I almost forgot. I found something yesterday in the house. It was behind an old dresser." Tugging out my wallet, I extracted a folded piece of paper.

Piper took it from me, and her whole face changed as she smoothed out the creases.

"Oh my gosh. I haven't seen this in ages."

"It was folded up like that when I found it," I added.

She touched the photo gently, like she was afraid it might disappear. "No, I'm the one who folded it. Used to keep this in my purse to remind me of better days, I guess."

Her lips parted slightly as she stared down at the image. It was her and Grace, maybe around eighteen or nineteen years old, with their arms around each other as they laughed. Caught in a moment of pure joy.

"I took this selfie of us during freshman year of college." Her thumb traced over the image. "Went to the drugstore the next day to have the photo printed out, and I pinned it to the bulletin board in our dorm room."

My upper body shifted to face Piper, which wasn't easy given the tight space on this loveseat. My arm draped over the backrest. "You and Grace were roommates in college?"

"You didn't know that?"

I shrugged, though the empty spaces in my chest echoed with the reminder of what I'd missed. There was far too much I didn't know about my siblings' lives.

By the time Piper and Grace were nineteen, I'd been years into my prison sentence. Totally cut off from them, in part by *my* choice. Furious at the world for everything that had been taken from me.

"There's been a lot to catch up on," I simply said. Most days since I'd returned to Silver Ridge, I tried not to think about all those missing years. Because when I did...

Fuck, it was a lot to even process.

"Grace and I had *way* too much fun." Piper looked up at me, her eyes glossy in the firelight. "There we were, two small-town girls in Fort Collins. Which isn't that big of a town anyway, but to us, it was a whole new world. She had this amazing scholarship covering all her tuition and expenses and felt like she had to study nonstop. So I had to drag her to all the frat parties. She was *such* a good girl."

"As any little sister should be," I grunted. "I don't want to hear otherwise."

Piper laughed. "I was more the kind to dance on the tables. Made sure Gracie didn't grow roots in the library with her nose in an accounting book."

"You were the wild one, huh? I buy that."

"I could get wild. On occasion." Her chin angled as she looked at me through her lashes, downright sultry.

Hell. If I wasn't in full view of her, I would've adjusted my cock in my jeans. I shifted around, trying to do it subtly.

She blinked, and the flirtation disappeared from her green eyes. "Until I met Danny my junior year. He was older, a dental student down in the Denver area. He was on campus visiting a former frat buddy. He seemed so polished."

I didn't like hearing about Piper with him, even if it had been over a decade ago. When I'd still been behind bars. But if she needed to talk about it, I'd listen.

"He fooled you. Can't blame yourself for that."

"In my defense, I didn't have the chance to know him all that well before I got pregnant. Ollie was the best accident to ever happen to me. But I've always had this daydream of going back to school to finish my English Lit degree."

"You could do it online. Same way I got my Bachelor of Fine Arts."

She grinned. "You have a degree? When did that happen?"

"I finished it when I was in Seattle. But when I started on the credits, it was whenever I had privileges in the prison library, mostly."

Piper's expression faltered. "Exactly how long were you... Sorry, never mind."

I lifted my hand to trace her jaw with my thumb. "It's okay.

I've told you before, I don't mind talking about it. How long was I in prison? That's what you were going to ask?"

She nodded.

"Ten years. My full sentence."

Her body went totally still. As in, I could actually see the moment her exhale cut short.

"Ten years?" she said when she started breathing again. "I know it's been fifteen since it all happened, but I didn't think about it exactly. How much of it you were behind bars."

"Time is weird like that. Those ten years felt like ten lifetimes when I was going through it, but looking back, it's like this strange blip in my life story. Parallel universe or something."

"Don't people usually get out early, though? For good behavior or however that works?"

My hand dragged over my beard. "Good behavior, sure. Problem was, my behavior didn't meet the US Army's definition of *good*. I had a lot of anger in me, Piper. Not just after I got to prison."

"Because of losing your mom? And your dad leaving?"

I gave her a soft smirk. "I'm not that hard to figure out, am I? I was an angry teenager, and an angry man when I joined the Army, hoping it would sort me out. Sometimes, I still am. To a lesser degree. You've seen it."

"But you've never seemed that way to me. Not now, not then."

I hadn't wanted to get into this. But Piper wanted to talk about it, so I had to give her a truthful answer. "I hid it around you and Grace. Even Teller and my brothers, to some extent."

When I'd been a soldier, being angry had sometimes been an asset. Lit a fire under my ass to be tougher, stronger, get shit done.

Unfortunately, it also interfered with my discipline and ability to follow orders. Superior officers tended to frown on that.

But I had to stay on topic. Otherwise we'd be here all night with the saga I could tell.

"After I got to Leavenworth, after all the shit that put me

there, I didn't see any point in trying to keep that anger at bay. My fellow assholes among the inmates got the brunt of it, and I ended up in the hole a few times. But then there was the time I punched an Army Corrections Specialist. A guard."

"Oh, Grayden." She winced. "Really?"

I had to laugh at her reaction.

"I promise he was the king of the assholes, and he kept getting away with it. Made a younger inmate his personal punching bag. Eventually, I couldn't stand for it anymore. I'm lucky I didn't get my sentence extended, but there was enough evidence the guard had been abusing his position."

But that was me. Reacting impulsively to try to protect someone, try to make this screwed-up world a little bit right. Often it didn't go well.

Maybe that was a lesson I didn't want to learn.

Piper's hand rested on my thigh, filling my blood with endorphins and helping push away the bad memories.

"I'm sorry that happened," she said.

"It was a wake-up call, actually. After I realized I wouldn't get out of there until my ten years were up, I got more serious about making something of myself. That's when I signed up for the correspondence courses and started getting college credits. Read a ton of books and really focused on my art. Did what I was supposed to. Just took it one day at a time."

"But ten years. I'm still trying to make sense of it. How you got through that."

"I didn't care for the alternatives, so I didn't have much choice."

When I glanced over at her, Piper's eyes were shining again, and then a tear slipped free.

Fuck me, I was making her sad.

Bringing the pad of my thumb to her cheek, I smudged the tear away. "I told you before, when you hear my whole history, I don't come out of it sounding like a hero. Just a guy who messed up every good thing in his life and took years to figure out how to start over again. Still working on that."

I sat back, pushing out a laugh that sounded more like a sigh.

"And now I'm a guy who hijacked the entire conversation. We were talking about you and Grace in college."

"Grayden." Piper's frown was still there, and still deathly serious. "The more I get to know the man you are, the more you're a hero to *me*."

Then she leaned over, put her palm on my chest, and kissed me.

I tilted my head, and my hands found the sides of her waist. Piper's lips were hesitant against mine at first. I let her control the kiss.

Then she shifted so our bodies were more aligned, her thigh draping over mine. My hands reached the edge of her sweater and dipped beneath. My fingers spread wide over the warm, smooth skin of her back above the waistband of her jeans.

Really, if I was the hero Piper thought, I would stop this right now, no matter how much I craved her. I was becoming a liability for her. This town had been looking down on me since the moment I returned, thinking I wasn't good enough for their golden girl.

But I didn't stop her.

Piper sighed against my mouth, her tongue licking against my lips. Which was all the invitation I needed.

My lips parted and drew her tongue inside, sucking gently on it. I fed her mine.

And I was just gone. Lost in her.

We tasted each other, and between the heat of the fire and the heat of want igniting my veins, I already felt like I might combust.

Another tug of my hands against her hips brought her closer. Piper straddled my thigh, and her crotch rocked against me with the movement.

Her eyes went wide as her head tipped back and a moan snuck from her lips.

Oh. She'd liked that, huh?

My conscience tried one last time to speak up. Just a week ago, I'd told her one or two secret hookups wouldn't be enough for me.

But if this was all I could ever have of her?

I rocked Piper forward again by the hips, nudging my thigh upward a little. She rewarded me with a gasp.

"Does that feel good, wild girl?" I murmured. "My thigh between your legs?"

Her eyelashes fluttered. Her lips were pink, swollen from kisses. "Amazing," she breathed. "But..."

"Do you want to stop?"

"*No*. Please, Grayden. Don't stop."

She needed this. Piper's day had sucked, mostly because of her ex, but I'd had my part in it. Least I could do was give her this.

Make her feel sexy and wild again. Beautiful and wanted.

Like Piper had said the first time I kissed her, no one had to know. Nobody could see. We were out of sight of the windows, though of course in full view of the rest of the empty coffee shop.

If I could have my way completely, I wouldn't just have Piper in secret. I'd hold her hand down the street and defy anyone who said I couldn't be enough for her.

But this moment, making her feel amazing, was better than nothing. I was desperate for this.

And on a day like today, I could be more than selfish enough to enjoy it.

Dipping my head to reach her neck, I dropped kisses to the skin there. Her pulse throbbed under my tongue. Her vanilla-and-flowers scent filled my lungs.

"Make yourself feel good," I whispered in her ear. "Use me."

"*Grayden*," she gasped, and my name had never sounded so filthy.

Piper held onto my shoulders and rode my thigh. Keeping my firm grasp on her hip with one hand, I pressed the heel of my other to the erection stretching along the seam of my jeans.

My cock was thick and swollen, the vein on the underside pulsing.

Then she grabbed my face, pulling me into another dirty kiss. Tongues sliding and teeth nipping.

She wasn't holding back, and fuck, did I love that.

It was just a preview of how uninhibited Piper might be in bed. How she could drive me crazy in all the best ways, matching my need for her with a voracious appetite all her own.

If only I would have the chance to see that.

"I can't believe we're doing this here," she said.

Neither could I. But unless she tapped the brakes, there was no way I could stop. Not now.

Piper reached for her waistband and popped the button on her jeans. "I need more. Please."

I wasn't sure at first what she wanted. If she intended for me to strip her jeans off and bend her over this loveseat, which I was tempted to do.

I imagined sinking my cock inside her, the haze of desire between us pushing away any doubt or hesitation. Seeing her come apart while I felt her shuddering with pleasure around my shaft.

"Your fingers." She took my hand and brought it to the juncture between her legs, though she hadn't stopped rubbing against my thigh.

Mmm. That worked too. "Whatever you want, wild girl."

My cock twitched with jealousy as I unzipped her fly and slid my fingers into her panties. My fingertips met hot, wet heaven.

I groaned, my eyes rolling back involuntarily.

"You're soaking for me."

I could only fit the tips of two of my fingers into that slick space inside her panties. Piper grabbed my wrist to angle my hand toward her clit, which drove my arousal even higher.

Loved how she knew what she wanted and made sure I gave it to her.

Her hips bucked wildly, sliding her clit over my fingers. Her eyes were closed, golden hair tumbling over her shoulders after falling out of its tie.

Firelight danced over her pale skin and her pink lips. Gorgeous.

And *mine*. For these few minutes, even if this was all I ever got, Piper was mine.

Her rhythm turned staccato. As she began to shudder and moan, I slid one finger deep inside her, feeling her squeeze around me.

My cock throbbed with envy.

When she stopped shaking, Piper slumped against me. "Oh my..."

I rubbed her lower back and kissed her temple. "Feel better? Less stressed?"

"Mmhmm." She lifted her head, green eyes glazed, but with easy contentment instead of fear or confusion. "That was hot. And kind of crazy. I wasn't expecting it."

"Neither was I."

"But I liked it. What happened to just friends?"

"Maybe we can have the occasional day pass for benefits," I said.

"Yeah? I'm up for that."

I pulled her into another kiss. Piper's hand trailed lazily down my body until she found my erection. Her fingers traced the outline of my shaft until she reached the head and circled it through my jeans.

I shifted beneath her, and my hips lifted. "Fuck," I breathed. Especially as she used her thumb to rub over the tip.

Then her nose scrunched cutely.

"What is that? Are you... Is that a piercing?"

TWENTY-FIVE

Piper

I RUBBED my thumb over the head of Grayden's cock again.

Oh, he had that bad-boy thing going, alright. Damn. More than I'd even known.

Through the layer of denim, I could feel something like metal. Judging from the deep groans that rumbled from Grayden's chest, it felt really good when I touched him there.

His eyelids were heavy over dark-brown irises. The gold flecks caught the light from the fire, practically glowing.

I really couldn't believe we'd done that. Especially after Grayden had stopped us last week. But it had been spontaneous and wicked and exactly what I'd needed.

After the day we'd had today, we both deserved some stress relief.

I'd felt shameless when I was riding him. Yet also more like *me* than I'd experienced in such a long time.

Not Mom or a business owner or an aggrieved ex-wife. Just a sexual being, enjoying the pleasure a man gave me and eager to give him pleasure in return.

And not just any man. Grayden.

Somehow our shared history had made it even better. The

way we always opened up to each other so naturally, like being close to him was the easiest thing in the world.

I wished it could always be this easy.

I was still rubbing his cock through his jeans. He put his hand over mine, trapping my palm against the heat of his erection.

"Want me to show you?" he asked.

Then the shrill ringtone of my cell shattered the moment. Just like that, the bubble around us evaporated, and the real world rushed in.

"Shit, that's the alarm I set for a quarter to seven." I climbed off Grayden's lap, zipping and buttoning my jeans. "I need to get Ollie. I'm sorry, I thought we had more time."

"S'okay." He picked up the tray from the table. "I'll help you clean up before you go."

I cringed. "But I'm leaving you, you know, unsatisfied." I nodded at the thick ridge in his pants, though it was rapidly shrinking.

He smirked. "I'm extremely satisfied. Come on, let's clean up after ourselves. Otherwise your employees might show up in the morning and think someone broke in."

Right. No need for me to explain why I'd left two dirty plates, two glasses, and the loveseat by the fireplace twisted at an angle.

I'd gotten pretty enthusiastic.

Clean-up didn't take long. Within a few minutes, Grayden had helped me put everything away and erase the evidence of our being here tonight. I made sure the fire was out, everything reset.

Last, I pinned the photo of me and Grace to the wall in my office.

As I shrugged on my coat and grabbed my purse, I turned to find Grayden zipping up his jacket.

My heart did a strange shimmy just from the sight of him.

His hair was even messier than usual, and the tension lines that typically creased the sides of his mouth were missing. Even though he hadn't gotten an orgasm. I owed him one.

I wouldn't mind giving him *lots* more orgasms than just one.

The occasional day pass for benefits. Would Grayden really be okay with that?

The minutes were counting down, but I couldn't help stepping closer and kissing him again. Grayden's large hands went to my arms, holding me gently as our lips met.

But it didn't feel the same as before. That perfect, easy connection. We were both more relaxed than when we'd arrived at Silver Linings, but the hesitation in Grayden's kiss said it all.

No matter what, things would never be simple or easy between us.

I pulled back. The question was there on the tip of my tongue. *Come with me to get Ollie?*

But I already knew he'd say no. It was the smart move. Grayden showing up with me would be a provocation to Danny.

I would never be a doormat where my ex was concerned, but why start another fight at the end of the day? Especially in front of our son.

"Want me to drive you to get your car?" Grayden asked. I'd left it parked closer to the police station.

"I'll get it in the morning. The park is super close, and Ollie and I like walking. Benefit of living right off Main Street in the center of downtown."

He smoothed my hair down, giving me one more kiss, but to my temple this time.

"Let me know when you're home?" he asked.

"Sure. I will."

I locked up on my way out, leaving no trace of our being here. It was possible someone had seen us arriving or leaving through the back alley behind the building. But after the day I'd had, it was hard to care.

On the street, Grayden headed toward his truck, while I jogged off toward the park.

I tried not to look back. *Tried*.

When I did, Grayden had turned around on the sidewalk, watching me go.

It was a short walk to the park. Traces of snow crunched under my boots as I marched between pine trees to reach the picnic area. A common meeting place for Danny and me when he used to live in Silver Ridge.

Of course, the jerk was exactly five minutes late. Not enough for me to complain, but a clear *screw you*.

Just trying to prove who was in control here. Danny did love his mind games.

"Mom!" Ollie shouted, waving.

Taking a deep breath to settle my nerves, I smiled. Ollie was the reason I put up with Danny.

Ollie was my reason for *everything*.

I would do whatever I had to, even somehow dealing with my ex, for my son's sake.

"Look, Dad bought me a model car kit at the gift shop!" Ollie pulled a cardboard box from a shopping bag.

"Amazing, Ollie-bear. That'll be a lot of fun."

Danny hung back a few feet. "We had a great time, didn't we, champ?"

Ollie nodded, admiring his model kit.

"Did you say thanks?" I asked.

"Yeah, thanks Dad!"

Instead of responding to our son, Danny eyed me. "How was the rest of your afternoon, Piper? Anything exciting?"

Anxiety rose in my throat.

Was that his usual asshole smirk, or did Danny know exactly what had happened earlier? The police showing up at Grayden's place. The planted drugs.

Guess what, Danny? My afternoon was even more exciting than you could imagine. Had a cozy meal by the fireplace and then rode Grayden's thigh all the way to paradise.

"I stayed busy," I said.

Danny's smirk got sharper. More vicious.

"How much longer are you staying in Silver Ridge?" I asked.

"Hoping I take off? What happened to begging me to take a more active role in Ollie's life?"

I shrugged, keeping my expression neutral. "I just need to know what to expect. That's all."

Our son was looking at the model kit, but I felt his attention on us. Those small ears were perked all the way up.

"I'm still deciding," Danny said. "As I told Ollie over dinner, I'm thinking hard about moving back to Silver Ridge for good."

The frozen grass was solid under my feet. Yet it felt like a pit had just opened beneath me.

"Oh? What about your dental practice? I thought you were just getting some momentum in the new location."

"There are always new opportunities. Nothing's ever permanent, Piper. You must've learned that by now."

After Danny said goodnight, Ollie and I walked toward home. Ollie's pace was slower than usual, and the plastic bag from the gift shop dangled listlessly from his hand.

I was still trying to get myself to relax again. So much for my brief stress relief with Grayden.

"You had fun?" I asked.

"Yep. My burger was good. I got the one with two patties."

My lips curved into a smile. "How do you feel about your dad maybe moving back to Silver Ridge?"

Ollie was quiet for a few steps. "I dunno. He might not mean it."

"In the past, he hasn't been good at keeping his promises. But I know you'd like to see him more."

I hoped the darkness hid the grimace I was making. I was a hypocrite. How many times had I asked Danny to be around more for Ollie? And now he might do just that, and it felt like a threat.

Things had changed, obviously. At best, Danny had put his hands on me. Frightened me. At worst, he'd tried to frame Grayden to send him back to prison.

But there was no way I could tell my kid any of that.

Our footsteps thudded quietly as we turned onto our street. "When we were having dinner," Ollie said, "Dad asked about Grayden."

"He did?"

"Dad doesn't like him. I think he wanted me to agree with him."

I glanced at Ollie's profile. Waiting for what he'd say next, because I didn't want to pressure him. Whatever my feelings about Grayden, Ollie had a right to his own.

With a sigh, Ollie finally said, "But I think Grayden's okay. You like him, right?"

"I do."

A swirl of emotions made me lightheaded. I liked Grayden so much. More than I probably should. Enough to confuse the heck out of me.

I didn't just like Grayden. I admired him. Plenty of people wouldn't have survived what he'd been through, yet he still approached the world with so much openness. Grayden had my friendship, regardless of what anyone thought.

And that included Silver Ridge PD and all the lawyers and judges in the world.

"At least Grayden's back in Silver Ridge to fix stuff with his family," Ollie said. "Even though Ashford won't let Maisie know him yet, Grayden's still here. He wants to try. When they give him a chance, he'll be ready."

"I bet so."

We reached our porch steps. Ollie paused at the top, looking thoughtful. "So I guess I'll wait for Dad to do the same. If he comes back to Silver Ridge and stays and starts doing what he promises, then I'll be happy. Because it'll mean I can believe him for real this time. But if he doesn't, then I'll know that too."

Tears pricked my eyes. I went to one knee, right there on the porch, and hugged him. "That's very wise. I'm proud of you, okay? And I love you more than everything in the universe put together. Times infinity."

"Okay, Mom," he snickered. "Can you help me pack for the trip with Uncle Callum? I couldn't find my Broncos sweatshirt."

"Of course. Let's get everything packed tonight so we won't be scrambling in the morning."

"I thought you liked doing things at the last minute. So you can run around and get your exercise."

I winked at him. "But I also like being unpredictable. Just to keep everyone guessing. Come on. Race you to the laundry room, because I bet your sweatshirt's in there."

It wasn't right that Ollie had to learn such hard lessons at a young age. The same kinds of lessons I'd had to learn.

Sometimes parents weren't reliable. Sometimes we trusted the wrong people, and we had to figure out how to put our broken hearts back together, but stronger this time.

And no matter how hard we tried, too often history repeated itself anyway. Exactly what I was afraid of.

Was it possible for things to be different? I wanted to believe that for Ollie. Wanted him to have a bright, happy future with so much love in his life.

But as for *me*... I was still too scared to hope for the same.

TWENTY-SIX

Grayden

AFTER I SAID goodbye to Piper, I didn't head home. Did you really think I was going to leave her to face Danny on her own? No way.

But I didn't want to cause problems for her either. So I would have to stay out of sight.

My truck drove along Main half a block behind her as she walked toward the park. Another car's headlights appeared behind me, probably wanting to drive faster than a crawl.

I sped up a bit and found a parking space that still allowed a view of Piper's blond head and wool coat.

She'd just walked into the park. Though it was dark out, there were plenty of streetlights to show her standing beside a picnic table.

Within a couple of minutes, Danny and Ollie came up the sidewalk to meet her.

As they talked, I could read the tightness in Piper's shoulders from all the way over here. My hand squeezed repeatedly into a fist as I watched.

Then Piper and Ollie walked away from him, heading toward home. Danny went in the other direction.

I let out an exhale. Good. Hadn't expected any more foolishness from Danny tonight. Still a relief to see Piper and Ollie safe and leaving his vicinity.

Piper wasn't really mine, despite the line we'd crossed at her coffee shop. But it felt right to be watching over them all the same.

My gaze drifted over to Danny's sandy-brown hair. He reached his Lexus, which was parked across the street from me, and got in.

His headlights flared to life, and he drove off.

Don't do it, O'Neal, I thought.

Why did I even bother lecturing myself when I so rarely listened?

I pulled out of my parking spot, made a U-turn, and started following him.

Danny quickly left the Silver Ridge town center and took the highway. There weren't many other cars out.

I stayed back far enough he wouldn't spot the make and model of my truck, in case he might recognize it.

About fifteen minutes later, Danny pulled into the gravel lot of a nondescript dive bar. One of a thousand, probably, that dotted Hart County. I pulled in after him, parking as Danny went inside the bar.

For a good five minutes, I stayed there in my truck. Tapping my steering wheel and weighing the option of just driving away.

Then I went inside after him.

The place was wood-paneled and dark, lit by green-glass light fixtures. Billiard balls clacked, and a hockey game played on a TV while country music played from another speaker.

A couple of heads glanced my way, but they lost interest fast. Between my scruffy grooming habits and battered work boots, I looked like I belonged here.

Unlike Danny Carmichael. I found him sitting at a booth with a beer in front of him and his nose in his phone.

"You're late," he said, as I slid into the bench seat across from him.

Then he glanced up and his tanned face went pale.

"Expecting someone else?" I asked.

He glanced around. "What the hell are you doing here, O'Neal?"

I spread my hands. "I was hoping we could have a civil, polite conversation. Unlike the last time we met."

"Civil and polite? Doesn't sound like you."

"Doesn't sound like you either. We'll just have to do our best."

He took a swig of his beer and thumped it down on the table, all tough and macho. "You going to tell me to stay away from my own kid again? Like you have any fucking right?"

Over the years, between my military service and my prison sentence, I'd seen all kinds of men put on shows like this. Trying to assert their dominance. Officers, grunts. Rich guys and poor ones. Guards and inmates alike.

It wasn't the superficial display that mattered. It was the mettle underneath, and in my experience, the quieter ones were usually the most committed and least afraid.

Danny was scared to death of me.

Was I a bad person for enjoying it?

"Look," I said softly, "I'm just a friend of Piper's. Just renting a house from her. You and I had a confrontation last week, and it got out of hand."

"Damn right it did." A few other people glanced over at his shrill tone.

"So I'm here to de-escalate the situation. If you're pissed off at me, that's fine. I get it. I just want to make sure you aren't going to take that out on Piper or Ollie."

Danny leaned back, sneering like he thought he had the upper hand. "Maybe you should be more worried about yourself. Heard you had a surprise visit at your place today. From the cops?"

My jaw tensed, and the vein at my temple pulsed. But I kept my calm. "Did you have something to do with that?"

"You can't prove anything. But let's say I did. It should serve as a warning. You claim to be Piper's protector, but it would be so fucking easy to take you down and send you back behind bars. You're nothing."

I laughed to myself, my temper cooling. His insults didn't bother me. My own brother had said worse.

But I still wanted him to leave Piper alone. For her, I was in the mood to play nice. Carrot instead of stick.

"Okay," I said. "You're right. I'm nothing much. I'll forget about any break-ins at my place or inconveniences those may have caused. If you'll agree to go back to how things were before, when you stayed gone. We both know you don't actually care about your son."

"Fuck you."

"What is it you really want?"

His eyes narrowed, but with interest instead of offense this time.

"I want what I was looking for. The jewelry box that belonged to Piper's mother. It was in that house, and Piper didn't want it. She wants nothing to do with her mom, so why should she care? And I promise, there's nothing of value to you in there either."

"But it's valuable to you?"

"I'm the only one who knows how to make use of it. So don't even try."

This mysterious jewelry box did pique my curiosity. But that was irrelevant, because I was fairly certain it was gone.

Also, it belonged to Piper, not him.

"I have no idea where that box is. Couldn't give it to you even if I wanted."

"Then how about this. Two hundred thousand, and I'll leave Piper and Ollie alone for good."

I blinked at him for several seconds, long enough for those words to sink in. "Two hundred thousand dollars. For Piper and Ollie."

Danny put his elbows on the table, hunching forward. "Obviously you don't have that kinda money. But your sister Grace does. Or rather, her boyfriend. Dane Knightly probably has 200k in one of his slush accounts as we speak. He's the type to pay for problems to go away. Pay me off, and I'll never see Piper or Ollie again. You can have them."

Darkness feathered at the edges of my vision. I placed my hands flat on the tabletop. Weighing my next words.

"It's bad enough you lost Piper. I'd almost feel sorry for you if I didn't know it was completely and utterly your fault. You had the most beautiful, intelligent, passionate woman and you fucked it all up."

"Piper's always been a whore, and she always will be."

I slammed my fists onto the table, making the whole booth rattle. Heads turned again. Danny's face flushed red, but I wasn't finished.

"But for you to talk about your son that way? Like he's a thing to be bought and sold? You're pathetic. I'm usually too cynical to believe in karma. But I sure as hell hope it's real, because when it comes for you, you're going to wind up a smear under someone's boot."

"Is that a threat?"

"You're not even worth it." I pushed out of the booth and walked away.

The door to my truck slammed shut behind me, testing the old hinges.

My fist wanted to hammer the dashboard, but that would just risk bruising my knuckles and breaking my poor old Dodge.

Fucking Danny Carmichael.

I'd met some worthless pieces of shit in my life, but he was gunning for first prize.

Danny didn't come out of the bar, and I didn't see anyone else go in while I sat there.

Who was Danny supposed to meet tonight? Had the person stood him up? Or seen me and taken off?

I wasn't even sure if it mattered. Either way, I wasn't sticking around here any longer.

But instead of driving out to my place, where I belonged, I drove to Piper's.

Her street was dark and quiet, despite how close it was to Main. Dim light shone through the front blinds of her place.

I pulled out my phone, remembering I'd asked her to text earlier.

PIPER

We're home.

What about you?

Yoo-hoo, helloooo? Grayden O'Neal, where are you? So you fool around with a girl and then ghost her? Harsh

ME

Sorry. Had something to take care of

Something more important than texting me?

Not really. Just got distracted. Glad you're home safe. Ollie had a nice time at dinner?

Nice enough. He's excited about the trip with Callum tomorrow

There was a pause while I debated what to write back. Then Piper wrote again.

Maybe I'll see you this weekend? Another day pass?

With a groan, I dropped my head back against the head rest.

Did I want to spend time with Piper while she was alone all weekend? Fuck yes. I wanted that. My cock definitely wanted that.

But was it a good idea?

I knew how hot we would be together. I'd seen more than enough evidence of that at Silver Linings tonight. Piper using me to take her pleasure, the sweet, desperate sounds she'd made. Of course I longed for a repeat of that.

But I was at a crossroads with her. If this kept going, I wouldn't be able to help falling for her.

I'd made that stupid quip about benefits when I wanted all of her.

The smart play would be to take a step back from Piper's life. That way, if she had to go to court to deal with Danny, he couldn't use my past against her. I would never be the reason she got hurt.

I had to stay strong. Do the right thing.

I'm not sure about my plans.

OK. We can play it by ear then

Sweet dreams, okay? Have a good night

With that, I forced myself to drive away.

TWENTY-SEVEN

Piper

"MOM, I FORGOT MY TOOTHBRUSH!" Ollie said from the back seat.

"Nope. You didn't. Because I grabbed it for you." I turned the car onto Callum and Zandra's street. "And your toothpaste."

Glancing in the rearview mirror, I saw Ollie flop against his seat. "Thank goodness."

My lips tugged into a fond smile. "If you forget anything, I'm sure Uncle Callum can get you a replacement this weekend in Denver."

Ollie's expression in the mirror said he was skeptical.

I pulled my Subaru up to the curb, right behind a fancy SUV. I knew that plate, and who else in Silver Ridge drove a shiny new Range Rover with a flower decal on the back window?

Grace was here.

Ollie hefted his travel pack on his shoulder. We walked into Callum and Zandra's place through the unlocked door.

"Hey, we're here!" A cacophony of voices greeted us, and then running footsteps.

"Ollie!" Maisie shouted, throwing her arms around him. "You have to come see Daisy the kitten. She's getting so big."

Ashford appeared in the entryway next, and I gave him a

tentative nod. "How's it going?" I asked. "Is Maisie going to Denver too?"

We both got out of the way so Ollie and Maisie could search out the kitten. Zandra's older cat, Chloe, prowled by, probably looking for a quieter place to relax.

"Callum invited her, but Emma has a music teacher conference this weekend. Maisie and I are going to drive out and join her."

"Sounds good."

"But Maisie really wanted to see Ollie, and we were already here having breakfast with Callum and Z this morning, so..."

"Ah. Got it."

This wasn't awkward. Not at all.

I hadn't seen Ashford in a few weeks, aside from the occasional interaction in passing, like when I picked up Ollie from the kids' martial arts class Ashford taught.

He and I had been close for years, but lately, there was an unspoken hesitation between us. And we both knew the exact reason.

I was sure he knew I was renting a house to Grayden. Probably that Grayden and I were friendly too.

But Ashford was not the type to talk openly about things. This time, I wasn't going to push. Not when I had so many complicated feelings of my own where Grayden was concerned.

Grace charged into the entryway next, drying her hands on a dishtowel. "Piper!"

I hugged her. "Hey, didn't know you'd be here this morning. It's a full house."

"O'Neal family breakfast," Ashford said.

At his words, Grace's pretty smile morphed into a tense straight line. "Not the entire O'Neal family," she muttered without even glancing at him.

Oof. If Ashford and I were awkward, Grace's attitude toward him was downright hostile.

Grace draped the towel over her shoulder. "Sorry, would've

invited you for pancakes too, Piper, but it came together at the last second. Mostly I showed up because I haven't seen you in weeks, and I knew you'd be bringing Ollie. Dane and I just flew in last night from New York."

"Yes, the life of the wealthy and glamorous."

Grace gave me a wry look through her pink-framed glasses. "More like workaholics. Dane and I have both been so busy. I've been neglecting you and Ollie, and I'm sorry about that."

"Nah, we've been fine. We wouldn't have made it for pancakes, anyway. Ollie got started on packing last night, but of course forgot almost anything practical. I had to grab the rest this morning. He'd packed his clip-on tie, for lord knows what reason, but forgot underwear."

With a laugh, Grace took my wrist and led me into Callum and Zandra's cute living room. Gnome figurines decorated the mantle over the fire, and Chloe lounged on the windowsill, orange tail flicking as we took a seat on the couch.

"So," Grace said, folding her legs under her. "Tell me everything. What's new with you?"

Aside from getting frisky with your oldest brother last night?

I half coughed, half laughed. Totally subtle. "Not that much."

I'd texted Grace about renting my house to Grayden, so that much wasn't news to her. But there was so much else she didn't know. Not least, the police incident yesterday.

"Danny's back in town," I added.

A concerned look crossed her features. "Is that a good thing?"

I opened my mouth, considering what to say. Because part of me *really* wanted to tell my best friend everything. Grace had been there for me over and over again in the past. I'd really been missing her lately.

But something held me back.

"He took Ollie to get dinner last night," I said. "Ollie had a nice time, but aside from that, I don't know how it'll go. If Danny's going to step up, or if he'll disappear again."

"Same old Danny, then. But at least he's trying, even a little."

"Maybe," I hedged. "We'll figure it out. Tell me about New York."

She chattered happily about Dane's mom and dad, who they'd been spending more time with. And the friends she'd made and the hidden gems she'd discovered.

After a few minutes, everyone started migrating toward the door. Mainly pushed along by Zandra, who was doing her best to keep Callum on schedule. He was usually pretty responsible. But with so many people here, he was in his element, making sure everyone was having fun instead of being a slave to the clock.

Then it was time for hugs goodbye, a few more kitten snuggles with Daisy, and Callum and Ollie got on the road.

Ashford and Maisie followed, heading out to meet Emma at her conference in the next county over.

When those exits were finished, Zandra collapsed on an armchair in the living room with a groan. "You both know I love Callum more than anything in the world, but I won't say no to a weekend of quiet."

On cue, Daisy streaked by.

"What were you saying about quiet?" Grace quipped.

"Hold on." Zandra jumped up. "She's got the zoomies. Don't know how she's still got any energy after this morning. But the last time Daisy was really worked up and I didn't distract her, our down comforter got shredded."

Zandra dashed from the room. Grace and I took up our spots on the couch again, laughing. Never a dull moment.

"What're you doing with your weekend?" Grace asked. "Almost three days of freedom until Ollie's back."

I shrugged. "Catching up on some things at Silver Linings, probably."

"Wait, do I need to force *you* to get out and have fun? What happened to my party-girl best friend?"

If only Grace knew. My wild side had been present and accounted for last night with Grayden.

But after I'd asked to spend more time with him this weekend, he'd basically blown me off.

I'm not sure about my plans.

And of course that was for the best, as I'd told myself a hundred times about getting involved with Grayden. Those words had worn a groove in my brain at this point.

But it hadn't made me stop wanting him.

"I'm still a free spirit," I defended. "I'm going to get crazy this weekend, don't you worry. I just got the weekly flier for Main Street Market, and Rosie put the Ben & Jerry's on sale. I'm going to stock my freezer with *my* favorite flavors only. Netflix marathon of all the shows with complex plots, curse words, and explicit sex. And then I'll soak in the tub for like a solid hour with nobody bugging me."

Grace giggled. "You've got a full schedule."

"You know it."

She chewed her lower lip. After all these years, I could read Grace like a classic novel. Something was on her mind.

Then she said, "I really appreciate what you've been doing for Grayden."

Did my smile look as strange as it felt? Could Grace read me as easily as I could read her? I hoped not.

"It's no trouble at all."

"But it means so much. Knowing he's got support. There are so many people in Silver Ridge who don't want him here, and that kills me."

Chloe stretched, leaping into the space between us and snuggling in. Grace petted the cat's soft fur and continued talking.

"If I had it my way, I'd be bugging Grayden every day," she said, "dropping by to see how he's doing and making sure he's got everything he needs. Or just to see him, because he's my big brother and I'm making up for lost time. But that would drive him up the walls."

"Maybe it's better that you've been busy in New York."

She huffed. "Grayden probably agrees. He wants to do this on his own. I guess I'm the same way."

"Wait, you O'Neals are stubborn? Alert the media."

"Ha, ha," she deadpanned, then stuck out her tongue. "I just want to snap my fingers and heal the rift in our family. But I can't. Grayden should be here whenever he wants, not sidelined. But if I invite Grayden to something, Ashford refuses to come."

"I picked up on some tension between you and Ashford."

"We're barely talking, P. If Grayden knew, he'd feel awful about it. The last thing he wants is to cause discord. Callum says Ashford needs more time, blah, blah, blah. But to me, it should be simple. Grayden is our brother, and he apologized. He deserves our forgiveness. Full stop."

Grayden deserved that and so much more. He'd spent ten *years* behind bars for a crime he didn't commit. It was incomprehensible to me.

And Grace didn't even know.

"I've said something along those lines to Teller. How they were best friends once, and Teller should talk to Grayden and give him a chance."

Grace blinked her chocolatey brown eyes. "That is so kind of you," she gushed. "You're the best, Piper."

Ugh, I was hardly being selfless. I wanted Teller to accept Grayden for *my* sake. Because there was something between Grayden and me, no matter how much I tried to avoid it. Assuming he was even still interested.

Maybe Grayden deserved more than I could give him.

Chloe stretched out across both our laps, turning her belly up in an obvious demand for more pets. Oops. We'd been neglecting her. I took over the belly rubs.

"We should all be able to count on each other, like we used to," Grace said. "You and Teller and me and my brothers. After this is fixed, I want smooth sailing for all of us. I don't want anything else to come between any of us ever again."

What would Grace think if she knew how close I was getting

to Grayden? How I craved his kiss and his arms holding me and his hot body all over me.

Also, I was dying to see his piercing. Feel it on my tongue, inside me...*Ungh*. It shouldn't be legal for a man to be that over-the-top sexy.

My own feelings were scary enough. The risk of getting my heart broken when I'd sworn never to allow that again. But it wasn't just my heart or Grayden's at risk. It was Ollie's. Grace's. Maybe the future peace of our whole family.

Getting involved with Grayden O'Neal would be risking everything.

So what was wrong with me that I couldn't stop thinking about him?

TWENTY-EIGHT

Piper

FRIDAY AFTERNOONS at Silver Linings were usually quiet. Most people were done with their work week and thinking about happy hour drinks by now.

But I had no interest in going out. I'd meant it when I mentioned ice cream and a hot bath to Grace. If Grayden didn't want to meet up with me, fine. I would make this weekend all about self care.

And perhaps a session or two with the vibrator I kept on the top shelf of my closet.

At Main Street Market, I picked up things I loved but didn't get often enough. Like a wheel of brie and some fig preserves, the hearty bread Ollie hated, and even a bottle of Colorado whiskey. Plus raiding the ice cream sale, of course.

After I got home, I was putting away my frozen bounty when a call came in.

The screen read, *Silver Ridge Police Department*. Same thing it always used to say when my brother was calling from his office at the station. Of course, it wasn't Teller calling this time.

A cold chill traced down my spine, and it had nothing to do with my freezer.

Should I let the call go to voicemail? But if there was a problem, ignoring it wouldn't make it go away.

"Hello?" I asked, shutting the freezer door and leaning against the counter.

"Is this Piper Carmichael?"

I recognized Susan Nichols's voice immediately. "Hello, Chief. It's me. What can I do for you?"

"I expect you know what I'm calling about."

I grimaced, thankful she couldn't see me. Anxious goosebumps broke out all over my skin.

"Huh?" I asked, oh-so-eloquently.

"We have a contraband drop box here outside the station," the chief said. "As you know. We recovered a package from inside, and our cameras observed you dropping off that package yesterday."

Breathe, I told myself.

Could I pretend I'd lost the call? Ugh, seriously, I was bad at this. I'd felt so rebellious and defiant dropping off that contraband. Where had my inner outlaw gone?

"Don't know what you mean."

Nichols let out a tired sigh. "Let's skip the song and dance, alright? We've known each other a long time. That's why I'm calling, because frankly, I'm concerned you're mixed up in something."

"Like what?" I sputtered, fully expecting her to say *drugs*. To accuse me of getting caught up in Grayden's nefarious drug ring.

"First there was the anonymous tip that came in yesterday about Mr. O'Neal. Your tenant. And then you dropped off a suspicious package. Not that hard to connect the dots."

"You can't prove it was me."

There was silence, but I could almost hear her rolling her eyes. Maybe I didn't have a future in crime after all.

"Piper, here's the deal. We ran a test on the contents of that package. It was powdered sugar."

"*What*?" I roared.

"Okay, ouch," Nichols complained. "You just screamed in my ear. That was loud."

"Sorry." My free hand fluttered in front of my face. "I'm just... you're sure? Powdered sugar?"

"The type you can get at most grocery stores. Nothing illegal at all. But you *thought* it was contraband, and I'd like to know why. I'd also like to know what it has to do with Grayden O'Neal and that anonymous tip we got about him. Because something weird's going on, and I don't like that."

Nichols sounded so much like my brother right now. How many times had Teller marched around, grumping about exactly this kind of thing? *I want to know what's going on in my town. Grr.*

But for me, a lot more about this picture was becoming clear.

The real question: should I tell Chief Nichols that Danny was behind this? I didn't have any proof. But if this could help Grayden...

"I think it was my ex. Danny Carmichael. He has a grudge against Grayden."

Another deep sigh. "Go ahead and tell me everything."

I hoped I'd made the right decision.

I'd told Chief Nichols pretty much everything that happened yesterday. Well, not the part about me riding Grayden's thigh at Silver Linings. That secret, I would take to my grave.

But I'd told her the rest, including how Grayden and I both believed Danny was behind the tip and the planted package.

It was far better that Danny hadn't actually planted drugs at Grayden's place. And it explained how Danny could get the money for a brick of narcotics—he didn't. It hadn't been real in the first place. Just a way to get the police to harass Grayden.

I had to give Grayden an update. This involved him too, so I owed him that much, didn't I?

Hey. Spoke to Chief Nichols, and you won't believe what she told me. Package was a fake. The powder was nothing but sugar 😒

Grayden's response took about five minutes to come in. I wasn't proud to say I checked my phone every thirty seconds until I finally saw the three dots appear.

Damn. Definitely good news. Scared us both enough

Right??? It was a big stupid hoax to make the police harass you. I told Nichols that Danny was behind it, and then I pretty much had to tell her why Danny doesn't like you. Because you defended me after Danny broke into your rental

There was a long pause.

Okay

Okay? Was this man serious? All I got was *okay*?

He didn't write anything else, and neither did I. Seemed like our conversation was over.

After that, I couldn't sit still. I warmed up some leftover soup for dinner and barely tasted it. Watched half an episode of some drama on streaming without remembering a single detail.

Callum had texted earlier that he and Ollie arrived in Denver. Ollie texted too, reporting they'd had tacos and churros for dessert, complete with chocolate sauce Ollie had finished with a spoon.

So everything was great with my kid.

But my weekend of relaxation and self care? Not off to a great start.

Maybe because Grayden's final word to me had been *okay*.

Nothing else about what we'd been through together yesterday. Or the open-ended invitation I'd given him.

Maybe I'll see you this weekend?

He knew I was alone right now. It was Friday night and I had no plans. And Grayden *knew* I wanted more of what we'd done last night, because I'd made that pretty obvious. If I texted him yet again, I would probably sound desperate.

See, this was why I didn't date. Grayden was tying me up in knots.

Somehow, I wound up at my kitchen island with that bottle of Colorado whiskey, a shot glass, and a pint of chocolate fudge brownie.

The whiskey lit up my throat with the best kind of toasty burn on the way down. And the chaser bite of ice cream soothed my tastebuds with indulgent, creamy goodness.

Mmm. Yum. Now this was more like it. The liquor and the ice cream made a dangerous combination.

Which probably explained how, half an hour and quite a few shots later, I found myself with my phone in my hand hitting Grayden's number.

"Piper?" he asked. "Are you okay?"

His deep voice worked its way under my skin, like always.

I sloshed another half-shot of liquor into the glass. "Are you mad at me?"

"What are you doing?"

Tossing back the whiskey, I coughed. "I'm asking if you're mad at me for talking to Chief Nichols."

"Are you drinking? Where are you?"

"I'm at home. Alone. Like I've been for hours. I'm not on mom duty, so yes, I'm enjoying an adult beverage. Now would you please answer the question?"

"No, Piper. I'm not mad," he said after a beat. "I could never be mad at you."

"That doesn't make any sense! Plenty of people get mad at me. I earn it. I have a very strong personality."

Grayden made a soft, amused sound. "I know. I've told you I like that about you."

Ah yes, he'd compared me to a natural disaster before. How flattering.

"Aren't you worried I told Chief Nichols about what you said to Danny? Threatening to break all his bones if he ever touched me again? And how you were choking him?"

My heart rate kicked at those memories. How ferocious Grayden had been, declaring himself my protector.

"I said what I said, and I did what I did. You can tell the police what you want. I will never ask you to lie about anything for me."

My spoon scraped the side of the ice cream pint. "Stop being so perfect."

There was that soft almost-laugh sound again.

"And don't laugh at me," I added.

"You're being very cute though. Bossy Piper is always fun, but Drunk Piper might be even better."

"I'm not drunk." I picked up the whiskey bottle and carried it, along with my phone, over to the couch. The cushions squeaked as I fell back against them, staring at the ceiling.

"Did you tell Chief Nichols about what Danny did to *you*?" he asked. "Did she ask whether you want to press charges?"

"Yes and yes. But it's like I thought. It would be difficult to nail him for anything aside from the trespassing, unless I want to go through a whole trial or something. Because he'll deny attacking me. You're my only witness."

"And I don't have a stellar track record. Any defense attorney would flay me alive on cross-examination. I'm sorry about that."

Same kind of thing that might happen if I went to court to revoke Danny's visitation rights. At least he hadn't actually been handling drugs.

"It sucks," I muttered. "But at least Nichols knows Danny has a vendetta against you. She's a good cop. Teller always trusted her."

He didn't reply to that. My head was getting all swimmy now.

Maybe I'd overdone the whiskey.

"Grayden, I had a crush on you," I said to the ceiling. "Did you know that?"

"You mean when you were younger? Yeah. I guessed." His voice was right there in my ear. Gravelly and intimate. So close yet so far. "I was way too old for you then."

"But not now." My eyes fluttered closed. "Last night was the hottest thing I've ever experienced. The way you touched me? You felt how wet I was. All slippery." The word felt downright erotic on my lips. How it forced my tongue against my teeth. "I've never come that hard."

My thighs squeezed together as arousal built between my legs. "I didn't even get to play with your piercing."

He groaned. "Piper, I..."

A loud sound outside made me sit up. "What was that?"

"What do you mean?"

"I heard something."

"Where?"

"Outside." Getting up on wobbly legs, leaving the whiskey bottle upright on the rug, I tiptoed to the nearest window. Everything was dark outside. My nearest neighbor's lights were off, probably having gone to bed.

"What kind of noise was it?" Grayden asked sternly. There was a rustling sound, like he was moving.

"A bang. Something breaking."

And now there was an electronic beeping. Where was that coming from?

"But it wasn't in your house?" Grayden asked.

"No. It sounded like it was coming from..." I moved into the kitchen, looking through the window over the sink. "My garage. The side door looks open."

The beam of a flashlight appeared, cutting through the darkness. Shit. I ducked down to hide. A cabinet knob dug into my back.

I understood that beeping now. The alarm panel for my home

security system. The garage was detached from my house, but it was still wired into the system.

"Grayden," I whispered. "Someone broke into my garage."

"Don't move, okay? Stay right where you are and call 911. I'm on my way."

TWENTY-NINE

Grayden

My truck's engine roared as I raced toward Piper's house. "Grayden?" she asked through my phone speaker.

"I'm almost there."

"Good," she replied breathlessly. "The dispatcher said they're sending a car to check it out too. I turned the house alarm to silent so it's not blaring in my ears."

"You're still inside? Doors locked?"

"Yeah. Obviously. I do have some sense. I've got Ollie's baseball bat too."

Piper had switched over to call the police, but I'd stayed on the line until she returned. While I didn't have much faith in Silver Ridge PD, I would call on my worst enemy if it meant protecting Piper.

When I reached her street, there was no sign yet of any lights or sirens. Pulling up to the curb, I switched off the engine. "I'm outside. I'm going to check out the garage."

"Be careful," she said.

"Now who's stating the obvious?"

Pocketing my phone, I walked at a quick pace toward her garage. I'd brought my own makeshift weapon, a tire iron from my truck.

Aside from that, I was unarmed, and I had no clue what I was walking into. But the vast majority of burglars ran at the first sign of confrontation.

Also, I had a good idea of who was inside that garage right now. Danny. Probably here in search of that jewelry box he was so intent on finding.

I'd warned the asshole about what would happen if he messed with Piper again.

My steps slowed as I neared the garage. Light bled from the windows of her house, but everything near the back was dark.

My boot crunched over something on the concrete. Glass. Someone had smashed out the light by her garage door. It was probably on a motion sensor.

A thump came from inside the small structure. I lifted the tire iron. Took a step closer to the door. In the faint light, the broken lock was obvious. Kicked in, which had probably been the loud noise Piper heard.

Suddenly a dark figure burst through the doorway. I leaped back.

"Hey!" I shouted, grasping for the guy's hoodie. My fingers closed on the fabric briefly. He stumbled, kicking his leg out. His boot caught me in the shin.

I lost my hold on him, and he took off, running fast down Piper's driveway.

Dammit. I hadn't seen his face because his hood was up.

I gave chase, but the guy had disappeared. A motion-sensor light flashed on in a neighbor's yard, and a dog barked.

Of course, the moment the guy was gone, a police cruiser turned onto the street with its lights flashing. The siren chirped.

The car stopped in the middle of the road, and a cop leaped from the driver's side. "Drop your weapon! Get down on the ground!"

Oh, fuck. He was talking to me.

I was quick to comply, dropping the tire iron and keeping my hands up as I kneeled on the cold concrete.

Wasn't this just the most predictable thing ever? I might've laughed if it wasn't so disheartening.

A knee landed on my lower back and knocked the wind out of me. My hands were wrenched behind me. Metal cuffs landed on my wrists.

"Got you this time," the officer said. "I knew you were a worthless piece of shit, O'Neal."

Just wonderful. It was Officer Bronski, the cop who'd shown up to my house yesterday with Chief Nichols, responding to the anonymous tip.

"Piper was on the phone with me when she heard the break-in," I said. "I came here to help. You're letting the real intruder get away. He literally ran off one minute ago."

"Shut your mouth. You can spout your lies to the judge."

Footsteps thudded on Piper's front porch and ran toward us. "What are you doing? Let him go!"

I turned my head to see her charging up to Bronski, her blond hair flying.

"Ms. Carmichael, go back inside. I'll take your statement in a moment. I caught the culprit, and—"

"What kind of idiot are you? I called Grayden and asked him to come here. Un-cuff him right now!"

It took a few more minutes to sort the mess out. Piper threatened to call Chief Nichols, and finally Bronski agreed to release me. I got up, brushing off my clothes. A few of her neighbors had stepped out of their homes, watching curiously.

Of course, there were no apologies from Bronski. He radioed to call off his backup.

"The intruder smashed the light on Piper's garage," I said. "Kicked in the side door and was messing around inside. I saw him. Shorter than me, dark clothing. Gloves too."

Bronski's eyes narrowed. "But you didn't stop him?"

"I tried. He got free and took off. I can show you where he ran. It's possible your people could still catch him."

Yet Bronski didn't ask for more details or call anyone else to join a search. Instead, he took Piper's statement about what happened with his face pinched up, sending me hate-filled glances every few seconds.

My fists tightened, so I shoved them in my pockets. I wanted to put my arms around Piper, to comfort her and make sure she was alright. But I didn't dare in front of Bronski. The guy didn't need any more ammo about the two of us.

Maybe I should've also told Piper about my friendly little chat with Danny at the bar last night, but that seemed pointless right now.

"Let's see the garage," Bronski said.

"Oh, you want to investigate?" Piper snarked. "By all means."

I decided to keep my mouth shut.

Piper's garage had clearly been rifled through. When we walked in and switched on the lights, there were some plastic storage boxes on the ground with their lids off, contents half spilled. Mostly Christmas decorations and random household stuff. Some camping equipment.

"I don't keep much out here," she said. "But obviously Danny was looking for something. No surprise there."

"*Danny*?" Bronski asked. "You know who did it? I thought O'Neal didn't see the guy in your garage."

"Grayden didn't need to see the person for me to know it was my ex. Danny Carmichael. He's in town. Go find him and ask what he was doing tonight."

The officer snorted. "Yeah, I'll get right on that."

THIRTY

Grayden

BRONSKI FINISHED up and left a few minutes later. After taking some photos, just in case, I helped Piper fix the mess in her garage.

The door was damaged, but she said there wasn't anything that valuable inside.

With an exasperated grunt, which was actually pretty cute, Piper stomped up her front porch steps and into the house. I followed after her.

She went into the living room and flopped onto the couch. "Once again, Danny gets away with his bullshit," she said.

I stood a few feet away, my hand absently rubbing my jaw. "I assumed it would be Danny too. But before, you said he wouldn't come here looking for your mom's things. Since you didn't keep anything of your mom's here."

"Who knows what's in his head? Nothing he's been doing makes sense."

"The guy I saw. His shoulders were pretty broad. Bulky. Danny is thinner."

"He was wearing heavy clothes, though. Right? That could've made him look bigger."

I nodded. "Possible." But I didn't like this uncertainty. Who else would've broken into Piper's garage? "Maybe Danny hired someone."

Which was even more concerning. Some unknown person involved in this situation, someone who might be even worse than Piper's ex.

With a groan, she put her hands over her face. "I wish I had that stupid jewelry box of my mother's. I would hand it over to Danny if it made all this stop."

Crossing to the couch, I lowered myself to the cushion beside her.

Immediately my mind went to last night at Silver Linings. And before that, the night I'd spent right here, well over a month ago now. When I'd barely known what to think of Piper as an adult. As a mom.

Now, I knew how incredible she was. How irresistible.

And how much she'd had to deal with, thanks to her ex.

"But if you give him what he wants this time," I said softly, "he'll come back wanting something else."

"I know." Her eyes were plaintive, and I wished so fucking much I could give her the answers to how to fix this. "Thank you for being here for me."

"Anytime."

"We were in the middle of a conversation before we got interrupted."

"I remember."

Oh, did I ever remember.

She'd been telling me about her teenage crush. And then about how she'd enjoyed what we did last night. *I've never come that hard*.

"You blew me off," she said. "After I texted yesterday."

"Just trying to do the right thing."

"Why is it right for us both to spend this weekend alone? Assuming you would be alone. You don't have *plans* with someone else?"

I smirked at her. "There's no one else I'd rather be with than you."

Probably shouldn't have said that.

I saw the moment those sea-green irises caught fire. Piper's nose brushed my beard, and she leaned into me. "Will you stay? Spend the night?"

My dick stirred, and my blood heated with longing. "All your neighbors saw us talking to a cop outside. They'll notice if my truck stays here all night."

"So what?"

"I almost got arrested in your driveway. There's no need for your name to get dragged in the mud along with mine."

"How many times do I have to tell you? I don't care what this town thinks of me. I'm a big girl, and I can handle a few rumors. I've grown up, in case you didn't notice."

"I've definitely noticed." My gaze moved over her, drinking her in.

"I can also make my own decisions. Bonnie and Clyde, remember? If you want me, then do something about it." She brought her lips to my ear and whispered, "Spend the night."

"You've been drinking."

"I sobered up."

But I could tell from her tone, from her mannerisms, that she was still feeling loose and hazy. She was far from wasted, but this wasn't Piper in her usual frame of mind.

She carded her fingers through my hair. "Kiss me?"

Nnngh. I wasn't nearly strong enough to resist her brand of temptation.

Somehow, without my permission, my lips wound up on hers. My tongue licked into Piper's mouth, and her tongue played sweetly with mine. It was a slow give and take.

When I finally found my self control again, I gentled the kiss and held her face in my hands.

"I want you. Of course I do. I've been completely caught up

in you since the night I slept on this couch. But you've been drinking, so nothing else is going to happen tonight."

She exhaled. "Alright, I get it. But if the whiskey's cock-blocking us anyway, you might as well have a drink with me."

A laugh snuck out of my chest. "Fine. One drink."

Piper reached down and snagged the whiskey bottle sitting beside the couch. Opening it, she tipped the long neck to her lips, her eyes not leaving mine. The amber liquid flowed into her mouth. But she didn't swallow.

Instead, Piper leaned close to me again. She brought her lips to mine, and I realized what she was doing.

I slanted my mouth over hers, and the spicy, toasty burn of the whiskey flowed over my tongue, laced with just a hint of Piper's flavor. My cock gave an answering thump, hardening against my fly.

Swallowing down the liquor, I licked my lips. Piper was still close enough that my tongue flicked over her lips too.

"You *are* wild," I rasped. "And fucking wicked. You trying to seduce me, Piper?"

"Do I really need to?"

"I'm trying to be good here."

She blinked with feigned innocence. "But I want to be bad."

I took the whiskey bottle, threw back another swig, and capped it before I set it aside.

"Hey, I want another shot too," she protested.

"Nope. You're done for the night."

"Then I'll have to kiss you some more. So I can taste it."

For now, I was done objecting. Our mouths collided again. Rough and hungry. Between Piper and the whiskey, it was all vanilla and oak and caramel spice. I loomed over her, and Piper lay back against the couch, our mouths never parting.

My sweet, intoxicating temptation.

Her thigh lifted between my legs. She brushed against my erection and whimpered into my mouth. Her hand went to the hard length in my jeans and squeezed.

"Let me suck you off."

I made a tortured sound. "You're killing me, Piper." As bad as she made me want to be right now, I had to draw the line somewhere. If she ended up regretting anything we did tonight, while she wasn't fully sober, I'd hate myself.

She lifted up to kiss me again. Her lips were pink and swollen. "At least show me your piercing. Please? I'm dying to see. If you say no, it's just mean."

Knowing I shouldn't, I popped the button on my fly and lowered the zipper. Pulled out my aching shaft. The pressure of just my hand made me want so much more, and my cock jumped against my fingers.

By habit, I toyed with the curved silver barbell that pierced my cock head. A Prince Albert.

Piper's lips parted as she stared. "Wow. Grayden, that's..."

"Okay?" Not everyone was into piercings.

Her gaze met mine. "So sexy I can hardly stand it. It feels good for you?"

I dragged my thumb over the top of the piercing, shivering at the sensation. "Very."

Piper raised her hand like she was going to touch me, but I caught her wrist.

"Not tonight."

She pouted. "You show me the hottest thing I've ever seen, and then tell me I can't have it?"

"Just gotta wait. Don't drink so much next time."

Her tongue flicked out to trace her lower lip suggestively. Such a little tease. "You're missing out."

"I have no doubt." An image flashed through my mind of that pink tongue licking my barbell, then her lips closing and sucking. Wetness welled at my tip.

Piper stretched out below me on the couch, her arms going over her head. "At least let me see you get off. Promise I won't touch. I'll just watch the show. I'm plenty sober for that."

Fuck me for my weakness. There was no possibility of me turning down that offer.

"Okay, wild girl. Only if you're good for me."

I brought my hand to her mouth. To that naughty, teasing tongue. Piper licked my palm a couple of times, and I wrapped my hand around my cock and started to stroke.

My mind went to the memory of her last night, so wild and uninhibited. This woman... I could already tell I'd never be the same. Not after her.

My fist worked up and down my cock. On every few strokes, I used my thumb to play with the barbell, loving the intense jolts of pleasure. My gaze moved over her, studying every beautiful feature.

Everything I'd ever been through would be worth it, if she could somehow be mine.

Piper's hand sneaked down to her shirt and tugged up the hem, revealing her smooth stomach. "Come on me. I want to see you. Want to feel it."

My movements sped up and my breath went ragged. The things she was doing to me without even a touch.

"Piper," I growled as the orgasm hit me. My cock pulsed with jolts of perfect, overwhelming pleasure, spilling over her stomach.

My fist slowed, teasing out the last few aftershocks.

Then Piper dragged a finger through my release and brought it to her mouth. Sucked her digit between her lips. Holy shit.

My cock gave another valiant pulse like it was trying to get hard again. If only.

I bent forward, hunching over her. My forehead rested against hers as I panted to catch my breath. "Can't believe how gorgeous you are. All covered in me."

"I love it," she said dreamily. When I pulled back to look at her, she seemed tired, but her focus was sharp. "You're staying, right?"

I nodded. Nothing short of a tornado would possibly drag me

away at this point. And luckily, tornados weren't an issue in this part of Colorado.

"Stay here," I said. "I'll be right back." Slowly getting up from the couch, my head still fuzzy from that intense climax, I went to the hall bathroom and found a washcloth. The water took a minute to warm up.

When I got back to the living room, Piper was dozing. She barely stirred as I wiped the washcloth over her belly in gentle strokes, cleaning her up.

After returning the washcloth to the bathroom to deal with tomorrow, I found some blankets in a linen closet.

"Hey, wild girl. Scoot over a little."

I managed to get us arranged on the couch, with me on my back and Piper curled into my side. She nestled her head against my neck, right under my chin.

Good thing the cushions were deep and oversized. Otherwise, I didn't see how we'd fit. I wasn't a small guy, and Piper wasn't a small woman.

We fit so perfectly together.

She hummed and wiggled around. Sinking deeper into the blankets I'd spread over us. My eyes closed, a contented grin on my lips.

"Grayden, I'm scared," she whispered.

My eyes shot open, and my heart squeezed. "Of what, sweetheart?" Did she mean Danny? The break-in? Officer Bronski?

"Of getting my heart broken."

Heaviness gathered in my throat. She'd sounded so vulnerable. "I know." I kissed her hair. "But I won't hurt you."

"How do you know for sure?"

"Because I'd rather die."

"I'd rather you hurt me than *that*," she slurred sleepily.

"I'd prefer neither. I'm not going anywhere. As long as you want me, I'm yours. I promise, I'm yours."

Piper burrowed against me. I had no idea if she'd heard that, or if she was already asleep. But to me, my words seemed to echo in the room like a vow. Like something far bigger than a few murmured sounds.

I was already hers. There was nothing I could do about that. I'd tried and failed to stay away. Now, I was all in.

So, I had to make her mine.

THIRTY-ONE
Piper

I WOKE up wedged between two couch cushions. And with a pounding headache.

Crap, what had I done?

Whiskey, babe. Too much whiskey.

I jolted upright as more of last night came back to me. Someone breaking into my garage. My shameless attempt to seduce Grayden into spending the night.

And then the image, hot enough to sizzle as I remembered it, of Grayden kneeling over me with his thick cock in his hand. His thumb flicking over his piercing. The heady scent of his arousal. And when he came...

"Piper? Hey. You're up." Grayden leaned against the archway into the living room. His hair and clothes were rumpled. Another brief image came. More a collection of sensations really. Snuggling up with him on the couch.

So he'd stayed.

"I was going to make some breakfast." He pointed a thumb in the direction of the kitchen. "How you feeling?"

I kicked off the blanket and got up, patting down my tangled hair. When I swayed, Grayden lunged forward to grab my arms.

"Somebody's hungover."

"Barely," I protested. But yeah. I was a little hungover. "Just means I had fun. Nothing some coffee and eggs won't fix."

"Good." He was close now. Touching me, practically holding me up. Warmth flooded my stomach.

"I'm glad you stayed," I said softly.

"Promised I would." He pushed strands of hair back from my cheek. "I didn't really have a choice about it, in the end."

"Because I'm bossy? Or because I fell asleep on you?"

His grin was knowing, but he didn't elaborate. "You remember what happened before the sleeping part, right?"

I glanced down between us in an exaggerated way, as if I was trying to get a glimpse of the goods, then lifted my eyebrows. Too bad he was wearing his jeans.

"Sure do. You nearly set fire to my brain with how hot you were. Nice show."

"I had a lot of inspiration."

Grayden's fingers held my chin as he angled his head for a kiss. He tasted minty. He'd probably found the extra toothbrushes under the bathroom sink. Hopefully I didn't taste too bad, but judging from the eager strokes of his tongue, he wasn't complaining.

But as he pulled back, I winced at the throb in my temples. Ow.

"Let's get you some food and medicine," he said.

"Don't forget the coffee."

Grayden took my hand and led me toward the kitchen. "I would never."

"Marry me," I slurred. Kidding around.

But the look he gave me. Oh boy. I'd rarely seen those dark eyes more intense.

He insisted I sit on a stool at the island while he found my coffee beans and got a pot brewing. I gave half-hearted instructions on how to use my machine and where to find everything.

The quartz countertop was blessedly cool when I slumped forward and put my forehead against it.

"Here." A glass of orange juice landed in front of me, along with a couple ibuprofen. "Take these. I'll scramble some eggs."

"Thank you." The OJ perked me up. While Grayden broke eggs into a bowl, I propped my elbow on the island counter. "I don't think I've ever had a guy make me a morning-after breakfast before. Danny certainly didn't, and these days, I'm always gone by the morning."

Grayden made a little grumbling sound, and the next eggshell broke into pieces in his fingers. I snickered.

"Am I distracting you?" I asked.

"No." He fished a piece of shell out of the bowl, then grabbed a paper towel to wipe his hands.

"You don't like hearing that I've been with other guys? I was married, Grayden. I have a kid."

"I'm aware." He grabbed a fork to beat the eggs. "I just think you should be treated better."

"It's my choice. I never spend a whole night if I go to someone else's place. And I never bring anyone here, even on the rare occasions Ollie is sleeping elsewhere."

"Except me? That what you're saying?"

I shrugged one shoulder, my stomach doing something strange. "You'd already slept here once before. You're different."

"Okay," he said, lips curving with amusement.

"Do you usually make women breakfast after you've...you know..."

He stopped stirring the eggs and cocked his hip. "You really want to hear about that?"

"I don't care."

"Okay." He was smirking like he didn't believe me.

I huffed. "Would you stop just saying *okay* like that's a real response? It isn't. It's a conversation ender."

"Maybe I don't want to talk about us sleeping with other people."

"What if I'm curious? You know about my big relationship mistake. I don't know anything about that part of your past."

"You haven't heard enough of my mistakes already?" he joked. "Hey, where do you keep your cooking pans?"

"The cabinet in front of you. In the kitchen island." The coffeemaker beeped, so I got up to pour a couple of mugs.

After heating the pan, Grayden poured the eggs in to cook, humming a quiet melody. I set a mug on the counter beside him and mainlined my first cup. I sighed as the caffeine made its way through my bloodstream.

He opened my fridge and bent to look around. Which gave me a great opportunity to admire his ass in his jeans.

"How about breakfast tacos?" he asked. "You've got tortillas and salsa."

"Yes, please. There's shredded cheese in the drawer too. And grab the salsa in the back. That's the spicy one Ollie hates."

"Excellent. I love spicy." Grayden set everything on the counter. Now that I was feeling mostly human, I helped him warm up the tortillas and assemble our plates. Then he added a few sprigs of cilantro from a bunch I'd bought last week and had forgotten about.

"Cilantro. Look at you, Mr. Gourmet."

"I'm no Callum, but I get by."

We sat at the kitchen table, knees bumping from how close we were sitting. The tacos were exactly what I needed. Carbs, fat, and protein. A little spice and that hint of freshness from the herbs.

Grayden polished off his taco and sipped his mug of coffee. "There isn't much to tell about my dating history. Never had a serious girlfriend in high school or when I was on active duty."

Oh. So we were talking about this.

"Once I was in prison, I got extremely well acquainted with both my hands. There are women who are into dating inmates, but I was *not* interested in anything like that. And after..." He tugged on his lower lip. "Life in general was rocky the first few years after my release. I wasn't much of a catch."

I pressed my knee firmly against his thigh. "How did you end up in Seattle?"

"Well, I didn't have parole or anything like that to deal with. I was a free man, supposedly. Came back to Colorado at first. Showed up in Silver Ridge, and I think you know what happened. Callum told me to get lost."

I frowned at my coffee. "I heard. Grace told me after she found out." She hadn't known until earlier this year.

"Cal changed his mind about wanting me here, of course, and I've never blamed him for what he said. But anyway, I decided on Seattle because the JAG officer who originally defended me lived there. He kept in touch with me over the years while I was inside. By the time I was out, he was working as a private attorney. Helped me get on my feet."

"It's great you had someone like that."

"Yeah. Thank God. He was kind of a father figure, I suppose. Didn't have many of those in my life."

"Are you still in touch with him?"

"He passed last year."

I reached for his hand. "I'm sorry. I wish I could've met him."

"You're sweet to say that." He smiled easily, lifting my hand to kiss the back of it. "Sweet in lots of ways. I've never felt like this about anyone else, Piper. I want you to know that."

No words came to me, my pulse going too fast.

"I'm going to fix your broken garage door," he said. "I've got some pieces of wood at my place and an extra lock. *Don't* say I don't have to. I know I don't. I'd like to."

I decided to be easygoing. "That would be very kind of you. Thanks."

He smiled and kissed my hand again. "Can I spend some more time with you after that? I'd really like to."

My face flushed, and I couldn't help rolling my eyes. He was being so...formal, suddenly. "I thought you weren't sure about your plans for this weekend."

"Only said that because I wasn't sure if I *should* see you more. I hate the thought of people judging you for your association with me."

"We're back to that topic again?"

"I will stop bringing it up. But only on one condition."

"Which is?"

Grayden scooted his chair out from the table and pulled mine closer to him. His legs opened, bracketing me between his spread thighs. He took both my hands in his.

"Let me take you out today. On a real date."

I started shaking my head, but more out of habit than meaning *no*. Because I wanted to say yes. And wasn't that terrifying?

"What am I supposed to wear?" I asked.

Grayden's smile was one of the biggest I'd seen on him. "How about jeans and a warm layer. Hiking boots too."

"We're going hiking? There's snow on most of the trails."

"Not hiking. Something else, if I can get it set up. Heavy boots will be a good idea." He sat forward and kissed along my jaw. I tilted my head to give him access.

Because I was just putty in this man's hands, apparently.

"Feel free to skip a shower," he murmured, all growly and sultry. "I'd love it if you still smell like me when we're out later."

The strange, unsettled feelings inside me turned to desire. A far more comfortable place for me.

With sex, I always knew what to do. And I knew my limits.

"Or you could shower with me right now," I said. "We can have fun getting clean and then dirty again."

"Later." His lips met mine, far too slowly. A tease of what else was to come. "Maybe after our date. I'm hoping to get lucky. Think I've got a shot?"

"We'll have to see how good this date is."

THIRTY-TWO

Grayden

THE BIKE's engine rumbled beneath me as I rode down Main Street. Milo had described the Kawasaki Ninja as a sweet ride, and so far, it didn't disappoint.

Since the distance between Milo's shop and Piper's house wasn't far, on mostly quiet roads, I hadn't bothered putting on the helmet yet. The cold wind ruffled my hair and settled me, bringing me into the moment.

It had been fifteen years since I'd last ridden, but the muscle memory was still there. My hands remembering before my conscious brain caught up.

Kind of like my first time having sex again after getting out of prison.

Though even that experience paled compared to being with Piper. And I hadn't even gotten her naked yet. Maybe tonight. If things went well.

She'd actually agreed to a date with me, and I didn't intend to fuck this up.

I pulled the bike into her driveway, pulled it around so I was facing the street, and switched off the engine. By the time I made it to her front door, she had it open, peering out curiously.

"Did I just see you ride up on a motorcycle?"

My boots thudded against the porch steps as I climbed them, hands in the pockets of my black canvas jacket. I could feel the stupid, irrepressible grin stretching my lips.

"Yep. Here to pick you up. You ready?"

She gestured at herself. "Now I see why you told me to dress warm. Where are we going?"

As I'd requested, she was wearing jeans and a soft-looking sweater with hiking boots. Her hair was styled into a simple braid, and a little makeup accented her gorgeous features.

Damn, she was so pretty. I forgot to breathe for a beat or two.

"You'll see. Let's go." I held out my hand.

She went inside to set her security system, locked the door, and then slid her slender fingers into my grip.

After breakfast, I'd fixed Piper's garage door like I'd promised. In the few hours since, I'd been working on getting our date set up.

Calling Milo had been the first step. I'd promised him hours of free tattoo work if he did me this favor, and also offered up my single credit card as insurance, in case he was worried about me being irresponsible. But he'd been great about it.

We're friends, man. Of course I'll hook you up.

From the bike's saddle bags, I pulled out a couple of helmets and a nylon jacket with protective padding for Piper. "Here. One of Milo's ex-girlfriends used to wear this riding with him, so it should work for you."

She slid her arms into the sleeves. "So that's where you got the bike? Milo?"

"Yep. Don't have to return it until tomorrow."

Her brows shot up. "Is this an overnight trip? I barely packed anything. Just my wallet and phone." She pointed at the small crossbody purse she wore over her sweater.

"Nope, I'll return you to Silver Ridge safe and sound by tonight. Ever rode a motorcycle before?"

"No. But I like trying new things."

"I bet you do."

For half a second, I hesitated to get closer, remembering we were outside. In easy view of her neighbors. But I'd promised to stop thinking about public opinion.

I pressed a soft kiss to her glossy mouth, then lifted her helmet to put it on. It would provide full coverage for safety, including a face shield to block the wind and sun. I'd brought gloves for her too.

Piper was precious cargo, and I wasn't going to take any unnecessary risks with Ollie's mom.

Anticipation zinged through my insides. For the rest of today, she was mine. And if I didn't screw this up, hopefully for a lot longer.

After strapping on my own helmet and tugging on gloves, I swung my leg over the seat and started up the engine. Piper climbed on behind me. No hesitation, despite it being her first time, and I loved that.

"Hold on tight!" I said over the engine rumble. She wrapped her arms around my waist, leaning into me.

We roared out of the driveway, and Piper shouted happily. My grin was so big it could split my face.

Instead of following the back roads, I took her right down Main Street. Heads turned to look as we went past. With our helmets on, nobody could see us, and I wasn't going all that fast. I wasn't a dick.

But this still felt like a couple middle fingers to the naysayers of this town. Piper holding tight to me, her delighted laughter in my ear.

"Just wait till we're on the highway," I said when we reached a stop sign.

"God, I better not fall off."

"You won't. You'll get the hang of it in no time. Just lean when the bike leans, okay? Do what I do."

Her arms squeezed tighter.

As we turned onto the highway and accelerated, she had me in a death grip for a little while. But pretty soon, Piper relaxed. Her arms stayed around me, but looser, and I could feel her shifting a little as she looked around.

With the wind and engine noise, it was too loud to talk easily now. But man, I'd always loved this. The feeling of flying down the road right in the middle of everything.

Trees flashed past us. Mountains rose up ahead.

I hoped Piper felt it too. Freedom. Out here, our pasts and who we were didn't matter.

After about half an hour, I pulled into a turn-out, following a narrow path. When we reached the picnic area, I parked the bike.

Piper jumped off first, tugging her helmet free. Her cheeks were flushed pink, eyes bright. "That was amazing!"

"Pretty great, right? You weren't too cold?"

"Nope. I loved every second of it." She bounced on her toes. "What's next? Where are we?"

"Thought we'd have an early dinner. I packed a picnic."

"Wow, this really *is* a date."

"I'm not fooling around," I deadpanned.

I'd tucked our food carefully into one of the saddle bags. There was a thermos of coffee, of course. I handed that to Piper and grabbed the tote bag I'd packed.

"Want to sit at the picnic table?" she asked.

"That would be far too predictable. Follow me, please."

"So mysterious."

"I've heard that's what people say about me. Don't want to disappoint." I shot her a glance and was rewarded with Piper's dazzling smile.

I led her away from the parking area. As I'd expected, this spot was deserted. There was snow on the ground and dusted over the trees, but the sky was pure blue with warm sun shining down in places.

We walked along the creek bank until we came to a large, flat rock. "Here. This should work."

From my tote bag, I pulled out a picnic blanket and spread it out. So our butts wouldn't freeze against the cold rock through our jeans.

"You thought of everything."

I winked. "Tried."

"Didn't know you could be so charming, O'Neal." Piper took a seat on the blanket. But when I unwrapped our dinner, she made a face. "Did you seriously bring us gas station hot dogs?"

"Okay, hear me out."

She nearly fell off the rock from laughing, and I grabbed her coat, suppressing my own grin.

"These aren't from the gas station. I bought the fancy all-beef dogs from Main Street Market. And the nice buns."

"You do always bring nice buns," she said with an innocent expression.

Fuck, she made me happy. Every minute I got to spend with Piper made me realize how empty my life had been. Reconnecting with Grace and Callum meant everything to me of course, but in a different way.

Piper made me feel like, for the first time in maybe ever, I was actually living.

"Take a bite before you judge," I said.

The hot dogs were still a little warm from the foil I'd wrapped them in. I'd also added whole-grain mustard, fancy sauerkraut, and hot sauce. Since I knew now that Piper liked some spice.

"You know what?" she said, still chewing. "These are killer. I'm a believer."

I opened a container of homemade potato salad flecked with dill, and we shared it with plastic forks. Same with the cup-lid on the thermos. Piper took a sip of coffee, eyes not leaving mine, and held the cup out to me.

Beside us, the water of the creek rushed along beneath the top layer of ice. Out of sight, but still there. Waiting for spring.

If I'd ever had a better meal, I couldn't remember it.

"What're Ollie and Callum up to today?" I asked.

Piper folded her legs, criss-cross style, and tugged her phone from her purse. "Callum texted me and Zandra this picture earlier."

I huddled closer to her to see the screen. It was a selfie of Callum and Ollie in front of a T-Rex skeleton. Ollie looked like he was having a blast, and Callum sported his usual crooked grin.

"They're at the natural history museum today. Checking out the dinosaurs and science exhibits. Tomorrow it'll be the Broncos game. It's an early kickoff, but they're driving back afterward, so they won't get home until late."

Piper put her phone away, still glowing with pride. Her love for Ollie was so easy to see.

"I'm glad Callum could do that with him," I said. "He hangs out with Ollie a lot?"

I'd noticed Ollie called him Uncle Callum. I was proud of my brother for stepping up like that and being a good influence in Ollie's life. Though clearly it was no hardship. Piper's son was a wonderful kid. Loyal and funny and smart.

"He does, as often as he can, and it means a lot to Ollie. Especially since Teller hasn't been around as much. Teller and Ollie have always been really close, and my brother's new life has been an adjustment."

"No wonder. Never would've pictured Teller with a celebrity." Pretty much the entire world had been talking about Ayla Maxwell's small-town love story when it first happened. I'd read the articles like everyone else. It had been strange to see clips of a TV interview Ayla and Teller did, seeing my former best friend so obviously in love.

"I wouldn't have either," Piper said. "But they're great together. Teller's the head of security for her new tour."

I took Piper's hand. Her fingers were cold, so I warmed them between my palms. "You know, Teller and I used to drive around Hart County sometimes when we needed to get away."

"Did you ever come here?"

"Yeah." I couldn't help my mischievous grin. "We brought

girls out here more than a time or two. Played some music, lit a campfire. Teller had some moves."

Piper barked a laugh. "Ha! I'm learning my brother's secrets. I'm not sure if I want to hear this or not."

"I won't scar you by revealing any more details. Just know, Teller was the popular one with the girls back then. I just tagged along."

"I don't believe that for a second."

I set our trash aside to pick up later and moved behind Piper. We were both facing the creek, and she leaned back against me. The sky was starting to take on color. The oranges and pinks of the sun beginning to set.

"I remember the year you and Grace both came along. Teller and I were around ten, eleven years old. First time I ever saw Teller cry was when I came over and he was holding you. He called you an angel."

Piper sniffled. "You're going to make *me* cry. I should tease him mercilessly about that."

"Callum wanted to hold you too. He was five, I think? Insisted on carrying you around like a doll, and you should've seen the way Teller hovered, afraid Callum would drop you."

Shit, I hadn't thought about those memories in years. When we were all such little kids. Innocent. Our parents had still been around then.

Piper turned her head. Not quite looking at me, but enough I could see her profile and the sadness in her eyes.

"People used to say I wasn't my dad's child. Do you remember that?" she asked quietly.

"Yeah. I remember." I kissed her forehead and closed my arms around her. She snuggled into my warmth. "People are shitty to say a thing like that to a little girl. Teller fought another kid at school once for repeating it."

"I think it's true though. My dad worked as an oilfield roughneck. People said the timing of my birth didn't add up. As I got older, Dad would take faraway jobs for longer and longer stints at a time. My mom said it was because he couldn't stand the sight of me."

Her mother had said that to her? What the hell?

"The day of my high school graduation," she went on, "when I was eighteen, my dad told me he was glad I'd finally grown up, so he didn't have to spend another cent on me. He never even spoke to me again before he died."

"I'm sorry, sweetheart." I wished I could hold her so tight there was no room left for the bad stuff.

She wiped her eyes. "See, I'm not good at dating. You brought me on a fun picnic, and I'm being so depressing."

"I want to know everything about your life, Piper."

"You know a lot already."

"You know my ups and downs too. Some things we just understand about each other. It's nice."

"Yeah," she whispered.

"Anything you ever want to talk to me about, happy or sad, you just lay it on me."

Her head tilted. "Will you kiss it better?"

"Always."

She put her hand on my cheek, guiding me down until our mouths met. It was just us, and in that moment, we were enough.

THIRTY-THREE

Piper

We gathered up our trash, and Grayden rolled up the picnic blanket.

"Where are we going next?" I asked.

"For someone who didn't want to go on a date at all, you're pretty into it."

"I'm into having a fun day with you, and hopefully getting laid at the end of it. That's all."

Chuckling, Grayden went to repack the saddle bags and pull out the helmets.

I'd never seen him smile as much as he had today.

I was having a great time with him. An amazing time. But it was easier if I didn't think about the *date* word and what it meant.

Also, why had I never ridden a motorcycle before? It was exciting and freeing, with a hint of danger. And sexy, with how close I had to sit behind Grayden, hugging him like my life literally depended on it.

I really hadn't meant to talk about my father. Those memories were some of my most humiliating. But Grayden hadn't blinked an eye. At least now he remembered that I'd been the subject of scorn and gossip in Silver Ridge before.

Why should I care what anyone said about me now?

The chinstrap of my helmet clicked into place, and I climbed onto the bike behind Grayden. He revved the bike's engine, and then we were off.

The wind caught the tail end of my braid as we rode down the highway. I held onto Grayden more loosely this time, simply because I felt relaxed. There was something peaceful about being in the wind and the cold, surrounded by the scent of pine and hearing the birds cry out as they flew overhead.

And the whole time, Grayden was so solid in front of me. All I had to do was hold on.

The sun disappeared behind the mountains. Light faded by degrees, the view getting narrower around us. We passed the occasional car, but mostly it was just us out on this highway winding through the landscape.

We pulled into the crowded parking lot of a restaurant. I wasn't even sure if we were in Hart County anymore.

The neon sign by the door flashed the words, *The Mangy Moose*.

"Where are we?" I asked with a laugh after Grayden switched off the engine and flipped up his face shield.

"You've never been here? The Mangy Moose is famous. At least, it used to be. I was just glad it's still here when I looked it up online."

"Another blast from your past?"

He pulled off his helmet, his hair tousled and wild. "Yep. Teller and I loved this place back in the day."

I was getting new insights into my brother today, which was an odd thought, considering I was on a date. But I liked hearing about Teller from Grayden's perspective. Seeing him smile at the memories.

It gave me hope that Teller might have the same fond memories too. That he could find a way to forgive Grayden. Or at least, remember him as more than just a disgraced former soldier.

We put the helmets away. Grayden held my hand on the way inside.

When we stepped through the doorway, an indie rock song greeted us, along with a giant trophy of a moose head above the bar. The tables were made of rough-hewn wood, and the rock concert posters adorned the walls.

"Is that the place's namesake?" I asked under my breath, nodding at the trophy. "Looks pretty mangy."

"I assume so."

"Does it seem the same as you remembered?"

"The moose, yes. The rest, not really." His hand moved to the small of my back. "They used to play classic rock. And they had wood shavings on the floor. This is much cleaner."

"Sounds like an improvement."

"I dunno. I liked that it was a dive." His eyes narrowed critically as he scrutinized the place. "There was this one regular who was always slumped on the stool in the corner. Like he was glued there. Great guy."

I was snickering at him as we pulled up seats at the bar. There were little hooks underneath to hang our coats, which Grayden also managed to complain about. Also the barstools were too comfy, apparently.

I smacked a kiss on his cheek, passing him a bar menu. "You're adorable." He pretended to grumble, but he put a hand on my thigh and squeezed.

"Hi! Welcome to The Mangy Moose." A bartender set a couple of glasses of water in front of us. She looked like she'd turned twenty-one yesterday.

"This place has been here a while, huh?" I asked.

"Yeah! The building's been here for ages. The bar was closed down, like, forever. It's a landmark. Part of the local history. The new owners bought it last year and restored it to its former glory. Let me know when you're ready to order. Be sure to check out our mocktail menu."

"Local history," Grayden grumbled after she walked away. "Makes me feel ancient. The old Mangy Moose would never have served mocktails."

I flipped to that page of the menu. "They look really good."

"I guess it's a smart idea. I don't want to ride the bike under the influence. And you drank enough last night."

I elbowed him. "Maybe you should stop complaining then."

"You could stop my complaining by kissing me." He nuzzled my neck. Warm, happy chemicals raced into my bloodstream.

I liked Grayden like this. Playful and affectionate. It was just hard to accept that this was for *me*. The only man I'd ever actually dated was Danny, and he'd never given affection easily.

Ugh, why was I thinking about my ex-husband right now? For even just a few hours, I wanted to forget he existed.

"Order me a mock-arita?" I asked. "I'll be right back. Going to visit the girls' room."

"Sure."

The bathroom was freshly remodeled with new tile and a trendy sink design. Yet another clue that this place was no longer a dive bar. Well, Grayden could grump about that if he wanted to. I was enjoying myself.

I did love a good dive bar, but I liked some frills and modern touches too.

When I emerged from the restroom a couple minutes later, the place had started to fill up, and an upbeat country song was playing. An older couple was dancing in an open area, broad smiles on their faces. The way they touched each other made me think they'd been together a long time.

Sliding onto my stool, I noticed a group of twenty-something women had arrived while I was gone. One had a plastic tiara with rhinestones spelling out *Bride*. Her friends were around her, passing out shots.

I hoped the bride-to-be had better luck in her marriage than I'd had. Maybe she'd be like that couple on the dance floor. Growing old together and still in love.

My chest did something funny. My heart thudding in an uncomfortable way.

I took a sip of the mocktail waiting in front of my seat. Grayden was already halfway through his. "The bridesmaids are staring at you," I said.

"The *what*?"

"The bachelorette party over there. You're the hottest man in this bar. You've got their attention."

"They can take it back. I don't want it."

"But it's so cute. See?"

He finally glanced over, and several of the women blushed and laughed, whispering to each other.

"You should dance with them. It'll make their night."

"Piper, I'm here with *you*."

"So?" I said with a laugh. "You should give the poor bride a thrill before she signs her whole life away."

Before Grayden could keep arguing with me, I went over to the bachelorettes and held up my glass. "Congrats to the bride! Ladies, anyone want to dance with my friend over there? He's available."

Grayden was giving me an unamused look from the other side of the bar.

When several of the women jumped at the chance, he went ahead and got up with them. The heated glance he sent my way conveyed a very clear message.

He wasn't happy about this, and he was going to pay me back for it later. But hey, I was having fun.

And if I felt a twinge of something like jealousy, seeing Grayden spin the bride around with a polite almost-smile on his face, that didn't mean anything.

Sitting back on my stool, I crossed my legs and finished the last dregs of my mock-arita.

"Hey, beautiful. Want to dance?"

I looked up to find a guy around my age standing beside me, his elbow on the bar. He wore a cowboy hat and a confident smile.

"Sure," I said. "Why not?"

A dance with a stranger didn't mean anything. Just like this "date" with Grayden didn't truly mean anything. It was just a fun night out. I hadn't had one of those in too long. I should make the most of it.

The cowboy gently held my fingers and led me toward the dance floor. He gave the impression of being a nice guy. Didn't hold me too close. His hand brushed the small of my back as he steered us around in circles, his pointed-toe boots moving gracefully to the music.

The song ended and flowed into the next. His grip on me loosened, but he didn't let go. "What's your name?" he asked.

A throat cleared, and a tall shadow appeared in our path. The cowboy had to jolt to a stop to avoid a collision.

"Sorry, she promised me the next dance," Grayden said.

The cowboy stood taller, puffing up a bit. "You sure about that?"

"She's my girlfriend, so yes."

The other man backed off immediately, raising his hands. "Didn't know." He disappeared through the small group of dancers.

Meanwhile, my body was reacting to the word *girlfriend*. Terrified and elated and annoyed at the same time.

I turned to Grayden. "I don't remember promising you any dances. Or agreeing to the *G* word."

He put his arms on my hips, smoothly pulling me into a sway. "Can't even say it, huh?"

I rolled my eyes. "There's no need to say it because it's irrelevant. I'm nobody's girlfriend."

"Okay."

A grumbling hum vibrated in my throat. But I let Grayden pull me further into the circle of his arms. It wasn't such a bad place to be. My nerves lessened just from being close to him, my body ending its resistance and melting into his warmth.

"I know what you were doing, Piper," he said, whiskers brushing my ear. "Making me dance with the bachelorette party. Dancing with that other guy."

"I wasn't trying to make you mad."

He pressed a soft kiss to the tip of my ear, making me shiver. "I know. To be honest, I wasn't happy seeing someone else's hands on you. Made me want to claim you as mine. But I wasn't mad. I'm completely calm. You know why?"

My tongue was heavy, so it wasn't easy to get the word out. "Why?"

"Because you're just scared, and that's alright. I'm a patient dance partner. But don't expect me to back off and give up. Unless you tell me you absolutely don't want me, then I'll keep on being here. Ready to dance when you are."

It didn't really seem like we were talking about dancing.

Even though the song was fast-paced and lively, we were swaying slowly. I was inside Grayden's shadow, completely protected.

I pushed out a laugh, and it felt so fake. "Don't go falling in love with me, O'Neal. I'm not that kind of girl."

"No promises."

His eyes were full of a soft kind of amusement, but he didn't seem at all like he was kidding. Instead, everything about him radiated sincerity.

I couldn't take it.

I had to glance away. My lungs were going all tight and strange, making it hard to get air. But I didn't want to leave the safety of his arms. Not yet.

My hands went from his shoulders to his chest, dragging over the fabric and the hard muscle beneath. "I guess I didn't like seeing you dancing with those girls."

"It was your idea."

"I know! But if you're my date tonight, I suppose I should be making the most of it."

We danced to the next several songs. Had another drink.

After a while, my arms went around his neck, and I kissed his tattoo, my tongue sneaking out to lick the inked skin. "Want to get out of here? Take me home? You were hoping to get lucky, and the signs are pointing to yes."

His large hand squeezed my hip. "Then let's go."

THIRTY-FOUR

Piper

THE RIDE back to Silver Ridge felt quicker. Less open-ended and free, more urgent.

I kept my arms tight around Grayden, my head as close to him as I could manage without knocking my helmet into his.

My feelings were kind of a mess right now, and I knew it. But what I wanted, more than anything, was to be close to Grayden. Skin to skin. To explore him and enjoy this connection we felt.

And hopefully not talk about what it all was supposed to mean.

The things he'd said at the bar... What was I supposed to do with all that?

The bike's engine rumbled as we turned onto my street. Grayden pulled up to my garage. "I'll open it," I said, and jumped off to use my code on the little keypad. The overhead door lifted.

He parked the bike inside. Dang, he was sexy as he took off the helmet and shook out his shaggy hair. Swung his long leg over the seat to stand up.

We packed the helmets back into the saddle bags along with my borrowed jacket. Then I closed up the garage.

"Didn't want the neighbors to see the Ninja parked in your driveway?" he asked.

"*No*. I wasn't thinking that at all."

"I don't have an issue with it. It's a smart move. They might think it's Milo over here instead of me."

I swatted Grayden's arm as we walked to the back door. "Should I leave the curtains open? So the neighbors get to witness firsthand that you're my overnight guest?"

I slid my key into the back-door lock. Grayden crowded behind me, his body flush with mine, and he pushed my braid out of the way to kiss my neck. The bulge in his jeans nudged my butt cheek.

"If you want to put on a show, wild girl, I'm game. But they'll get an eyeful, considering what I have planned for you."

Yes, all of me responded. My body, my mind.

None of my confused feelings mattered when sex was the main focus.

I wanted Grayden to make me forget everything else tonight but how much we craved each other. Everything but desire and sweat and all the ways we could give each other pleasure.

The door opened, and we stumbled inside. I quickly punched in the alarm code, shutting off the system. We both kicked off our shoes.

Grayden was still touching me, and it felt more like a necessity than a possessive gesture. Like he couldn't resist this pull any more than I could.

He spun me to face him, his hands going to either side of my neck. His fingers massaged the tension in the muscles there, right where the base of my neck met my shoulders.

Grayden's mouth slanted onto mine, yet this kiss wasn't as urgent as I'd imagined it would be. We'd been building up to this for weeks. Finally getting naked together. But he was clearly in no rush. His lips slowly caressed mine.

Then he whispered, "Hi," like we hadn't been together for hours. Like this moment was something brand new.

"Hi," I murmured back.

"I'm so fucking happy to be here with you, Piper."

My next inhale caught in my lungs.

The first time Grayden had spent the night here, at my house, he'd needed a friendly face. I'd wanted to help him out more for Grace's sake than anything else. Or so I'd told myself.

And last night, the second time Grayden had spent the night, he'd been here to comfort me. To make me feel safe.

But this, right now, really was something new. We were here because we both wanted to be. This was just about *us*.

"I'm happy too," I said, ignoring the riot in my chest. Sex with Grayden could be special without it having some huge, life-changing meaning. I just had to forget about everything else and let myself enjoy it.

"Do you need anything?" he asked. "Glass of water?"

"I need you to take me to bed."

"I can do that." He tapped my hip. "Jump."

My brain took a half-second to catch up. Then I put my arms around his neck and jumped. Grayden caught me, hands bracing where my butt met my thighs. My ankles crossed behind him.

I loved how strong he was. Given my height, I'd been with men who were shorter than I was, and size wasn't a big issue to me. But the way Grayden could lift me so easily was nice too. More of a turn-on than I'd expected.

"You were kidding about leaving the curtains open, I assume?" he asked with a smile, and I laughed.

"Not actually an exhibitionist."

"We did get pretty naughty in your coffee shop. Someone could've caught us. Those windows were right there."

Arousal slid lazily along my spine. But the abstract idea of getting caught was far more exciting to me than the reality. It wasn't my kink.

"I want this to be just for us."

"Good. That's how I want it too." The gold flecks in his eyes shone. "Whatever we do tonight, it's ours. Tell me everything you want, and I'll give it to you."

Grayden carried me down the hallway. The house wasn't very

big, not much bigger in fact than the place I was renting him. Though of course I'd made every inch of this house personal to me and Ollie.

"My bedroom's at the end," I said.

"I figured it wasn't the room covered in Lego models and comic books."

Grayden carried me through the open door and set me on my feet. The lights were off in here, so I went to my nightstand and switched on the lamp.

This room was my sanctuary. The walls were a dusky blue with white wainscoting. My bed had a white duvet cover and tons of pillows in striped decorative cases. A low-slung upholstered chair sat in one corner next to my bookcase, which had a variety of used paperbacks from Silver Linings and well-worn hardbacks of my favorite classics.

I'd never had a guy here. Certainly not to spend the night.

Sudden shyness made me press my hands to my stomach. Which was *not* like me when it came to sex. Usually I was fast and eager to get things going. Maybe because I never had an entire night to share with a partner, but still.

Grayden walked toward me. "Beautiful room for a beautiful girl."

His next touch was soft, once again. A caress of his fingers moved from the crown of my head, over my hair, and down to rest on my collarbone.

"Can I undress you?" he asked.

My reply came out shaky, and I hoped Grayden didn't notice. "Yes."

Taking my hands, he walked backward and pulled me along with him. When he reached the chair by my bookcase, he sat. I stood between his open knees. Grayden stared up at me with a slight smirk that was just a touch wicked.

He was still holding my hands and tugged me forward until I kneeled on the chair, straddling his lap.

His fingers slid beneath my sweater. "Arms up."

My sweater came off. The tank top beneath. My bra. He removed one layer after another without stopping. My breaths came in shallow pants.

"Want you so bad," he murmured. "Look at you."

Then Grayden was kissing my naked breasts. His tongue laved my nipple. His lips sucked the bud, and his brown eyes flicked up like he was checking how much I liked it.

Oh, I liked it.

I gasped and dug my hands into his hair. The air of my bedroom was a little cold against my back, yet the heat inside me and radiating from him was making sweat bead over my stomach.

His mouth moved to my other nipple and sucked until I was rocking my hips. Grayden's cock was hard underneath me.

I wanted him naked, but I also didn't ever want to move from this spot.

When both my nipples were deep pink and beaded and wet from his mouth, he sat back. His gaze was pure fire as he took me in. That shyness came over me again. Making me self-conscious, which was so weird for me.

Grayden unbuttoned my jeans and lowered the zipper, revealing the pink triangle of my panties. With my legs spread like this as I sat on his lap, he couldn't undress me much more than that. But he didn't seem to mind.

He dragged heavy breaths through his nose and out again, his hands on my hips, thumbs barely grazing the silky fabric of my panties. Building up the anticipation.

"You're gorgeous, Piper. I can't get over it. So fucking perfect."

"I'm not perfect."

I liked myself, and I rarely worried about things like stretch marks from my pregnancy or how my breasts weren't as perky as they used to be before motherhood.

But the way Grayden was looking at me just seemed to strip me bare. And I wasn't even naked.

"Perfect for me," he said, as his fingers caressed a stretch mark on my stomach. "Every bit of you."

Absurdly, tears burned behind my eyes and in my throat. My eyelids closed and I breathed through it. Grayden pressed kisses to my exposed skin.

"Stand up for me?" he finally asked, barely a whisper. And I did it without a conscious thought. Something about Grayden was so commanding without him even trying.

He slid my jeans over my hips and down my legs. I stepped out of them, toeing off my socks too. His fingers hooked the elastic of my panties and dragged them down.

When I was totally naked, he brought one index finger to the juncture between my legs. Testing and teasing.

"I love how wet you are already for me. How do you want this to go? You can boss me around if you want, Piper. My manhood can take it. Or..." He leaned in, his lips brushing my hipbone. "You can lie back and open your legs for me, and I'll make it good for both of us."

My breath quickened, but the tension in me was melting away. Turning me soft and pliant in his hands. "I don't want to think right now. Want you to take whatever you like from me."

Grayden stood, his hands on my hips, his body pressing close to mine. Though of course he was still fully clothed.

He turned us both so we'd switched places.

Then he went to his knees on the rug, dragging me along with him to sit in the chair in front of him.

I spread my knees and leaned back against the upholstered back of the chair. He groaned, nostrils flaring. "That's it, wild girl. Show me everything."

Just like that, any trace of shyness disappeared, and I felt like myself again. Someone who loved sex and wasn't ashamed of that. And I knew that sharing this with Grayden would be incredible, so why hesitate?

His hands cupped the undersides of my knees. He leaned forward, tongue already darting out, and he laved over my core.

Then he paused, licking his lips like he was savoring the taste of me.

I found the boldness that lived inside me. Grabbed his hair and urged him forward again. I felt the smile on his lips and the huff of his laugh as he gave me what I wanted. Hot, uninhibited, open-mouthed kisses, right where I was most sensitive.

My hips tried to buck forward. But his grip on my thighs was firm enough I couldn't move. His tongue explored, flicking my clit and delving inside me.

I panted and moaned and shouted his name. Shameless.

Grayden certainly didn't have any shame about eating me out, either. His mouth and tongue moved like he couldn't get enough. Like I was the best thing he'd ever tasted, and he wasn't going to leave a single drop behind.

"Wait, wait," I said breathlessly.

His mouth went to my inner thigh and pressed a kiss there. "Yeah? You okay?"

"I want to come at the same time as you. Want your cock in my mouth."

"Fuck, Piper, I love the way you think."

Grayden stood up, pulling at his shirt. He stripped it over his head, tossing it aside, and went for his jeans. Without pausing, he shoved down his boxer briefs, revealing his thick, straining cock.

He was finally getting naked, giving me a chance to see all of him, and it was happening way too fast.

Before I could take a good look, he grabbed my hands and pulled me up against him. Then I was in the circle of his arms again. Our bodies zipped together. It was just the two of us with absolutely nothing in between. His cock pressed along my belly, all silky and hot.

"Can't believe I get to be with you like this," he said.

"You can't believe it? I told you about my crush on you. My younger self would be losing her mind."

"I'm hoping to make you lose your mind in just a few minutes."

Grayden gazed down at me with equal parts tenderness and desire. But the weight of who we were was present too. The past and everything that had happened to bring us here.

We were completely stripped down, and I'd never felt so safe. Just standing here with him, looking into each other's eyes, was the most intimate thing I'd ever experienced.

I was the first to break eye contact. Sinking to my knees, I dragged my hands down his chest and stomach, admiring his tattoos along the way. But I had another destination in mind.

When I reached his cock, I brushed my lips up and down his shaft, then licked at the curved barbell. The metal was smooth under my tongue.

Grayden moaned, his hips thrusting forward a little to nudge his cock head over my tongue again.

My palms braced against the taut muscle of his thighs as I closed my lips around the head of his dick. My tongue kept flicking at the piercing, and my cheeks hollowed. A burst of salty flavor hit my tastebuds.

With a desperate sounding groan, his fingers slid into my hair and rubbed my scalp. "That's enough for now, wild girl. Your mouth is too much. I won't last. I need to get my mouth on you too."

Grayden turned me around so he was behind me and nudged me toward the bed. I crawled to the middle and lay back against my elbows. With his brown eyes dark and intense, he kneeled on the bed and prowled toward me on his hands and knees.

His hard cock bobbed between his legs. Between the tattoos and the piercing and just *him*, it was the sexiest thing I'd ever seen.

As he reached me, he rolled onto his back and patted his chest. "C'mere. Straddle my face and show me heaven again."

I loved how Grayden could say something filthy, and it came out sounding sweet.

Swinging my leg across him, I lined myself up so his cock was right in front of my mouth. His hands gripped my thighs, kneading the flesh and spreading me wider. I felt him reach for a pillow and shove it under his head.

When I felt his tongue between my legs, I dipped my head and licked all around the tip of his cock.

Then I was pretty much insensible. Lost to a knife's edge of pleasure. I loved the weight and feel of his cock between my lips. The way the hum of his moans vibrated against me.

I tested out different ways of tonguing his piercing until his stomach muscles tightened and his hands squeezed my hips, his mouth licking and sucking relentlessly on my clit.

I was far drunker than I'd been last night, and I hadn't touched a drop of alcohol.

"Need you to come for me," he rasped. "Fuck, I'm so close." He brought his fingers to my clit and started rubbing, his fingertips sliding easily through my wetness.

I pulled off of him, gasping, and stroked him with my hand. "Me too. Oh, Grayden, I'm—oh—"

My eyes rolled back involuntarily. My legs shook, and I felt the orgasm racing toward me. Unstoppable. I already knew it was going to wreck me.

My mouth closed around Grayden's cock again, sucking to the same rhythm as the waves of pleasure overtaking me.

His tongue pushed inside me. The climax hit and pulled me under. I was floating and sinking and tumbling, and the only thing keeping me on this earth was him.

Grayden's cock started to pulse against my tongue a few moments later. I swallowed everything he gave me.

A perfect circle. Just him and me.

THIRTY-FIVE

Grayden

SUNLIGHT SPEARED MY EYELIDS. I was under a pile of blankets with something warm and soft and just the right amount of heavy on top of me.

Piper burrowed her face against my chest, making a sleepy sound.

I stroked her back and sighed with contentment. Last night, I'd had big ideas about keeping her up all night. Like my cock was her personal amusement park, and I had to take her on every possible ride.

Ha. After we'd given each other earth-shattering orgasms, we'd both been too wrecked to stand. Much less gear up for round two. We'd managed to stumble to her bathroom to get ready for bed. But after that, we both passed out.

I hadn't slept that soundly in a long time. Not since sleeping on her couch on Thanksgiving night with a stomach full of good food. But her bed was far more comfortable.

Having Piper pressed naked up against me, using me as a pillow, had been best of all.

She shifted. With her cheek still on my chest, she looked up at me, and I dipped my chin to look down at her.

"Morning," I said.

Her eyelashes fluttered as she blinked. "Hey."

My heart squeezed. She barely had to do a thing to get that kind of reaction from me.

I rolled so I was on my side. She tucked up against me. My arm lifted the blankets higher around us.

Piper traced her fingers over the tattoos on my upper chest. Then followed the designs across to my shoulder and down my arm. "You shouldn't be this sexy. It's wise you keep these covered most of the time. Women would be throwing themselves at you constantly. Gay men too."

"You haven't seen me in the summer. I'm usually less clothed."

"Is that a warning? You'll be waving this sexy around all over the place when June hits?"

I liked that she was talking about the future, even indirectly. "Doesn't matter. I won't be looking at anyone except you."

Piper's teeth dug into her lip, and her gaze moved away. Maybe I'd said too much, suggesting we would still have something going on months from now.

But it wasn't easy to hide how I felt. I didn't ever want to lie to Piper.

"I used to be a string-bikini girl," she said. "When Grace and I used to drive out to the lake a million years ago in the summer."

I ran my hands down her body beneath the blankets, mapping her curves. "I'd love to see that. We should do that sometime when it's warm. Go to a lake. Does Ollie like to swim?"

I knew I was pushing my luck. Piper chose the avoidance route, sitting up and dangling her legs off the bed, arms stretching up. "I'd better get the coffee started or I'll be a zombie all morning."

"You don't seem that zombie-like."

"The orgasm last night and lots of sleep helped. But I'm running on fumes now."

"Stay here. I can give you another orgasm. I'm fully stocked."

"Coffee first." She popped up, sending me a coy glance over her shoulder and wiggling her round butt cheeks.

After grabbing a fleece bathrobe, Piper went out to the kitchen. I threw on my jeans and followed.

Unlike yesterday, when she'd been hungover, Piper was all smiles this morning. She made the coffee, and I threw together breakfast again. An omelet this time with shredded cheddar and some roasted red peppers from a jar in her fridge. A little more fresh cilantro.

We ate at the counter. It felt casual and easy. The kind of morning I could get used to. Ollie wasn't here, but of course he was on Piper's mind. She checked her phone and found some texts waiting.

"They're already up and getting food before the big game." She showed me the latest selfie of Callum and Ollie decked out in Broncos gear. They were all wrapped up to face the cold. I smiled at Ollie's goofy expression.

Hell, I missed the kid. I really did. His attitude and his big personality. While I loved having Piper to myself for a while, I could imagine the three of us on a Sunday morning like this too. Relaxing and laughing. Going for a walk and playing keep-away in the park.

Was I an idiot to hope for that? To dream of Piper giving me that kind of chance?

Probably. But hope was free. Disappointment hurt, but so did all the shit that life dealt out whether you hoped for better or not.

I had hope where Ashford was concerned, too. My ideal future didn't just have Piper and Ollie in it. It had both of our families together. Acceptance.

That happy ending seemed a long way off. Maybe it was nothing but a pipe dream. The kind that could break your heart just from how real it seemed before true reality crashed down.

But I wanted so fucking badly for it to be real.

After breakfast and more coffee, we wound up in the shower

in Piper's bathroom. The shower was like the rest of her house. Not huge, but inviting and cozy.

I stood behind her and kissed the wet droplets that ran down her neck.

My cock was throbbing and swollen against her lower back. Balls heavy and full. Like I hadn't come last night at all. She made me so hard. Especially because of how much Piper clearly enjoyed sex. Her mouth made me crazy, not just her talented lips on my cock but the things she said.

She arched her back and wiggled against me. "Want you."

"Here? Or your bed?"

"Right here. I can't wait. I need your tongue again. Please."

Nngh. My cock thumped from how horny and desperate she sounded.

I turned her to face the shower wall. "I'll give you what you need."

"I know. I trust you."

Fire ignited in my veins, flames licking the underside of my skin. She'd said those words to me before, but not like this. Not like she was putting something precious in my hands.

"That means a lot to me. Your trust. I'll take good care of you."

Piper could pretend this was just about sex if that made it easier for her. But to me, my promise was about so much more than today.

"Hands on the tile, sweetheart. Spread your legs."

Kneeling on the ground behind her, I gripped the backs of her thighs. Used my thumbs to spread her open more. Piper arched her spine.

Oh, that was heaven alright.

I moaned and closed my eyes at the first taste of her. Just as good as last night. But I didn't think either of us were in the mood to drag this out. For one, we had the water heater to consider.

So I was merciless. Sliding my tongue over her clit with the pressure that had made her scream last night.

"Like that," she moaned. "Please. Just like that."

My blood was thick with arousal. My cock begged for attention, but not yet. Not until I had her falling apart on my tongue. Adding my fingers, I sought out the perfect movements that would take her apart.

"There! Don't stop." Piper cried out, convulsing around my fingers and tongue.

I gentled the pressure but kept giving her what she needed until her legs tried to close, and I let her go. She leaned against the shower wall.

Standing, I grabbed the bottle of conditioner and slicked my cock. "Can I use your thighs, wild girl?" I didn't have a condom, and it was important to me that we have that talk. Now wasn't the time. I was way too close to the edge.

"Mmm, yes. That sounds hot. Do it."

My cock slipped and slid as I thrust between her clenched inner thighs. Piper was just the right height for me, the perfect combination of flirty and sweet and filthy. She kept urging me on. Begging for more.

I came with a roar of her name on my lips, my head swimming as black spots stole my vision.

Perfect.

I would've taken Piper back to her bed to spend the day there. But I had to return Milo's Kawasaki Ninja before he decided I'd taken off with it.

Piper stopped to kiss me as I sat astride the bike, ready to fire it up. "Maybe we could borrow it again sometime?" she asked.

"Yeah. I bet we can. Have a special place in mind for our next date?"

Her cheeks pinked. "Just thinking about how sexy you look riding it. That's all."

"Okay. I'll make it happen." I winked and pulled the helmet on. Piper could play coy all she wanted. She'd brought up a next time, and that was enough for me right now. "See you in a few."

Piper followed me to Milo's shop in her Subaru. I was going to return the bike, but from everything she'd said, we weren't going to say goodbye just yet. We still had hours and most of the day until Ollie and Callum would return.

The motorcycle shop had a closed sign in the window when I pulled up, but Milo's head popped through the door a moment later. "Hey! I'll pull up one of the garage bay doors. Pull in."

I rode the bike inside and parked it where he pointed. The shop was full of bikes in various states of repair, tools, and parts. The place smelled of metal and grease and a hard-day's work.

"Hope you weren't waiting for me," I said, placing the borrowed helmet on a table. "I slept in."

He laughed knowingly. "Nah, I was just in here tinkering. Dealing with some paperwork before the week starts. Your date went well, I take it?"

"It did."

I hadn't mentioned to Milo that Piper was my date, but I had a feeling he could guess after seeing us together the other day.

"I really appreciate this," I added. "You're a good friend, man. Anytime you need a favor, just ask. You're first on my list for ink when my studio's open."

He nodded, but something darker passed across his features. A moment of uncertainty.

"What's up?" I asked. "Need a favor sooner?"

He hesitated, then shook his head. "No, nothing like that. But there's something you might wanna know. That cop who was with Chief Nichols when they responded to the drug tip at your place? Chad Bronski?"

My shoulders tensed. Officer Bronski, who despised me for existing. "Yeah, what about him?"

"He was in here yesterday afternoon with his pal Dillon Kirby, picking up a couple dirt bikes that were in for maintenance. They were talking about you."

"Dillon? Is that the same kid who works at Silver Linings?"

"Yep. He works there. From the way they were shit-talking you, I'm guessing Dillon isn't president of your fan club?"

"Hardly. Officer Bronski's the president. Dillon Kirby is the chief executive officer."

Milo snorted. "Well, Bronski said you were prowling around Piper Carmichael's house on Friday night."

"Fuck's sake," I muttered. "That was someone else. A guy broke into Piper's garage, and she called 911. Bronski barely lifted a finger to find the real culprit. He let the guy get away."

Milo held up his hands. "Look, I knew it sounded like bullshit. I piped up, telling them Piper's your girl and that must be why you were at her place. I mean, I assume she is, right? That's who you were out with yesterday?"

The muscle in my jaw worked. Piper had said, over and over, that she didn't care who knew about us spending time together.

"I'm not sure I can say Piper's my girl. I'd like her to be. But yes, she was with me yesterday. I was only at her place on Friday because I was invited."

He crossed his arms, nodding along. "Exactly what I figured. But anyway, when I said that, Dillon seemed pretty pissed off. He clearly didn't like hearing it. Just wanted to give you a heads-up."

"A heads-up that certain people don't like me in this town? It's not news, but I appreciate it. Hey, you won't believe what was actually in that suspicious 'drug' package planted at my house."

I told Milo the brick of powder turned out to be powdered sugar. He thought that was seriously messed up, considering how much trouble it caused me in the short term. But funny in a sick way.

"So you still think it was Piper's ex Danny?" Milo asked.

"I'm sure of it. He all but admitted it to me later that night. Then he said he'd take a payment of two hundred grand in exchange for Piper and their son. Said I could have them if I paid him off."

Milo whistled. "Dude. That's fucked."

"Couldn't agree more. It could've been Danny behind the break-in at Piper's garage on Friday too."

"He's that desperate for money?"

I dragged a hand over my beard. "I don't know. I have no idea what's in that man's head. He's essentially a coward, though. Sneaks around and threatens and tries to intimidate Piper, but I think he'll back down."

I'd seen Danny put his hand on Piper's throat, and I wasn't going to forget that. But I'd known many violent men in my past. Ruthless killers. I simply didn't believe Danny Carmichael was one of them.

I would protect Piper and Ollie from him, but Danny would slink away soon enough. Like a rodent seeking out the shadows.

Milo blew out a breath, shaking his head. "You know, I'm impressed. For someone who hasn't been back in town long, you've made a lot of enemies." He clapped me on the shoulder. "Let me know if you ever need backup."

"Thanks."

THIRTY-SIX
Piper

I SMIRKED at Grayden as he got into the passenger seat of my car. "Thought I was going to have to drag you out of there. Was Milo trying to talk you into buying the Kawasaki?"

"Something like that." Grayden leaned in for a kiss. "Missed you."

"It was only fifteen minutes."

But I missed you too, I thought. Ridiculous as that was.

I felt giddy. Waking up next to Grayden had been amazing. Comfortable and warm and just...nice. And sexy, obviously. I'd enjoyed the chance to admire him some more at a close distance.

It made me nervous when he talked about us doing things together in the summer. Bringing Ollie along, which was something we'd do if we were in a serious relationship.

I'd resisted the idea of being with someone for so long. But with Grayden...

I shook off that train of thought, not ready to follow where it could lead.

"Where should we head next?" I asked. "Back to my place?" I gave him my best flirty smile, remembering the steamy shower we'd taken an hour ago.

Everything we'd done together so far had been hot. But Grayden's cock still hadn't been inside of me yet. If this weekend ended without a chance to get underneath him, I'd be seriously disappointed.

He twirled a lock of my hair around his finger. "Let's stop by my place. I'd like to show you something."

"Is it sex-related?"

His head tipped back with a laugh. "You have a one-track mind, Piper. No, it's not about sex. But we could break in my futon afterward."

"Let's do it. I haven't had futon sex since college."

His thumb brushed my nose and then my lips, his expression so full of affection I had to glance away.

"You make me so damn happy," he said. As if that was a normal thing to say during...whatever this was. Were we still on the date? Was this just a wild sex weekend now?

I put my car in gear and pulled onto the road. "And then we can grab lunch."

"Okay."

I rolled my eyes. He was doing it again. Saying "okay" in that weird, complicated tone. Like he knew things I didn't, and that fact amused him.

It was just a couple of turns to reach Grayden's street. *Our* old street, though every time I visited the house, it felt less like the place where I'd grown up. Grayden was turning it into something different. Something better.

I parked across the street from the house, since I was pointed in that direction. Grayden unlocked the door, leading the way inside. He went to the wood stove to get the heat going.

Last time I'd been here, we'd been freaking out about the police visit and that fake package of drugs. Today, I actually looked around the front room. There was fresh paint, and the flooring was finished. Also an antique-looking desk piled with papers.

"This is what I wanted to show you." Grayden put his hand on my back, ushering me toward the desk. "Here."

They were sketches. Several of a mountain landscape with the buildings of Main Street nestled at the bottom. It was Silver Ridge.

I spotted my coffee shop, the details of the building perfectly accurate.

"Grayden, these are so good."

"I've been brainstorming for a mural to paint on the big wall there, behind the desk. But I got inspired yesterday, before I picked you up for our date, and I tried it from a different angle."

He handed me another sketch. This was a more stylized view of Main Street, close-up, less realistic. There was a single row of buildings, some of the most iconic businesses. Like Hearthstone Brewing, Main Street Market, and the souvenir shop that carried the weirdest stuff.

Silver Linings was front and center. Again, not realistic, since my building was on a corner.

But clearly, realism wasn't the point of this drawing. There were evergreens and aspens growing all around the buildings, and the road was a meadow full of wildflowers instead of concrete.

There were people too. Just rough depictions. But I spotted a kid doing a trick on a skateboard in front of the coffee shop. He was leaping into the air with one hand on his board. The sight made me grin.

"There's a lot more I want to add," Grayden said by my shoulder. "But what do you think?"

"I don't know much about art."

"You know design. Your house is beautiful, and so is Silver Linings. You have a great eye. Imagine this is the first thing people see when they walk into the studio."

I set down the sketch, turned to Grayden, and wrapped my arms around his neck. "They'll be blown away. It's incredible. You're incredible."

I'd said that last part without over-thinking it. Grayden beamed at me. "So are you." He kissed me. One of his hands was in my hair, the other on my hip.

The kiss turned from sweet to dirty in seconds. His tongue licked into my mouth. Our bodies pressed close.

Then there was a creaking sound and an intake of breath. "*Piper*?"

I broke the kiss with Grayden and shifted toward the sound.

Grace stood in the open front doorway. Her hand was still on the knob, and she was frozen there with a look of horrified shock on her face.

"Gracie." Grayden touched his mouth, like he was realizing exactly how much his sister had just seen. Just a kiss, but that kiss had felt like *everything*. What was she going to think?

"I was stopping by to say hi. I was going to knock, but I saw you inside through the window, and the door was unlocked, and... Oh my God, I'm sorry."

Grace spun and dashed out the door.

Crap.

"I'll go." Grayden started to follow.

"No, it should be me." Grace was my best friend. Basically my sister.

I had to explain why she'd just caught me with her brother.

Grace had left the house, but she hadn't gone far. I spotted her in the driver's seat of her SUV. She was just sitting there staring at the steering wheel. Hadn't even switched on the engine.

I tried the passenger door. It opened, so I slid into the seat. "Hey."

Grace barely glanced at me. "I just thought I'd stop by and see him. I should've texted first. Not just walked inside."

"No, Grace, it's fine. I'm sure Grayden would love to see you. We just happened to be..." I waved my hand. "I didn't mean for you to find out this way."

"I'm guessing you would prefer I didn't find out at all. And I'm feeling the same way. You and my brother?" She sounded shocked and maybe a little disgusted. Which didn't make me feel too great.

"It surprises me too," I said.

Except I'd had a crush on him since I was fifteen years old, so I'd certainly imagined a scenario like this. I'd been smart to never tell her about that.

Grace's hands gripped the steering wheel. Like she wanted to strangle something. I hoped it wasn't me.

"I probably shouldn't even ask, but how long has this been going on?"

There was so much she didn't know. I had to start at the beginning if there was any way she might understand.

"Well, he spent the night at my house on Thanksgiving."

"*Thanksgiving*? The same night he got to town, the two of you..."

"*No*. Hold on, no. That's not what I meant." This wasn't going well. I brushed my hair back. "On Thanksgiving, I saw Grayden in his truck. I was pretty sure he didn't have a place to stay, so I offered my couch. After what happened with Ashford that night, I wanted to make sure Grayden was okay."

Grace's throat moved as she swallowed. "Alright. That makes sense. Why didn't either of you mention that before now?"

"I don't know. He was embarrassed, I think. He didn't want you and Callum worrying about him. And after that, he started renting the house from me. There was one day that Danny showed up here, and Grayden..."

I squeezed my eyes shut. It was hard to get all of this out.

"What happened, Piper?"

"Danny broke in here looking for something. I caught him, and Danny attacked me."

"*What*?"

"But Grayden stopped him. He was there for me. And after that, we kept getting closer, I guess. Nothing really happened between us until just a couple days ago, though."

I was leaving out the time Grayden first kissed me, but she probably didn't need an exact play-by-play.

Grace breathed, seeming to process everything I'd said. "I heard something about police showing up here the other day. I was actually going to ask Grayden about it. Did that have something to do with Danny too?"

"Yes," I said on an exhale. For once, I was thankful for the Silver Ridge gossips. They'd caught Grace up on recent developments. "Danny's trying to punish Grayden for protecting me. It's completely stupid, but you know my ex."

She rubbed her face beneath her glasses. "So Danny has been back in town, and he's been harassing you. Worse, he *attacked* you. Are you okay?"

Tears burned in my eyes. "Yeah. I'm okay."

Because of Grayden. He'd made everything better.

"Can I hug you?" she asked, tears in her eyes too.

"Of course." I leaned over, and Grace and I hugged tightly. This was why she'd been my best friend my whole life. Because, no matter what, even when we fought, she still loved me.

Yet I'd kept these secrets from her.

Guilt made nausea rise in my throat. "I'm sorry, Grace. I just didn't want to scare you. Or for you to think you needed to fix it for me. You've already been through so much."

She pulled back, frowning. "So you and Grayden both don't want my help?"

"It's not like that."

"Sounds like that. And then you and Grayden, you've been... I mean, that kiss didn't look like your first."

"He spent the night at my place again last night. But not on the couch."

She groaned and dropped her head in her hands. "I cannot believe we're discussing this. *Gross*."

"I've discussed my sex life with you plenty of times before."

"But not involving my *brother*!" Grace swatted my arm.

A giggle snuck up my throat. She looked like she was holding back a laugh too. Then her expression smoothed out.

Her glasses had gone crooked, so I reached out and straightened them for her.

"Thanks," she said.

"You know I love you. Always."

"And I love you." She took my hand and squeezed it before letting go. "I'm confused, though. Is Grayden just convenient? I mean, I know Hart County isn't huge, but there have to be other attractive men out there."

"Okay, ouch. Are you trying to ask if I've already slept with all the other available men in our county?"

She snorted. "You said it, not me."

"I changed my mind. I hate you."

Grace laughed and flipped me off.

"But Grayden's trying to get back on his feet," she went on. "Trying to get settled again here. Why him? Why *you*? Piper, I don't want to sound like I'm judging either of you, okay? But if the two of you wanted a no-strings arrangement, couldn't you look elsewhere? Not my brother? Not my best friend?"

"You sound pretty hypocritical. Dane is Ashford's best friend."

"Okay. Fair. But we didn't keep it a secret from Ashford. And even from the beginning, it wasn't just casual between Dane and me. I might've pretended it was, for like five minutes, but it always meant something deeper. Right away, we had feelings for each other."

"Who says I don't have feelings for Grayden?" I blurted, without even thinking.

Grace's eyes widened. She stared at me. "What are you saying?"

Panic flooded me, making me want to run from the vehicle. Somehow I managed to stay put. "I don't know."

"Are you serious about Grayden?"

"I don't *know*."

"Where do you see this going? Like, a relationship? Love?"

My head fell back, and I groaned. I had a negative knee-jerk reaction to that word. At least its romantic sense.

But.

But.

"Piper, you're the woman who swore up and down, on pain of death, that you would never fall in love again. Or have a relationship. All you would ever do is no-strings."

"I meant it," I said desperately.

"I know we had that no-dating pact, and I broke it when I fell for Dane. Of course I want the same for you. But I just didn't expect it. Didn't really think it was possible, given how adamant you were."

"I didn't either. Until...him."

That admission cost me. It rearranged things inside of me that I'd thought were fixed in place. Atrophied, even. Grayden made me imagine a different possibility for me.

But imagining wasn't enough to make it a reality. Real life was cruel and hard. Men you trusted could end up hurting you. *Breaking* you.

But.

"Okay," she said softly. "I get it now."

"You do? Because I don't. I'm so confused."

Grace reached for my hand again and held it. "I was confused about my feelings for Dane, too. Remember what you told me? You said I should trust myself. Trust my instincts."

"Well, what did I know!"

She smiled. "Fear will lie to you, babe. But your heart tells the truth. Listen to it."

THIRTY-SEVEN
Grayden

I PACED AROUND the front room, keeping an eye on Piper and Grace through the window. They were sitting in Grace's SUV. Just sitting there and talking.

At one point they hugged, which seemed like a positive indication. Grace had run out of here, but she hadn't driven off. Wasn't yelling, far as I could tell.

Of course she wouldn't. Grace wasn't angry like that. Like me and Ashford.

I still worried I had hurt her, though. I never wanted to hurt my sister. Some of the biggest decisions I'd made in the past had been designed to avoid hurting Grace.

And yet I'd ended up hurting her anyway by being out of her life for so many years. Sometimes a guy couldn't win.

After about ten minutes, Piper and Grace both got out of the vehicle and approached the house. I thought about pretending I hadn't been watching them. But what was the point of that? So I opened the door for them and stood aside.

"Hey, Gracie," I said as she walked into the house again.

"Hi. Sorry about earlier. I should've called ahead or something."

"Don't be sorry. You're always welcome here."

"That's pretty much what I told her," Piper said.

I shut the door and touched Piper's back, running my hand down her spine over her sweater. I wanted to kiss her and ask how she was feeling, but my sister's presence stopped me. For the moment, anyway.

"We good?" I murmured to Piper instead.

She didn't answer. Grace turned and faced us, arms crossed over her coat. She was glancing from Piper to me.

"Can we talk?" I asked Grace.

"I was going to suggest that."

Piper took a step away from me, and my hand fell back to my side. "I'm going to call Ollie and Callum," Piper said. "Should be kick-off pretty soon. I want to say hi."

Grace nodded at her, and the two of them shared a serious look.

Well, shit. My stomach churned, nervous about what exactly the two best friends had been discussing in that SUV. Piper was already so skittish about us having a future.

"We can sit in the kitchen," I offered after Piper stepped outside. "Not much seating in here just yet."

"It's looking great, though. Wow. I can't believe this is Piper and Teller's old house." Grace glanced around the room, stopping beside the desk to study my drawings.

"Sketches for a mural. It'll go on that big wall. This area will be reception. Don't have a studio name yet, but I'll work that into the mural."

Hell, I was rambling. Time to get to the point. I was the older brother here, and I owed it to my sister to make this easier for her.

"Grace, it wasn't my intention to keep this a secret." *This*, obviously being my dating Piper.

She shrugged. "I get it. Piper said it's pretty new. Whatever's happening between you two. You went on a date yesterday?"

"We did." I was glad Piper had told her. "She means a lot to me. I didn't expect any of this when I came to Silver Ridge, but I care about her."

She took a slow breath. "Good. If you didn't, I'd have to punch you in the nose or something, and I already know how much that would hurt my hand."

A laugh burst out of my chest.

"I'm ready to sit down now," she said, leading the way to the kitchen. When she reached the table, Grace took a seat and folded her hands on the table like this was a business meeting.

My stomach dropped. I felt like a guy called into the boss's office to get fired.

I slowly dragged out the chair across from her and took a seat. "Are you supposed to give me the bad news?"

"Bad news?"

"I just barely got Piper to agree to go out with me. I pushed for too much, didn't I? Moved too fast. She's scared." This wasn't Grace's fault, of course. Just that her showing up gave Piper a ready excuse for why we couldn't work out.

Grace's mouth dropped open. Closed. Opened again. "She's scared, yes. That's true. But there's no bad news. Not right now, I mean. This is... I'm still trying to get used to the idea."

I exhaled. Alright. So I still had a chance. "I'm sorry. Not sorry for what I feel for Piper. But sorry this is hard on you. I know it's complicated."

"That's the thing about love. It actually makes complicated things seem really simple."

"I know what you mean. Wait, did you say love?"

What exactly had Piper said to her out there?

Grace gave me a hard look, sitting forward. "You know Piper and Ollie are a package deal, right? If you want to be with Piper, you have to think of her son too."

I rested my arms on the table and scooted my chair closer. I couldn't believe we were talking openly about me and Piper being together. It gave me a hell of a lot of hope. "Absolutely. Ollie's an amazing kid. He detested me at first, not that I can blame him for being skeptical."

"Kids are honest."

"Yeah, that's something I admire about Ollie. The kid made sure I knew he had his eye on me."

"Callum told me he saw you and Piper and Ollie having dinner at Hearthstone. But I didn't think... I guess I just didn't see this coming. Not even close."

"Do you have a problem with it?"

Tears filled her eyes. "I'm just afraid of losing you again. I couldn't take that."

I reached across the table to put my hand on her arm. "You won't lose me. No matter what happens between me and Piper. I came here for you and Callum and Ashford and our family, and I'm staying."

"What about Teller? He and Piper are my family too. *Our* family."

I glanced at the table. This same damn table where Teller and I had sat so many times. "I haven't spoken to him yet. I don't expect him to approve of this. Of me with Piper. But I have to try, Grace."

There were plenty of other factors too, and I wasn't sure how much of that Grace knew. Like Danny's threats and my need to protect Piper and Ollie from him.

I could've protected them as a friend. Set my true feelings aside and been the better man. Refused to risk upsetting the rest of our families. Refused to tarnish her reputation in Silver Ridge with mine.

But this, what I felt for Piper, was undeniable.

Grace sent a glance toward the back of the house, where Piper was on the phone with Ollie. "Are you in love with her?" Grace whispered.

"That's where I'm heading."

She blinked, and those tears hovering in her eyes fell. "Oh, Grayden. Then I want this for both of you. It won't be easy for Piper, though. You have to be patient with her."

"I'm planning on it. I'm glad she has you." I already loved my sister like crazy, but I adored her all the more for being such a good friend. "Proud of you," I said. "I'm sure Ashford and Callum deserve a lot of credit for how great you turned out."

"Hey, I'm awesome all on my own."

"Of course you are."

She grabbed both my hands. "And you were around for plenty of important things when I was growing up. You were there for all of us when mom died. You stepped in when dad left. Nothing that happened afterward takes away from that."

Dammit, now I was getting choked up.

Grace deserved the whole truth. Every ugly reason that I'd cut off contact when I was in prison.

She'd probably had enough revelations today. I wanted her to keep looking at me like I was the big brother she loved. But we'd just been talking about Ollie's brash honesty. I could take a page from the kid.

"Gracie, you know you can ask me anything, right? Anything about what happened. My arrest, my prison time. All of it. I don't want to keep secrets from you."

She was still gripping my hands, but her eyes drifted to the window over the sink. "Do you want me to ask?"

No. Yes. No.

I was a coward for making this her decision. But that same old hesitation held me back. I never wanted to hurt Grace, that was a given, and this *would* hurt her.

"It won't be easy to hear. Or easy to say."

"Then it can wait. You served your time, Grayden. That includes the years you spent after getting out, thinking we never wanted to see you again. We've been through enough sadness. We're still going through it because Ashford is so damn stubborn."

"I don't blame him."

Annoyance flashed across her features. "I kind of do, but I'm trying not to. Maybe when Ashford's ready to listen, you can tell all of us about those awful years and what happened. But I just want us to be a little bit happy in the meantime. Okay? I want you to try to make this work with Piper."

"I will."

Grace stood up, opening her arms. I got up and pulled her into a hug. Had to bend way over to do it because she was so small.

"Fair warning," she said against my shoulder. "If you break Piper's heart, I might have Dane hire someone to kill you."

I chuckled into her hair. "And if she breaks my heart?"

"She'd better not. That's all I have to say."

THIRTY-EIGHT

Piper

AFTER I FINISHED CHATTING with Ollie and Callum, I stayed in the backyard for a long time. My head and my heart were both a mess.

I'd told Grace I had feelings for her brother. She'd handled it surprisingly well. I, on the other hand, couldn't stand still.

Could I have a relationship with Grayden? Let myself fall for him? Invite him, not just into my life, but into Ollie's? Even if I could be willing to risk my heart, what about my son's?

Just the fact I was considering it was mind-blowing.

After a while, Grayden opened the back door and stepped outside. He came over to me, his hands in his pockets.

"Grace took off. She wanted to see Dane. Said she'd like to tell him about us, and I said yes. Hope that's fine."

"Of course. Yeah."

"How was your talk with her?" he asked.

"I was going to ask you the same thing. It was alright. She was surprised, obviously, but she understands now. Grace is the best."

"She is." Grayden shifted his weight, looking at me like he was trying to read something in my face. "Can I kiss you?"

"You don't really have to ask at this point. We're probably past that."

"You seem pretty tense, though."

"I'm not."

My shoulders were up near my ears.

"Piper," he murmured, and closed the distance between us. Cupped my face in his hands. "Whatever's spinning through your head right now, it's okay. We don't have to figure it all out yet."

Grayden pressed his lips to mine briefly. Then came in for another soft kiss. And another. Giving me the chance to breathe in between.

I felt my shoulders dropping. My defenses lowering. Exactly what always happened when I was around him.

"Do you want some lunch?" he asked. "I can whip up a couple of my world-famous hot dogs. Got the ingredients in the fridge."

"World famous, huh? Word got around that fast?"

"Hey, this is Silver Ridge. People talk. Or I could take you out to Hearthstone. Doesn't matter to me. Just as long as I get to be with you. We're still on our date."

"Is it still our first official date? Or did we move on to the second?"

"You're up for a second date?"

My heart kicked in my chest. "I could be persuaded."

We had the rest of the afternoon and early evening to be together before Ollie returned home. After Ollie was back, I'd have more time to think and figure out what to do about the future.

The big, scary, unknown future. That might just include Grayden as my boyfriend.

Grayden smiled and kissed me again, more thoroughly this time. Overwhelming me and leaving me breathless.

"My place," I said. "I don't want lunch. I'd much rather have you."

When we reached my house, I shut and locked the door. Grayden was giving me another *look*. Searing me with that intense gaze of his. Like he was trying to see into me.

I wanted him inside me, but there was only one way I could handle right now.

"Kiss me?"

"Coming right up."

Grayden took my mouth in a blistering kiss. We were alone again, behind closed doors. Just us. Everything felt easier when we were like this.

"Tell me what you need, Piper," he said between kisses.

His question was bigger than this moment. I knew that. I hadn't missed the deeper meanings of the things he'd been saying since yesterday.

"Need you to fuck me. Show me how it would feel..."

"Hmm?" he prompted, kissing my neck as his hands traveled the length of my body. "Tell me."

"Show me how it would feel if I were really yours, and you were mine."

Grayden picked me up. I wrapped myself around him. He carried me to my bedroom, kicking the door shut. Set me gently on the mattress and lowered himself on top of me, still showering me with kisses.

His fingers popped the button on my pants. I helped, lifting my hips for him to pull them off. Then he pressed himself onto me again, the thick bulge in his jeans rutting against the crotch of my panties. The way he rocked his hips was dirty and a little rough. Exactly what I needed to get out of my head and focus on this moment.

"You want my cock thrusting inside you, wild girl? You want to feel me?"

"Yes," I moaned. "I need it. Give it to me."

Grayden sat back to yank his shirt over his head. I wiggled my sweater up and off while still lying flat on the bed.

I loved every detail of Grayden's body. The tattoos, the

dusting of dark hair on his chest and along his stomach. All the hair on his legs and forearms and his beard. So blatantly masculine.

He opened the fly of his jeans and pulled his cock out, stroking. His tip was deep purple, and his piercing glistened in the low, warm light of my bedroom. We'd left the lights off, and afternoon sunlight bled around the edges of my curtains.

"So hot," I breathed.

His fingers toyed with the barbell in his cock head, tugging the curve of metal back and forth. Grayden made a low sound like the feeling of it was pure ecstasy, and somehow I felt it in me too. That jolt of wicked pleasure.

I wanted more. Everything.

He lowered himself to the mattress, moving down until his shoulders fit between my legs, and he pressed a kiss to the crotch of my panties. Then ran his tongue over the fabric, getting it even wetter than it already was.

"Grayden," I gasped. "Please."

"Condom?"

"Drawer. Over there."

While Grayden reached for my nightstand, I stripped my panties off and unhooked my bra, tossing both garments somewhere on the floor. He pawed around in the drawer before turning back to me, giving me a heated, predatory look.

"What is this?" He held up my little bullet-shaped vibrator. His amused smirk told me he definitely knew what it was.

"It's nothing," I said in a teasing tone.

"Do you use this to make yourself feel good, Piper?"

"Sometimes." I usually kept it better hidden, but since I was alone this weekend, I'd put it in my nightstand. That had been way back on Friday, when I hadn't known if I'd see Grayden or not. So much had changed.

"Do you want to see?" I asked.

A feral growl rumbled from his throat. "Fuck yeah, I do."

He handed me the vibrator. I stretched my other arm over my

head and let one of my knees bend and fall open. My hair fanned over my pillows.

"You are so gorgeous." His gaze devoured me. Consumed me and gave me life at the same time.

I switched on the vibrator and brought it between my legs. The first buzzing touch made me shudder and whimper. But as I kept going, sliding it just where I needed it, my breaths came faster and I lifted and lowered my hips.

Still watching me, Grayden got up and pushed his jeans all the way down. Then his boxer briefs. When he was naked, he kneeled on the bed again. Right between my legs. He gripped his cock and stroked a few times, stopping to thumb absently at his piercing.

I hadn't even noticed that he'd grabbed a condom. But he held it up with his free hand. "I'm happy to use this if you want me to. You make the call. I'm negative."

"Same. I haven't been bare with anyone since..." I felt myself frowning, my body going cold. "Sorry." Last thing I wanted in my head right now was my ex-husband.

Grayden tossed the condom to the mattress and crawled up beside me. He took the vibrator from my hand. "I've never been bare with anyone. But I want you like that, Piper. So fucking bad. I want to feel you on my cock. Claim you. Do you want that?"

"Yes," I whispered, relaxing again and leaning into him. We were side by side. Skin against skin.

The vibe was still buzzing quietly. Grayden brought it between my thighs and slid the toy up and down over my clit. My head fell back against the pillow. "Oh, like that. Again. Please."

"Tell me when you're close. Right on the edge. Okay?"

I nodded, moaning at the jolts of pleasure spreading over my body. "It's so good."

Moving so he kneeled between my legs, he kept teasing the vibe over my clit. Withdrawing the toy and advancing. Until I couldn't stand it anymore. "I'm going to come. Please don't stop. Keep it right there. I—"

Grayden pulled the vibe away, downright evil, and I was about to tell him so.

But then he lined up his cock head at my opening and pushed inside. He thrust shallow and fast, angling his hips, and intense pleasure detonated inside me. Stealing my words. My breath.

I grabbed for my pillow over my head and just held on as wave after wave crashed over me.

Panting, Grayden slowed his thrusts, looking down at me with a satisfied smirk. "I think you liked that."

"A little."

"Nothing little about what's happening here, sweetheart."

He slid his shaft all the way into me, seating himself fully. I wrapped my legs around his hips. Dug my hands into his hair and pulled him down to kiss me.

Grayden was all around me. Filling me. His kisses were deep and hypnotic. A little messy too, like this was affecting him as much as me. He wasn't even moving, and still the sensations were overwhelming enough to have my heart thrashing.

When he finally broke the kiss, he lifted onto his arms to stare down at me. And I had an excellent view myself. His strong body above me, his hair wild and hanging into his face.

His hips shifted, and I whimpered at how incredible it felt. His cock pulled out a bit more, then surged forward. I squeezed his hips with my thighs.

I didn't ever want this to end.

He kissed me again for a while, pairing the caresses of his lips and tongue with flicks of his hips. Drawing out the pleasure.

I felt like a sparking live wire, and he was sharing all that electricity. Like I was made for this, and Grayden was the only man who'd ever fit me so exactly.

Even just breathing felt wonderful. Filling my lungs with something beautiful and sweet. Because I was breathing him in, and he was breathing me.

I had to be delirious with these thoughts I was having.

I only came back to reality when he pulled out. "What're you doing?" I asked.

He nudged my hip. "Roll over for me. On your belly."

I did. Grayden pushed my legs apart, and his cock slid easily back inside me. My moan was shameless, but it just felt so right.

My head turned to the side, and Grayden's chest rested lightly against my shoulders. He felt deliciously heavy against me, though he was holding up most of his own weight.

He kissed my hairline. My ear.

Then he stroked his cock inside me again, and I felt his piercing hitting a spot on my inner wall that made me arch into him. The sound I made was guttural and primal. Made of nothing but sex.

"More," I moaned. "More."

"You like my cock, wild girl?"

My snark broke through the haze of lust in my brain. "Obviously. Give me more, or I'll flip you over and reverse cowgirl you to within an inch of your life."

Grayden belly-laughed, and I felt it inside me. "We're definitely doing that sometime. Fuck. Maybe I want that right now. I can't decide."

"*Grayden.*" I wiggled back against him.

"Alright, alright. Calm down, you needy thing. I've got you."

He pumped his cock with smooth, sure movements. It felt so good I almost couldn't take it. I was moaning and begging. But the best part was the way Grayden was falling apart too. His body was slick with sweat, radiating heat, as he panted and groaned into my ear. Giving me so much pleasure, but using me for his pleasure too.

I reached back to grab his hip and feel the flex of his muscles with every thrust.

"You gonna come for me again?" he growled.

"I'm so, so close."

"I'm trying to hold out for you, but you just feel too damn good."

Suddenly Grayden withdrew and flipped me onto my back. He pushed my knees open and sheathed his cock inside me again. Then I noticed he had my vibrator in his hand.

He thumbed it on and held the vibrating toy against my clit.

The climax hit me hard and fast. Making my entire body clench tight and shudder. Almost immediately, I felt Grayden's cock pulsing in answer.

His hips rocked against me a few more times, his rhythm faltering as he groaned huskily.

Grayden tossed the vibe aside and fell forward onto me. His arms snaked around me, his mouth seeking mine. He was still inside me, and I was wrapped around him, and I couldn't tell where I ended and he began.

That should've been terrifying to me. But in that moment, I didn't want any separation from Grayden. I wanted to believe we could have this closeness forever. And neither of us would ever let the other be hurt, ever again.

THIRTY-NINE

Grayden

We took a long, leisurely shower. I couldn't keep my hands off her. My mouth either. We washed each other and kissed and laughed.

I'd never had sex like that before. Like we were both completely in tune.

I was so fucking gone for this woman.

By then, we were starving. Piper and I made pasta in her kitchen. She pulled on a tank top and sweats, and I was just wearing my jeans. I wanted to keep this sense of intimacy between us for as long as possible.

"You're making it difficult to cook," she said with a laugh.

"I get it, but the thing is, I need to be holding you. This is not negotiable." I tickled the side of her neck with my beard.

She giggled and turned in the circle of my arms to face me. Which led to making out. My cock firmed up optimistically, but I doubted I could come again so soon. Not after I'd already gone off three times in the last twenty-four hours. I wasn't twenty anymore.

"Shit! The onions are burning." Piper grabbed for the wooden spoon.

We finally got lunch made and sat down to eat at the table. I pulled her chair as close as possible.

I took a bite of penne and chewed, thinking. After I swallowed, I said, "I should tell Callum about us, since Grace knows. You okay with that?"

She set down her fork. "Yeah. Grace handled it pretty well, after the initial shock. Callum's not going to stumble in on us kissing. So he'll be fine with it too. Don't you think?"

I wasn't so sure. Callum was easygoing most of the time, but he was fiercely protective of those he loved. I wouldn't want him to be any other way.

He truly loved Piper like a sibling. Of that, I had no doubt.

"I think it'll be alright, once I explain things to him. But I need to do it sooner rather than later. He should hear it from me first."

"How about you tell him tonight? After he drops Ollie off?"

"You want me to stay that long?"

She looked down at her plate. "Yes. Why not?"

I'd been looking for signs constantly of where Piper's head was at. It wasn't easy to tell. I mean, reading her cues during sex had been second-nature. She didn't make a secret of what she wanted, which I loved.

But when it came to *us* outside the bedroom, what was our status? Would she agree to be exclusive? There was no question I wanted that, but I didn't know if Piper was ready.

Sometimes patience was easier said than done.

"What exactly should I tell Callum?" I asked. "Can I tell him we're dating?"

Piper stirred her pasta with her fork. "I guess. Sure, that's fine."

I tried not to take her lack of enthusiasm personally. "Piper, I want to be with you. In case I haven't been clear. But I also don't want to push you too fast. I told you I'd wait, and I will. Just know I'm serious about you. In fact, I'm pretty crazy about you."

"I..." Her eyelashes fluttered and she looked up. Those pale-green eyes met my gaze and held. "Okay."

My eyebrows lifted. "Not sure how to take that. 'Okay' isn't a real response."

She pushed my shoulder, and I laughed. "Now you see what it's like," she said.

I held on to her chin and kissed her, a smile on both our lips. She hadn't pushed me away or insisted relationships weren't for her.

We were dating. Officially. Also, having the hottest sex on the planet.

Seemed like progress.

Piper put on a movie, and we curled up on her couch. It was a comedy of some kind, and I didn't pay it the least bit of attention.

I was just savoring this. Having her in my arms. But the clock kept ticking down.

Piper was thrilled she would see Ollie soon, of course. She showed me every photo Ollie texted from the game and the start of the drive back home.

Ollie had sent one selfie sitting in Callum's passenger seat, covered in new Broncos merch. He was wearing a foam finger that barely fit in the frame. Then a picture of Callum driving and flashing a peace sign along with a huge smile.

I couldn't wait to see them either. Especially Ollie, partly because I was really starting to care about the kid. And partly just because Piper adored him so much. It was amazing to see the affection between them.

It made me think of my own mom. She'd loved us deeply. It killed me that Piper never had that, and all the more touching to see her give everything to her son.

I wanted to give everything to both of them.

It was around ten o'clock when Callum's truck drove up.

Piper had been tracking their progress, so she and I were waiting on the porch. We went down to the curb as soon as the truck pulled up.

Callum parked and went around to the passenger side. He extracted a sleeping Ollie from the seat. "Conked out an hour ago," he whispered, holding out Ollie's bag to Piper.

"I've got it," I said, taking the strap of the duffel. Callum did a quick double take, just now noticing me standing there.

Piper smoothed back Ollie's hair. He was out cold. "Thank you so much, Callum."

"We had a blast. I'll carry him inside."

Callum and Piper went in first, and I brought up the rear, setting Ollie's bag in the living room. There was some laughter while Piper tugged off Ollie's shoes and Ollie woke up, flopping around in Callum's arms.

"Good, you're awake," Piper said. "You can brush your teeth."

"I'm not awake, Mom."

"Are you sleep talking?"

"That's a thing!"

"But sleep arguing is not."

They went to Ollie's bedroom. I listened to them from the living room, leaning my shoulder against the wall with a stupidly happy grin on my face.

Fuck, I wanted this. Little family moments. The small, perfect memories that added up day after day to a good life.

My eyes burned as I imagined it.

Could I really have that with Piper and Ollie? Would she open up enough to let me?

Callum came out of Ollie's room first. "Hey. Didn't expect to find you here." He gave me a quick hug.

"I was hoping we could talk. Do you have a couple more minutes?"

Callum clapped a hand on my shoulder. "Yeah, big bro. Can't

stay out too long or Zandra will kill me. But I've always got time for you."

We went out to the front porch. Callum rested his weight against the railing, and I stood with my arms crossed over my long-sleeved shirt. I hadn't bothered with a coat. The cold was welcome. Sharpened my mind so I could hopefully say the right thing.

"Ollie talked about you a lot this weekend," Callum said.

"Oh?" My head lifted. "He did?"

"Yeah, man. I heard about the skateboarding trick for the ages that went epically wrong. And how you helped him out after."

I stuck my hands in my back pockets. "Ollie kind of hated me before that. I earned a few points."

"More than a few. He also mentioned Piper liking you, and I wondered what was up with that. How much he was exaggerating because he's nine, and how much was accurate."

"Uh, that's what I wanted to talk with you about. Piper and I are dating."

Callum was quiet, and his expression didn't change.

"Grace found out today," I added. "So I wanted to tell you. Wasn't sure how you'd feel about it."

"Does it matter how I feel about it?"

"It does. I want to be with Piper, and if she's on the same page, nothing's going to stop me. But I do care what you think, and if you need me to talk it through with you, I will."

His face scrunched up. "Well, I don't love it. It's fucking weird, honestly."

"Which part?"

"All of it!" Callum took off his Broncos cap and put it on again, backwards this time. "But let's start with the fact that you haven't been back in Silver Ridge more than a few months. Is this why you really came back? Because you secretly had designs on Piper?"

"*No*. Not remotely. She was still a kid the last time I saw her before...everything. I came back for you and Ashford and Grace.

A hundred percent. And for *me*. So I could have a life here. Earn a life here."

"And this thing with Piper just happened?"

"Yes and no. I felt drawn to her right away. To who she is now. I tried to stay away from her, I swear to you I did, but in the end my heart wouldn't let me."

"Your heart."

He huffed, shifting his weight with his hands on his hips. The porch creaked beneath him. I could tell he was building up to something.

"Piper doesn't date. You know that, right? She's committed to being single. So this is some kind of fling. Do you know what you're risking if it doesn't end well? Ashford hasn't even forgiven you yet. Grace and I are just getting to know you. This could fuck up *everything*."

Okay, so Callum was being more difficult about this than Grace had been. As I'd known he might.

Part of me wanted to get defensive. But I couldn't do that with my little brother. I could not allow this to put new barriers between us. And I couldn't let go of Piper either.

"I understand you being skeptical. Completely. But we *are* dating. Piper agreed that I could tell you those very words tonight. She knows I'm serious about her, that I want to be in a relationship with her, and she's nervous. I'm not denying that. But she's at least open to it."

Callum sat down against the railing again. Like that news had shocked him so much he couldn't stay standing.

"She's open to being in a relationship," he said. "With *you*."

I had to laugh at that. "Yes, with me. Can't help who you fall for, can you?" I held up my hand. "Not that Piper feels that way about me yet. But I'm sure as hell falling for her."

"Wow. I really hope, for all our sakes, that this works out." Callum pushed out a breath. "Geez, listen to me. I sound like an asshole. You just want to be happy, and you deserve that. You and Piper both deserve that."

A huge weight lifted. Sounded like he wasn't completely against this.

I was just grateful to be back in Callum and Grace's lives. And lucky they were both so forgiving, even if Callum tended to resist at first.

"You're happy, right? With Zandra?" I asked.

His expression softened. "So happy. She's my whole world."

"That's what I'd like too. With Piper and Ollie, if I'm lucky. I know you love them, and I swear I won't hurt them."

"I also love you." He wiped a hand down his face. "This thing with you and Piper will take some time to get used to, but I'll get my shit together. Okay? I'll be rooting for you."

"Thank you. That means a lot. I love you too."

Callum opened his arms. "Alright, bring it in. We need to hug it out, and then I need to go home and see my girls."

"Girls? Who else is there besides Zandra?"

"Chloe and Daisy, man. Our fur babies. Gotta go home and get some kitty-cat snuggles. From Z most of all."

I laughed and clapped him on the back as we hugged.

Then he pulled back and gave me a more pensive look. "There's other stuff we need to talk about, huh? Stuff about the past."

I nodded. Same thing that had been on my mind earlier with Grace.

"Grace hasn't wanted to push the issue," Callum said, "and I don't really want to rock the boat either. But I don't think Ashford will be able to move forward until he knows everything. Like, why you cut off ties with us after your sentencing, when you should've needed us most. Why you refused to defend yourself or even explain."

The lump in my throat made it tough to speak. Callum and I had never spoken so openly about those subjects, even indirectly.

Which was ironic, since it was always in the back of my mind. In all of our minds, probably.

"I can tell you tonight," I said. "Right now."

He took a step back, recoiling slightly before his sheepish smile returned. "Not tonight. I need to get home. But soon."

"Soon," I agreed. "Whenever you're ready."

He patted my arm once more before heading to his truck. I stood on the porch, my arms crossed.

Callum and Grace both seemed to know, at some unconscious, instinctual level, that nothing would be the same after I told them the whole story. They wouldn't ever look at me the same.

Maybe I was the one who wasn't ready.

FORTY
Piper

THE FRONT DOOR OPENED. I heard Grayden's footsteps on the tile. I'd been scrolling my phone and pretending to read random articles while sitting on the couch, but really, I'd been waiting for him to come back inside.

He stepped into the living room. "Ollie's asleep?"

"He surrendered to brushing his teeth, but he went out like a light when his head hit the pillow. How'd it go with Cal?"

Grayden came over and sat beside me. But he left some space between us, and I didn't like that. I put my legs up on the couch so my bent knees would touch his thigh.

"Was it bad?" I asked.

"Nah, not bad. Callum's not thrilled with the idea of you and me together, but he said he's rooting for us."

A blush crawled up my neck. "That's good."

"It is." Grayden draped his arm over the back of the couch. "Do you have an early morning tomorrow? Should I get going?"

"No, stay." I reached for him instinctively, like I might physically keep him from leaving.

Who was this needy, possessive woman who'd taken over my body?

"You should stay the night. Have breakfast with me and Ollie before I take him to school. I'm not due at Silver Linings until after that."

"You sure? I would love to, but it seems like a big step."

My logical side wanted to deny it, but the flutters inside my body agreed. It was a big step. I still wanted it. "You should sleep on the couch. Ollie knows you've done that before, so it won't be such a shock. But I want him to get to know you better."

Grayden brought his hand to my cheek. I leaned into the touch. "I want this so fucking badly, Piper. I have to be honest."

"You're always honest with me." Even with the fear still waging a war inside me, I knew that about Grayden with zero doubt.

"Am I, though? I haven't lied to you about anything, but I still haven't told you everything you need to know about me."

"Grayden—"

He brushed his thumb over my lips. "No, don't make excuses for me. I should've told you all of it already. You said weeks ago that you don't know who I am. And really, you still don't."

"I don't believe that. The past isn't everything."

He pulled me closer and kissed my forehead. "That's the irony, though. You can't say the past doesn't matter if you don't know what it is. You studied literature. You know all about irony."

I laughed even though I felt like I might cry. Something amazing was happening between us, something I'd believed was impossible for me. I just wanted to savor that. Why was Grayden trying to mess it up?

"All you have to do is listen," he said. "Please?"

"Okay. I will."

I tucked my head beneath his chin. He put his arm around me.

And then, after a few loaded moments of silence, he started talking.

FORTY-ONE

Grayden

"FIRST FEW YEARS in the Army, my anger fueled me. I told you that. I was kind of an asshole. Didn't make many friends. Joining the military seemed like the best option for me, for a whole host of reasons, but I missed everyone here too. It was like I hated Silver Ridge, and I also felt like huge parts of me were missing, not being here. Does that make any sense?"

"I think so."

"Teller and I hadn't enlisted together, but we were stationed the same place at first. Then his career took off pretty fast while I was barely skating by. We started to grow apart. He tried to be a friend and understand what was going on with me, but I didn't let him in."

Piper traced a finger over my thigh, drawing a pattern on the denim. "Teller never told me that. He's always been pretty quiet about his years of service."

"Well, most of this he didn't know. I met this skinny kid named Aaron Drummond. He reminded me of Callum and Ashford, but he had anger like mine boiling inside him. Aaron despised his father, like I did. I befriended the kid. Tried to keep him out of trouble. And we just clicked. I started to feel more settled, like I'd needed a younger brother around to set a better example for."

She smiled against my chest.

"Aaron's background wasn't like mine, though. Like yours and mine. He came from money. At that point, I didn't know exactly who his father was or what he did for a living, but Aaron told me he'd grown up privileged. I thought that difference between us didn't matter. In fact, it bonded us even more. Having a similar experience with uncaring fathers even if we'd grown up in the opposite circumstances."

I huffed a soft laugh.

"Also, Aaron let me borrow his Yamaha Supersport. That elevated his status in my head too."

"I bet," Piper said.

"Things were actually looking up for a while. I wasn't getting chewed out by my superior officers as much, and Aaron met a girl he really liked. Got engaged when they found out she was pregnant. But he still had a chip on his shoulder. When Aaron drank, his anger came to the surface, and I was usually the guy trying to pull him back."

She stroked my hand, threading our fingers together and apart. So sweet and soft, and yet she gave me the strength to keep talking.

"One night, though, I was the one getting drunk and belligerent. It was the anniversary of my mom dying. We went to a bar on base. I proceeded to get shit-faced. Some other soldiers were in the mood to get rowdy, I guess, so I decided to oblige. There was a certain guy who was especially awful. Private Ricker. His favorite hobby was saying shit to rile Aaron up. But that night, everything the man said was riling *me*."

My heart was beating hard. I wondered if Piper could feel it.

"Even now, I don't have a clue what set me off. But I threw the first punch. I remember that, clear as day. Everything that happened afterward was a result of that one stupid impulse. I started it, and that's something I can never take back."

"You didn't mean to."

"But I did, Piper. I punched Ricker in the face with everything I had. That would've been enough to earn me a reduction in rank and confinement, if not worse. I'm still so fucking ashamed of it. Losing control like that."

She lifted her head to look up at me. I averted my gaze to the wall, my expression stoic, but the racing of my heart and the emotion in my voice probably spoke volumes.

"I told you," I said. "I'm not the hero in this story."

"Doesn't sound like there's a hero at all. Just people messing up and being human."

My eyes squeezed shut for a second. "Suppose so."

"Someone died in that fight?" she asked.

She could see where this ended. The night my entire life had shifted and gone off track.

I nodded. "It got chaotic fast. A dozen of us brawling. Glass breaking, fists flying. Within minutes, somebody shouted that the MPs were on their way. Time to get out of there, but I couldn't find Aaron. I hoped he'd already bailed, and I ran out the back."

I took an unsteady breath.

"That's where I found Aaron. He had Private Ricker on the ground. Whaling on him. Ricker was bloody and unconscious. I dragged Aaron off him and didn't think. Just told him to go. Run. The MPs got there less than a minute later."

"They blamed you?"

"I told them it was me." My voice was raw. "So many things flashed through my head right before. The fact that Aaron was engaged with a baby on the way. The fact that I'd thrown the first punch and started the stupid fight. Aaron was like my kid brother. I had to protect him, like I would've done for Ashford or Callum. I was responsible."

"You were drunk. Hardly in your right mind to make a confession."

"Didn't matter. A dozen witnesses could confirm I'd punched Ricker in the first place. My knuckles were torn up already. It all fit. But I didn't know Ricker would die. I wasn't thinking through all the consequences. What it would really mean for me."

Pain bled from my voice. The shame and guilt that had wracked me all these years.

She put her hand over my heart. "But Aaron just left you to twist in the wind? What the hell? How could he do that to you?"

I rubbed my cheek against her hair, taking comfort in her even more than I was giving it.

"When I learned Ricker had died, I realized how badly I'd screwed up. Not that I wanted Aaron to suffer, but at that point, I could've been on the line for murder. I'd never see my family again. I thought about changing my story, but why would anyone believe me? So I tried to get in touch with Aaron. My only hope was that he'd come forward and confess."

"But he didn't."

"Nope. His father showed up to see me at the stockade, where I was being held."

"The father Aaron despised?"

"Exactly. Aaron had called him for help. Told him everything. Turned out, his father's a big-shot attorney with high-powered clients and friends. People with serious political power. He told the MPs he was my lawyer, so he could talk with me privately. Aaron's dad said I had two choices. If I tried to tell anyone the truth about what happened, he would destroy me and everyone I cared about. And I'd still go to prison anyway because he'd make sure I was courtmartialed and found guilty for murder. Or, I could accept a plea deal from the prosecutor and keep my mouth shut."

"Oh, Grayden," she whispered. Her fist tightened on my shirt, as if she wanted to absorb some of the pain I was feeling. "So that's why you pled guilty to manslaughter instead. Refused to explain what really happened to your siblings."

"Yes."

"Why did you cut off all contact with everyone, though? Your siblings and Teller."

Teller had tried to speak to me a few times, but what could I possibly say? It had been easier to put up a brick wall of silence. Same as Ashford and Callum and Grace. I'd refused to speak to any of them after my sentencing.

"I was too ashamed. Just...fucking broken. I'd done something impulsive for someone I thought of as a brother, and that destroyed my entire life. I thought it would be better for you all if you forgot about me. I know I hurt everyone, and I'm so sorry for it. So sorry."

A tear streaked down her face.

"Piper, I understand if you don't see me the same way after this. I should've told you before, whether you wanted to hear it or not."

She pushed back a little from me. "You think I'm that judgmental? I'm sorry it happened to you, but even more than that, I'm furious. I want to know the full name of Aaron's father and anyone else who was involved. So I can..." She waved her hands. "I don't even know. Something terrible because they deserve to get what's coming to them. You didn't destroy your life. It was stolen. It was *stolen*, Grayden."

I brushed her tears with my thumb as they kept falling.

For years, I'd hated myself for throwing that first punch. For taking the blame for my so-called friend.

The story wasn't as bad as it might've been. Better than my worst critics in Silver Ridge believed, anyway. I wasn't a killer. But I'd still blown up my life. I'd made choices that had terrible consequences and hurt the people I loved.

"What if you hadn't survived your prison sentence?" she asked. "If we'd never had this chance..."

"C'mere." I pulled her into my lap. "I hate making you cry. Ollie's not going to be happy with me. He doesn't want you to be sad, and neither do I. I haven't even told you the rest of it yet."

"I can't talk anymore," she said. "Can't feel anymore."

"What can I do?"

"You don't have to do anything. Nothing you told me changes what you mean to me."

It was the best thing she could've said. I hadn't been sure what Piper would think. But she wasn't pushing me away. Instead she wished she could avenge me. I adored her for that, even though I'd given up a long time ago on my record being cleared.

Piper saw past my mistakes. She still wanted me. That meant everything.

She straddled my lap and kissed me. I kissed her back, pulling her up against my body. My cock responded to her proximity, hardening against my thigh. But this wasn't even about sex. It was just the need to be close to her.

"Take me to my bedroom," she said against my lips.

Was it possible to fall for someone this quickly? It had happened little by little over the last couple of months, and then in a cascade effect over the last few days. The more I knew about Piper and how she viewed the world, the deeper I fell.

It had to be possible. Because I was completely and utterly in love with this woman.

I picked her up and carried her. Piper rested her head on my shoulder. When we reached her room, I set her on the bed and closed and locked the door.

We undressed quickly. I just wanted to be skin to skin with her, and she clearly wanted the same.

Piper pushed back the covers. We crawled beneath them, and my blood quickened when she was pressed fully against me. Warm, smooth skin. Her golden hair, light brown eyelashes. I wrapped my arms around her and held her close, gazing into her green eyes. She did the same to me.

"So beautiful," I murmured. "How do you get more perfect every time we're together?"

I'd never been in love before. Never felt anything like this. For a lot of my life, I'd never believed I could have something, some*one*, this pure and soft and beautiful.

But Piper was right here in my arms. This was the third time we'd been naked together in Piper's bed, and every time, it had felt more and more like a place I could belong. There was no way I could ever let her go.

I couldn't tell her yet, because she wasn't ready to hear it, but hell. I desperately wanted to tell her.

I love you.

We kissed slowly. Trailed hands over bare skin. She lay on top of me, long hair falling in a curtain. I rolled us so I was above her, my erection nudging her stomach.

"We'll have to be quiet," I whispered.

When I slid inside of her, she sighed and put her hands on my face. We kept kissing and touching as our hips rocked.

Piper felt like home.

Still kissing her, I rolled us again so she was on top. She sat up to ride me. Her eyes were still a bit red around the edges from her crying, and that did things to my chest.

"Want to make you feel good," I said. "No more tears, okay?"

She draped herself over me and nodded, her hair brushing my shoulders. "You said you won't hurt me, and I believe that. But I won't hurt you either, Grayden. I want to keep making you happy."

"Just be with me, and you will."

She was killing me. Tearing me down to my base elements and building me back up again. Before coming back to Silver Ridge, I hadn't expected much from the remainder of my life. I'd had small hopes. Like finding solace and peace, having a few genuine friendships. My art. Some kind of relationship with my siblings.

But with Piper, I felt like I had a shot at my wildest hopes coming true.

FORTY-TWO

Grayden

SOMETHING POKED MY SHOULDER.

"Grayden? Hey, are you awake yet?"

I opened one eye and saw Ollie peering down at me. He poked me again, this time on my forehead.

"Ow."

"Oh, good. You're awake."

Making a sound halfway between a laugh and a groan, I sat up on the couch. "Good morning. Did you sleep well?" I asked.

"Yeah." He bounced on his toes. "Did you?"

"Until about two minutes ago, yep."

"My mom's still sleeping. Her alarm hasn't gone off yet, but sometimes I get up before her. Then I saw you out here."

I braced myself for more questions. What was I doing here? Why had I spent the night?

But Ollie seemed to be taking it in stride. "Hey, do you wanna see the chemistry kit Uncle Callum bought me at the museum in Denver?"

"He—heck yeah. That sounds awesome."

"Were you going to say hell? You can say that around me. It's okay."

"Right, I almost forgot how mature you are."

While Ollie ran to his room, I stopped by the bathroom. Despite the fact that I'd been up late with Piper, and we'd had a difficult conversation, the guy in the mirror wore a happy smile.

I started the coffee in the kitchen. Ollie talked me through the detailed instructions of his science kit, which seemed to be focused on making slimy stuff that would gross out adults.

"Should we make some breakfast for your mom?" I asked.

"Yeah, she would like that. She's always in a rush in the mornings."

"What would she like to have?"

He put on a thoughtful face. "Probably chocolate chip pancakes. With chocolate syrup on top."

"Really? Your mom's big on chocolate for breakfast?"

"Loves it."

I felt that huge grin on my face again. "Okay. We'd better get started."

After finding some pancake mix in the pantry, I had Ollie measure out the milk. "You kept my mom company over the weekend?" he asked as he stirred the batter.

"I did. We had a nice time." Wow, was that an understatement. It had been the best three days of my entire life. "Sounds like you did too."

"Yeah." He tilted his head and peered at me through his dark blond bangs. "Maybe the next time I hang out with Callum, you can come too. Since he's your brother and all."

"I would love that."

By the time Piper wandered out of her bedroom, we had a stack of pancakes ready, and Ollie was setting the table. "What's all this?" she asked. "Is it my birthday or something?"

"Nope, just Monday." Ollie smiled at her. "I better get the chocolate syrup!"

I handed Piper her coffee. We sat at the kitchen table to eat, and the quiet beauty of this moment hit me.

Piper's knee touched mine beneath the table and she smiled behind the rim of her coffee cup. Like she could feel it too.

Ollie shoveled down his breakfast in about five minutes and dashed off to get ready for school. I got up to rinse the dishes, and Piper leaned against the counter beside me.

"Hi," she whispered. She cast a glance over her shoulder, making sure we were alone, and leaned in for a kiss. It was far more chaste than heated. Full of tender affection.

"I'll miss you today," she said.

I stroked her cheek. "I'll miss you more."

I thought of Danny Carmichael and the twisted offer he'd made me. *Pay me off, and I'll never see Piper or Ollie again. You can have them.*

Piper and Ollie weren't his to bargain with anyway. But they were priceless.

Danny would always be Ollie's father, but I hoped I could have a role in Ollie's life too. If I earned it.

"I'll see you soon," I said after another quick kiss. I'd be counting the minutes.

But a few days apart might be a good thing. It would give Piper a little time to consider all I'd said to her this weekend.

"Do you want to come over for dinner tomorrow?" she asked.

My heart did a flip in my chest. The things this woman made me feel. "Absolutely."

"Where's your backpack?" Piper called out, grabbing Ollie's lunch from the counter.

The sound of running feet echoed through the hall. "Am I taking the bus today, Mom?" he called out.

"Doubt it, Ollie-bear. Pickup at the bus stop was five minutes ago. I'm driving. Let's roll!"

I smiled and picked up Piper's coat, holding it open for her to slide in. "Anything I can help with?" I asked. "Want me to look for the backpack?"

"Nope, we're just about set. Come with us. I'll drop you off at your place after I take Ollie to school."

"Nah, that's alright. You've got enough on your plate, and I could use a walk."

"That's like, eight miles!"

"I'm capable of walking eight miles. Looks like a beautiful day out there. I could use some exercise. I've spent way too much of the last few days horizontal."

Her frown shifted at the edges, almost turning to a smile. "I don't like the idea of you walking along the road. It's not safe."

Ollie still wasn't here, so I kissed her forehead. I liked when she was protective of me. "I'm not actually going to walk the whole way. I was thinking I'd stop by Callum's, and he or Zandra can probably give me a ride. I'll be fine."

Once Piper and Ollie were both piled in her car, they took off for school. I waved goodbye from the sidewalk.

This morning had been wonderful. I wanted so many more just like this. A million at least. Except, if I was lucky, waking up next to Piper in bed rather than on the couch. Maybe driving Ollie to school myself on my way to my studio.

Could that really be my life?

I whistled, hands in the pockets of my coat, as I started down the sidewalk. A shiny car turned onto the road, heading in my direction at a fast clip. I barely gave it a glance. Enough to notice it was a Lexus.

The next moment, the Lexus veered toward me. Jumped the curb. Shouting and cursing, I leaped out of the way. The car took out a mailbox and slammed into a truck in a neighbor's driveway.

I landed hard on my side after avoiding the vehicle. For a couple of seconds, I was frozen with shock.

What the *fuck*?

That was Danny's car. Had he just tried to *kill* me?

I shoved to my feet and lurched toward the vehicle. The figure at the driver's seat was slumped over. Not moving.

I reached the door and tried the handle. It opened. The airbag had deployed. Danny Carmichael lay against the white fabric, barely conscious.

I would've assumed the airbag had stunned him. Except for the blood soaking the lower half of his shirt and the driver's seat.

"Hey!" someone shouted. "Holy shit, my truck! What the hell, man?"

I turned and saw a guy running toward us from the nearest house. The owner of the truck Danny had just t-boned, I assumed. "Call 911!" I shouted. "He's injured."

"Is he drunk? He just destroyed my new Silverado!"

"I don't think the injury is from the accident. Just call for an ambulance! Hurry!"

I yanked off my jacket and held it against Danny's side, where blood was still pumping from some kind of wound. From the amount, he'd been bleeding for a while. Driving like this. Had he been heading to Piper's house?

I hated this man for what he'd done to Piper and Ollie. How he'd treated them. But he was still Ollie's dad. I knew exactly how it felt to lose a parent, and I didn't want Ollie to go through that.

"Don't you dare die, you asshole," I growled. "You'd better fucking hang on."

FORTY-THREE

Piper

As I STEPPED into my office and started up my computer, I felt like I was walking on clouds. Not even the ever-present stack of invoices and bills could get me down.

Pulling out my phone, I sent off a text to Grayden.

> Dropped off Ollie at school. He kept talking about making pancakes with you on the drive. He had a great time. Maybe we can do that again soon?

I kept typing, even though he hadn't responded yet.

> Let me know when you're home, okay? So I know you didn't actually walk along the two-lane highway and have an unfortunate meeting with a delivery truck?

Ugh, I regretted that sentence the moment I wrote it.

I shouldn't joke about something bad happening to him. Grayden was a grown man and capable of getting himself home.

Was I coming across as too needy? I hadn't been in a position like this in...*ever*. Having a crush on a guy, wanting to be with him constantly. Wanting to know where he was and if he was thinking of me. If he was okay.

Even in the early days with Danny, it hadn't been anything like this.

Last night, after Grayden had told me how he ended up in prison, my heart had been overflowing with too many things. I'd felt something like heartbreak before, after Danny dashed all my hopes of love, but there was no comparison.

My heart truly broke for Grayden and what he'd lost. What those people, the Drummonds, had taken.

I'd tried to show Grayden what he meant to me. Show him that nothing he'd told me gave me any doubts about him.

Then this morning, the way he'd smiled at me conveyed nothing but relief and happiness. I loved making him feel that way.

There was a knock at my office door, and Rina poked her head in. "Hey, Piper. The payment system is being weird again."

I sighed. "Coming."

After solving that problem and dealing with a few other issues, I returned to my office, where I'd left my phone. There was a message from Grayden waiting.

As I read it, a fist closed around my heart.

Piper, Danny's at the hospital. He's hurt. Don't know what happened. But I found him.

WHAT??? Where are you?

I called Grayden. No answer. My stomach was in knots.

My phone rang in my hand, but I didn't recognize the number.

"Hello? This is Piper," I said breathlessly.

"Ms. Carmichael? I'm a nurse at Hart County General Hospital. I'm very sorry to call like this, but it's about your husband, Daniel Carmichael."

"Ex-husband," I corrected automatically. But the rest of my brain was frozen in shock.

"Daniel has been admitted as a patient," the nurse said. "You're listed as his emergency contact."

"What happened?"

"I can't give too many details over the phone. He was brought in about an hour ago, and his injuries are serious. The doctor needs to speak to someone as soon as possible."

"Oh my God," I whispered. "Okay, um, I'll come." My heart was in my throat.

"Drive safely," she added. "Come to the front desk at the main entrance and give your name. Someone will be ready to bring you back."

I tried calling Grayden again. Voicemail.

What on earth was happening?

I drove way too fast to the hospital, calling Grayden's phone again and again. Finally I gave up and called Grace instead. "Danny's hurt, and Ollie's at school, and I don't know where Grayden is—"

"Piper, slow down, okay?" Grace asked. "Tell me exactly what happened."

"I don't know!"

"Just start at the beginning."

Hart County General was a good half hour away, even driving at top speeds. When I finally reached the hospital, they took me to a family waiting room. I felt like I was going to crawl out of my skin.

They told me Danny had been *stabbed*. That news blindsided me. And Grayden had found him? It just didn't make any sense.

And Ollie. My baby was at school instead of with me. He was going to be terrified. I wanted him here. I had to hold him, know he was safe.

But I was stuck here, waiting for news while Danny was in surgery.

About an hour and a half later, Grace and Ollie came rushing in.

"Momma," he sobbed as I caught him in my arms. "Is Dad okay? Aunt Grace said he's hurt."

I locked eyes with her over Ollie's shoulder. "He's in surgery right now. The doctors are helping him."

"But—"

"That's all I know for right now, Ollie-bear. I'm sorry."

Grace's eyes held mine. *Grayden*, I mouthed silently. She shook her head. I'd told her over the phone that Grayden found Danny and texted me, but hadn't been answering his phone.

So she didn't know where he was either.

"Callum's trying to see what he can learn," she said. "I texted our whole group thread. We'll figure out what's going on."

But an hour later, we still had few answers. Ollie was watching videos on an iPad Grace had brought, because she was a genius.

I wanted to pace across the waiting room. Curse to let out my frustration. But I couldn't. I had to keep myself together for my kid. Couldn't let him see me coming apart at the seams.

Why hadn't I heard from Grayden yet? Was Danny going to be okay?

Even through all our difficulties, I'd never wished for him to disappear from Ollie's life. Our son deserved better than that. I would never wish physical harm on Danny either.

Stabbed. Who could have done this?

Finally, a doctor came in and motioned for me.

Ollie looked up as I stood. "Mom?"

"Stay with Aunt Grace for a minute. I'll be right back."

We stepped just outside. "Ms. Carmichael?" the doctor asked. She looked young, mid-thirties maybe. "I'm Dr. Richardson. I was part of the surgical team working on Daniel today. I understand he's your ex-husband?"

"Just tell me how Danny is. Please."

She nodded. "He sustained two stab wounds to the abdomen.

The blade penetrated deeply enough to cause significant internal bleeding and lacerated his spleen. We performed emergency surgery to control the bleeding and remove the spleen. He tolerated the surgery, which is encouraging."

"So he's going to be okay?"

"He's stable right now, which is different from okay." Her voice was gentle but careful. "He lost a substantial amount of blood before he arrived, and his body has been through serious trauma. He's receiving more transfusions, and he's on a ventilator to support his breathing. We also have him sedated. We're giving his body the best possible chance to begin healing without additional stress. We'll be watching closely for any signs of complications."

I covered my mouth with my hand. "How long until he wakes up?"

"We'll start to wean the sedation after twenty-four to forty-eight hours. It's the next seventy-two hours that are most critical. It's difficult to give an exact recovery timeline. But he's being monitored constantly, and our team is doing all we can."

I felt numb. All the anger I'd felt at Danny, all the pain he'd caused me and Ollie both… I would never have wanted it to end like this.

"My son. I mean, our son. He'll want to see Danny. Is that allowed? He's nine."

She gave me a sympathetic look. "We'll allow a short visit with you accompanying him. But your son might be frightened by what he sees."

A breath punched out of me.

"Is there anyone else we can call for you?" Dr. Richardson asked. "Does Danny have any other family we should notify?"

"Not really. No. But I have family. They're helping me."

"That's great. If Danny's condition worsens, we may need you to make decisions. Do you understand?"

"Yeah. I do."

I understood perfectly. Danny had nobody but me and Ollie. He'd burned every other bridge, and we were the only ones left.

I didn't want to care about what happened to him. It would be so much easier if I didn't care. If I were as callous to Danny as he'd been to me.

Damn it, Danny, I thought.

Dr. Richardson said a few more things, but I barely heard the words. She walked away, and I leaned against the wall of the hallway.

Who could have attacked him? And why?

I pulled out my phone and tried Grayden's number again. It rang and rang.

I was about to go back into the waiting room when a different voice said, "Excuse me, Ms. Carmichael?"

Two Silver Ridge PD officers were heading my way down the hall. One of them I'd seen around, a rookie who'd moved to town recently.

The other was Officer Chad Bronski.

Oh, hell. This day just kept getting better, didn't it?

"You're here about Danny?" I asked.

"We have a few questions," Bronski said stiffly. "You're aware your ex-husband was stabbed multiple times?"

Good thing Dr. Richardson didn't have this guy's bedside manner.

"I'm aware. I got here to the hospital as soon as I heard. Grayden O'Neal texted me that he found Danny hurt, but I haven't been able to reach Grayden for hours."

Bronski shared a glance with the rookie. "What's your connection to Grayden O'Neal, exactly?"

"He's my..." I didn't even know what to call him. The man I craved having near me? The man I trusted and cared for more than anyone who didn't share my blood?

"My very close friend," I finished.

Bronski snorted at his notepad. I swear, I almost decked him.

"Do you know where Grayden is?" I asked. "Are the police interviewing him or something?"

"Or something." Bronski's mouth slid into a vicious smirk. "O'Neal is a person of interest. He's being questioned in connection with Danny Carmichael's attempted murder. Or, I guess, murder if your ex doesn't pull through."

FORTY-FOUR
Grayden

THE DOOR to the interrogation room opened, and Chief Nichols stepped in again.

"Mr. O'Neal. I brought you some more water. Can I get you anything else to eat?" She set a water bottle on the table.

"Not hungry," I grunted. The sandwich they'd brought me earlier sat on the far side of the table, barely touched. "I'd like my phone."

It had been hours since I'd texted Piper. She had to be worried. I also had no idea if Danny was alive. Nichols had refused so far to tell me. I had no idea what Piper was going through right now. She was probably at the hospital.

I needed to be with her.

Nichols pulled out the chair across from me and sat. "Speaking of your phone. Would you unlock your screen for us to take a look? That could help speed this along. We're just trying to get to the bottom of what happened."

"No. I will not. As I said before when you asked. If you want access to my phone, get a warrant."

Like I wanted the police reading my texts with Piper and my brother and sister. Those were personal.

Chief Nichols shrugged sadly, as if this was out of her hands. As if she wasn't in complete control here.

"Maybe in a while then. First, though, I have some more questions. Let's go over the events of this morning. Starting with when you woke up."

"It's the same as I said before. I've told you all of this." My voice shook with simmering fury.

I was trying so damn hard to stay calm, but my anger was rising. That old siren's call in my head. I breathed through it.

"One more time," Nichols said. "We have to be sure to get it right."

Beneath the table, my hand squeezed into a fist against my thigh. "Fine."

I started with waking up on Piper's couch. Making pancakes with Ollie. Sitting and eating with him and Piper.

The beautiful morning we'd spent, which had morphed into *this*.

I'd been here for ages. I wasn't sure exactly how long.

The police had arrived on the heels of the ambulance earlier. I'd been covered in Danny's blood, and the cop had taken one look at me and asked me to come to the station for routine questioning. They had to get my statement.

My clothes were now in an evidence bag somewhere. They'd given me sweats and a long-sleeved tee to change into. Both were too tight on me.

Before we'd started talking, Chief Nichols had read me my rights. Theoretically, that meant I could be a suspect. But it seemed absurd.

Danny had nearly run *me* over earlier. He'd already been bleeding out. Looked like he'd been stabbed. I'd tried to stop the bleeding and got medical help.

In fact, I was pretty sure I'd *saved* him. Assuming he survived.

This room brought back too many memories, all of them awful. I wasn't necessarily claustrophobic from my years of imprisonment, but I hated being stuck behind a locked door without it being my choice.

The police could keep me here for a while to carry out their investigation, but this was getting ridiculous.

"I waved goodbye to Piper and Ollie as they drove off," I recounted. "Started walking down the sidewalk."

"Because you were going to walk to your brother's house."

"*Yes*. As I've said. Then Danny's car suddenly drove down the street and nearly hit me. I jumped out of the way. He hit a truck belonging to Piper's neighbor, and the neighbor came outside to see what happened. I told him to call 911."

"But you had the door to Danny's car open already, correct? Before the neighbor came outside."

"Yeah, because I thought Danny had just tried to run me over. He was slumped forward. I opened the door and saw the blood."

"He was already bleeding? You're sure."

"Of course I'm sure," I said through gritted teeth.

"You didn't injure him? Maybe by accident?"

"*No*, I did not. I didn't do a damn thing to Danny Carmichael."

"But you and Danny have had confrontations before, haven't you? That's what Piper told me a few days ago. After the incident with the fake drugs? The anonymous tip claiming you were dealing? Piper thought Danny was behind it."

I leaned back in my chair. Right. Piper had spoken to Chief Nichols about that. "Danny and I don't get along. That's true. He's no fan of mine."

"According to Piper, you helped her when Danny was getting aggressive with her."

"Yes," I bit out.

"You wanted to protect Piper and Ollie from Danny, right? That's understandable. I wouldn't blame you if you wanted to stop him from hurting Piper again. Or his son."

Shit, I knew what she was trying to do.

Maybe it was time to invoke my right to an attorney. But I knew how that would look.

I didn't respond to Nichols's question.

She opened a file folder she'd brought with her. Glanced over the contents. "I have a witness statement that you met with Danny at a bar last Thursday evening. Things got heated. You argued."

My stomach churned. I said nothing, and Nichols went on.

"You and Danny were speaking, and you got angry. Slammed your fist on the table. You said something about crushing him under your boot."

Hell, the old timers at the bar that night had been listening to every word, huh? I wondered how Nichols had heard about the incident.

But it didn't matter. I didn't bother to correct her about misquoting me. I hadn't directly threatened Danny that night at the bar.

I'd been in the wrong place at the wrong time earlier. I had no idea why Danny had been driving down Piper's street, bleeding from a wound in his side.

But from the minute the local cop had seen me there, recognized my name, I apparently became the number one suspect.

They couldn't pin this on me. There was just no way.

"We took fingerprints from the scene," Nichols said. "I'd like to bring in someone to get copies of your prints now. Your prints are in the national database, obviously, given your criminal record. But this will be quicker and easier for our techs."

"Do I have a choice?"

"It'll be easier if you just agree. The more you work with us, the quicker we can rule you out as a suspect. If you didn't do this."

My mouth was stone dry, but I didn't reach for the water. "Fine. Go ahead and take my prints." What difference did it make, anyway? My prints and DNA were forever on public record.

Nichols called another officer in for the printing. I stared at the dark ink as it smudged my fingers.

Usually ink on my hands meant I was working on a sketch. Ink represented my artwork. The very thing that had saved my soul during my darkest days.

But this ink was a stain. An accusation of guilt.

Bands of anxiety were tightening around me. Dread increasing by the second, sinking down to my bones.

Piper wouldn't believe I'd done this to Danny. Right?

But she'd seen me lose my temper with her ex. The day I found Danny with his hand on her throat, I'd done the same to him. Slammed him against a wall and nearly cut off his air supply. She'd had to tell me to stop.

I'd told her about my anger problems before my prison sentence. The incident at Leavenworth when I'd punched a guard. Piper had said she understood. She didn't judge me for those mistakes.

But she'd had that moment of doubt when she saw the package of so-called drugs at my place.

If she believed me capable of stabbing her ex, like I was some kind of violent thug, it would destroy me.

I sat there, listless, as the tech finished the fingerprinting. Nichols had sat silent across from me the entire time.

When we were alone again, the chief said, "Was Piper afraid of Danny? She sounded pretty angry at him the other night, when I spoke to her on the phone."

Can you blame her? I wanted to say, but managed to keep quiet.

"Did she tell you she was afraid? Did she ask you to keep Danny away from her and Ollie? Maybe for you to get rid of him for her?"

"*No,*" I blurted, fury heating my skin like a furnace.

Fucking hell. Over the last hour or so, I'd come to terms with how bad this looked for me. But now Nichols was dragging Piper into it? Trying to pin guilt on her because of me?

I knew Chief Nichols was manipulating me. But that didn't make it any less effective.

Because I would do *anything* to protect Piper. Do anything to keep from hurting her.

Even something monumentally stupid.

FORTY-FIVE

Piper

"Mom, I want to stay," Ollie begged.

"You can't, buddy. Aunt Grace is going to take you back to Silver Ridge. You need to sleep, and if you feel well enough, there's school in the morning."

"*School?*" He spit that word out like a curse. "But what if Dad needs me? What if *you* need me?"

I hugged him close, knowing I absolutely would need him. His humor and his big spirit and the way he cut through the b.s. of adulthood and spoke the truth. My son was such an amazing kid.

About half an hour ago, I'd taken Ollie to Danny's hospital room to see him. Danny had never looked so diminished. Helpless. Ollie had cried and held his dad's limp hand, and it had cracked my heart down the middle.

Danny had to make it. For Ollie. He owed it to our son to survive.

"I'm the mom, and that means I have to take care of you. I have to make this decision for us. That's just how it is. Even if it sucks."

It wasn't an easy decision, sending Ollie home. But I was afraid he'd hear someone talking about Grayden and the suspicion around what had happened. On top of the stress of seeing his dad hurt and just being here, that would be too much.

Ollie's mouth ticked up just a little at the corner. "It does suck. But you'll be here at the hospital with Dad? He doesn't have anyone else."

"I'll be here."

Not for Danny. He hadn't earned my loyalty. But I would do this for Ollie. Because Danny was my son's father, and Ollie couldn't do this himself.

"I won't be alone," I added. "Uncle Callum's on his way. He's bringing dinner for me."

"I guess I could make a card for Dad."

"That's a great idea."

Ollie looked up at Grace. "Can we get art supplies on the way home? And chicken nuggets?"

She ruffled his hair. "Sure can. And I've got some cookie dough at home. We can bake cookies together."

Ollie shrugged. "I guess that could be cool."

"If you want, you can come back to the hospital tomorrow," I said. "Instead of school. Okay?"

I hugged him one more time, and then Grace. "Please tell me if you hear anything about Grayden," I whispered in her ear.

"Dane's working on getting a lawyer here for him," she murmured back. "For now, we just know Grayden's still at the police station. But we'll be okay, Piper. We'll figure this out."

"You stole my lines." I'd always been the one telling her we'd be okay. But right now, I wasn't so sure.

My insides were twisting all over the place as I pulled back. I waved to them as they walked toward the exit. There were messages on my phone, and I kept skimming over them. But none were from Grayden.

Memories echoed in my brain. Like the day Grace and I found out, in our first year of high school, that Grayden had been arrested. That feeling of despair and loss.

I couldn't take it if today ended the same way.

About twenty minutes later, the door to the family waiting room opened. "Dinner delivery has arrived," Callum announced.

He walked in laden with takeout bags. His easy smile and backward cap were familiar sights, and they calmed me.

"Thanks. You're a lifesav—"

My voice cut off as I saw who'd just walked in behind him. Ashford.

And *Teller*. Holy crap. My big brother was here.

"Teller!" I rushed over to him and closed my arms around him, squeezing my eyes shut as tears threatened. "How did you— What are you doing here?"

"Grace has been texting the group thread since this morning. The minute I saw her first message, I got my butt in gear. Knew I had to be here for you."

"But what about Ayla? She's on tour. She needs you."

He laughed softly. "She was the first to insist I come to Hart County. She sends her love. Luckily we were in Salt Lake, so it was a quick trip for me. Arranged a private flight and got here as soon as I could."

I put my face against his shoulder. Tears leaked into his jacket. "Thank you."

Remembering Callum and Ashford behind me, I wiped my eyes and turned around. "Hey, Ashford," I said. "Thank you for coming."

He glanced down sheepishly. "I'm here for you. Always."

I reached out for a hug. A flash of surprise crossed Ashford's face, but his embrace was as fierce as my brother's had been. Ashford wasn't the effusive type when it came to emotions. But I'd never doubted that he cared about me and Ollie.

I was frustrated with him for his stubbornness about Grayden. But that would never diminish the love I felt for Ashford.

"Grace really wants to be here too," Callum said. "We were conferencing on the drive. How would you feel about Ollie staying at Ashford and Emma's place tonight? Zandra's planning to join them, and Dane was talking about going over there."

"Fine by me," I said. "Sounds like a full house."

But this was what we did. We banded together when things got tough. I'd joked about this being the Lonely Harts club, but none of us were ever alone.

Except Grayden, my heart reminded me.

Ashford glanced around the waiting room. There'd been an older couple in here earlier, as well as a family with a baby, but they'd all disappeared.

"People are saying Grayden's the one who attacked Danny," Ashford said. "Is there any way that's true?"

Callum's arms crossed, his frown giving little away.

I felt my expression go hard. Bright, hot anger rose to the surface of my skin. "Do you want it to be true?" I asked. "So you can get rid of him once and for all?"

Ashford shook his head. "That's not fair."

"A *lot* isn't fair," I countered.

"We're not making any assumptions," Callum said. "I don't think Grayden could have done this. But there's obviously a lot we don't know. Grace said Danny's been harassing you? You didn't tell us?"

A heavy hand rested on my shoulder. My big brother. "We're not trying to gang up on you," Teller said. "You don't have to talk about this right now. You should try to eat. You've been here all day, right?"

"I have." My voice wobbled, and I cleared my throat. "I've sat through a doctor telling me Danny might not survive. I've answered awful questions from rude, incompetent police."

Teller's eyebrow lifted. He knew I was talking about his department.

"And I've been worrying all day about Grayden," I went on. "Because I know he didn't do this. I know it in my heart and my gut and my soul. He told me earlier he'd found Danny hurt, and Grayden doesn't lie to me. He..."

I felt the three of them staring at me.

Callum knew Grayden and I were dating. I had no idea what

he'd told the others. It wasn't something I intended to keep from Teller.

But there was no way I could describe what Grayden meant to me. How everything had shifted between us over the last few days.

Grayden had been some part of my life since the day I was born. First as my best friend's brother. My older brother's best friend.

And then, as a terrible absence.

It would be impossible to explain how important he was to me now, and how quickly it had happened. Grayden's good heart, though? To me, that was beyond question.

Suddenly, I knew what I had to do.

I grabbed Teller's sleeve. "I need to talk to you."

We went out to the hallway. There was a vending machine area with terrible coffee, and I found a deserted corner. The hum of quiet activity and other nearby voices filled the air.

"Do you have anything to share about you and Grayden?" Teller asked.

Ugh. He was using his dad voice. Teller wasn't even a father yet, but if and when he and Ayla decided to start a family, he was ready.

"We're dating. He wants to be with me, and I...I want to be with him. Ollie likes him a lot too."

Teller wiped a hand over his face. "Piper, I realize what a big deal it is for you to be open to a relationship again. But why *him*?"

"I'm not a teenager rebelling with the local bad boy. Don't treat me like one."

Teller held up his hands. "I just don't understand how this happened."

"I hardly do either. Grayden and I just fit. It's our history and who we are now. Everything. You and Ayla weren't a likely couple, in case you forgot."

He gave me a look. "Grayden has a history of violence. Did you forget *that*? Chief Nichols is interrogating him right now because he's suspected of putting your ex in this hospital. I know you don't believe that, but..."

"If you knew everything, you would have as much faith in Grayden as I do." Then the wording my brother had used clicked in my mind. "Wait, have you spoken to Chief Nichols?"

Teller glanced around. "I have. Yes. I called her on my way to town. She gave me an update. Very unofficially, since I can't be involved in the investigation given my connection to Danny and Grayden."

"Tell me what you know."

"Piper, I can't—"

"Spill it."

He put his hands on his hips. "There's plenty of circumstantial evidence. Grayden's motive is clear. He's protected you in the past. He's had confrontations with Danny."

I groaned. "And I'm the one who told Nichols about it." I'd been trying to do the right thing, and I'd given the police information to use against Grayden.

"But Susan—I mean Chief Nichols—is far from certain," Teller said, dropping his voice even lower. "She couldn't tell me much, but she's seeing what she can get from questioning Grayden. The department is working on gathering evidence. They also have to investigate the possibility that you were involved, regardless of how ridiculous we know that is."

"*What?* Me? You didn't lead with that?"

"I didn't want to scare you by mentioning it first thing."

But if Grayden was worried I might get pulled into the investigation, what would he do to protect me?

God, I hoped he wasn't that foolish. Not after everything he'd been through in his past.

I poked my finger into Teller's chest through his jacket. "You're going down to the station, and you're going to help Grayden. I don't care how. You're going to do it."

This was why I'd pulled Teller aside in the first place. He knew everything about police procedure. There had to be something he could do.

"Piper, I cannot interfere with this investigation. It would be a gross violation of my duties as a member of Silver Ridge PD."

"Then quit! I don't care! Grayden is alone down there. He didn't do anything to Danny. I *know* it. If I didn't have to stay here, I'd be at that station right now raising hell."

"I'm sure you would," Teller said with a smirk.

"So you're going to do it for me. Don't you dare argue. Get down to that station and help the man who was once your best friend."

Before it was too late.

FORTY-SIX

Grayden

I WAS EXHAUSTED, and if I drank another cup of disgusting coffee, I'd wind up with an ulcer.

The door to the interview room opened, and I dragged my head up. Chief Nichols was back, holding another file folder. "Mr. O'Neal, can I get you anything? Do you need a restroom break?"

"Had one an hour ago. Had some dinner too. I'm good. But you must be sick of this song and dance. Could we at least get some music? Might break the monotony."

She didn't respond to my suggestion, but a muscle in her cheek twitched.

I'd been going back and forth about trying to end the interview. They couldn't keep me here forever. But if I demanded an attorney or asked to leave, it was entirely possible Nichols would decide to arrest me instead.

I couldn't imagine she had enough evidence, because I hadn't *done anything*, but that didn't always matter, did it?

And my other deeper fear was that, if I left, they might go after Piper and drag her in here instead of me.

"Just a few more questions," Nichols said, taking her seat across from me. "I truly appreciate your patience."

The chief opened the file folder and turned it around to face me. There were photos inside. Despite my mental fatigue, I couldn't help leaning forward to study them.

"The Pine Cone Motor Lodge," I said.

"You recognize it? The sign's not visible in this photo."

"I stayed there a little while. Right after I got back to Silver Ridge." What did this have to do with anything?

"Daniel Carmichael has been staying there as well."

"Is that important? I haven't been near that motel in over a month at least."

She flipped to the next photo, placing another beside it. "Do you recognize either of these items?"

There was a knife covered in blood. A sweatshirt with Seattle written across it. Looked like *mine.* But the white letters were smudged with red.

I said nothing.

"We found these items at the Pine Cone Motor Lodge, thrown into some bushes. We believe this knife is the weapon used against Mr. Carmichael."

My pulse was racing, but I still couldn't tell whether this news was good or bad.

Chief Nichols folded her hands. "From other evidence in the parking lot of the Pine Cone, it looks like that was the scene of the stabbing. Mr. Carmichael drove away, possibly to escape the attack, and for some reason headed toward his ex-wife's house. And that's where he ran into you. Well, not literally."

"Thank fuck for that," I muttered. "So you finally believe I'm telling the truth?"

"A recording on a neighbor's doorbell camera helped. It shows exactly what you described. Mr. Carmichael nearly hit you as his car careened off the road. Likely because he was losing consciousness. You opened his door and tried to render aid. Our medical examiner hasn't completed his report, but he agrees Mr. Carmichael had lost significant blood before that point. You couldn't be the attacker."

I dropped my head into my hands, going faint with relief. "Why are you telling me all of this?"

"Because I just had a witness identify the knife used in the attack." She tapped the photo. "We've now confirmed it came from Piper Carmichael's garage."

I sat up with a jolt. "*Piper*? She had nothing to do with any of this. She and her son were at their house all night with me."

Nichols shook her head. "No, I'm not accusing Piper of anything. Piper reported a break-in at her garage a few days ago."

"Yeah. I was there. Officer Bronski's smooth police work helped the culprit get away."

"Our current theory is that someone attacked Mr. Carmichael and intended to frame Piper. *And* you. If this Seattle sweatshirt is indeed yours?" She pointed at the other photo.

"I have no idea." I wasn't ready to give up anything just yet. How could I know that sweatshirt was mine, based on some photo?

Could this possibly be a trick? An elaborate ploy to get me to make an incriminating admission?

It didn't seem like it, though.

"I had more than one break-in at the place I'm renting from Piper. The first was when Danny broke in looking for something he wanted. A jewelry box that belonged to Piper's mom. Piper told you about that already. The second was whenever the fake package of drugs was planted, and you know about that too. But I thought Danny was responsible."

"Do you have any idea who'd want to harm Daniel Carmichael and frame you and Piper?" Chief Nichols asked.

"*No*. None whatsoever." Then I thought of my confrontation with Danny at the bar last week. Again, Nichols knew about that. But there was something else. "When I saw Danny on Thursday night at the bar, he said, 'You're late', before he looked up. Like he'd expected someone else. I have no idea who he was meeting."

"We'll look into that." Nichols took out her phone and typed out a note. "God willing, Mr. Carmichael will recover soon and be able to share what he knows. I'm sure this process hasn't been pleasant, but your cooperation has been very helpful."

"I'd say you're welcome, but..."

"I'm afraid I need more, though. I'll be asking Piper the same thing. If you think of anything else, any reason someone would try to frame you, please share it. We have no idea if Mr. Carmichael was the real target, or you, or Piper. We have no idea what this person is really after. Or what they might do next."

Nichols had a few more questions for me. But finally, she gave me back my phone and told me I could go.

"Do you still have my card with my number?" she asked. "In case you think of anything?"

"I'll figure it out." I just wanted the hell out of here.

And I wanted, more than anything, to see Piper.

Someone opened the interview room door for us. Nichols waved me forward, and I stepped out into the hall.

Then I stopped short. Teller Landry was leaning casually against the wall just outside the interview room.

"Susan," he said, nodding at Nichols.

"Hey, Teller. Can you see that Mr. O'Neal gets where he needs to go?"

"Plan to."

"Do I get a say in this?" I asked.

It was the first time I'd seen Teller in about fifteen years, and I was just leaving a police station after spending last night at his sister's house. I had no idea if he'd want to slug me for touching her or what.

The hell was he doing here?

Chief Nichols winked, like we were all friends. "Officer Landry is here as a private citizen today. I think you two should have a chat."

"That's what I was hoping for." Teller's light-green eyes, the same as Piper's, were serious. But angry? Ready to dismember me for defiling his baby sister?

Not so much.

We walked toward the exit. The other officers and staff members stared, and I noticed Officer Bronski wasn't here. Maybe he'd leave me the hell alone next time we crossed paths.

In the parking lot, Teller said, "Piper sent me. She's been very worried about you."

As he spoke, I saw the notifications on my phone. Piper had called and texted. So had Callum and Grace. The only other friend I really had was Milo. I wondered if he'd heard about what happened.

We got into Teller's truck, and I sent off a quick text to Piper.

Hey sweetheart, I'm sorry it took me so long to respond. I'll catch you up on what happened today. I'm fine. Teller's taking me somewhere to chat. So if they don't find my body...

Just kidding. Mostly.

I miss you and I hope you and Ollie are okay. Let me know where you are. I'll see you soon.

Seconds later, she wrote back.

Thank God. I'm at the hospital. We're okay. Just want to see you 🧡🧡🧡

"I didn't even know you were in town," I said, tucking my phone away for the moment. "Don't think Piper knew either."

"I dropped everything and got here as soon as I could today. Danny isn't my favorite person, but I knew Piper would need support."

"Good. Glad she has that from you."

"Of course she does," Teller said. "She's my sister."

This was awkward. Things used to be so easy between Teller

and me. Another lifetime ago. But we'd grown apart even before I went to prison.

I'd heard about Teller being wounded as a Green Beret. The scars on his face hinted at that story. Piper had mentioned he and Ayla lived in Silver Ridge part time now, spending the rest of their time in LA or traveling.

His life couldn't have been more different from mine. I didn't know Teller at all anymore. It was impossible to imagine ever getting back to the camaraderie we used to have. The brotherhood.

My sleeping with his sister probably wasn't helping.

I had to be upfront about it. If only because I preferred to be on offense right now than defense.

"I haven't told Piper this yet, but I'm in love with her."

Teller cursed, and his truck swerved slightly within the lane.

"Not what you wanted to hear?" I asked.

"Man, what do you expect me to say? Congratulations?"

"That might be nice, actually."

His jaw tightened, and he tapped one finger against the gearshift. "Are you sure you're in love with Piper? Or is it what she represents? A chance to get back a piece of what you lost."

I frowned at the window as trees whipped past. "I don't love an idea. I love *her*. Everything about her. I love Piper's sense of humor and her love for her son and her passion for life. Her kindness. Some people think empathy is for suckers. That's not the world I want to live in. In my life, I've had some time to sit around and contemplate what really matters. Not claiming to have any profound answers. I've made plenty of mistakes and taken wrong turns. But Piper...she's *everything* that matters for me."

Teller was quiet for a long moment.

"That was quite a speech."

I glared from the side of my eye. He was smirking. "Fuck you," I said, but there wasn't much bite to the words.

"Can't imagine the Grayden O'Neal I used to know being so damn talkative."

"It's called eloquent. That's the word you were looking for. Eloquent."

He snickered, and just for a few seconds, it was like a couple decades had disappeared from the gulf between us.

I crossed my arms. "Where are you taking me, anyway? Am I about to meet my end off some cliff? A chief of police can probably cover up a crime better than anyone."

"Let's not even joke about that."

"Why? Because you and I have tended to be on opposite sides of the justice system?"

"No. Because I may have interfered with the Silver Ridge PD investigation today, and I'm trying not to feel bad about it."

"*What*?"

He shrugged, one hand steering us through the curves in the road. "I bent the rules. Piper asked me to come to the station and see what I could do for you. I convinced Chief Nichols to interview me as a witness. That way, she could show me exactly what evidence they had against you. Technically, I was just sharing what personal info I had on those subjects. I didn't expect to have useful information."

"Nichols mentioned a witness identifying Piper's knife. That was you, wasn't it?"

"Yeah. But I was just telling the truth. And it's Ollie's camping knife, actually. I bought it for him."

Teller explained what had gone down over my dinner break. After he'd seen the photo of the knife, he'd called Piper for permission to check her garage. He and Nichols had driven to Piper's house. They'd found the leather sheath and holster, all part of a fancy camping knife set Teller gave Ollie for his last birthday.

But no knife.

"When I got to the station a couple hours ago," Teller said, "I had no idea if I could help or not. By then, Chief Nichols was starting to have serious doubts about your guilt. The timing and events just didn't add up. It's clear the stabbing took place at the Pine Cone, and you weren't there."

"I was at Piper's."

"Yeah, I heard," he said tightly. "Anyway, the perp tossed the knife, along with that Seattle sweatshirt, as false clues. It's sheer coincidence you wound up discovering Danny slumped in his car."

A damn lucky coincidence, in a weird way. I couldn't have stabbed Danny at his motel and also waved goodbye to Piper and Ollie at the same time. And then jumped out of the way of his car minutes later on Piper's street.

"I'm just glad I could provide one more piece of the puzzle," Teller said.

"Before that, you thought I did it. Didn't you?"

He took a long breath. "I had to entertain the possibility."

We drove in silence for a while. I still had no idea where we were heading, but it was outside Silver Ridge. Made me think of the drives Teller and I used to take. Talking, laughing. Just being there for each other.

Finally, I said, "I get it. You don't know me. I'm just a violent ex-con to you. An ex-con who's trying to get his hooks in your sister, from your perspective."

Teller pulled us into a bright parking lot.

"You're more than that," he said hoarsely. "You were my friend, as Piper keeps reminding me. You were family. Just like Ashford, Callum, and Grace are to me. But you...with all the shit that happened with our parents, you and I stood shoulder to shoulder. We tried to take care of the others. For a while there, I counted on you, and I think you counted on me too."

"I did. You were my fucking brother." I blinked at the windshield as my eyes stung. "I messed that up too, even before my arrest, and I'm sorry for it. Sorry for a lot of things. Maybe that doesn't mean much to you, but—"

"No, it does," Teller said. "Remorse isn't a weakness. It's

cowards who hide behind lies and excuses. It takes strength to admit when you've done wrong."

He turned and looked at me, and the barrier behind his eyes shifted. Like he was really considering me for the first time since we'd met in the station hallway earlier.

"Piper keeps telling me to listen to your side of the story. Do you want me to do that? Do you think it'll make a difference?"

"You have to decide for yourself. I've told Piper nearly everything. I need to tell my siblings the whole story. It's long past time. Might be easier if I can tell all of you at once, but I still don't know if I can get Ashford into the same room as me."

Teller pointed at the large building in front of us, and I finally registered where we were. Hart County General Hospital.

He'd brought me to Piper. That had to be a positive sign.

"Everyone's here," Teller said. "Even Ashford. They're here for Piper."

"Because she's amazing." She deserved everything. All the love in the world.

"But from what I've seen, her faith in *you* hasn't wavered for a single second. That's what convinced me to go to the station and try to help you. If anyone can convince Ashford to listen and give you a chance, it's her."

FORTY-SEVEN

Piper

I MANAGED to get a few bites of food down. Callum and Ashford tried to keep me distracted. But my anxiety was through the roof.

I was probably driving Teller insane with my constant messages.

ME

Any news yet? What's happening?

TELLER

New evidence in the investigation. Good chance Grayden will be able to leave soon.

OMG THANK YOU WHEN???

You're hurting my eyes with the all caps

I'm conveying a sense of urgency

Oh is this important to you? Hadn't noticed

Relax and take care of yourself. You'll see Grayden soon.

I forced myself to set down my phone. It was still hard to

breathe. I wouldn't be able to relax until I saw Grayden with my own eyes. Could touch him with my own hands.

Finally, Grace got back to the hospital. She'd made sure Ollie was settled at Emma and Ashford's.

"Dane brought over the cookie dough from our place, so you can imagine how popular he'll be with Ollie and Maisie," Grace said, settling into the chair beside me. "He's going to help them bake. I told Emma and Zandra to have a fire extinguisher ready."

"Will he wear an apron? We'll need some photo evidence."

Grace took out her phone. A text had just come in from Zandra: Dane in a frilly apron, with Maisie and Ollie aiming spatulas at him like they were ready for battle.

The picture made me smile, and yet the ache in my heart only worsened.

The new additions to our family over the years had brought us closer and made us stronger. Now, I couldn't imagine Dane, Emma, Zandra and Ayla not being in our lives.

Ayla wasn't here, obviously, but she'd sent me a few personal texts expressing her love and support.

I checked my phone again. Teller had written about ten minutes ago. I hadn't heard the notification.

Leaving with Grayden any minute now. As soon as he's out of his last interview. We'll head to the hospital

Thank you I love you you're the best big brother ever

Remember that the next time you get grumpy at me

"Teller and Grayden are on their way," I said to Grace.

"Oh, thank goodness." She hugged me, wiping her eyes.

A little while later, Callum and Ashford strolled into the waiting room. They'd been on some kind of snack mission. "The vending machine near the maternity ward has the best stuff," Callum announced. "Check out this haul."

He dumped an armful of cookies, cakes, and chocolate bars on an empty seat.

Grace greeted her brothers. That tension between her and Ashford was still there. A strain in her expression when she hugged him, pulling back lightning fast.

"Piper, have you heard any news about Grayden?" Callum asked.

"Teller said Grayden's been released."

"Thank fuck," Callum breathed, sinking down in his seat. He grabbed a packet of cookies.

But Ashford hadn't said a word.

With everything else that had happened today, all the terrible ups and downs, I'd officially had enough.

"Teller's bringing Grayden here," I said, glaring at Ashford. "Are you going to leave?"

"Do you want me to?"

"Of course we don't," Grace cut in. "But you're the one who's refused to see him."

Ashford glanced to the side, his knee bouncing, hands flexing. Like he might take off any second.

"I'm here for Piper," he said. "That's it."

Callum stood up abruptly. "Grace, want to help me look for decent coffee? I have a theory it's got to be in this hospital somewhere."

She rolled her eyes. "We're having a grown-up conversation right now, Cal."

"Yeah, which might be easier one-on-one." He gave her a complicated look. Grace scrunched up her face. Callum wiggled his shoulders.

Their silent sibling communication was really weird sometimes.

But whatever Callum had been conveying to her, she finally

got it. Grace jumped up. "Coffee. You're right, Piper loves good coffee. Let's try to find some."

As they left, Ashford was shaking his head. "So you're my one-woman intervention, is that right? Everyone thinks I suck, and it's your job to tell me so."

I moved to the seat beside him, handing him a chocolate bar. "I'd rather call it an open dialogue between friends."

He ripped the candy wrapper and took a bite. When he finished chewing, he said, "I just don't get it. How easily you all trust him again."

"It wasn't easy."

Ashford's mouth tightened into a flat line. He set the rest of the candy bar aside.

"You know what wasn't easy? Going through all the shit I did without my older brother. Maisie being born. My wife dying. Everything that happened when Emma came into our lives. For the last fifteen years, I haven't had an older brother at all."

"If you let him explain—"

"*Fuck that*, Piper," he hissed. "Grayden abandoned us just like our father did. He abandoned *me*, and *I* became the oldest brother whose job was to take care of everyone else. And you know what? I did it. I stepped up."

Ashford was keeping his voice down, but every word was raw and bleeding with emotion. Like a knife blade to his soul.

"You did," I said.

"So don't sit there and tell me I should forget all that pain."

"Grayden was in pain too. So much. There are important things you don't know. He tried to come back here after he got out of prison, and Callum sent him away."

"I already know. It was too late then. Too late now."

"But you're still hurting, aren't you? What if the rest of us are right? Grayden wants to be your brother again and make up for what went wrong in the past. What's the harm in just hearing what he has to say?"

"What's the *harm*? If I trust him, accept his empty apologies, he could let us down all over again. I'd be the biggest idiot in the world."

"You don't want to get hurt again."

"Of course I fucking don't." He glared at the wall. "I can't let Emma or Maisie get hurt because of him either."

What he was saying sounded so familiar.

"I've been hurt deeply, and I was scared to ever risk that happening again," I said.

I didn't just mean Danny. It was my mom. My dad, or at least the man who'd raised me and given me the name Landry, even if he didn't accept me as his.

They'd all broken my heart in different ways. I bore those scars.

"But over the last couple months, I've seen things differently. Because of Grayden. When we reach out for something, when we make that leap and open our hearts, we might not get there. The person we're reaching for might not reach back. We might fall. But the part where we take the risk? That's when we're most alive. That's the moment we can fly."

I had no idea where all that had come from. Maybe I'd been taking the advice I once gave Grace. Trust your instincts. I'd spoken from the heart, and the heart didn't lie.

A hundred different emotions flashed in Ashford's eyes, like they were battling to come to the surface.

"Piper?" a deep voice said. A voice that resonated everywhere inside me, filling my loneliest spaces.

Grayden stood in the doorway to the waiting room.

I leaped up, a tear streaking down my cheek. He caught me in his arms and pushed his forehead against mine, holding me tight.

"You're here," I said.

"Finally, right?" he murmured, and I smiled sadly.

Then Grayden pulled back, looking past my shoulder. "Ashford."

I turned and tucked myself against Grayden's side. Ashford

nodded at his brother with a neutral expression. Nowhere near friendly. But not angry either.

The last time they'd met, on Thanksgiving, Ashford had almost hit him. This was definitely a step in the right direction.

"Can we talk in a bit?" Grayden asked him. "I have some things to tell you all. You, Callum, Grace. Teller as well."

Ashford grunted, standing up. "Maybe. In a few minutes. I'm going to call Emma."

"You're not leaving though?" I asked.

"Nah. I'll be right back."

We moved aside so Ashford could step out of the waiting room. Then another family came in, so I took Grayden's hand and tugged him down the hall.

I pulled him into the first quiet alcove we found. Grayden and I spoke over each other. I was trying to tell him how worried I'd been, and he was trying to say something about evidence.

But words were inadequate anyway. There was no way to describe the storm happening inside me.

So I just decided to kiss him.

He pressed me into the wall as our mouths moved together. I grabbed onto his jacket, and his fingers dug into my hair. His kisses stole my breath and gave me life at the same time.

Eventually we had to stop, gasping. Grayden put his forehead against mine. I wanted to cry and laugh and just...hold on.

I had to hold on.

"You're okay?" I asked.

"Yeah. I was more worried about you. I should've been here with you."

"Hardly your fault."

He sighed against my hairline. "Nah, I suppose not. How's Danny doing?"

I put my head on Grayden's shoulder. "Alive. We saw him earlier. He's still sedated. Stable but not out of danger. There's nothing I can do for him, obviously, but I'm staying here because

Ollie can't. I need Ollie to know I did all I can. Danny doesn't have anyone else."

"How's Ollie handling it?"

"He's scared. But he's brave."

"He is. You're an incredible mom. And far more than Danny deserves, but anyway. You know that." Grayden smoothed back my hair. "Piper, there's something I haven't shared with you. Last Thursday, after Danny showed up at Ollie's school and took him to dinner, I followed Danny to a bar. I confronted him. It got heated."

My mouth dropped open. "You didn't tell me? Why?"

"Danny said some pretty despicable things. I didn't want to repeat them. But today, the incident came up with Chief Nichols. She was pretty convinced I'd attacked Danny to protect you and Ollie from him. Not such a far-fetched idea. Either that, or you'd asked me to do it."

"And I'd told her everything about Danny threatening me." I cringed. "I *was* terrified you'd do something stupid to protect me. Like confessing and telling Chief Nichols I had nothing to do with it."

He kissed my temple. "I thought about it. For all of two seconds. I wouldn't leave you like that, Piper. It's you and me."

"Bonnie and Clyde," I murmured.

"Shouldn't joke about that anymore. Not within hearing of anyone from Silver Ridge PD. Aside from Teller, but I doubt he'd be laughing."

Yeah, I didn't think my brother would enjoy that particular reference.

Grayden breathed deeply, and his brown-and-gold gaze met mine. "My biggest fear was that you'd believe I hurt Danny. You've seen me angry before. You've had your doubts about me before as well."

"Not anymore," I said. "Not for one second today. You told me you'd found him like that, bleeding, so I knew it was true."

The only way Grayden would strike out against my ex was in

self-defense or defense of others. I knew that in my bones. Grayden wasn't a violent man.

He cupped my face. "I'm so damn lucky to have you."

"Maybe it's luck. Or maybe you're finally getting what you deserve. People who care about you and have your back."

"God, I want to deserve you. Thank you for sending Teller to the station. It helped. Sounds like you went to bat for me, and I love you for it."

The word gave me an electric jolt. *Love.*

My first reaction, even after what I'd said to Ashford about opening my heart, was to pull away. To hide, as if that would keep me safe.

But I wanted *more*. I wanted to leap. And it wasn't even that scary. Because I already knew Grayden would catch me.

"I'll go to bat for you every time," I said. "You might be stuck with me."

"Best news I've heard all day." Grayden's lips curved. "There's new evidence about Danny's attack. So much I need to explain. But I think there's something else I have to do first. Something that's long overdue."

"Talking to Ashford and the others? Like you mentioned to him?"

"Do you think Ashford will listen?" he asked.

This morning, I would not have been optimistic. But now?

"He went to call Emma, and I'm sure she's encouraging him to sit down with you," I said. "Also, he didn't curse you out when he saw you a few minutes ago. Progress."

"Hey, I'll take it. I'll round everyone up, and hopefully, Ashford will be willing."

"Do you want me to be there?" I asked.

"I need you there." He took my hand and laced our fingers. "Not sure how I survived so long without you, but I need you, Piper. Whatever this is, I don't think there's a cure."

"Sounds serious."

"Nah, I think it sounds wonderful."

FORTY-EIGHT

Grayden

IT WAS ALMOST midnight when we piled into a small conference room. Apparently, Callum had gotten to know several nurses when Zandra's grandfather had been hospitalized last year. My youngest brother could charm his way into or out of pretty much anything.

But Ashford wasn't here.

I stood up. "I'll look for him."

"No, I will," Teller said. "I'll be right back."

But that same moment, Ashford stepped into the doorway. "I'm here. Was planning to spend the night at the hospital anyway for Piper, so we might as well do this."

I nodded at him. Ashford avoided my eyes, leaning against a wall instead of taking a seat.

But that was fine. He was here, and that was all that mattered.

Piper sat next to me, a hand on my thigh beneath the table. Teller took the seat beside her. Grace and Callum were right across from us.

I finally had the chance, after all these years, to tell them the truth about everything. Fuck, I was dreading it.

This had been a long, painful day for all of us. And it wasn't over yet.

I knew I was a strong person. I'd had to be to survive all I'd been through. But Piper's presence beside me gave me a whole new kind of strength.

She made me feel like the hero she believed I was. A man who made mistakes, but those mistakes didn't have to define me.

"I had a friend named Aaron Drummond in the Army."

I started there, and I told them everything. Every brutal detail. All the things I was ashamed of, like throwing the first punch in that bar fight.

Grace gasped, covering her mouth when I described finding Aaron covered in blood, standing over an unconscious Private Ricker.

She cried when I told them about my impulsive confession of guilt. Callum had an agonized look on his face.

Ashford... It was impossible to tell what he was feeling.

The funny thing was, my voice got stronger as I kept going. With every ugly detail I shared, the weight on my soul got lighter. They would know exactly who I was, and if any of them decided it was too much, it would hurt. But at least I'd be living fully in the open.

By the time I got to Aaron's lawyer father and his threats, Grace hammered her fist on the table. She was just as furious as Piper had been. Callum got up and paced across the tiny room, hands digging into his hair.

"This is fucked," Callum said.

Ashford shifted his weight, still leaning against the wall. "So this lawyer guy threatened us if you didn't take the fall? You really think he could've done something?"

I nodded. "Silas Drummond worked in Washington. He knew generals and congressmen. I looked him up online once. He was golf buddies with the Secretary of Defense. You and Cal were both in the service. There's no telling what he could've done. And even if I changed my story, I would've struggled to prove my innocence at the trial. I thought your lives would be better if I played along."

"Better without you?" Ashford said. "How the hell could you think that?"

"Because Drummond promised he could *help* you if I kept my mouth shut."

Everyone in the room went quiet. Piper's hand tightened on my thigh. I hadn't told her this part.

For my sister, it might be the hardest of all.

This, right here, was the reason I hadn't volunteered the full truth before now. It would kill me to hurt my baby sister.

"Help us *how*?" Ashford demanded.

"He said he'd make sure you and Callum had good assignments anytime you had a change of station. He could help your military careers. Put a thumb on the scale in your favor."

Callum dropped his face into his hand.

"And Grace..." I met my sister's sweet, open gaze. "He offered to give you a full ride to college. He set it up as an anonymous scholarship through the high school."

The color drained from her face. "*No*," she whispered.

"I'm so sorry, Gracie." My voice broke.

"I didn't earn my scholarship? That was...blood money?"

"I wish you didn't ever have to know. I don't want to hurt you or make you feel—"

Grace got up and ran from the room. Piper squeezed my shoulder and then went after her.

Okay, I'd known this would suck. But it *really* fucking sucked.

Grace and Piper had great memories of their college days together. Grace was proud of her degree. And I'd just tainted those memories.

"Is that all of it?" Ashford asked. He was staring at the carpet. "Every last thing?"

"Yes," I spit out. "It's enough, don't you think?" Enough for them to second-guess the idea of ever forgiving me. But at least it was done now.

Teller blew out a breath. "And I thought I had some baggage in my past. I have nothing on you, Gray."

His use of my old nickname gave me a glimmer of hope. He'd used to call me that when we were friends. He wouldn't be using that name if he was disgusted by my story, right?

But what about my brothers?

Callum spoke first. "I hate everything you just told us. It's all so wrong. But I'm upset for *you* and what those people did to you. This can't be the end of it. There's no way this Silas Drummond guy and his son can get away with it."

I shrugged. "It's been so many years. I just care about you guys. I've never wanted to make excuses, but I hope you can understand the choices I made. And forgive them."

"Anything that needs forgiveness," Callum said firmly, "you already have mine."

Teller put his hand on my shoulder, his expression saying everything I needed from him. Maybe we weren't friends again just yet, but I saw understanding. He nodded once.

All three of us looked to Ashford.

His face was hard as stone. He walked toward me. I saw every ounce of pain I'd felt reflected back at me.

Looking at Ashford had always been like looking into a mirror of my past. A better version of myself.

Instead of saying anything, he opened his arms.

Choking back tears, I stood up and hugged him. He clapped me on the back, pulling me tighter. We had years to catch up on, probably some more difficult conversations ahead. But the wall between us was gone, crumbled at our feet.

A moment later, the door opened again, and Grace was there. Her pretty face was tear-streaked, but she hugged me next, burying her face against my chest.

"I didn't know where that money came from," she sobbed. "If I knew..."

"Please don't feel guilty. If you hadn't gotten that money, everything else would have turned out the same." At least one tiny good thing had come from it, though I knew Grace wouldn't see it that way right now.

I caught Piper's eye in the doorway. She'd been out there comforting my sister. Her best friend. Once again, I saw no judgment from her. Only a bittersweet, encouraging smile.

I loved Piper so fiercely in that moment. So intensely. We were part of the same history, the same found family, and that just made our connection sweeter.

"I love you, Grayden," my sister said.

"I love you too. I love all of you. I wasn't there for you before, but that changes now."

Callum and Ashford both put their hands on my arms where I was holding Grace.

It felt like I was finally coming out of a long, dark night. The first rays of sun had appeared when Grace and Callum came back into my life.

And then Piper. My heart and my soul had truly come alive because of her.

But now, my new beginning was really starting.

FORTY-NINE

Piper

WE STAYED up half the night in the family waiting room, reminiscing.

Grayden and Teller shared stories about the Mangy Moose, back when it was a filthy dive that didn't check IDs. Then they started in on Callum about his antics as a kid.

We passed around the rest of the snacks Callum had raided from the vending machine. Grace and I chimed in with the things we'd overheard as kids when our brothers hadn't known we were listening. *Ha*.

Ashford was quiet for a lot of it, but he cracked a few smiles. Brought up their mom, and then the reminiscing had turned more heartfelt and sad.

Yet it meant so much. The four O'Neal siblings, able to share these memories together. The good and the bad. I loved having Teller there too. All the people I'd grown up loving. Who'd given me happy memories of childhood instead of just darkness.

Eventually, I passed out with my head on Grayden's shoulder.

My dreams were hectic. Full of shouts and confusion. My mom and dad were yelling at each other. Arguing about me. *Again*.

Then it was Ashford shouting, then Danny. Men and women

in uniforms, but I couldn't tell if they were trying to help me or drag me toward the danger. Hands reaching, trying to pull me away from my son.

I dreamed Ollie and I took shelter in a quiet room. And Grayden was suddenly there. Like he'd just appeared, an answer to a prayer I hadn't known I made. But he held us. Kept us warm and safe.

The danger was still outside, but with Grayden, I wasn't afraid to face it.

I blinked, opening my tired eyes. Beige walls, nondescript chairs. My back was killing me from sleeping in a weird position, half sitting and half sprawled over the man beside me. *Ow.*

Then I noticed Grayden's breathing was shallow. I glanced up and found him looking back at me.

"Morning," he murmured. "Everyone else is still asleep."

Teller and Ashford had pulled chairs across from them to prop up their feet. Grace had her head on Callum's shoulder, and Callum was snoring quietly. A few other people in the waiting room, those who'd stayed overnight like us, were just beginning to stir.

A hum of noise came from outside the waiting room. The hospital day was off and running. Any moment, a doctor or another family would step into the room, dealing with their own personal nightmare. But there hadn't been any news about Danny since yesterday, and I assumed that was good. Meant he was still stable.

I sat up a little more. Grayden was leaning way back in his chair, head against the wall. I put my head against the wall as well, the two of us inches apart.

"Strange day yesterday," I said.

"Very. Would not want to live that one over again. Except maybe the parts after midnight."

"That was today, technically."

After he'd told the others his story.

The revelation about Grace's scholarship had gutted her. I

finally understood why Grayden feared the truth would make her feel guilty. She'd thought she earned that money through her academic record, and it turned out to be payment for her brother's freedom.

She'd sobbed in my arms in the hallway. She hadn't wanted Grayden to see her fall apart like that.

"I would've given up anything if it would've brought Grayden back to us," she'd said.

"We can't change what happened. But he's here now."

"I know." She'd wiped her tears away. "I have to go back in there. I don't want him to think I'm mad at him."

Because, no matter what, Grace chose love where Grayden was concerned. She was true to her name.

We were all ragged after yesterday. My nerves were raw and my heart was bruised. But seeing the four of them, even Ashford, hugging Grayden had been beautiful. Same with seeing him and Teller together. All those wounds weren't healed yet, but I was sure we'd get there.

"Today's a new day," I said.

"Sure feels like it." Grayden's hand rose to press against my cheek. His thumb moved over my cheekbone. "I love you, Piper."

Everything inside me stopped. "What did you say?"

Because it couldn't have been what I thought I'd heard. Just coming out of the blue like that.

"I'm in love with you." His gaze still held its usual intensity, but the flecks of gold were softer. Liquid. His hand was warm and dry against my skin. "Might be telling you that too soon. But I can't help it. After all the confessions last night, I'm an open book. The barriers are down. I love you."

My lower lip trembled. "Okay."

He huffed a laugh and leaned in to kiss me deeply. The kiss held all those same words. I felt them like a mantra repeating in my head.

I love you.

"Gross. Get a room," Callum said sleepily.

"Agreed." Ashford stretched his arms over his head.

"I think they're cute," Grace said on a yawn.

Teller was blinking away sleep and intentionally not looking at us. "Anyone want a breakfast sandwich?"

Grayden and I both laughed. He nuzzled his nose against mine, then let me go. "Great idea. I'll come with you, Teller."

Grace wiped her face and smacked her lips. "My mouth tastes yucky. Does anyone have a mint?"

I grinned affectionately at all of them.

Yesterday had been agonizing. The waiting and not knowing. Today was going to be so much better.

We took turns going back to Silver Ridge to get cleaned up. Ollie was anxious to come back to the hospital, so Teller said he'd swing by Ashford and Emma's place to pick him up. Ollie would be thrilled to see him.

Grayden and I were able to go to my house and take a quick shower. There wasn't much time to enjoy each other, but we made the most of it. Kissing and washing each other and relaxing under the warm spray.

He loved me. I couldn't believe he'd said that.

He didn't seem upset with my ridiculous response either. *Okay*. A non-response, conversation ender. Probably because I just didn't have the words yet to give him the reply he deserved. The reply I wanted to be able to give him.

But someday. I wanted to say it someday. *Me*, the founder of the Lonely Harts club. The woman who'd sworn she would never, ever say those three words to a man again.

Wild.

After freshening up, it was back to the hospital. No change yet in Danny's status, but the doctor who spoke to me said things were looking good.

Ollie and I went in to see Danny again, and Ollie put a card next to his hospital bed with elaborate drawings inside.

"So that'll be the first thing Dad sees when he wakes up," Ollie said.

"He's going to love it, Ollie-bear."

He'd damn well better love it.

Back in the waiting room, Grayden and Teller were talking with their heads together. They both smiled when Ollie ran in. My heart swelled.

At one point, while Teller played some kind of game with Ollie on his phone, Grayden and I had a few minutes to talk about the "new evidence" he'd mentioned yesterday in Danny's case.

We went to that quiet alcove again. Grayden told me about the bloody knife and sweatshirt the attacker had left at the Pine Cone Motor Lodge. How Teller had identified the knife as Ollie's, and he and Chief Nichols had found the empty knife sheath in my garage.

"Unbelievable," I said. "That's why the person broke into my garage. I should've noticed the knife was missing."

"It was probably mixed in with your camping gear. You thought it was Danny looking for your mom's jewelry box again."

But it had been someone plotting to stab my ex. Why? And why frame me and Grayden for it?

"One thing keeps popping up in my mind," Grayden said. "Danny drove toward your house after the attack."

"It's strange. Why wouldn't he call 911? Try to find medical help? Did he have something in his car he was trying to hide?"

"Doubt it. I figure Nichols would've mentioned that to Teller." Grayden tucked my hair behind my ear, like he just wanted an excuse to touch me. "I'm not trying to give your ex any credit, but I wonder if he thought he was dying, and all he could think of was seeing you or Ollie one last time."

I huffed. "Can't imagine that."

"Weird things happen in a guy's brain when he thinks he'll never see his family again," Grayden said. "Who knows?"

But now that idea was stuck in my head too.

We talked a while longer about Grayden's interrogation yesterday and all he'd learned. Then we returned to the waiting room to kill more time.

Thank goodness I had employees I could rely on to run Silver Linings. I checked in a few times over the phone, and my team assured me they were fine.

Ashford, Callum, and Grace came and went. They had their own responsibilities. Zandra and Dane stopped by, bringing food and company.

But as the day wound down, heading toward dinner, it was just Teller, Grayden, Ollie and me. I napped with my head against Grayden's chest.

Until Grayden's hand rubbed my back, and a new voice said, "Ms. Carmichael?"

I sat up. A nurse stood in front of me.

"Daniel is awake and breathing on his own now. You and your son are welcome to see him."

"He may be confused from the sedation," the nurse warned as we walked toward Danny's room. "And he'll have trouble speaking. But he's doing very well so far. Ollie, your dad is clearly a fighter."

More like an ornery jerk, I thought. I kept that to myself.

Grayden was walking with us. Just before the doorway, I turned to him. "You'll wait out here?" I asked. Teller had stayed in the waiting room to call Ayla.

"Not going anywhere." Grayden reached out and his hand brushed mine. Ollie's eyes followed the movement, but mostly he was dancing back and forth with excitement.

"Dad!" Ollie cried the moment we stepped into the room. I put my hand on his shoulder.

"Remember, he's weak," I said. "Better go easy on him."

Ollie slowed down and shuffled to the side of Danny's bed. "Dad? It's me. Oliver."

A sad smile pulled at my lips.

Danny's eyes opened halfway. The ventilator and bags of transfusion blood were gone, but he still barely looked like himself.

Ollie reached out and gently put his small hand over Danny's, and there was a hint of some kind of emotion in my ex's eyes.

"I made you a card, Dad. Did you see?"

Danny nodded his head, just slightly, which made Ollie grin ear to ear.

Ollie started talking rapid fire, catching up Danny on the hospital, the nurses, the cookies he and Maisie had baked with Dane. Anything and everything.

"Uncle Teller's back, isn't that cool? Mom's been staying here at the hospital almost the whole entire time, so you wouldn't be alone. Even though they have terrible coffee. Grayden's been with her. He's her boyfriend."

So Ollie had noticed Grayden and me sitting together. I hadn't told him we were dating, but yeah. Kids picked up on plenty. Especially mine.

My jaw tightened, and my gaze met Danny's. I lifted my chin defiantly.

After a while, Danny's eyelids drooped. I told Ollie to meet Grayden out in the hall. "I just need to say a few things to your Dad real quick. Okay, Ollie-bear?"

When Ollie stepped out, I closed the door behind him.

There were so many things I could say to my ex. I could ask if he'd ever cared about us at all. I could ask why he'd driven toward our house when he was bleeding out.

Even if Danny were able to speak, there was no way I'd get a satisfactory answer.

"Do you know who attacked you?" I asked. "Just nod or shake your head. Yes or no."

He shook his head slowly. No.

Was that true? I had no idea.

"Grayden probably saved your life. I heard the nurses talking. If no one had slowed the bleeding right when he did, you'd probably be dead."

Danny didn't respond. His eyelids drifted closed, but I sensed he was listening. I went closer.

"Things have been bad between us for a while. You haven't been a good father. You've been an asshole to me. But things are going to change, do you hear me?"

I picked up Ollie's card and set it on the bed, right on Danny's lap. "You almost died, and nobody was here for you but me and Ollie. I was only here for his sake, not yours. Against all odds, your son loves you. He's still willing to give you another chance. I really hope you realize what a rare, precious gift that is."

Grayden had proven to me that second chances were real. I was getting my second chance at love. Grayden had a second chance at a relationship with his siblings.

I wanted to believe Danny could change. That he could earn his new chance too.

"I'm with Grayden now. But you'll always be Ollie's father. He needs you. If you can step up and be the dad Ollie deserves, then you'll be welcome in our lives. If you don't? Then we're finished. The next time the worst happens, you really will be alone."

I turned around and walked out. Grayden and Ollie were waiting for me in the hallway. My guys.

When the three of us were together, especially with our families around us, I felt like I could face anything.

FIFTY

Piper

"Hey, um, Grayden?" Ollie stuffed another bite of pancake into his mouth.

"Yeah, what is it, Big Air?"

Ollie laughed at the new nickname. "Can I ask you a question?"

"You just did." He winked. "Go ahead and ask another."

It had been two days since Danny had regained consciousness at the hospital. He was recovering slowly but surely. Ollie and I had been driving out to Hart County General each day to visit him, usually with Grayden coming along.

Yesterday, Ashford had brought Maisie to the hospital to meet us. For the first time, she'd met her Uncle Grayden. She'd been hesitant as he went down to one knee, holding out his hand for her to shake.

I swear, that moment would be etched into my mind forever. How beautiful it was. How *big*.

All of us adults had been fighting back tears, while Maisie and Ollie immediately said they were bored and asked to check out the gift shop.

After we got home from the hospital, Grayden and Ollie had skateboarded in the driveway for the rest of the afternoon. Or rather, Grayden sat and clapped loudly whenever Ollie attempted a trick.

They'd watched online videos of skateboarders to get ideas. *Yikes.*

But I'd also witnessed serious safety discussions, and Grayden made sure Ollie wore his helmet. Grayden started calling him Big Air after Ollie made an especially impressive jump off the curb.

I loved seeing them together.

In fact, I couldn't remember when I'd ever been this happy.

Ollie took another bite of pancake and asked his question. "Are you going to move in with us?"

I nearly choked on my sip of coffee and started coughing.

Grayden smirked at me and reached for my hand under the kitchen table. "That's probably a question your mom needs to answer."

"Grayden has his own place," I said, once I'd stopped coughing.

"Then why does he keep sleeping on our couch?"

"Well...he..."

"I've been stressed the last few days," Grayden said. "Makes me feel better to be near you guys. You're pretty much my favorite people. And I have several contenders on my list, so that's saying a lot."

And there went my heart, melting like syrup into pancakes.

Ollie nodded. "Mom and I have been stressed too."

"Do you mind me hanging around?" Grayden asked.

"Nah, it's alright. If you moved in, we could practice skateboarding tricks way more. Can we do that today? It would be *great* for my stress levels."

Grayden and I exchanged an amused glance. This kid. "Sorry, bud. You're going back to school today. Skateboarding will have to wait until after."

Ollie rolled his eyes. "Stupid school."

After breakfast, we did our usual comedy of errors trying to get out the door. But finally, we made it into the car.

Grayden came with us, sitting in the front seat. We'd swung by his place a couple days ago so he could grab some clothes and toiletries, but his truck was still parked under the carport there.

When I pulled to the front of the drop-off line, Ollie jumped out with his backpack. He trotted into the school and waved.

"I'm worried the other kids will be talking about Danny," I said. "And about you."

"He's ready for it. He's strong, like his mom."

I'd been answering plenty of difficult questions from my kid. He knew Danny had been stabbed and that we didn't know the identity of the assailant.

He also knew the police had questioned Grayden, but that Grayden had only helped Danny.

Mom, why do people do things like that? Ollie had asked. *Why do they hurt each other? Not like in a movie but for real.*

I did my best to answer. Then Ollie had gone to Grayden for advice.

Ollie had listened with rapt attention as Grayden tried to explain why people did bad things. He didn't have any magical answers either. But somehow, Grayden had made Ollie feel secure. Grayden's experience with prison gave him a unique perspective, and my kid had picked up on that.

Seeing Ollie grow to trust him was an amazing thing.

I drove away from the school. Grayden reached for my hand and rubbed his thumb over my knuckles. "Are you headed to Silver Linings today?"

"Not yet. I need one more day. It's been..." I took a deep breath. "So much."

"What would you like to do? Spa day? Hang out with Grace? I can make myself scarce if you need some time."

"No. I just want to be with you today."

We'd either been separated or had other people around us almost constantly since Danny's attack. I wanted to relax with Grayden and just be.

He was my boyfriend now, after all, according to Ollie.

Grayden hadn't pushed for labels. Boyfriend was okay, though. I didn't hate it.

We were at a stop sign. Grayden leaned over to kiss me. Someone tapped their horn behind us, and I started driving again, laughing. Oops. As if there weren't enough rumors swirling about Grayden and me. We were putting on a show for the other elementary parents.

"Want to head to my place?" he asked. "I could use your help with something. It'll be fun. At least, it will be fun for me."

"Now I'm intrigued."

"Right there," Grayden said. "Hold that position. Just like that."

I tried not to crack up. I'd never been a life model for a drawing before. "My hair is tickling my cheek."

"Don't move, wild girl. Stay still for me."

A giggle threatened to erupt. My lips closed to keep it in.

"Be good," he warned, eyeing me over the top of his glasses.

I stuck out the tip of my tongue.

We'd arrived at Grayden's house a few minutes ago. He'd dragged me inside and moved me around like a doll, finding the light he liked best.

After he said he wanted to draw me, I'd assumed he would take out a sheet of paper.

But instead, he'd started sketching directly on the blank wall behind his desk. The future site of the mural he'd been planning the last time I was here. That had been just a few days ago, the same day Grace had walked in on us kissing.

Now, both our families knew about us.

I watched him from the corner of my eye. My hair was up in a messy bun, and I wore jeans and a plain sweater. Grayden had handed me an empty coffee cup to hold. He was sketching me just like that.

"Are you sure you want me in the middle of your mural?" I asked.

"Completely. You're the first piece, and I'm going to build the rest of Main Street around you."

My skin flushed. Nobody had ever made me feel the way Grayden did. Adored. Cherished.

At one point, I realized he'd stopped drawing. He was watching me through those naughty, sexy glasses of his.

"What?" I asked.

Grayden took off his glasses, set down his drawing pencil, and walked toward me. His fingers were smudged with charcoal.

"Just can't believe you're mine."

He put his hands on my hips and tugged me into him. His mouth slanted onto mine, and without breaking our kiss, he took the mug from my grasp and set it on the desk.

"I've been thinking all day about getting you naked again," I confessed, when we broke for air.

"Good, because I've had my mind on the exact same thing."

He led me to the sunporch. Warm sunlight streamed through the blinds. We undressed each other and lay naked in a tangle on his futon. Kissing and caressing, trying to find the perfect alignment of our bodies.

Grayden licked along my collarbone, his stiff pierced cock dragging over my stomach. I traced my fingers over the tattoos on his chest and arm and wrapped my legs around his waist.

His lips kissed their way down my body, stopping to suck my nipples and lick every stray freckle.

"Look at all this pretty, untouched skin. Ever thought about getting ink done? Here. Or here."

I hummed, enjoying the softness of his mouth and the contrasting scratch of his beard. "I'm always worried I'll have regrets. That I'll get a tattoo and then decide I don't like it. How did you know you'd want yours forever?"

"Just a leap of faith, I guess."

Before Grayden, I wouldn't have been able to imagine what

that meant. I used to be the girl who danced on tables, who drank too much and got wild with a man I'd just met.

But actually choosing to take a risk on *forever*?

"I'll think about it," I said. "If I get a tattoo, I will definitely hire you to do it."

"Thank goodness. Might hurt my feelings otherwise." He winked, then inched even lower and dipped his head.

I gasped and grabbed onto his hair.

Grayden's tongue teased my opening while he massaged my clit with the pad of his thumb. Then he switched, his tongue flicking over my sensitive bundle of nerves while his fingers worked inside me.

When he finally pushed his cock into me, gliding through my wetness, I was moaning and panting like a wanton thing.

He was gorgeous like this. Sunlight illuminated the contours of his skin and tattoos as his hips rolled, our bodies meeting again and again.

I loved when he took over. Took what he wanted from me. I was always happy to boss a man around in bed to make sure I got what I needed, but with Grayden, I trusted him enough to just let go.

With Grayden, I felt completely free. His wildness was a perfect match for mine.

He kissed me tenderly at the same time that his thrusts got rougher. I moaned into his mouth. In a swift, filthy move, he pulled out and flipped me to my stomach, his palm smacking my butt cheek. I gave him a heated look over my shoulder.

"Watch it," I said teasingly.

"Like you don't love it."

"I'll smack *your* butt next time."

"Just try me, wild girl."

He pinned me with his body, and his cock slid inside me. That piercing. *Ungh*. The head of his cock rubbed inside me, driving the spiral of pleasure even higher.

"So good," I moaned.

"You want more of this cock? Should I keep giving it to you?"

"Yes, please, yes," I cried.

His chest pressed against my back, and Grayden kissed behind my ear. His hips were doing wicked things, angling his cock just right to have hot pleasure cresting toward me, making me shake in anticipation. But he also reached for my hands, curling his fingers over mine in a way that was so intimate and caring.

"I love you," he murmured in my ear. "Fuck, you're making me come, Piper. Need you to come with me. Squeeze my dick with that sweet pussy."

His dirty words and rampant thrusts drove me over the edge. We both yelled, and the futon bumped rhythmically against the wall. I felt myself tighten and convulse around him as his cock jerked.

Later, when I was wrapped up in Grayden beneath his blankets, I heard my phone buzz.

"I don't want to move," I mumbled. "But I should check that."

"I'll grab it." Grayden jumped out of bed, fully naked, and went to fish my phone out of my purse. "Geez, it's cold out here."

I laughed. "Hurry up and get under the blankets again."

He climbed into bed and pulled me against him while I checked the notification. "Teller wrote."

I read the message aloud.

> Arrived in Austin for Ayla's next show. She says hi and that she misses you all. Spoke to Chief Nichols and got an unofficial update on the investigation. Since Danny doesn't remember much, they've hit a dead end. If you think of any more details…

Grayden huffed, his breath warm against my shoulder. "I appreciate Teller's help. But it's the police department's job to solve Danny's attack, not ours."

Over the last couple days, Danny had recovered enough to be

moved to a regular room and to be interviewed by Chief Nichols. He'd said he remembered being attacked by a man in a ski mask as he walked out of his motel room that morning.

But Danny had claimed to have no memory of anything else, including driving toward my house. No idea who would want to harm him or frame us. He'd said he wasn't meeting anyone the night Grayden confronted him at the bar.

Danny was lying. Or his memory was truly spotty after the trauma of his injuries. Either way, he wasn't helping solve the case.

An officer from Colorado State Patrol had been assigned to guard Danny's hospital room. Just in case the assailant tried again.

But since Danny's stabbing, there hadn't been any further incidents or break-ins.

Grayden kissed my shoulder. "Do you know if Danny will be released from the hospital soon?"

"Another week, at least. They're monitoring for infection. After that, he'll be able to leave, but he'll probably need someone to check up on him. Help with driving and wound care and stuff like that."

His hospital stay would be expensive. I didn't know the extent of Danny's financial problems, but this had all started because he needed money. There was no way he could afford an in-home nurse or anything like that.

He would also need a better place to stay than the Pine Cone.

"You've done more than enough, Piper. Someone else can help Danny."

"He doesn't have anyone. That's the thing. His parents are gone, and he doesn't speak to anyone in his family. I assume he still has friends, but nobody's bothered to come see him. Who else is there but me?"

"I'm here. I'll play Danny's nursemaid for a little while. He'll *love* that."

I laughed. "I'm being serious."

"So am I. I plan to be in your life for a long time, so Danny will have to get used to me. I can even take Ollie to visit him, if you're alright with it."

"You would do that for me?"

He kissed my temple. "That and more. Anything. But Danny has to apologize to you for everything, or none of us are lifting a damn finger for him."

"My thoughts exactly."

FIFTY-ONE

Grayden

As I WALKED toward Milo's shop, I spotted him outside, wiping down the bikes for sale.

"Afternoon," I said.

The guy jumped, shoulders hunching as he turned toward me. "Oh, Grayden. Hey. Been a few days."

Geez, he seemed tightly wound today. "It has. Funny story, except not so funny..."

Milo grimaced. "Dude, I heard all about it. I came down with a brutal stomach bug on Monday and was out of commission until yesterday. Finally poked my head out of my own house, and bam, heard the news about what happened to Danny Carmichael and you being questioned by the police."

So that explained why he looked so pale. At least I didn't have to catch him up.

"I was going to call you and see how you're doing," he said guiltily.

"Nah, you get a pass if you were sick. It's been a tough week so far. But it's been getting better."

I'd been spending every moment possible with Piper and Ollie. Yesterday had been his first day back at school, and Piper and I had been able to forget the world and just be together for a while.

Then, after school, we'd had dinner together at their house. Roasted chicken and potatoes. Ollie had shown me his favorite comic books before bedtime, and then Piper and I relaxed and watched a movie on her couch. Well, *watch* was a loose term. Mostly, we'd made out like teenagers.

All in all, a pretty much perfect day. Except for the part where I went back to my place to sleep. I was seeing the benefits of Ollie's suggestion that I move in. But we weren't quite there yet.

Soon, I hoped.

With Piper's okay, I'd given Ollie my number to program into his phone. So far, he'd texted me a meme this morning that I couldn't understand. I'd smiled so big when that notification popped up.

I'd spent my morning working on my mural. I had plans with Piper and Ollie later this afternoon. We would meet up for Ollie's after-school martial arts class, which promised to be a good time. Best of all, Ashford was the teacher.

My relationship with Ashford had a long way to go. But being able to hang out with him, to just be brothers again, was the best feeling in the world.

"Anyway, thought I'd stop by to say hello," I said. "Could I take another look at that Ninja you loaned me? It's still for sale, right?"

A smile broke over Milo's face, making him look more like his usual self. "Yeah, man. Come on. Let's talk."

We walked to the next row of bikes, and we batted around some numbers. I wasn't ready yet to make a big purchase, not until my studio was open. But I had ideas about taking Piper out on another ride before long.

Maybe we'd even hit up the Mangy Moose for more of those mocktails.

Milo rested a hand on a nearby sport bike. "So I hear Danny's recovering?"

"He's doing as well as can be expected. Or so the doctors say. Piper's been there for him at the hospital far more than he deserves."

"And the attack? Does Danny remember what happened?"

That tense, distracted look had reappeared on Milo's face.

"If he does, he's not talking," I said. "But Piper thinks he knows a lot more than he's saying. She suspected Danny was up to something even before the attack."

"Right. You said he broke into your place."

"He did, at least once." I scrubbed my hand over my beard. "Actually, I've been thinking a lot about the day I met you. When Earl and Zach found the drugs?"

Milo laughed nervously. "The fake drugs, you mean?"

"Yeah."

This was my other reason for stopping by the motorcycle shop today. My brain had been turning over the events of the last several weeks. Chewing on those details like a piece of gristle.

Something had been bugging me, and it just wouldn't go away.

We now knew Danny hadn't broken into Piper's garage. That had been someone else. The would-be killer, who'd stolen the knife used to stab Danny. We also knew my Seattle sweatshirt had wound up in the hands of that same attacker.

The question was, *how*? Had Danny really planted the fake drugs at my place?

Or somebody else?

Before I could ask another question, someone called out, "Hey, Milo?"

We looked over. Dillon Kirby, Piper's employee from Silver Linings, stood several yards away.

Geez, was that stomach bug going around? Because Dillon didn't look well either. He looked like warmed-over shit.

"How's it going, Dillon?" Milo asked, walking between the motorcycles toward him.

Dillon dug a hand into his greasy hair. Dark circles ringed his eyes. "Can I talk to you?"

He glanced past Milo's shoulder, scowling at me, and the rest of that sentence was implied. *In private*. Whatever Dillon wanted to discuss, he didn't want me around for it.

"Sure." Milo gave me an apologetic smile. "I'll be right back, Grayden. Feel free to look around at the other bikes. Unless you need to take off?"

"I'm good. I'll be here."

Milo and Dillon walked toward the shop's front door and into the small reception area.

But I didn't stay put. I wanted to know why Dillon looked so stressed.

As soon as the shop's front door closed, I walked along the building to get closer. The two bay doors to the garage were closed today, probably because it was chilly out.

I paused beside the shop's front window and leaned against the stucco exterior wall. An upper frame of the window was open for ventilation, which meant I could hear everything they were saying. If I craned my neck, I could just see them without risking them spotting me.

"Have you seen my brother?" Dillon asked.

"I haven't." Milo's voice was tight. "I was out sick for over two days."

"So he hasn't been here?"

"No, and that's obviously an issue. Nobody's seen him, and he won't respond to my messages. I was going to call *you* to find out what the hell's up with him. He's stressing me out."

Dillon muttered a curse. He grabbed his head and shifted his weight from foot to foot. The picture of anxiety. "You think *you're* stressed? He told me something was up a couple months ago, but when I've asked lately what's going on with him, he denies anything is wrong."

I remembered how Dillon had been hanging around with Chad Bronski, the Silver Ridge cop who hated me.

Could *that* be the brother Dillon was talking about? Not all brothers had the same last name. They could have different fathers.

Mentally, I went back to the details that had been bugging me. The intuition that there was an obvious connection, and yet I was missing it.

So far, all I had were a lot of disjointed threads. Dillon was one of them. Bronski was another. My new friend Milo.

The fake drugs.

Then there was Danny. The break-ins at my place and Piper's garage. Danny's stabbing and his reluctance to confess what he'd really been up to in Silver Ridge.

"You guys aren't all that close," Milo said.

"But after everything our family has been through, I know my brother. I'm afraid he's into something really bad this time, Milo. Really, really bad."

Dillon asked Milo to contact him if his brother showed up. Milo agreed.

I stepped over to a nearby Harley, pretending to admire the leather and chrome, and Dillon stormed out of the shop. He jumped in a car and took off.

Milo came out a couple moments later, sighing heavily.

"Sorry," he said. "Thanks for waiting around. As you can probably tell, I'm having a shitty day."

I nodded. "No fun to be sick and have to catch up on work."

"No kidding."

I glanced in the direction Dillon had driven. "I may have overheard some of your conversation. Who's Dillon's brother? Is it Chad Bronski?"

Because a weird theory had just popped into my head. It was bizarre and totally far-fetched. But the truth was often pretty strange.

What if Dillon and Bronski had set me up? Planted those fake drugs, stolen my Seattle sweatshirt. And then Bronski pretended to receive an anonymous tip about me.

And the intruder in Piper's garage. Bronski had shown up in response to Piper's 911 call, conveniently the closest officer available. Then just happened to let the intruder get away.

I was sure Dillon had a thing for Piper. What if he'd planned to get rid of Danny and me in one fell swoop? Framing me for Danny's murder?

Except Danny's attacker had tried to frame Piper too. Hard to imagine Dillon being involved in that, unless he'd gone full crazed stalker.

Milo gave me a confused look. "No, Dillon and Chad are tight, but they're friends. Dillon's brother is Zach."

"*Zach*?"

"Yeah, man. Zach Kirby. You remember him, right? He and Earl came with me to your place to meet you. Zach and Dillon remind me a little of you and Ashford, actually. They haven't always gotten along. But I think Zach has been trying. He works on Dillon's dirt bike here at cost."

Zach. He and Earl had found the fake drugs.

Dillon hated me, and Zach was his brother.

"The Kirby family has been through some terrible things," Milo went on, oblivious to where my mind had gone. "Not really my business, but just saying. Usually, Zach has been a solid worker. But he hasn't shown up here for work in days. With me out sick as well, it's been a clusterfuck. We've had to cancel appointments, and..."

Milo stopped, squinting at me.

"Grayden, you okay?"

"Not sure. Is Earl around? He working today?"

"Sure, he's in the garage. Working his butt off to pick up slack. I really need to get in there and help him. Why?"

"This will probably seem odd. But I need to ask him a question."

FIFTY-TWO

Piper

MOST OF THE TIME, I loved being at Silver Linings. This place was such a part of me. I was one of those lucky people who'd turned her passion into her job.

But today? Ugh, why couldn't we just close already? I wanted to go pick up Ollie from school. Grayden had made plans to meet us at O'Neal Martial Arts for Ollie's Brazilian Jiu-Jitsu class, which Ashford taught.

We were going to watch the class, then grab dinner with Ashford, Emma, and Maisie. Seriously. I could not wait.

"You keep checking the time on your phone," Rina said. "If you want to meet your hot-ass man for sexy times, you can just go. Have fun and send photos." She added a wolf whistle.

I glanced at the dining area, where a couple of people were enjoying afternoon coffees. A prim older woman pinched her lips at us in disapproval.

"I appreciate the enthusiasm, Rina," I said. "Not sure that's a work-appropriate subject, though."

"Hey, you're the boss. You would know."

The news about Grayden's and my relationship was out. There were also some lingering rumors about Grayden being responsible for Danny's attack, despite Grayden having a clear alibi.

Then again, the townsfolk of Silver Ridge despised Danny, so that rumor probably scored Grayden a few points in their eyes.

The minutes ticked by toward closing time, and Rina and I worked on the afternoon checklist. I was checking our inventory of oat milk when she said, "Hey, Piper? I've been meaning to mention something."

"Oh?"

"I feel conflicted though. Like, I'm not the type to badmouth another employee, and that's not what I'm trying to do. But I'm just concerned, you know?"

I turned away from the supply shelf and faced her. "I can't read your mind, Rina. You'll have to be more specific. What's going on? Who are you concerned about?"

"It's Dillon," she said quietly. As if someone might overhear, though our customers had left and it was just us in the shop. "The past few days, while you were out dealing with your family stuff, he hasn't been acting like himself. Burned half the batches of croissants. And yesterday, he switched salt for sugar in a batch of scones. Thankfully we noticed before serving any."

"Okay, yeah. That's definitely bad." Today was Dillon's day off, so another of my employees had handled the baking. I hoped he was alright. "Thanks for letting me know, Rina."

I had to tread carefully about personal questions with my employees. Maybe the baking mishaps meant nothing. Everybody screwed up sometimes. But if Dillon had an issue and needed time off, I hoped he would talk to me instead of suffering in silence.

I made a mental note to give Dillon a call later in my office.

About ten minutes before closing time, the bell on the door jingled. "Welcome," I said automatically, then did a double-take when I noticed who it was.

Zach Kirby.

"Hey, Zach. Haven't seen you in here in a long while."

"Piper." He rubbed his face, eyes darting around. "Yeah, I'm not much of a coffee drinker. But I could use a bottle of water. And maybe one of those blueberry muffins."

Sometimes I forgot that Zach was Dillon's older brother. The two of them shared the same dark hair as their mom. Zach had graduated from Silver Ridge High the same year as Grace and me.

Dillon was much younger, and as far as I knew, he wasn't that close to Zach. Or so the local gossip went. I'd mentioned Zach to Dillon a time or two, but Dillon never said much. And I almost never saw the two of them together.

But maybe that had more to do with their family's past tragedy than anything else. While hardship could bring a family together, it could just as easily tear it apart.

Given my discussion with Rina just a few minutes ago, though, it was hard to imagine Zach's appearance was a coincidence.

I grabbed the tongs and opened the bakery case. "Were you hoping to see Dillon here? He's not working today."

"Actually, I'm here to see *you*."

"Me?"

His gaze moved around the shop again. "It's a little sensitive."

If this wasn't about Dillon, there was only one other subject I could think of. The incident last week, when Zach and his coworker Earl had found the fake drugs at Grayden's place.

Couldn't imagine why Zach would want to talk about that.

I passed him the muffin in a paper bag, along with a bottle of water. "On the house. How about you come back to my office? We can chat there."

"Great. Thanks, Piper."

We passed Rina, who was tidying the kitchen. I opened the office door, going in first, and Zach closed it behind him.

"Have a seat." I grabbed some stray papers from the chair across from my desk, then squeezed over to my desk chair. "It's tight in here."

"Nah, no worries." He set the water and muffin on my desk. Then rubbed his palms against his oil-stained jeans.

Now that we were alone, Zach seemed even more anxious. I noticed sweat stains under the arms of his work shirt.

"So? Is this about Dillon?"

"Uh, this is going to sound strange. But it's actually about Danny."

"My *ex* Danny?"

"Yep, that's the one." Briefly, Zach's eyes glinted with something I couldn't interpret. "I hear he's in the hospital."

My arms crossed. "Everyone's probably heard that."

"See, thing is, there was an item he promised to sell me. And with him out of commission, in the hospital and all, we didn't get to finish that transaction. It's important to me. I thought maybe you could help me with it."

All I could do was stare at him. This made absolutely zero sense.

I'd suspected Danny wanted my mom's old jewelry box for some scheme. But I'd never imagined *Zach* could be involved in it.

"What kind of item?" I asked. "Was it a jewelry box?"

His features sagged with relief. "Yeah, that's it. Do you have it?"

"Why do you want it? What exactly did Danny claim was inside?"

"That's kind of private. I just need what Danny promised. I'll pay."

"You'll pay," I repeated in a monotone.

He lifted his hands, squirming in his seat. More sweat beaded at his temples. "Look, I know I don't seem like I'm flush with cash. I'm not. But my mother has money. She's not all that generous with it, as I told Danny. But for this, I can figure something out."

"Your *mother*?"

"I just want this settled." His eyes bored into me, turning hard. Same blue as Dillon's, but a lot less kind. "I told Danny we could pay ten thousand."

Did he mean *dollars*?

In high school, I'd thought Zach was cute. Dark hair, those blue eyes. He'd been a loner, a bad-boy type who'd naturally attracted me. Rode a motorcycle and everything.

But his family had been rich, and I'd literally been from the wrong side of the tracks. Nowhere near brave enough in those days to ask out the wealthy, quiet bad boy.

Aside from those fleeting impressions, I hadn't known him well at all.

Then the Kirby family nearly lost everything. That awful fire killed their father and older sister. Destroyed their home. I'd felt terrible for the Kirbys. Even now, their mom still lived on the same massive property, but all alone.

A memory popped into my head. Something I hadn't thought about in years.

About a month after the fire, I'd seen Zach in the school hallway and stopped to tell him how sorry I was.

If you need anything, I'd said.

Until I'd seen the look on Zach's face. Pure hatred. Like *I* had been the cause of his suffering.

Same way he was glaring at me right now.

"Look, I have to get this done today," he said. "*Now*. My offer is ten thousand. If that's not enough for you—"

I laughed incredulously. Not because this was funny, but because it was so strange. "I don't have the jewelry box."

"Danny demanded a lot more, and I told him what would happen if he fucked with me. Don't test me, Piper."

All at once, the room telescoped around Zach, like he was finally coming into focus. What I saw was not good. Not at all.

"It was you," I breathed. "You're the one Danny was supposed to meet with."

Zach was probably the person who'd attacked Danny too. Broke into my garage. Tried to frame me and Grayden.

Holy. Crap.

It didn't matter why. Not right now. Didn't matter that none of this made sense.

I had to get out of here.

I lunged for the door, but Zach leaped up and blocked my path. I gasped.

My hand searched my back pockets for my phone. But it wasn't in my jeans. Wasn't in my apron either. I'd left it on the counter when I was chatting with Rina.

Rina. She was still here. I opened my mouth to scream.

Zach pushed me back, his hand slamming over my mouth. "Yell for your employee, and I'll do to her what I did to Danny."

My eyes bugged. I wanted to gasp for breath, but struggled to get enough air with Zach's hand on my face.

"Will you give me the jewelry box or not? I'm going to move my hand. Stay fucking quiet."

As soon as the obstruction was gone, my chest heaved a few times. Pulling in oxygen. Then I whispered, "I don't have it. I swear to you, Zach. I have no idea what any of this is about. Whatever Danny told you, it has nothing to do with me."

His eyes narrowed with hatred again. "It has *everything* to do with you."

FIFTY-THREE

Grayden

I WALKED with Milo through a door and onto the work floor. Earl looked up from the Yamaha he was servicing.

"Earl, got a minute for Grayden?" Milo asked.

"Sure." He grabbed a rag to wipe his hands. "Been meaning to stop by your place, O'Neal. I'm about halfway through a new piece with that fabric you gave me."

Milo tilted his head toward me. "Earl considers himself a fabric artist. Not a quilter. Just FYI."

Earl pointed at him. "Damn right. Want to see a progress photo?"

"Another time," I said. "I have a question for you. It's about the day you, Milo, and Zach stopped by. When you took the fabric with you."

His face scrunched behind his unruly beard. "You want me to pay for it or something?"

"No, not at all. I just need to know. Was it you who found that package that looked like drugs? Or was it Zach?"

"Uh." The big man thought. "It was Zach. I was poking through one crate of fabric, and then he tapped my shoulder. Showed me that brick of powder inside another box."

"Did you happen to see a sweatshirt with Seattle written on it?"

"I dunno. Maybe? Why all these questions?"

Milo was watching me curiously too. I didn't want to make an unfounded accusation against their friend. But the evidence was lining up, and I didn't like where it led.

"Why did you all come see me that day in particular?" I asked. "Did you ask Zach to come along? Or..."

"It was Zach's idea, now that you mention it." Milo tugged at the zipper pull on his leather jacket. "He said he'd heard about a new tattoo studio going in. And I realized you were my old classmate and Ashford's brother. Seriously, why is this important?"

"Because a Seattle sweatshirt disappeared from my house at some point. I have no idea when, since I didn't notice it was gone. Then it turned up at the scene of Danny Carmichael's stabbing. I have an alibi, as the police have already confirmed."

Earl held up his hands. "Whoa, I've got nothing to do with any of that."

"It's also a pretty big coincidence that those drugs turned up when you all were at the house," I went on. "I immediately assumed Danny Carmichael was behind it. That he'd broken in again. But now? After somebody attacked him and tried to frame me?"

I didn't even mention the part about Ollie's camping knife.

"Wait, do you suspect *Zach*?" Milo asked. "You're making it sound like he planted the fake drugs. Why would he do that? Or go after Carmichael? Yeah, he's been a shitty employee lately, but you're talking about attempted murder."

"I don't know why. All I know is that something is going on with Zach, and that he had the opportunity to plant the fake drugs *and* take that sweatshirt." He could've hidden the shirt in Earl's fabric and gotten it later.

Earl and Milo were both shaking their heads. They didn't want to believe their friend could do any of this, and I understood. Didn't change the facts.

I probably had to go to Chief Nichols about this. The police were supposed to be handling this investigation, and I'd refused to do their job for them. But it seemed like I was doing it after all.

I checked the time on my phone. I'd been here far longer than I'd planned. It was almost time for me to meet Piper and Ollie at Ashford's martial arts class. I could tell Piper what I'd discovered then.

"I know you're both tight with Zach," I said. "Maybe I'm wrong about him. I hope I am." I doubted it. "But if you could keep my theory to yourselves, I'd appreciate it."

Milo and Earl just glanced at each other.

It was entirely possible they'd tell Zach my suspicions, and Zach would skip town. But there was nothing I could do about that.

My phone rang in my hand. It was Ollie.

"I need to take this. I'll be right back." I went through the reception door and then out to the lot, squinting at the bright afternoon sun. I felt the smile on my face as I answered. Ollie'd had my number programmed in his phone for less than a day, and here he was calling me.

It didn't even occur to me that something could be wrong.

"Hey, Big Air. Finished with school for the day?"

"I'm outside at the pickup circle. My mom was supposed to get me, but she's not here. She's really late and didn't answer her phone. Is she with you? I'm going to be late for Jiu-Jitsu!"

An icy sensation slid down my spine. "Hold on. Back up. Are you alone?"

"My teacher's still here. She tried to call Mom too."

I raced toward my truck. "I'll be there soon, okay? We'll figure out what's going on."

FIFTY-FOUR

Piper

"Where are we going?" I asked, trying to keep my voice steady. Playing along. For now.

I should've fought him harder. Shouldn't have let him take me. But it had all happened so fast.

Zach didn't look at me. The main commercial district was behind us, and he gunned his engine, taking us away from town. Toward the foothills.

"You want to know what this is really about. I'm going to show you."

"But how long will this take? My son is waiting for me."

Ollie was probably scared. And what about Grayden? Did he know I was gone?

What the heck was I going to do?

At Silver Linings, I had just wanted to get Zach out of there. He'd told me he would harm Rina. It would've been easy for him to walk into the kitchen, grab a knife, and hurt her. Just like he'd done to Danny.

My stomach roiled, dizziness hitting me as bile rose in my throat.

Zach had pushed me through the back door to the coffee shop, and I hadn't fought him. His beat-up sedan had been right there in the alley. Like he'd been planning a quick getaway, which freaked me out even more.

Like he'd always planned to force me to go with him.

I'd almost run right then, but Zach had grabbed my wrists and manhandled me into the car. He'd started the engine and peeled off, roaring straight through any stop signs.

Now, unless I wanted to leap from a moving vehicle, I couldn't leave this car. I had to stay calm. If Zach lost control at this speed, it would not be good.

"Does Dillon know what's going on?" I asked. "Rina said he's been stressed."

"He probably knows something is up." Zach squeezed the steering wheel. "I told him...some of it. Because I had to. But I've tried to keep him out of it."

"Why don't you take me to my mom's old house? That's the last place Danny saw the jewelry box. We can look for it. I'll let you have it, okay? For free. I don't even want it."

"That's where Grayden lives," Zach said, eyes fixed on the road. "Did you forget I've been there? Do you think I'm fucking stupid?"

He swerved the car in the lane, and I closed my mouth on a scream, grabbing the dashboard.

"No! I think you're...you're going through something. Let me help."

"What I'm going through is your fault, Piper. It's *always* been your fault. First your mother, what she did to my family. Then your idiot ex-husband. If Danny hadn't—"

Zach cut off abruptly. The car sped up on the narrow two-lane road as he accelerated.

"What? What did Danny do?"

"Poked his greedy nose where it didn't belong."

He'd mentioned my mother. What could my mother have done to the Kirby family? They'd suffered a terrible tragedy, but my mother had nothing to do with it. The Kirbys had been wealthy and respected. I doubted my parents had ever spoken to them.

The road climbed in elevation. We roared through the foothills, continuing upward through twists and curves.

I had to get away from Zach somehow. And yet part of me also had to know what was behind Zach's anger. His hatred of me. What had I ever done to him?

Miles later, we turned onto a dirt path. The car bumped over rutted potholes. I had no idea where we were. Forest grew all around us. I didn't see any buildings.

"Did Danny contact you about this jewelry box?" I asked. "He claimed it was valuable, right? Offered to sell it?" I was going partly off of what Zach had said, partly off what I already knew about my ex. His latest money-making scheme.

"He didn't just offer to sell it," Zach spit out. "He blackmailed me. Said I could buy that box from him along with everything inside, or he would make sure everyone in Silver Ridge knew about it."

Knew about what? I wanted to demand.

"I couldn't let my mom go through that," Zach added.

"But it was my mother's jewelry box. Did she have something of your mom's?"

He aimed a sneer at me. "Yeah, you could put it that way. Barbara Landry, your slut of a mother, took something of my mom's."

FIFTY-FIVE

Grayden

I'd already been to Silver Ridge Elementary a couple of times with Piper to drop Ollie off. My truck's engine whined as I pulled up, brakes squealing. Ollie stood in front of the school with a young woman tapping her foot beside him.

She headed over to meet me as I jogged toward them. "You're Grayden O'Neal? I'm sorry, but you're not on the pickup list. I already called Grace O'Neal, since she's one of Ollie's emergency contacts."

"Grace is my sister."

Ollie stood there with his oversized backpack on his shoulders. He looked like he was just barely holding back tears.

I crossed the distance between us. "You okay, Ollie?"

"I'm worried about Mom."

"Me too. But we'll find her. We'll get this all fixed."

He threw his arms around my neck. "I'm glad you're here."

I hugged him back. "I'm glad too. Now, let's go over what happened, and we'll keep trying your Mom."

From what Ollie and his teacher said, Piper was supposed to show up at school half an hour ago. Within a few minutes, Grace's SUV pulled up and parked behind my truck.

I waved to her, though I also had my phone to my ear. I was trying Piper's number again.

All kinds of bad scenarios were flying through my head. Could Piper have fallen and hurt herself? Could the coffee shop have been robbed? Maybe she'd gotten sick. Passed out.

Fuck, my heart wouldn't slow down.

"Hi, this is Piper's phone," a voice said. Not Piper.

"Rina?" I asked.

"Yeah. Is this Grayden? I saw your name on the screen."

Grace was talking to Ollie's teacher now. I nodded at her, but kept my ear to the phone line.

"It is. Where's Piper? Why did you answer her phone?"

"She left it here at Silver Linings. It was on silent, but I heard the buzzing."

I gripped the bridge of my nose. "She's late to pick up Ollie from school. Have you seen her?"

"She was here a little while ago. It's really strange, actually. She went back to her office with Zach Kirby, Dillon's brother, and then I knocked on her door to ask a question, and nobody was there. She'd just *left*."

My breath had stopped. The whole world had fucking stopped. "She was with Zach Kirby? *Why*?"

"I don't know. She wouldn't have left without saying goodbye to me, and no way without her phone. And I didn't see Zach leave either. I think maybe they both went out the back door. But you see what I mean? It's weird."

The phone slipped from my ear.

Grace came over to me, dropping her voice. "Grayden, what is going on?" she murmured. "Please tell me you know where Piper is."

I shook my head. "We have to find her. I have no idea what's really happening, but I think she's in danger."

FIFTY-SIX

Piper

Zach drove along the next curve in the path, and the trees opened up, revealing a wide, flat clearing. A grand two-story house sat in the center.

Once, it had probably been breathtaking, given the architecture and the surrounding views.

Now, half the home was a burned ruin. Blackened and exposed to the elements.

My pulse thrummed so fast it felt like one continuous blur. My body rioting internally even as I was frozen in fear.

"Your family's old house. It's still here?"

"Mom never could tear it down. We built a new house down there." He pointed.

Below the Kirbys' old home, there was a steep drop-off with a broad view of a valley peeking between the trees. This clearing had been carved right into the mountainside.

I'd never been out here to the Kirby property. But I'd heard it was huge and had been in their family for generations.

The car bumped along as Zach drove us up to the ruined house and parked. "Why are we here?" I asked.

"This is where I found out. That day, my mom was out of town with Dillon. Taking him to some baseball tournament. My sister Jeanine was out with friends, and my dad was home doing... whatever the hell he used to get up to. Drinking, probably. He had the beautiful family, the house, the fancy car. Nothing was enough for him."

Zach pointed at a blackened mass beside the house.

"That was the garage. I used to sneak cigarettes behind it in high school. So I was back there, just minding my own damn business, when a truck pulled up. You want to know who it was?"

I didn't respond. Deep down, I knew I should be fighting my way out of this car. Doing anything to get away. But I was stuck in that seat, unable to move until I heard the end of Zach's story.

Maybe some part of me had guessed what he was going to tell me.

Your slut of a mother took something of my mom's.

"Your father," Zach hissed. "Frank Landry. He got out of the truck. Banged his fist on our front door until my dad answered. I snuck around the side of the garage to listen. That's when I found out."

"Found out what?" I whispered.

But I was pretty sure I knew.

"That my father was actually *your* father too. Your mom and my dad had an affair. I always figured you didn't have a clue."

"I didn't." I shook my head as numbness seeped through my veins. But at the same time, I'd always known the truth about me. The rumors that I wasn't my dad's. And definitely from the way Dad treated me.

I just hadn't known it was Mr. Kirby.

"Landry had just found out. Sounded like your mom had finally told him. I guess Landry knew your mom was a slut, because everyone in town knew that, but he hadn't known about my dad's part in it. He was there to confront my dad. Took a swing at him. But my dad ducked. Shoved the door closed. Landry stood there screaming at him until he finally gave up and left."

"So you're my brother. Dillon's my brother."

Zach's head turned sharply, his face a snarl of disgust. "Fuck, no. You're not our sister. *Jeanine* was our sister."

My eyes stung with angry tears. "It wasn't my fault. I couldn't help being born."

"But if not for you..." Zach slammed his fist against the dashboard, making me flinch. "You and I were born the same year. Months apart. You realize that?"

Hot shame rose to the surface of my skin, even though I knew I didn't deserve it. I had so many people who loved me. Teller, Ashford, Callum, Grace. And Grayden. We knew everything about each other, the bright spots and the ugly.

Grayden *loved me.*

I had to get out of this. I had to get home to Grayden and Ollie.

Could I use Zach's phone? Or maybe trick him into getting out of the car, then take his keys?

"You said Danny was blackmailing you," I said. "Is this why? He found out about the affair between your dad and my mother?"

"He found some jewelry box in your mom's things. Said it had proof inside. DNA tests would be proof too, but there's no way any of us would've consented to that. But whatever Danny found, it would stand as proof to the people of Silver Ridge. My mom would be humiliated."

"But Danny didn't have the jewelry box. He was looking for it."

"I didn't know that at first, did I? I just knew he had to be telling the truth. Because I'd known since high school what you really were."

FIFTY-SEVEN

Grayden

"Nobody's at her house," Dane said through the phone. "Have you found anything?"

"Not at Silver Linings." I'd gone to the coffee shop, hoping to pick up her trail somehow. Piper's car was here, but there was no other sign of her.

Grace was with Ollie. Our other friends and family had joined me in scouring Silver Ridge for Piper, and they were spreading the word around town that she was missing. Milo and Earl were helping too, driving out to Zach's place to look for him.

Nothing.

So I was in my truck, engine running, trying to figure out where to go next.

I'd never felt anything like this. So powerless. Not even when I'd first been arrested and the MPs were interrogating me. Not even when Silas Drummond gave me that terrible ultimatum or on my first day at Leavenworth.

I had to find Piper.

I'd survived a hell of a lot in my life, but I didn't think I could survive losing her.

"We need to call the police," Ashford said. He was on the line too. He'd canceled his martial arts class when he heard about Piper.

I put my truck in gear. "Do it. But don't expect me to wait around answering their questions."

Another call came in. Milo. Driving aimlessly along the road, I switched over and said, "Found anything?"

"I just had an idea," Milo said. "When Zach has a lot on his mind, he sometimes goes to their family property. There's a house where the Kirbys used to live before the fire. They never tore it down."

"Wouldn't Dillon or their mother look for him there?"

"Their mom, I don't know. But Dillon wouldn't go there. I went there once with Zach, and that place seemed...haunted. If he's trying to avoid people, that's where he would go."

"Tell me how to get there," I growled.

Milo gave me the general directions and promised to send an exact address to my phone. My truck careened down the highway as I accelerated.

"Can you call the police?" I asked. "Give them the information? Dane and Ashford were already planning to contact Chief Nichols."

"Yeah, man. I will. You're going to the Kirby property by yourself? If Zach's there and he really kidnapped Piper, he's gone off the rails."

"I'm going to help Piper. Whatever it takes."

"Do you want me to let Dillon know you're heading there? Or..."

"Do whatever you think is right," I said. "But it won't be good for him if he gets in my way."

I didn't care what I had to do. Nothing was going to keep me from her.

Unless I was too late.

FIFTY-EIGHT

Piper

"When did Danny contact you?" I asked.

"Couple months ago. It started with phone calls. Once he realized I already knew my dad was your father, he figured I was hooked. He didn't admit until later, after I asked for his alleged proof, that he didn't have the jewelry box in hand."

It was bizarre to think Danny had known the identity of my real father and kept it to himself.

Had he found that jewelry box at my mom's house after she died? He could've seen this "proof" about my parentage then. But why wouldn't he take the box right away?

Everything had been pretty chaotic in those days. Planning the funeral, trying to pack up my mom's stuff. I'd stuffed most everything in the basement to deal with later. Maybe Danny had assumed he could find that box later, too. If he ever decided to make use of it.

And now, years later, Danny had done just that. He hadn't paid child support in six months. He'd somehow gotten himself into dire financial trouble and decided to use this knowledge about me to his advantage. To blackmail the Kirby family with Mr. Kirby's dirty secret.

But that jewelry box was nowhere to be found.

"Does Dillon know?" I asked.

"I told him about you after Danny contacted me. I didn't want Danny to get to him first. Dillon was upset, because he'd admired our dad. But he already liked you. He started working for you with no idea what you'd done to our family."

Heat flared again in my face. I hadn't done a thing to them.

But it didn't seem like Dillon had judged me the way Zach did. If anything, he'd been more friendly over the last couple months. More protective of me.

Because he knew I was his older sister.

"Did you plant the fake drugs at Grayden's house?"

Zach waved a hand dismissively. "Dillon's friend Chad came up with the idea."

"Officer Bronski." That jerk. He'd helped set Grayden up?

"Chad didn't like Grayden coming back to town, given his criminal record. Dillon didn't like that Grayden had been hanging around you."

Which was why Grayden assumed Dillon had a crush on me. I'd known that was ridiculous. But not the true reason why.

"I agreed to help them set up their little stunt to make Grayden look bad. Put doubts in your mind about him. But really, I wanted a look at your mom's old house. By then, Danny had admitted he didn't have the jewelry box, but he claimed you'd taken it."

"If I'd had it, wouldn't I have discovered the truth about my mom and your dad?"

Zach wiped a hand over his face. "I don't fucking know, okay? Your ex-husband clearly thinks he's smarter than the rest of us. He thought you couldn't figure it out so easily."

That definitely tracked. Danny was arrogant enough to believe it.

What was inside that box? A secret compartment? A note written in code?

"That day, meeting Grayden, I realized he had a thing for you." Zach shrugged. "The moment he saw the drug package, he blamed Danny. So the rest was pretty clear. What I should do."

So he took the sweatshirt from Grayden's place. And it had to be Zach who'd broken into my garage. He'd stolen Ollie's knife. And then...

"I offered Danny ten thousand dollars to go away and leave us alone," Zach said. "But that wasn't enough for him. He wanted more. Even after he failed to produce the proof from this mysterious jewelry box, he still demanded more."

Zach glanced over at me.

"You should be grateful to me," he added. "If Danny hadn't survived, he'd be out of the picture. You'd be free of him."

Chills sheeted my skin. Zach was talking openly about trying to kill Danny.

"But you tried to frame me and Grayden for it."

He turned away and stared at the half-destroyed house again. "Had to have somebody to blame. You and Grayden made sense. Why the hell *not* you?"

"Then why come to me today? Why ask about the jewelry box? Nobody knew what you'd done to Danny."

"Because there was still the risk you had the box. And maybe I just wanted to look in your eyes and see if you knew the truth. If you had any idea how much you'd destroyed, just by existing."

He was going to kill me. Really, I'd known it all along. But fear and confusion had kept me here, frozen. The hatred in Zach's eyes, making me desperate to know *why*. As if listening to him, hearing every cruel thing, would somehow defuse his anger.

Same way I used to listen to my dad's hurtful words and just take it. Or my mom's. Or Danny's. But that wasn't the real me. I was strong. I'd always been so much more than what any of them said about me.

No. More.

I couldn't sit here and wait for the worst to happen.

Balling my right fist, I swung. My knuckles connected with Zach's nose, and he screamed.

I lunged for the door handle, pawing at the lock to get it open. Then I was outside, sprinting through the cold winter air. The scent of pine was sweet in my nose, but underneath, I imagined there was something darker. A hint of old charred wood.

I ran.

Footsteps pounded behind me. A few moments later, Zach's stocky body crashed into me, sending me sprawling in a patch of dead grass. The impact knocked the wind from my lungs.

Zach pinned me down. He rolled me over, and his face was a mask of cruel rage.

"Why do you hate me so much?" I said, struggling to speak. "I never did anything to you."

"Because it's your fault she's dead! I knew Dad was in the house, but Jeanine wasn't supposed to be there. She wasn't supposed to get hurt!"

Shock turned me numb, all the way down to my bones.

Zach looked shocked too. As if he hadn't expected to confess any of that.

"You started the fire," I said as the truth dawned on me.

He kneeled over me, holding my wrists. A tear rolled down Zach's cheek and splashed onto my skin.

"I was so pissed off at my father. Wanted to punish him for cheating on my mom. So I went in the garage. Used my cigarette to ignite some greasy rags I'd shoved under his car. I didn't know the fire would spread so fast."

He sat back, letting go of me. His dark eyes were filled with horror, and I couldn't bring myself to look away.

"The fire spread to the house. Later, they said Dad was drunk. He must've been drinking after Frank Landry left. He didn't realize what was happening. And I didn't know...I swear, I didn't know..."

I started edging away from him. Slowly at first. I didn't want to startle Zach, but it seemed like his mind was a world away.

"Jeanine had come back early from her friend's house. She

was asleep inside. If I knew, I would've gotten her out. I would never have started the fire. I swear. I loved my big sister."

I got up, ready to run again, and Zach caught the movement.

"You should've died, Piper, not her. You never should've been born."

He launched himself at me. Caught hold of my sweater. We spun as I tried to shove him away from me.

Only then did I realize we were heading toward the steep slope of the drop-off. Where the mountainside fell away.

FIFTY-NINE
Grayden

SOMEHOW I PULLED up the GPS coordinates of the Kirby property while not slowing my speed. Milo had texted me a GPS pin for the old Kirby house, the one that had burned down.

I remembered Piper telling me about the tragedy in the Kirby family. How Dillon's—and apparently, Zach's—father and sister had died in the fire, and the arsonist was never found.

But why the hell would Zach take Piper there?

Why would he attack Danny at all?

My truck turned onto a dirt path. My old shocks were no match for these potholes, but I kept going as fast as I could manage. When I'd climbed the curving road, I pulled into a clearing with a half-burned hulk of a house.

There was a car parked in front of it, both the driver's side and passenger doors open wide.

My brakes protested as I pulled behind the car, threw my gear into park, and leaped out.

Then I heard a scream.

My boots pounded the dried grass. "Piper!" I shouted, racing toward her.

She and Zach were fighting. He'd grabbed hold of her sweater, and she was trying to get away.

They both lost their footing. Stumbled over uneven ground.

Before I could reach them, Zach and Piper fell and disappeared.

A roar of anguish ripped from my throat. It looked like they'd just gone over a fucking *cliff*.

I reached the beginning of the slope and skidded to a stop. There were remnants of a railing here, but most of it had fallen into disrepair. It hadn't done anything to stop them from falling.

But below me, Piper clung to a tree root.

"Grayden!" she cried.

A seventy-foot drop yawned beneath her. At the bottom, the slope gentled, leading down toward a valley. But that first drop was the kind that could break someone's neck.

And that seemed to be exactly what had happened to Zach. He lay sprawled on the rocks below, his neck at an unnatural angle.

"Hold on," I shouted, getting down on my stomach. I reached for Piper, but my fingers couldn't quite touch hers.

With a shout of effort, Piper pulled herself up higher.

My hand closed around her wrist, and I pulled her up to flatter ground. I collapsed back with her on top of me. Just holding on to her as tightly as I could.

That had been too close.

Piper was crying. "Is Zach—"

"He's dead. The fall killed him."

She shuddered. "Where's Ollie?"

"He's safe with Grace."

For several long moments, we just lay there. Breathing.

Then Piper crawled up my body and held my face. "I know I'm a mess, but I'd really like to kiss you. You saved me. You saved me."

I smoothed my fingers through her hair. "You saved yourself. I was just there to take your hand."

Our mouths met in a fierce kiss. Like we could purge the terror and confusion if we just pulled each other close enough.

"How did you find me?" Piper asked, when our kiss broke.

"Milo. It was his idea to check here. I'd already figured out Zach might've planted the drugs and stolen my sweatshirt. I just don't understand why. Why would he do this? Why did he bring you here?"

"He's my half-brother. He and Dillon both are. I mean, Zach *was* my half-brother." She sobbed into my chest.

Before Piper could explain that revelation, a truck peeled into the clearing, skidding in the dirt. Piper and I both sat up.

Dillon got out of the truck and raced toward us. "Piper! Where's Zach?" He looked panicked, and his eyes narrowed as he saw me. "Milo said you guys could be here, but why? What the hell's going on?"

I jumped up, heading Dillon off. "You need to back up."

All I knew was that Zach had tried to hurt Piper. Dillon might intend the same.

But Piper put a hand on my back. "Grayden, it's okay."

"You're crying," Dillon said to her. His face crumpled. "What happened? Where's Zach? I've been looking for him. Then Milo said he could've kidnapped you, but that's bullshit, right? Please say it's not true."

Piper reached back and laced our fingers together. I stayed right behind her.

"I know about the affair between your dad and my mom," she said. "Zach told me. He brought me here and told me everything. He tried to kill Danny a few days ago."

"Oh God," Dillon whispered. "When I heard about the stabbing, I was afraid...but I wasn't sure..."

He didn't look like a twenty-something man anymore. Dillon looked like a scared little kid.

"I wanted to tell you, Piper. About you being my sister. Zach told me not to. I'm sorry."

"I know. It's okay. But there's more." She took a step toward him. I stayed close, ready to lunge if Dillon lashed out. "Zach was going to hurt me. I tried to run, and Zach followed me. We fought and...he went over the edge."

Dillon started to move toward the slope, but Piper touched his shoulder.

"Don't look. He's gone, okay? You don't want to look."

Dillon fell to his knees, tears streaming down his cheeks. Piper kneeled and wrapped him in her arms, and he dropped his face to her shoulder.

She was holding him up. Being the strong big sister the poor kid needed. So I went to my knees too and put my arm around her waist. Making sure that she could lean on *me*.

The wail of sirens drifted through the air, but none of us moved from that spot on the grass.

"Mom!" Ollie cried.

He started running, and Piper caught him in her arms. "Ollie-bear. Hey, bud. I love you so much."

"I was scared."

They hugged for a solid minute. Then, to my surprise, Ollie let go of his mom and hugged me around the middle. "Thank you for finding her."

We were at the Silver Ridge PD headquarters. I'd spent way too much time here a few days ago, and certainly hadn't expected to be back so soon. But this time, I was in the waiting area along with a whole crowd of people.

Grace had brought Ollie here because he couldn't wait to see his mom.

Shortly after Piper had told Dillon his brother was dead, a police car rolled up. Milo had called them, like I'd asked. After the reports that Piper may have been kidnapped, they'd agreed to send a car to check the old house at the Kirby property.

As of now, the county coroner and crime scene techs were probably working on the scene. Piper had given a short statement, the cop told us to head to the station for a full interview. So here we were.

Dillon hadn't been in any state to drive, so the three of us had piled into my truck to drive back to town. But along the way, we'd pulled off to the side of the road for Piper and Dillon to talk. She'd wanted him to wait to hear the rest of her story, but the kid had insisted.

Dillon had only known bits and pieces about Danny's blackmail plan from his brother. A few days ago, he'd worried Zach could be involved in Danny's stabbing. But he'd wanted to talk to his brother before making any accusations.

Dillon admitted to scheming with Zach and Chad Bronski to plant the fake drugs at my house, though. He'd confirmed that what Zach said was true. Even if he'd had no idea that Zach stole my sweatshirt or the knife from Piper's house to frame us.

But the worst part by far was when Piper recounted the true events of the night of the fire. How Zach was the one who'd started the blaze without knowing his sister was inside the house. How he'd blamed Piper for living when Jeanine had died.

It was horrifying. Even with all I'd been through with Ashford, he hadn't actively wished me harm. How could anyone know Piper, see how much sunshine she brought into this world, and want to snuff her out of it?

But maybe that was the very thing that had tortured Zach for years. Knowing she was his sister without being able to acknowledge it. And losing his other sister because of his own tragic actions. The guilt must've eaten him alive.

"Can we go home, mom?" Ollie asked.

"Not yet, buddy. Chief Nichols wants to ask me some questions about what happened today."

"What did happen?"

Piper met my gaze. Then turned back to Ollie. "I'll tell you everything I can. But I need you to stay with Grace and Grayden for now. And keep being brave. Can you do that for me?"

His chest lifted and he nodded. "I will. I'll be right here when you're done."

Then he reached for my hand and held it tight. It felt like he'd reached right into my chest and taken hold of my heart.

It wasn't just Grace and me in the waiting area. Ashford and Callum were here too. All my siblings, together again, and not for a fun reason. Last time it had been the hospital after I'd told them everything about my past.

And here we were again, reckoning with dark family secrets. Piper's this time, instead of mine. But with all this support, we were going to make it through just fine.

Unfortunately, there weren't enough seats for all of us in the waiting area, especially when Zandra showed up with food from Hearthstone. Ollie stayed right by my side, and we talked quietly.

At one point, an older woman ran into the station and demanded to see Dillon and Zach.

"No, I don't want to go to a private room," she shouted. "An officer already came to my house and was spouting lies. I have to see Zach and Dillon. *Please.*"

So this was Mrs. Kirby.

Dillon had already gone back for his interview. The station wasn't very big, and it seemed like Chief Nichols's team was working overtime tonight.

Mrs. Kirby was going through her own personal hell, and it seemed like she was here alone. But Grace jumped up immediately, heading over to speak to her. Within a couple of minutes, she'd convinced Mrs. Kirby to go with her into another room.

Thank goodness for my little sister. She was small, but she had one of the biggest hearts I'd ever encountered.

I couldn't imagine Mrs. Kirby would want to hear from me. If she even knew who I was, she probably didn't have a good impression. But I could tell her that the O'Neals and the Landrys would treat her and Dillon like family too. If she was ever willing.

Piper had already accepted Dillon as her brother within the last couple hours since she'd learned the truth.

I never should've doubted the strength of this family's love and acceptance. But now that I'd finally opened up to them, I knew our bond was unshakable. Just like I knew my love for Piper was infinite. The most profound thing I'd ever felt.

Listen to me, getting all philosophical.

SIXTY
Grayden

"Mr. Carmichael, you have a visitor."

I followed the nurse into Danny's room. He looked hopeful for a split second before his frown sank into place.

"Oh, it's you."

"It's me." I walked to his bed and held out a paper bag. Danny looked at it like I might be handing him a rattlesnake.

"What's that?"

"Rice pudding. I brought you lunch. They said you can only eat soft foods."

"I hate rice pudding," he grumbled.

"Just eat it, asshole. Or I will. It has cinnamon."

The nurse smirked at us as she checked Danny's vitals. He reluctantly took the bag.

Danny was moving around more easily now. Supposedly he'd be released in a few days.

"Piper and Ollie are at the nurse's station, giving out thank-you gifts for everyone taking care of you," I said. "They should be here in a couple minutes. But I figured you and I could have a chat first."

"I heard about what happened with Zach Kirby yesterday. The police have already been here to talk to me."

Danny's nurse left the room, and I went and closed the door. He took out the container of pudding and stared at it.

"If this is your way of poisoning me, it'll be pretty obvious," he said.

"Do I *want* to poison you for everything you did? No comment. But I'm not going to. I do have some questions though. Like why the fuck you didn't tell us earlier that Zach Kirby was involved in this mess."

Slowly, he took off the container's lid and dipped the plastic spoon inside. "Why do you think?"

I supposed it was obvious. If Danny had admitted to blackmailing Zach, he would've been admitting a crime. But because he'd kept silent, Piper had almost died.

Fury boiled in my gut as I thought about it.

"I didn't know he'd go after Piper. I swear."

"Did you know it was Zach who stabbed you?"

"Not for sure. He was wearing a ski mask. Jumped me as I left my motel room, just like I told the police before. But I suspected it was him. Didn't think he was a danger to anyone except me."

"Right, because you rarely think of anyone but yourself." I paced over to the window and scowled at the parking lot.

Couldn't believe I had to keep dealing with Danny Carmichael. But he was Ollie's dad, so I'd have to keep dealing with him for the rest of my life. If I was lucky.

"Piper wants answers," I said, still facing the window. "I'm trying to save her the discomfort of getting them directly from you."

"What else do you want to know?"

There was a hint of humility in those words. I glanced over my shoulder at him. Danny took a small bite of the pudding.

"How did you first find the jewelry box?" I asked.

"Piper's mom was in hospice care. Mrs. Landry was pretty incoherent toward the end, but she said something about a man she'd loved. She seemed to think I was Teller at one point. Told me to find a locket in her jewelry box and give it to Piper after… uh, she died."

"Did you find this locket?"

"Yeah. The jewelry box was at Mrs. Landry's house on her nightstand. I found the locket and realized what it meant. It had a picture of Piper's biological father inside. Bruce Kirby."

"But you didn't tell Piper? Or give her the locket?"

"I left it in the box. I meant to tell her about it. I really did."

I snorted derisively. "Sure."

"I *did*. It's not like I set out to be a shitty husband and father, okay? Piper just needed so much all the time. It was constant demands and pressure."

"All she needed was to be loved," I bit out.

Danny stirred the spoon in the pudding. "Maybe I just didn't have that in me."

It struck me how incredibly sad that was. Danny was a pathetic excuse for a husband and father, but maybe he was finally starting to understand that about himself.

"After Mrs. Landry died, I went to look for the jewelry box again. But the box was gone. I assumed Grace or Callum or one of Piper's friends had already packed it up to store with Mrs. Landry's other things in the basement. So I decided to just leave it alone. Piper's mom didn't have a detailed will or anything, so nobody knew about the jewelry box."

"And you figured it might be useful someday."

He didn't bother denying it. "I'm deep in debt. Had some big investments that didn't pan out, and when I tried to make the money back, those opportunities didn't pan out either."

"In other words, you gambled everything away."

"The exact details don't matter, okay? I'm about a month from bankruptcy. I'm going to lose my dental practice. I remembered Mrs. Landry's locket, and that was my Hail Mary."

"Blackmailing the Kirby family."

"Yeah, and look where it got me." Danny pointed at himself. "I nearly died."

"So you were supposed to meet with Zach that night at the bar, right? When I showed up instead? You lied about that."

He shrugged.

"That night, you mentioned the police showing up at my place," I added. "How did you know?"

"From Zach. He'd said something about it when we were arranging the meeting. How he'd seen Piper there with you." He pushed the pudding cup away. "I realize you hate me, and I'm not too fond of you either, O'Neal. But I'm not the same man I was. That has to be something you can understand. Fucking up your life and trying to come back from it."

I crossed my arms. I didn't like thinking of myself and Danny as remotely the same. I'd never intentionally hurt a woman or a kid I was supposed to love.

But I'd screwed up before. I'd lived with that shame. I also believed anyone could change. If they wanted to.

"Can't I start over?" Danny asked quietly. "I could be a better person. A better father."

"If you think starting over is the same as everyone else magically forgetting what you did, then no. That won't happen. But if you're really willing to do the work, then you can earn a place in Piper and Ollie's lives. Just don't expect *me* to go anywhere."

Danny rolled his eyes. "I guess that would be too much to hope for."

"I will always protect Piper and Ollie. I'm going to give them all the love they deserve, and then some more. But if you can be a positive presence in their lives, then I'll make room for you. I might even help you. I would suggest you start with apologizing to them. And you'd better fucking mean it."

He looked at me curiously, like he couldn't quite figure me out.

The door opened, and Ollie's head popped in. "Hi, can I come in?" He glanced between me and his dad.

I walked over and patted Ollie on the shoulder. "I was just giving your dad his pudding. I'm done. I'll go find your mom."

Danny worked to sit up a little higher on his pillows. "Hi, champ. Come in. There's some things I'd like to say to you."

Last night, after Piper had finished at the police station, our closest friends and family had gathered around us and brought dinner over. Teller had spent time on the phone with Piper as well. He'd wanted to fly out again, but Piper had insisted he stay on tour with Ayla.

Tonight, it was just the three of us again at Piper's place. Ollie was in his room. Piper and I were in the kitchen putting together a stir fry.

Simple moments. But we all needed this. To feel safe and do quiet, normal things.

"Interesting conversation with Danny at the hospital," Piper said as she chopped a bell pepper. "He apologized to me and Ollie. I think he actually meant it."

He better have, I thought, but just nodded. "Good. How are you feeling?"

"Sad," she whispered. "Overwhelmed. But lucky too. Grateful you're here."

"No place I'd rather be."

I hadn't shared everything Danny told me with Piper yet. Later, after Ollie went to bed, we'd have time to sit and talk it all through.

"Dillon texted me earlier," she said. "He's with his mom. They're mourning, of course. He's not ready to see me again just yet, but he said he will. He doesn't blame me for anything. He wanted to make sure I knew that. He's nothing like Zach."

I set down the spoon I'd been using to stir the vegetables. Wrapped both my arms around Piper.

Earlier today, we'd also received word that Officer Chad Bronski was suspended without pay for his involvement in placing the false report against me. I had no idea if he'd be fired or what. Honestly, I didn't really care. Chief Nichols could deal with him.

Ashford had assured me he was spreading the truth far and wide: I was a good guy who'd gotten a bad rap. I'd reminded him I wasn't entirely innocent. But he just countered that *nobody* was entirely innocent.

Ashford had also said he and Dane were looking into hiring a private investigator to go after Silas and Aaron Drummond. Maybe even clear my record. That seemed pretty far-fetched to me.

But if Ashford thought I was worth the effort, that meant a whole lot.

"Mom? Grayden?"

Piper and I separated, though we hadn't been doing anything but hugging. Ollie stood near the kitchen island. We hadn't even heard him approach.

He held a polished wooden box in his hands. Looked like a jewelry box.

"Ollie-bear? What's that?"

"I heard Dad and Grayden talking about it in Dad's hospital room. I didn't know it was important, I promise."

"Is that Grandma's?" Piper asked breathlessly. "Where in the world did you get it?"

Ollie's eyes filled with tears. "I'm sorry, Momma. I just wanted to pretend it was a treasure box so Maisie and me could play pirates. I took it from Grandma's house when she was getting really sick, but I didn't mean to keep it."

Piper swayed against me. I put my hand on her back. "Let's all go sit in the living room," I said, then put my other hand on Ollie's shoulder, smiling in a way I hoped reassured him.

Seemed like we were about to solve another mystery.

After switching off the stove, we went to the couch with Ollie sitting between us. He handed the box to Piper, and she cradled it in her hands without opening it.

"You're not in trouble, honey," she said. "Did you have this in your room the whole time since Grandma died?"

"Maisie and I played with it some. We were always careful to put everything back inside. I kept it in my toy box. Kind of... hidden, I guess. Like pirate treasure. But then I forgot about it. I wasn't trying to keep it from you. Dad said Grandma wanted you to have it."

Piper's gaze locked with mine, full of shock.

"That's what Danny told me today," I said. "I was going to share all of it later. Didn't realize Ollie was listening, not that I mind." I winked at him.

With shaking hands, Piper opened the lid. A jumble of items lay inside. Some tangled necklaces, a couple pairs of hoop earrings. Odds and ends.

The locket lay tucked into a soft velvet cloth, like it was truly a treasure.

"It was always wrapped up like that," Ollie said excitedly. "I think Grandma did it. I think this necklace was special to her. Mom, is that the one Dad meant? That Grandma wanted you to have?"

Piper wasn't saying anything. She seemed overcome with emotion, so I nodded.

"Looks like it, Ollie," I said. "That's a locket."

Piper opened the clasp. There was a tiny photo in the hollow of the pendant. Two blond children. Teller holding Piper.

"Is that you and Uncle Teller?" Ollie asked.

"Yes, that's us. But I thought..."

Ollie reached to take the locket from her hands. "Here, Mom. Look. There's another picture inside, underneath. Maisie's the one who found it."

With his small fingers, Ollie plucked out the tiny portrait of Piper and Teller. Just as he'd said, there was another photo beneath.

"Is that Grandma? She looks really young."

Piper stared at it for a long moment. A tear slipped down her cheek.

"That's my mom. And Mr. Kirby." She pointed at the faces of the adults. "And I think that's me."

"You're the baby they're holding?" Ollie asked. "Whoa."

From the angle, it looked like Kirby had been holding the camera. He and Mrs. Landry both wore bittersweet smiles. Like this was a stolen moment, and they knew it wouldn't happen again.

Ollie bounced on the cushion. "Because it was a secret, right? That Mr. Kirby was really your dad? That's why this photo was hidden."

Piper had tried to explain last night about why Zach Kirby kidnapped her. She'd told Ollie the vague outlines of the drama between the Kirby and Landry families, leaving out some of the darkest parts. Like Zach setting the fire that killed his father and sister, or how he'd meant to kill Piper.

She'd said Zach fell by accident and died. Which was essentially true.

Piper was breathing hard. I could tell she was trying to keep from falling apart in front of her son.

"You're probably right, Ollie," she said. "Thank you for showing this to me. I'm glad to have it."

"You're not mad?"

She hugged him. "No, baby. Not mad at all."

Piper smiled through dinner, but her mind seemed far away. After she got Ollie into bed, she and I sat on the couch again.

She took the locket out of the jewelry box and opened it, looking again at the hidden picture inside.

"Why would my mom keep this?" Piper whispered. "I guess she must've loved him, but she couldn't be with him. Maybe that's why she was so miserable the whole time I knew her. That's why she hated me."

I pulled her against me. Piper's head tucked beneath my chin. "But she kept that locket like it was precious," I said. "She could've kept a photo of just him, but it wasn't. It was the three of you."

Damn. Life really was complicated, wasn't it?

Piper sniffled and wiped at her tear-streaked face. "There was this big presentation we did at school one year. Seventh grade, maybe? We each had a role saying something about Colorado history, and most everyone's parents came. Zach spoke right before me, because we were in alphabetical order. K before L. My parents didn't show."

She took a breath, and I stroked her hair.

"But afterward, Mr. Kirby saw me standing alone and walked over. He said..." She swallowed. "He said I did a great job. I should be proud of myself, and my mom and dad would be proud if they were there."

A sob burst from Piper's throat. I crushed her to my chest.

There was no way I could make this better except hold her. So that's what I did. I held her and told her, over and over, that I loved her.

"Sleep in my bed with me?" she asked.

It would be the first time I slept in her room with Ollie in the house. Another big step. But if she was ready for that, I was ready too. "You want me to wake up next to you?"

"I just need you, Grayden. I don't think I could make it through all this without you."

"You don't have to. I'm going to take care of you tonight. Don't worry about another thing."

I knew I could spend the rest of my life taking care of her. Loving her. And it would still barely scratch the surface.

Actually, that sounded like a pretty good plan.

SIXTY-ONE

Piper

It was spring, and Grayden was finally ready to open his tattoo studio.

At least, he would be ready tomorrow. Today was a special preview just for me. I felt like a very lucky girl. That was how Grayden made me feel every day.

But I'd been looking forward to seeing his mural for over two months now. The man had been so secretive about it.

I parked in front of Grayden's place and got out. It had completely transformed in the last several months. Fresh new paint in a vibrant green. Repairs to the roof. A new stone walkway, which led to the porch.

But the most prominent feature of all was the wooden sign hanging from the eaves of the porch.

Roses & Thorns Tattoo Studio. All in hand-painted lettering. My man definitely had some talented hands.

As I walked up the steps, the door opened, and Grayden stepped outside with a gorgeous smile on his face. I loved how much he smiled now. It wasn't a rare occurrence anymore.

"You ready to come take a look?" he asked.

"I've been ready for ages."

"You can't rush art. Or county inspectors."

"Maybe, but I was starting to wonder what you've really been doing in there."

He took both of my hands. "You just want me sitting around your house while you're at work? Waiting for you to get home?"

"Preferably naked."

"That could be a problem, considering all the spare keys you've given to our family."

I giggled, and he leaned in for a kiss.

"You know I'm kidding. You've been working your butt off getting this place ready, and I'm so excited for you." I squeezed his hands. "I love the name. *Roses & Thorns*. It's perfect."

It captured Grayden perfectly. And not just him. Our lives. All the good and bad that this house represented, along with the house across the street.

Our history. Our childhood.

But also, our incredible future that was ready to bloom.

"If you don't take me inside to see the mural, I might have to push you out of the way."

"Alright, alright. Don't get all worked up. We're going."

Grayden walked backward, leading me by both of my hands. His tall frame blocked the view through the doorway at first.

But then he stepped aside, and I saw the wall behind the desk. It wasn't blank anymore. Wasn't just some rough outlines either, like the last time I'd seen it.

The wall was a riot of color. It looked like the sketches Grayden had shown me of Main Street, but brought to fantastical life. Familiar architecture, but with trees and flowers growing everywhere. Silver Ridge turned wild.

He'd incorporated the name of his studio into the meadow at the bottom, as if the letters were woven from thorny vines and roses.

At the center was Silver Linings Coffee, and standing out front was *me*.

A painted version of Grayden stood beside me, his arm around me as he looked at me adoringly. And Ollie was just to the right of us, doing a trick on his skateboard with his trademark smile.

I put my hands over my mouth as I went closer, admiring all the details. There were more people, plenty of them recognizable. But so many intricate abstract elements too. As if there was another layer to the painting underneath.

It was absolutely breathtaking.

"What do you think?" Grayden asked quietly behind me.

I spun and threw my arms around his neck. "This place should be a town landmark. You should charge an entrance fee just to let people see it."

"You don't think the landlady will be angry that I painted all over the wall?"

I pretended to think. "I hear she takes sexual favors, so as long as you put that hot body of yours to use..."

"I'm really glad I'm not renting from Dixie Haines."

Dixie was a family friend and one of our local real estate moguls. Who was also nearing eighty years old. I snorted and hid my face against his chest as I laughed.

The last couple of months had not been all smiles and laughter. It had been pretty brutal, learning the truth about my parentage and about Zach. While pretty much everyone in town now knew that Bruce Kirby had been my biological father, very few knew Zach had been responsible for his father and sister's deaths. What would be the reason to spread such a horrible thing around?

But Dillon had told his mom the entire truth. Just weeks after the day Zach died, Dillon and his mom left Silver Ridge and hadn't been back. I'd texted with Dillon and spoken to him on the phone several times since then, but we had no plans to see each other just yet. Even though I wanted to.

As Grayden knew well, sometimes it took families time to be ready to reconnect. But whenever Dillon wanted to see me, I would be here.

But the rest of our family had been amazing. Teller had taken another break from Ayla's tour to come see me and spend quality time with Ollie. Ayla had even made a quick trip here over a weekend.

That had really been something. The Landrys and the O'Neals and all their significant others, together for the first time. Just like Grace had been dreaming of.

Even Danny had been there. Which was even more astounding, given all the hard looks my brother gave him.

It would be a very long time before Teller, Grace, and our other family members were ready to trust Danny. Heck, I didn't fully trust him yet. I had way too much experience with him for that.

But he'd braved their disapproval and sat with Ollie, who'd been ecstatic to have his dad there with the rest of us. Danny was making a real effort. Even if he was still pretty surly about it.

He was also still recovering from his wounds, as well as dealing with a bankruptcy and renting a cheap apartment on the edge of town. And true to his word, Grayden had been the one to go over and help Danny those first few weeks after he left the hospital.

If you heard Danny tell it, you'd think having Grayden as his nurse was the worst punishment the world could devise.

But from Grayden, I'd heard the word *karma* thrown around several times.

Danny didn't deserve Grayden. Sometimes I wondered if *I* deserved him, because Grayden was the best man I'd ever known. Every day, my feelings for him grew.

He was everything I'd never believed I could have.

And I was finally ready to tell him so.

"You're still up for your first tattoo today?" Grayden asked, giving me another soft peck on the mouth. "You don't have to."

"I want to! Definitely."

"Okay." He grinned. "I've got the room all set for you. Did you decide on a design?"

I pulled a piece of paper from my pocket and unfolded it.

Before, I'd had no idea what kind of design I'd want permanently inked on my skin. Seemed like I'd been waiting for a sign, and now, I had it.

"This is what I was thinking." I handed him the paper. "A heart, but better than the one I drew here. I'd love if you draw one for me? With vines and flowers, like your mural. If that's okay."

"Absolutely. I'd love to do that for you." He hadn't taken his eyes from the paper. "And these names on the sides?"

On either side of the heart, following the curves, I'd written the names *Oliver* and *Grayden* in my messy script. "Maybe you can fancy up the font too?" I asked. "This is just my best attempt."

His brown-and-gold eyes lifted to meet my gaze. "You sure you want my name there? Absent tattoo removal, that's going to be there forever."

"I know. That's the idea. You're already in my heart forever. I love you."

Happy tears filled my eyes. It was the first time I'd told him, even though I'd felt it for a while. Grayden had been so patient with me.

He cupped my face with his hands. "I love you too, sweetheart. With my whole heart and soul."

We kissed for a while longer, but then Grayden got down to business. He put on his glasses and sat down at the desk, where he sketched my tattoo free-hand. It was exactly what I'd asked for.

Then he put the design into his computer and printed it on some kind of tattoo printer thing.

Grayden showed me to a back room. In fact, the room that used to be my bedroom. Of course, it had been transformed as much as the rest of the house.

"Have a seat."

I told Grayden I wanted the tattoo near my right shoulder blade. He transferred his design to my skin and showed me in the mirror.

I already loved it.

He wore his glasses as he worked, his handsome face a mask of concentration. I'd worried the needle would hurt, but the rhythmic pulsing of it actually lulled me into calm. More than anything, I trusted Grayden. I knew I was completely safe in his hands.

But as he kept working on inking his design into my skin, my calm state of mind gradually turned to a constant state of arousal. I loved that he was marking me. Putting his name into my skin along with his beautiful design.

I was so hot for my man right now.

When he finished, he showed me the final result in the mirror. I met his gaze in the reflection. "Is it weird that I'm insanely turned on?" I asked.

His mouth shifted into a slow grin. "Not that weird. How about I bandage you up, and we can do something about it?"

"Keep your glasses on?"

"That can be arranged."

"You're so sexy. I can't wait. I need you right now."

"Settle down," he murmured in my ear. "You need to be patient for my cock. Such a wicked girl."

I bit my lip and looked at him over my shoulder. "Too much?"

"Never. You're my wild girl, and I don't ever want to tame you. Just want to stay right here by your side. Forever."

Epilogue

Grayden

"If I'd known we were coming to a celebrity wedding," Piper said, "I would've worn a different outfit."

I kissed her temple. "You look gorgeous in anything, and you know it."

She shrugged. "Maybe. I like hearing you say it though."

It was a beautiful July day. We were in Hartley, the county seat, to witness the nuptials of Teller and Ayla. Not that we'd been expecting it.

Last night had been the final show of Ayla's tour. She'd sold out Red Rocks Amphitheater near Denver. Today, we'd been planning to meet her and Teller in Hartley for lunch. The whole crew had been invited. The O'Neal clan and all their significant others, plus a bunch of Teller's other friends and coworkers from Silver Ridge PD.

Little did we know, we would cross the street to the justice of the peace for Teller and Ayla to get married.

Now we were on the courthouse steps, waving goodbye to Teller's truck. A few of us had hastily decorated the back window with a bunch of hearts and flowers and the words *Just Married*.

A year ago, I couldn't have fathomed that I would be standing here. Not just an invited guest to Teller's wedding to a pop star, but with his sister on my arm. The love of my life.

Or that she'd have my name tattooed on her shoulder, clearly visible in her sundress.

"Party at Silver Linings!" Piper shouted. "Coffee and treats are on me!"

Our friends and family cheered, especially Maisie and Ollie.

"You might want to warn your employees this crowd is heading to the shop," I said.

And maybe some reporters too, from the looks of it. Teller and Ayla had fooled the paparazzi with their surprise wedding, but people were catching on fast.

The happy couple had already zoomed off to their newly renovated home, but the rest of the world would probably assume they'd be with us.

Piper smiled. "Already texted. Let's go party and celebrate love." Then her nose wrinkled. "The old me would never believe I just said that."

"But the current you is a fan of love, right?" I asked.

She rubbed her nose against mine. "Of course. Because I'm so ridiculously, completely in love with you, Grayden O'Neal."

"Ew, Mom," Ollie said, laughing as he ran by us.

We all piled into vehicles and headed back to Silver Ridge. Wildflowers were blooming everywhere, and I tried to memorize the lush, summer landscapes along with Piper and Ollie's smiling faces.

I wanted to draw them later. Maybe paint a new mural on the side of my studio building. The neighbors wouldn't mind that, right?

Since I'd opened my studio in the spring, I'd been doing brisk business. Milo and Earl had been a couple of my first clients. Ashford and Callum had gotten ink from me too, along with tons of other Silver Ridge residents I could've sworn had given me dirty looks in the past.

But all that was forgotten. I was back in the town's good graces. Back in the lives of everyone I loved, which was far more important.

I'd also pretty much moved in with Piper and Ollie. While I still had my space in the back of the studio, I spent every night with them. We felt like a unit.

Pretty soon, I hoped to make our arrangement more official. But for now, I'd just been enjoying all the simple pleasures of every day with them. Like skateboarding with Ollie, making Piper her coffee in the mornings, and sharing in all their laughter and love.

About an hour later, we'd taken over Silver Linings. The party spilled out onto the sidewalk, and Piper opened up the doors of the coffee shop to invite in the sunshine. Everyone was in a jubilant mood.

So I was surprised to see Dane and Ashford heading over to me with serious expressions. There was a glint of something fierce in Ashford's eyes.

"What's up, guys?" I asked.

"So it turns out today's a momentous day for more than one reason." Ashford held up his phone. It was open on what appeared to be a live video. He was streaming a broadcast from a cable news channel.

As I watched, the world around me stopped.

"*Silas Drummond, a well-known attorney in Washington, D.C., and a major political donor, has been arrested today on charges of bribery and making false statements to the FBI,*" the news anchor said.

The video showed Drummond, far older than I remembered, being escorted from his massive home by police.

"What the fuck," I said under my breath.

I walked outside with Dane and Ashford, and we moved away from the crowd. "I've known this could be in the works for a while," Dane said. "Didn't know it would be today until minutes ago."

Ashford gripped my shoulder. "I thought you'd want to see it live."

I looked from Dane to my brother. "But *how*?"

I'd known Dane hired a private investigator to look into Drummond. But to actually see him arrested...not for what he did to me, obviously, but for *something*. It was indescribable.

"When my investigator started digging into Drummond's secrets," Dane said, "there was a whole lot to find. We turned over everything to law enforcement, and they took over. I'm shocked it all happened so fast. Sometimes these things take years."

"Tell him the rest," Ashford prompted.

Dane nodded, a sly grin curving his lips. "My investigator also got in touch with Silas's son, Aaron Drummond."

My stomach twisted. Aaron, my former Army friend. The man I'd taken the fall for.

"I've been working with some lawyers who are experts in federal criminal law," Dane said. "They're going to try to overturn your conviction, and Aaron is willing to speak on your behalf. Seems he's been wracked with guilt all these years over what he and his father did to you. He's ready to sign an affidavit admitting everything. Including that he killed that soldier in the bar fight fifteen years ago, not you."

My knees went weak, and I leaned against the wall of the building. "Holy shit."

"Aaron won't serve any time," Dane went on, "and he knows that. The statute of limitations for manslaughter or lying to police is long past."

Ashford scowled. "It's bullshit that he can get off so easy. But if Aaron's testimony will help get your conviction reversed..."

"Then I'll take it," I finished. "I can't believe it. Thank you. Both of you. You didn't have to do this for me."

"Sure we did," Dane said. "You're family."

Grace ran outside. "Did you tell him?" she asked, then sprinted toward me.

There were lots of hugs. Too many to count. I still had a long way to go toward getting my conviction overturned, but I'd never expected to get even this close to vindication. Or to have so many people in my life who cared to make it happen.

Then Piper came outside. Her face said Grace had told her the news. We walked toward each other and kissed like we were in some movie, and the emotional music had crescendoed.

This certainly felt like a happy ending.

Piper

I woke to an empty bed. But that wasn't very surprising.

I sat up, yawning and patting down my messy hair. Voices drifted in from somewhere beyond my bedroom door. Again, not surprising.

Grayden had a habit of getting up early to spend time with Ollie in the mornings. While I loved waking up next to Grayden, I loved walking out into the living room and finding them chatting over a comic book even more. Or in the kitchen making chocolate chip pancakes with flour dusting the counters and laughter filling the air.

I pulled on my robe over my pajamas and stopped by the bathroom to splash water on my face.

Looking at myself in the mirror, I couldn't help but smile. Life was good.

Silver Linings was doing better than ever before. My new baker had started experimenting with pastry recipes that had people lining up before we even opened.

I'd also started taking online courses toward finishing my college degree in literature. Grayden had been the one to inspire that, reminding me that it was never too late to pursue something I'd once dreamed about.

Though of course, a lot about my life felt like a dream come true.

I headed out to the kitchen and found the table already set. There was a plate with eggs and bacon waiting for me, and a mug of coffee sat beside it.

Both Grayden and Ollie were smiling at me in a way that seemed almost conspiratorial. Ollie was practically bouncing on his toes, dancing around the way he did when he was particularly excited about something.

"Good morning," I said slowly, looking between them. "What's going on?"

"Nothing," Ollie said, his grin widening.

"Just breakfast," Grayden added, leaning against the counter with his arms crossed.

I narrowed my eyes at them. "You two are acting weird. Did I forget something? Is there some big event today?"

They exchanged knowing glances, and Ollie giggled.

"Seriously, what is happening right now?" I asked, though I couldn't help smiling at their obvious excitement.

I went over to Grayden and kissed him on the cheek, then pulled Ollie into a hug. "I love you both, you know that?"

"We love you too," Ollie said, pushing me away playfully. "Now go sit down and have your coffee."

"My coffee?" I raised an eyebrow. "Since when are you this concerned about my caffeine intake?"

"Just drink it, Mom."

I looked again at Grayden, who was trying to maintain a neutral expression but failing miserably. The corner of his mouth kept twitching upward.

"Okay, fine. I'm going. You weirdos." I moved to the table and pulled out my chair. Then reached for my coffee mug, lifting it to take a sip.

And that's when I saw it.

Underneath where the mug had been, sitting on the table, was a ring.

My breath caught in my throat. I set the mug down carefully, staring at the delicate band with its small but beautiful stone catching the morning light.

"What..." I looked up at Grayden, my heart hammering. "What's going on?"

Grayden crossed the kitchen and kneeled down beside my chair. He took my hand in his, his dark eyes meeting mine.

"Piper," he said, his voice steady but soft. "You and Ollie are everything I could've dreamed of or hoped for. During the darkest times in my life, even when I didn't think I had any hope left, something got me through. Maybe I sensed back then, somehow, that life would bring me to the two of you."

Tears were already streaming down my face.

He picked up the ring, holding it between us. "Will you marry me?"

"Yes." The word burst out of me before he'd even finished. "Yes, of course, yes."

Ollie let out a whoop of celebration, jumping up and down. "Gray, I told you she'd say yes!"

Grayden slipped the ring onto my finger, and I launched myself at him, wrapping my arms around his neck. He caught me, pulling me close as I sobbed into his shoulder.

"I love you," I whispered. "I love you so much."

"I love you too."

When I finally pulled back, Ollie crashed into both of us, his arms around us in a fierce hug. I held them both, my son and my future husband.

Grayden had always felt like part of my family, even when I was young. But now, the three of us had a bond together that went beyond any words or description. Nothing would ever tear us apart.

Grayden was going to be Ollie's stepfather. He would love my son and take care of him. I'd already seen how wonderful he was with Ollie.

Grayden would be my husband. My happily ever after.

And I was going to be Piper O'Neal. The thought made me laugh through my tears. The O'Neals and the Landrys. We were already family in the ways that counted, but soon, it would be legal too.

"Can we have pancakes now?" Ollie asked, still wrapped around us. "To celebrate?"

"We're having eggs and bacon," I pointed out.

"But pancakes are great on the side. Everyone knows that."

Grayden laughed, pressing a kiss to the top of Ollie's head. "Chocolate chip?"

"Obviously."

I looked at the two of them. At the ring on my finger that promised a bright future. I remembered the first night Grayden stayed here with us, back on Thanksgiving, less than a year ago. Before so much had happened.

This felt like the end of one chapter of our story. But for our family, it was only the beginning.

The end.

A Note from Hannah

I can't believe it's the end of the series.

From the time that I wrote Ashford's story in book 1, I knew Grayden would be the key to this series. The brother who would eventually come home and heal all the wounds the O'Neal family was still struggling with. But it's been pretty emotional to finally write this book and see it all unfold, not just in my head but on the page.

Piper's been the heart of the series all along, so I hope you feel she got the happy ending she deserved! It's been an emotional ride, right? She had unfinished business too, both with Danny and her parents' secrets. But Grayden was there for her exactly when she most needed him. That's why I love writing romance. We get to see beautiful happy endings for the main characters, even if real life doesn't always deliver them.

Many thanks as always to my incredible writing group, my beta and ARC readers, and to my fans who keep reading and enjoying my stories. Thank you for sticking with me! I'll have more stories for you soon.

Until next time—

Hannah

More from Hannah Shield

Hart County

Starcrossed Colorado (Ashford & Emma)

Moonlit Colorado (Dane & Grace)

Stormswept Colorado (Teller & Ayla)

Sunkissed Colorado (Callum & Zandra)

Homeward Colorado (Grayden & Piper)

Last Refuge Protectors

Hard Knock Hero (Aiden & Jessi)

Bent Winged Angel (Trace & Scarlett)

Home Town Knight (Owen & Genevieve)

Second Chance Savior (River & Charlotte)

Iron Willed Warrior (Cole & Brynn)

One Last Shot (Dean & Keira)

West Oaks Heroes

The Six Night Truce (Janie & Sean)

The Five Minute Mistake (Madison & Nash)

The Four Day Fakeout (Jake & Harper)

The Three Week Deal (Matteo & Angela)

The Two Last Moments (Danny & Lark)

The One for Forever (Rex & Quinn)

Bennett Security

Hands Off (Aurora & Devon)

Head First (Lana & Max)

Hard Wired (Sylvie & Dominic)

Hold Tight (Faith & Tanner)

Hung Up (Danica & Noah)

Have Mercy (Ruby & Chase)

About the Author

Hannah Shield writes spicy, suspenseful romance with pulse-pounding action, fun & flirty banter, and tons of heart. She lives in the Colorado mountains with her family.

Visit her website at www.hannahshield.com, where you can join her newsletter to receive bonus content and hear about new releases.

www.ingramcontent.com/pod-product-compliance
Lightning Source LLC
LaVergne TN
LVHW041054080826
845145LV00007B/1574

* 9 7 8 1 9 5 7 9 8 2 4 6 5 *